Contents

THE HAUNTED MONASTERY   1

THE CHINESE MAZE MURDERS   109

THE HAUNTED MONASTERY

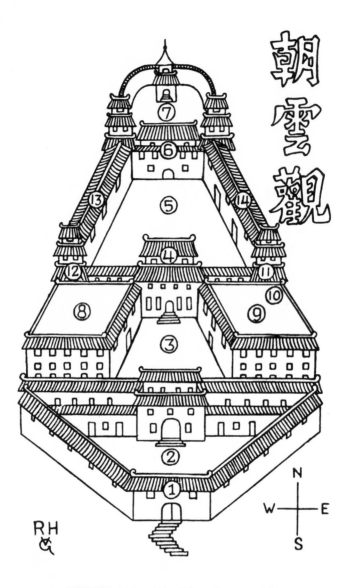

朝雲觀

SKETCH MAP OF THE MONASTERY

1. *Main Gate*
2. *First Court*
3. *Temple Court*
4. *Temple*
5. *Central Court*
6. *Abbot's Quarters*
7. *Sanctum*
8. *West Wing*
9. *East Wing*
10. *Judge Dee's rooms*
11. *Store-room*
12. *Master Sun's Tower*
13. *Gallery of Horrors*
14. *Monk's Quarters*

DRAMATIS PERSONAE

*It should be noted that in China the surname—here
printed in capitals—precedes the personal name.*

Main characters:

DEE Jen-djieh, magistrate of Han-yuan, the mountain district where the
Monastery of the Morning Clouds is located.

TAO Gan, one of Judge Dee's Lieutenants.

Persons connected with "The Case of the Embalmed Abbot":

True Wisdom, abbot of the Monastery of the Morning Clouds.

Jade Mirror, former abbot of the same monastery.

SUN Ming, a Taoist sage, former Imperial Tutor, who lives retired in the
monastery.

Persons connected with "The Case of the Pious Maid":

Mrs. PAO, a widow, from the capital.

White Rose, her daughter.

TSUNG Lee, a poet.

Persons connected with "The Case of the Morose Monk":

KUAN Lai, director of a theatrical troupe.

Miss TING, an actress.

Miss OU-YANG, an actress.

MO Mo-te, an actor.

I

The two men sitting close together in the secluded room, up in the tower of the old monastery, listened for a while silently to the roar of the storm that was raging among the dark mountains outside. Violent gusts of wind were tearing at the tower; the cold draught penetrated even the solid wooden shutters.

One of the men looked uneasily at the flickering flame of the single candle that cast their weirdly distorted shadows on the plaster wall. He asked in a tired voice: "Why do you insist on doing it tonight?"

"Because I choose to!" the second replied placidly. "Don't you think that today's feast is a most appropriate occasion?"

"With all those people about here?" the first asked dubiously.

"You are not afraid, are you?" his companion asked with a sneer. "You weren't afraid on that former occasion, remember?"

The other made no reply. Thunder rumbled in the distant mountains. Then there came a torrential downpour. The rain clattered against the shutters with a rattle as of hail stones. Suddenly he said: "No, I am not afraid. But I repeat that the face of the morose fellow looks familiar to me. It worries me that I can't remember when or where I . . ."

"You distress me!" the man opposite him interrupted with mock politeness.

The first frowned, then resumed: "I wish you wouldn't kill her, this time. People might remember, and start wondering why three . . ."

"It all depends on her herself, doesn't it?" His thin lips curved in a cruel smile. Rising abruptly he added: "Let's go back, they'll notice our absence in the hall below. We must never forget to act our parts, my friend!"

The other got up also. He muttered something but his words were drowned in another roll of thunder. It seemed very near, this time.

II

Farther down in the mountains on the southern border of Han-yuan, that thunderclap made Judge Dee lift his head in the pouring rain and anxiously inspect the dark, wind-swept sky. He pressed himself close to the side of the high tiltcart, drawn up under the cliff that overhung the mountain road. Wiping the rain from his eyes he said to the two coachmen who stood before him huddled in their straw rain cloaks: "Since we can't go on to Han-yuan this evening, we'd better pass the night right here in our cart. You could fetch some rice for our evening meal from a farm in the neighbourhood, I suppose?"

The elder coachman pulled the piece of oil-cloth closer to his head, the ends were flapping in the strong wind. He said: "It isn't safe to stay here, sir! I know these autumn storms in the mountains; it's only just beginning! Soon there'll be a real gale. It might blow our cart over into the ravine on the other side of the road."

"We are high up in the mountains," the other coachman added. "There is not a hut or farm for miles around; there's only the old monastery up there. But of course you wouldn't like to . . ."

A flash of lightning lit up the wild mountain scene. For one brief moment Judge Dee saw the high, scraggy mountains that loomed on all sides, and the red mass of the old monastery, towering on the slope above them, on the other side of the ravine. There was a deafening clap of thunder, and all was dark again.

The judge hesitated. He pushed his long black beard further into the fold of his drenched travelling cloak. Then he made a decision.

"You two run up to the monastery," he said curtly, "and tell them that the magistrate of this district is here and wants to stay overnight. Let them send down a dozen lay brothers with closed litters, to carry my womenfolk and luggage up there." The elder coachman wanted to say something, but Judge Dee barked: "Get going!"

The man shrugged his shoulders resignedly. They set off at a trot; their storm lanterns of oiled paper were two dancing spots of light in the dark.

Judge Dee felt his way along the tilt cart till he found the step ladder. He climbed inside and quickly closed the canvas flap behind him. His three wives were sitting on the bed rolls, their padded travelling cloaks drawn close to their bodies. In the back of the cart the maids cowered among the bags and boxes. Their faces white with fear, they pressed close to each other at each peal of thunder. It was dry inside, but the cold wind blew right through the thick canvas of the hood.

As the judge sat down on a clothes box, his First Lady said: "You shouldn't have gone outside! You are wet through and through!"

THE HAUNTED MONASTERY
and
THE CHINESE MAZE MURDERS

Robert Van Gulik

THE HAUNTED MONASTERY
and
THE CHINESE MAZE MURDERS

TWO CHINESE DETECTIVE NOVELS
With 27 illustrations by the author

DOVER PUBLICATIONS, INC.
NEW YORK

This Dover edition, first published in 1977, is
an unabridged and slightly revised republication
of the following novels by Robert Van Gulik:
The Haunted Monastery, as published by Art
Printing Works, Kuala Lampur, in 1961.
The Chinese Maze Murders, as published by
N. V. Uitgeverij W. van Hoeve, The Hague, in
1957.

International Standard Book Number:
0-486-23502-5
Library of Congress Catalog Card Number:
77-73303

Manufactured in the United States of America
Dover Publications, Inc.
180 Varick Street
New York, N.Y. 10014

"I tried to help Tao Gan and the coachmen to fix that broken axle," he said with a wan smile, "but it's no use; it'll have to be replaced. Anyway, the horses are tired and the storm is only beginning. We'll stay the night in the Morning Cloud Monastery. That's the only inhabited place in this neighbourhood."

"Do you mean that huge red building with the green-tiled roofs we saw high up on the mountain slope, when we passed here two weeks ago?" his second wife asked.

The judge nodded.

"You won't be too uncomfortable there," he said. "It's the largest Taoist monastery in the entire province, and many people visit it during the religious feasts. I am sure they'll have good guest quarters."

He took the towel his third wife gave him and tried to rub his beard and whiskers dry.

"We'll manage all right!" his First Lady resumed. "During our holiday in the capital we were so spoilt in your uncle's mansion that a little hardship won't matter! And it'll be interesting to see what that old monastery looks like inside!"

"Perhaps there are spooks!" his Third Lady said with a smile. She moved her shapely shoulders in an exaggerated shudder.

Judge Dee knitted his thick eyebrows.

"There isn't much to see," he said slowly. "It's just an old monastery. We'll have the evening meal in our room and go to bed early. If we leave tomorrow morning at dawn, as soon as the grooms of the monastery have replaced the axle, we'll be back in Han-yuan before the noon rice."

"I wonder how the children have been getting along!" his second wife said in a worried voice.

"Old Hoong and the steward will have looked after them," the judge said reassuringly. They talked about household matters till loud shouts outside announced the arrival of the men from the monastery. Tao Gan, one of Judge Dee's lieutenants, poked his long, gloomy face inside and reported that four litters were standing ready for the ladies.

While Judge Dee's three wives and their maids got into the litters, the judge and Tao Gan supervised the lay brothers as they rolled large boulders up against the wheels of the cart. The coachmen unharnessed the horses, and the cortège moved along the winding road, the rain clattering on the canvas roofs of the litters. Judge Dee and Tao Gan trudged along behind them—they were drenched to the skin anyway! In this strong wind it was no use trying to unfold their oil-paper umbrellas.

As they were crossing the natural bridge over the ravine, Tao Gan asked: "Isn't that the monastery which Your Honour planned to visit some time ago, in order to make inquiries about those three young women, called Liu, Huang and Gao, who died there last year?"

"It is," the judge replied soberly. "It's not the kind of place I would choose to stay overnight together with my womenfolk. But it can't be helped."

The sure-footed litter-bearers went quickly up a steep flight of slippery steps, zig-zagging up through high trees. Judge Dee followed close behind them, but he found it difficult to keep up with their pace. He was glad when above him he heard a gate open on creaking hinges. They entered a large, walled-in front courtyard.

The bearers carried the litters up a second flight of steps at the back of the court, and put them down under a high archway of blackened bricks. A group of monks in saffron-coloured robes stood waiting for them there, carrying lampions and smoking torches.

Judge Dee heard the main gate through which they had entered close with a resounding thud. He suddenly shivered. He thought he must have caught a bad cold in the rain. A short, corpulent monk stepped forward and bowed deeply in front of him. He said in a brisk voice: "Welcome to the Morning Cloud Monastery, Your Honour! I am the prior here, at Your Honour's service!"

"I hope our sudden visit doesn't inconvenience you," Judge Dee said politely.

"It's a signal honour, sir!" the prior exclaimed, blinking his slightly protruding eyes. "It adds splendour to this auspicious day! We are celebrating the foundation of our monastery, as we do every year on this day. This is the two hundred and third time, Your Honour!"

"I didn't know that," the judge said. "May your monastery prosper for ever and ever!" A gust of cold wind blew through the archway. He cast an anxious eye at his ladies who were stepping down from the litters, assisted by the maids, and resumed: "Please lead us to our quarters. We all need to change our clothes."

"Of course, of course!" the small prior exclaimed. "Follow me please!" As he led them into a narrow, dark passage, he continued: "I hope you won't mind the steps. I'll take you to the east wing by a roundabout way. There are many sets of steps, but it'll at least save you from going outside again and getting wetter!"

He went ahead, holding a paper lantern close to the floor so that Judge Dee and Tao Gan could see the steps. A novice followed, carrying a lampion on a long stick, and Judge Dee's wives brought up the rear together with six lay brothers who carried their travelling bags and boxes, suspended on bamboo poles over their shoulders. When they had gone up the first flight of stairs and turned a corner, it had grown very still; nothing was heard any more of the storm outside.

"The walls must be very thick!" Judge Dee remarked to Tao Gan.

"They knew how to build in those days! And they didn't grudge expense!" As they began another steep ascent, Tao Gan added: "But they made far too many stairs!"

After they had climbed two more flights of stairs, the prior pushed a heavy door open. They entered a long, cold corridor lighted by a few lanterns hanging from the thick, age-blackened rafters overhead. On their right was a blind plaster wall; on the left was a row of narrow, high windows. Here they again heard the gale blowing outside.

"We are now on the third floor of the east wing," the prior explained. "The steps on the left there lead down to the hall on the ground floor. If Your Honour listens, you can hear faintly the music of the mystery play they are performing there now!"

The judge halted and listened politely. He could vaguely hear the beat of drums coming from far below. It was soon drowned by the rattle of the rain against the shutters. The wind was gaining in force. He was glad they were inside.

"Round the corner ahead there," the prior went on in his quick, clipped voice, "are Your Honour's quarters. I trust you won't find them too uncomfortable. Presently I'll take Your Honour's assistant down to his room on the floor below, where we have a few other guests staying." He motioned the novice with the lampion to precede them, and they went on.

Judge Dee looked round. His wives and the maids were just emerging at the head of the stairs at the end of the corridor. He followed the prior.

Suddenly a particularly violent rush of wind blew open the shutters of the window on his left, and a gust of cold rain came inside. With an annoyed exclamation Judge Dee leaned outside and grabbed the swinging shutters to pull them shut. But then he stood stock-still.

The window in the wall of the building opposite stood open, and across the dividing space of six feet or so he looked into a dimly lit room He saw the broad back of a man wearing a close-fitting iron helmet, trying to embrace a naked woman. Her face was covered by her right arm; where the left should have been there was only a ragged stump. The man let go of her and she stumbled back against the wall. Then the wind tore the hooks of the shutters from Judge Dee's hands, and they slammed shut in his face. With an oath he pushed them open again, but now he saw nothing but a dark curtain of rain.

By the time he had the shutters fastened, Tao Gan and the prior had stepped up to him and helped him to secure the rusty bolts.

"You should have let me do that, Your Honour!" the prior said contritely.

The judge remained silent. He waited till the women and the bearers

had passed by them, then asked: "What is that building over on the other side there?"

"Only the store-room, Your Honour," the prior replied. "We had better..."

"Just now I saw one of the windows there standing open," Judge Dee interrupted him curtly. "But someone closed it very quickly."

"Window?" the prior asked astonished. "Your Honour must be mistaken! There are no windows on this side of the store-room. There's only a blind wall. This way please!"

III

Silently Judge Dee followed him around the corner. There was a dull pain behind his eyes; evidently he had caught a head cold. Moreover, he had been looking through the grey curtain of the falling rain, and it had been only one brief glance. He felt feverish; it could have been a hallucination. He gave Tao Gan a quick look, but apparently his assistant had seen nothing. He said: "You had better go and change, Tao Gan! Come back here as soon as you are ready."

The prior took his leave with many bows. He walked back to the stairs together with Tao Gan.

In the spacious dressing room his First Lady was giving directions to the maids as to which of their boxes should be opened. His two other wives were supervising the bearers, who were busy filling the bronze brazier with glowing coals. The judge looked on for a while, then walked on to the bedroom beyond.

It was a very large room with only a few pieces of solid, old-fashioned furniture. Although thick draperies were drawn over the windows, he could hear faintly the sounds of the storm outside. A huge bedstead stood against the back wall; heavy curtains of antique brocade hung down from its carved ebony canopy, high up near the raftered ceiling. In the corner he saw a dressing-table of blackwood, and next to it a small tea-table with four stools. Except for a large bronze brazier there was no other furniture. The floor was covered by a thick, faded brown carpet. The room didn't seem very inviting, but he reflected that when the brazier was burning and all the candles lighted, it would probably not be too bad.

He pulled the curtains of the bedstead aside. It provided ample room for himself and his three wives. As a rule he didn't like them all sleeping

THE FIRST LADY DIRECTS THE MAIDS

together. At home each of his wives had her own separate bedroom, and he either passed the night there or invited one to his own bedroom. As a staunch Confucianist he thought that to be the only proper arrangement. He knew that many husbands slept with all their wives together in one bedroom, but Judge Dee thought that a bad habit. It lessened the women's self-respect and did not make for a harmonious household. However, when travelling it couldn't be helped. He went back to the dressing room, and sneezed several times.

"Here's a nice padded robe for you!" his First Lady said. And softer: "Do I give a tip to those lay brothers?"

"Better not," the judge whispered. "We'll leave a gift to the monastery when we take our departure tomorrow." Louder he added: "That robe'll do!"

His second wife helped him to change into the dry garments after having warmed them over the brazier.

"Give me my new cap!" Judge Dee said to his First Lady. "I'll have to go down now and say a few polite things to the abbot."

"Come back here quickly, please," she said "We'll make some hot tea, then have our meal here. You had better get to bed early; you are looking pale. I think you have a cold coming on!"

"I'll be up as soon as I can," Judge Dee promised. "You are right, I don't feel too well. I must have caught a bad cold." He tied the black sash round his waist; then his ladies conducted him to the door.

Tao Gan was waiting for the judge in the corridor, together with the novice carrying a lampion. His gaunt assistant had changed into a long gown of faded blue cloth, and he had a small square cap of well-worn black velvet on his head.

"The abbot is waiting for Your Honour in the reception room downstairs," the novice said respectfully when they were entering the corridor that led to the staircase.

Judge Dee halted in his steps. He said: "We'll go there presently."

He stood listening for a while. The sound of the rain seemed less than before. He unfastened the shutters of the window through which he had seen the weird scene. Only a little rain blew in from the darkness outside. He waited till a flash of lightning lit up the building opposite. He saw a solid brick wall directly in front of him. Higher up there were two windows of a tower; below the blind wall continued into the deep well that separated the two buildings. Thunder rumbled again. He closed the window and remarked casually to the novice: "Beastly weather! Lead us now to the store-room opposite there!"

The novice gave him an astonished look. He said doubtfully: "We'll have to go a long way, Sir! We must first descend two floors to get to the passage that connects the two buildings, then we must go up again two . . ."

"Lead the way!" Judge Dee ordered curtly.

Tao Gan gave the judge a curious look. Seeing his impassive face, however, he refrained from asking the question that was on his lips.

They descended the dark stairs in silence. The novice led them through a narrow passage; then they went up a steep staircase. On top was a landing, surrounding a large square well. The heavy scent of Indian incense wafted up through the lattice work screen that lined the well on all four sides.

"Deep down there is the nave of the monastery's temple," the novice explained. "Here we are on the same level as Your Honour's floor in the east wing." Entering a long, narrow corridor he added: "This leads to the store-room."

Judge Dee stood still. Smoothing down his long black beard he looked at the three high windows in the plaster wall on his right. Their sills were only about two feet above the floor.

The novice had pushed a heavy door open. He preceded the two men into an oblong, low-ceilinged room. The light of two candles shone on piles of boxes and bundles.

"Why are those candles burning here?" the judge asked.

"The monks go in and out of here all the time, sir, to fetch the masks and the stage dresses," the novice replied. He pointed at the row of large wooden masks and gorgeous brocade robes that covered the wall on their left. The wall on the right was taken up entirely by a wooden rack, stacked with halberds, spears, tridents, flagpoles and other paraphernalia used in the mystery plays. The judge noticed that neither wall had a single window; there were only two small ones in the back wall opposite them. He estimated that those two windows must be facing east, in the outer wall of the monastery. He turned to the novice and said:

"Wait for us outside!"

Tao Gan had been surveying the room, pensively playing with the three long hairs that sprouted from a wart on his left cheek. Now he asked in a low voice: "What is wrong with this store-room, Your Honour?"

Judge Dee told him about the weird scene he had witnessed when looking out of the window in the guest building opposite. "The prior remarked," he concluded, "that there is no window in the wall of this store-room facing the building where our quarters are, and apparently he was right. Yet I could hardly have dreamt it all! The naked woman must have lost her left arm some time ago, for I didn't notice any blood. If I had, I would have rushed to her at once to investigate, of course."

"Well," Tao Gan said, "it shouldn't be too difficult to find a one-armed woman; there can't be many of them running about in this monastery. Could you see anything of the furnishings of the room, sir?"

"No. I told you I got only one brief glimpse, didn't I?" Judge Dee said crossly.

"In any case it must have happened here in this store-room," Tao Gan remarked cheerfully. "I'll examine the wall; perhaps there's a window concealed behind all those spears and banners there. Perhaps even a trick window."

Judge Dee followed his assistant's movements as he busied himself about the arm-rack. Tao Gan pulled the dusty silk banners aside, looked among the shafts of the spears and tridents, and occasionally rapped the wall with his hard knuckles. He went about it quickly and efficiently, for this work belonged to his former trade. Tao Gan had originally been an itinerant swindler. One year before, shortly after the judge had taken up his post as magistrate of Han-yuan, he had extricated Tao Gan from a nasty situation, and then the wily trickster had mended his ways and entered Judge Dee's service. His wide knowledge of the ways of the underworld, and his skill in locating secret passages and forcing complicated locks, had proved very useful in the tracking down of elusive criminals, and helped the judge to solve more than one difficult case.

Leaving Tao Gan at his work, Judge Dee walked along the left wall, picking his way among the bags and boxes piled on the floor. He looked with distaste at the grotesque masks that were ogling him from the wall. He muttered half to himself, half to Tao Gan: "A weird creed, Taoism! Why should one need all that mummery of mystery plays and pompous religious ceremonies while we have the wise and crystal-clear teachings of our Master Confucius to guide us? One can only say for Taoism that it is at least a purely Chinese creed, and not an importation from the barbarous west, like Buddhism!"

"I gather that the Taoists had to institute monasteries and all that in order to be able to compete with the Buddhist crowd," Tao Gan remarked.

"Bah!" the judge said angrily. His head was aching; the clammy atmosphere of the room penetrated even his padded robe.

"Look at this, sir!" Tao Gan suddenly exclaimed.

The judge quickly joined him. Tao Gan had pulled a gaudy silk banner aside that hung against the wall near the large antique cupboard in the farthest corner. Under the dusty plaster that covered the brick wall one could still distinguish the outline of a window.

Silently the two men stared at the wall. Then Tao Gan looked uncomfortably at Judge Dee's impassive face. He said slowly: "There was indeed a window here, but it must have been walled up a long time ago."

Judge Dee looked up with a start. He said in a toneless voice: "It is near

JUDGE DEE AND TAO GAN IN THE STORE-ROOM

the corner of the building. That means that it's about opposite the window through which I looked out."

Tao Gan knocked on the wall. There was no doubt that it was solid. He took out his knife and with its point pried loose a piece of the plaster that covered the bricks with which the window had been blocked. He probed into the grooves among the bricks, and along the outline of the window. He shook his head perplexedly. After some hesitation he said diffidently: "This monastery is very old, Your Honour. I have often heard people say that mysterious, inexplicable things will sometimes happen in such places. Scenes of times long gone by are seen again, and . . ." His voice trailed off.

The judge passed his hand over his eyes. He said pensively: "The man I saw indeed wore a helmet of a type that is obsolete now; it was used by our soldiers more than a hundred years ago. . . . This is strange, Tao Gan, very strange." He thought for a long while, staring at the brick wall. Suddenly he looked hard at Tao Gan and said: "I think I noticed a suit of armour of that same antiquated type among the stage costumes hanging on the wall. Yes, there it is!"

He walked up to a mail coat with iron breastplates moulded like crouching dragons that was hanging under the row of leering devil masks. A pair of iron gloves and the empty scabbard of a long sword hung by its side.

"The round, close-fitting helmet belonging to that outfit is missing," Judge Dee went on.

"Many of those costumes are incomplete, sir. Just odd pieces."

The judge hadn't heard him. He continued: "I couldn't see what the man was wearing on his body. I had the impression it was something dark. He had a broad back, and he was quite tall, I think." He looked at Tao Gan with startled eyes. "Almighty Heaven, Tao Gan, am I seeing ghosts?"

"I'll go and measure the depth of the window niches," Tao Gan said.

While he was gone, Judge Dee pulled his robe closer to his body; he felt shivery. He took a silk handkerchief from his sleeve and wiped his watering eyes. He reflected that he probably had fever. Could it have been a hallucination?

Tao Gan came back.

"Yes," he said, "the wall is quite thick, nearly four feet. But still not thick enough for a secret room where a man can play about with a naked woman!"

"No, it isn't!" Judge Dee said dryly.

He turned to the old cupboard. The black-lacquered double doors were decorated with a pair of dragons, facing each other and surrounded by a pattern of stylised flames. He pulled the doors open. The cupboard was empty but for a pile of folded monks' cowls. The design of the two dragons was repeated on the back wall. "A fine antique specimen," he remarked to Tao Gan, then added with a sigh: "Well, I think that for the time being we better forget about the scene I saw, or thought I saw, and keep to the problems in hand. Three girls have died here in this monastery, and that has happened during the past year, mind you, not a hundred years ago! You'll remember that the one called Liu was said to have died from illness; Miss Huang committed suicide; and Miss Gao had a fatal accident—they said. I'll utilize this opportunity for asking the abbot for some more information about those three cases. Let's go down!"

When they stepped out into the corridor, they found the novice standing stock-still close to the door, peering ahead of him and listening intently. Seeing his pale face, the judge asked astonished: "What are you doing?"

"I . . . I thought I saw someone looking around the corner over there," the novice stammered.

"Well," Judge Dee said testily, "you said yourself that people are coming and going here all the time, didn't you?"

"It was a soldier!" the boy muttered.

"A soldier?"

The novice nodded. He listened again, then said in a low voice: "A hundred years ago there were many soldiers here. Rebels had occupied this monastery, and fortified themselves here together with their families. The army took it, and slaughtered all of them—men, women and children." He looked at the judge, his eyes wide with fear. "They say that on stormy nights like this their ghosts walk here and act over again all those horrible scenes. . . . Can't you hear anything, sir?"

Judge Dee listened.

"Only the rain!" he said impatiently. "Take us downstairs; there's a draught here!"

IV

The novice led them through a maze of passages down to the ground floor of the east wing. Downstairs was a spacious corridor, lined with high, red-lacquered pillars, decorated with intricate gilded wood carving. It represented dragons sporting among clouds. The floor boards had been polished to a beautiful dark sheen by the felt shoes of the countless feet that had passed there during past generations. When they arrived in front of the assembly hall, Judge Dee said to Tao Gan: "While I am talking with the abbot, you go to the prior and tell him about that broken axle. I hope they can mend and replace it tonight." Then he added in a whisper: "Try to get from the prior or someone else a good floor plan of this dismal place!"

The reception room was located near the entrance to the main hall. When the novice showed the judge in, he noticed with satisfaction that the room was well heated by a brazier heaped with glowing coals. Costly brocade wall-hangings kept the warmth inside.

A tall, thin man rose from the gilded couch in the back of the room and advanced across the thick carpet to meet the judge. He was a stately figure, looking taller still because of his long flowing robe of yellow brocade and a high yellow tiara, decorated with red tassels that hung down his back. As the abbot bade him welcome, the judge noticed that the abbot had curious, slate-coloured eyes that seemed as immobile as his long, austere face, smooth but for a thin moustache and a short, wispy beard.

They sat down in high-backed armchairs by the side of the couch. The novice prepared tea on the red-lacquered table in the corner.

"I feel embarrassed," Judge Dee began, "that my visit coincides with the big commemoration festival here. You'll have many guests staying in the monastery. I greatly fear that my staying here overnight will inconvenience you."

The abbot fixed him with his still eyes. Although their gaze was directed at him, Judge Dee had the weird impression that in fact it was turned inward. The abbot raised his long, curved eyebrows. He replied in a low, dry voice: "Your Honour's visit doesn't inconvenience us in the least. The east wing of our poor monastery has on the second and third floor more than forty guest rooms—though none of those is of course good enough for accommodating such a distinguished guest as our magistrate!"

"My quarters are most comfortable" the judge assured him hastily. He accepted the cup of hot tea which the novice offered him respectfully with both hands. He had a throbbing headache now; he found it difficult to formulate the usual polite inquiries. He decided to come directly to the point and said: "I would have given myself the pleasure of visiting this famous monastery soon after I had taken up my duties in Han-yuan. However, all through the past summer pressing official business prevented me from leaving Han-yuan. In addition to benefiting by your instruction and admiring this interesting ancient building, I had planned also to ask you for some information."

"I am entirely at Your Honour's service. What information might be required?"

"I would like to have a few more details about three deaths that occurred here last year," the judge said. "Just to complete my files, you see!"

The abbot gave the novice a sign to leave. When the door had closed behind the youngster, the abbot said with a deprecating smile: "We have more than a hundred monks living here, Your Honour, not to speak of the lay-brothers, novices, and occasional guests. Human life being submitted to the limitations set by Heaven, people fall ill and die, here as everywhere else. What particular deaths might Your Honour be referring to?"

"Well," Judge Dee replied, "going over the files in my tribunal I found, among the copies of death certificates forwarded to Han-yuan by this monastery, no less than three that referred to girls from outside. I gather that they had come to stay here to be initiated as nuns." As he saw the abbot knitting his thin eyebrows, he added with a quick smile: "I don't recollect their names and other particulars. I would have looked them up before coming here, but since my present visit was quite accidental . . ." He did not finish the sentence, looking expectantly at his host.

The abbot nodded slowly.

"I think I know what cases Your Honour has in mind. Yes, there was a young lady from the capital, a Miss Liu who fell ill here last year. The learned Master Sun personally treated her, but . . ."

He suddenly broke off and looked fixedly at the door. Judge Dee turned around in his chair to see who had come in, but he only saw the door close again.

"Those insolent actors!" the abbot exclaimed angrily. "They come barging in without even bothering to knock!" Noticing Judge Dee's astonished look, he quickly resumed: "As usual we have hired a small troupe of professional actors to assist the monks with the staging of the mystery plays that are performed on our commemoration day. They also play interludes, mainly acrobatics and juggling, and provide other light entertainment. They are quite useful, but they know, of course, nothing of monastic rules and behaviour." He angrily stamped his staff on the floor and concluded: "Next time we'll dispense with their services!"

"Yes," Judge Dee said, "I remember now that one girl of the surname Liu died of a lingering disease. May I ask you, just to get my record straight, who performed the autopsy?"

"Our prior, Your Honour. He is a qualified physician."

"I see. Wasn't there another girl who committed suicide?"

"That was a sad case!" the abbot replied with a sigh. "Quite an intelligent girl, but the very excitable type, you know. She suffered from hallucinations. I shouldn't have admitted her to begin with, but since she was so eager and since her parents insisted . . . One night Miss Gao had been very nervous, and she took poison. The body was returned to the family, and she was buried in her native place."

"And the third? I seem to remember that that was also a suicide, wasn't it?"

"No, it was an unfortunate accident, sir. Miss Huang was also a talented girl, deeply interested in the history of this monastery. She was always exploring the temple and adjacent buildings. Once the balustrade on the top floor of the southeast tower gave way when she was leaning over it, and she fell down into the ravine that borders our monastery on the east side."

"There was no autopsy report attached to Miss Huang's documents," the judge remarked.

The abbot sadly shook his head.

"No, Your Honour," he said slowly, "the remains could not be recovered. At the bottom of the ravine there is a cleft over a hundred feet deep. Nobody has ever succeeded in exploring it."

There was a pause. Then Judge Dee asked: "Is the tower she fell from the one built on top of the store-room? In that case it's right opposite the east wing, where my quarters are."

"Yes. It is." The abbot took a sip from his tea. Evidently he thought that it was time to conclude the interview. But Judge Dee made no move to take his leave. He caressed his long side-whiskers for a while then asked: "You don't have nuns staying here permanently, do you?"

"No, fortunately not!" the abbot answered with a thin smile. "My responsibilities are sufficiently heavy without that! But since this place, quite undeservedly, of course, enjoys a high reputation in this province, many families which have daughters desirous of entering religion, insist that they be initiated here. They receive instruction for a few weeks, and when nun's certificates have been bestowed upon them they leave and settle in one of the nunneries elsewhere in our province."

Judge Dee sneezed. When he had wiped off his moustache with his silk handkerchief, he said affably: "Many thanks for your explanations! You'll understand, of course, that my questions were a mere formality. I never thought for one moment that there had been irregularities here."

The abbot nodded gravely. The judge emptied his teacup then resumed: "Just now you mentioned a Master Sun. Is that by any chance the famous scholar and writer Sun Ming, who a few years ago served in the Palace as Tutor of His Imperial Majesty?"

"Yes, indeed! The Master's presence greatly honours this monastery! As you know, His Excellency had a most distinguished career. He served many years as Prefect of the capital, and retired after his two wives had died. Then he was appointed Imperial Tutor. When he left the Palace, his three sons had grown up and entered official life, so he decided to devote his remaining years to his metaphysical researches, and chose this monastery as his abode. His Excellency has been staying here now for two years already." He nodded slowly, then went on with evident satisfaction: "The Master's presence is a signal honour indeed! And far from keeping himself aloof, he takes a most gratifying interest in all that goes on here, and regularly attends our religious services. Thus His Excellency is completely conversant with all our problems, and never grudges us his valuable advice."

Judge Dee reflected ruefully that he would have to pay a courtesy visit to this exalted personage. He asked: "In what part of the monastery has the Master taken up his abode?"

"The west tower has been placed at his disposal. Your Honour will presently meet the Master in the assembly hall, as he is watching the performance there. Your Honour will also see there Mrs. Pao, a pious widow from the capital. She arrived here a few days ago together with her daughter, called White Rose, who wishes to enter religion. Then there is also a Mr. Tsung Lee, a poet of note, who has been staying here for a few weeks. Those are our only guests. A number of others cancelled their intended visits because of the inclement weather. There's also the theatrical troupe of Mr. Kuan Lai—but of course Your Honour won't be interested in that lowly crowd."

Judge Dee angrily blew his nose. It had always struck him as unjust that people in general considered the stage as a dishonourable profession, and actors and actresses more or less as outcasts. He had expected from the abbot a more humane attitude. He said: "In my opinion actors perform a useful task. They provide at low cost suitable amusement for the common people and thereby enliven their often drab lives. Moreover, the historical plays acquaint the people with our great national past. An advantage, by the way, which your mystery plays are lacking."

The abbot said stiffly: "Our mystery plays bear an allegorical rather than a historical character. They are meant to promulgate the Truth, and can therefore in no way be compared to common theatricals." To take the edge off his remark he added with a smile: "Yet I hope that Your Honour won't find them lacking entirely in historical interest. The masks and costumes used were made over a hundred years ago in this monastery; they are valuable antiques. Allow me to lead Your Honour to the hall now. The performance has been going on since noon today, and now they are at the last scenes. Later a simple, meagre meal will be served in the refectory. I hope that Your Honour will graciously consent to take part in it."

Judge Dee hardly enjoyed the prospect of sitting in on an official banquet, but as the magistrate of the district where the monastery was located he couldn't possibly refuse.

"I accept with the greatest pleasure!" he replied jovially. They rose and the abbot led him to the door.

When they were outside the abbot quickly looked up and down the semi-obscure corridor. He seemed relieved at seeing it completely deserted. He politely led the judge to a high double door.

V

Upon entering the enormous hall they were greeted by the deafening sounds of gongs, cymbals and some strident stringed instruments. They came from the orchestra of monks who were seated on a small platform on the left. The age-blackened roof of the hall was supported by a number of high thick pillars, among which were sitting over a hundred monks. The light of dozens of large paper lampions shone on their yellow robes.

The monks rose respectfully as the abbot led Judge Dee along the open path in the middle to a raised platform by the side of the stage in the back of the hall. The abbot sat down in a high-backed armchair of carved ebony, and bade the judge to be seated on his right. The third chair, on the abbot's left, was unoccupied.

The small prior came forward and reported that Master Sun had left, but that he would be back soon. The abbot nodded. He ordered him to bring fruit and other refreshments.

Judge Dee looked curiously at the magnificent pageant that was being enacted on the stage, which was lit by a row of red lampions. In the centre stood a high seat of gilded wood, on which was enthroned a handsome woman dressed in a red and green robe, glittering with gold ornaments. Her high chignon was decorated with a profusion of paper flowers, and she held a jade sceptre in her folded hands. Evidently she represented the Fairy Queen of the Taoist Western Paradise.

Eight figures, seven men and one woman, dressed in gorgeous long robes of embroidered silk were executing a slow dance in front of the Queen, to the measure of the solemn music. They represented the Eight Immortals of the Taoist Pantheon, doing homage to their Queen.

"Are those two women nuns?" the judge asked.

"No," the abbot replied. "The Queen is played by an actress of Kuan's troupe; Miss Ting is her name, I think. During the interval she did a rather good acrobatic dance, and juggled with cups and saucers. The Flower Fairy is Kuan's wife."

Judge Dee watched the pageant for a while but found it rather boring. He reflected that perhaps he wasn't in the right mood for it. His head was throbbing and his hands and feet were ice-cold. He looked at the box over on the other side of the stage. It was enclosed on three sides by a lattice screen, so that the two women sitting inside could not be seen by the audience. One was a portly lady rather heavily made up and wearing a beautiful dress of black damask, the other a young girl, also dressed in black, but not made up at all. She had a handsome, regular face, but her eyebrows were thicker than is thought becoming to a woman. Both were watching the performance in rapt attention. The abbot who had been following Judge Dee's gaze said: "That is Mrs Pao and her daughter White Rose."

The Judge saw to his relief that the Eight Immortals were descending the stage, followed by the Queen, who was led off by two novices dressed as pages. The music ended with a loud beat on the large bronze gong that reverberated through the hall. An appreciative murmur rose from the crowd of monks. Judge Dee sneezed again; he thought there was a nasty draught.

"A fine performance!" he remarked to the abbot. Out of the corner of his eye he saw Tao Gan step up to the dais. He came and stood behind Judge Dee's chair and whispered:

"The prior was busy but I had a talk with the almoner, sir. He claims that they have no ground plan of this place."

Judge Dee nodded. The hall had become quiet again. A powerfully built man with a broad, mobile actor's face had appeared on the stage. Evidently he was Mr. Kuan, the director of the troupe. He made a deep bow in the direction of the abbot, then announced in a clear voice: "By the leave of Your Holiness, we shall now, as usual, conclude the performance with a brief allegory. It represents the trials of the human soul seeking Salvation. The erring soul is played by Miss Ou-yang. She is harassed by Ignorance, played by a bear. Thank you!"

The astonished murmur from the audience was drowned in a mournful melody, interspersed with wailing blasts of the long brass trumpets that echoed through the hall. A slender girl dressed in a white robe with wide sleeves ascended the stage and started to execute a slow dance, turning round and round so that her sleeves and the trailing ends of her red sash fluttered about. Judge Dee looked intently at her heavily made-up face, then tried to get a glimpse of the girl in the box on the other side of the stage. But the portly lady was leaning forward, so that he couldn't see her daughter. Astonished, he said to Tao Gan: "That isn't an actress; that is Miss Pao, the girl who was sitting over in that screened box there!"

Tao Gan raised himself on tiptoe. He said: "A young girl is still sitting there, Your Honour. Next to a rather fat lady."

Craning his neck, Judge Dee had another look at the box.

"Yes, so she is," he said slowly. "But she is looking as scared as if she had seen a ghost. I wonder why that actress has made herself up so as to resemble Miss Pao. Perhaps she . . ."

He suddenly broke off. A big man dressed as an awe-inspiring warrior had appeared on the stage. His tight-fitting black costume accentuated his lithe, muscular body. The red light shone on the round helmet on his head and on the long sword that he whirled round. His face was painted red, with long white streaks across his cheeks.

"That's the man I saw with the naked girl!" Judge Dee whispered to Tao Gan. "Call the director here!"

The warrior was a superb swordsman. While dancing around the girl he made several quick passes at her with the long sword. She evaded the thrusts gracefully. Then he moved closer to her, stepping deftly to the measure of the drums. His sword swung close over her head, then came down in a wicked stroke that missed her shoulder by a hair-breadth. A sharp cry came from the ladies' box. Judge Dee saw that Miss Pao had risen and was gazing with horror-stricken face at the two figures on the stage, her hands gripping the balustrade. The portly lady spoke to her, but she didn't seem to hear.

The judge looked at the stage again.

"One wrong move and we'll have an accident!" he said worriedly to the abbot. "Who is that fellow anyway?"

"He is an actor called Mo Mo-te," the abbot replied. "I agree that he comes far too close. But he's being more careful now."

The warrior had indeed stopped his attacks on the girl. He was now executing a series of complicated feints some distance from her. His painted face flashed weirdly in the light of the lampions.

Tao Gan appeared by the side of Judge Dee's chair, and presented Mr. Kuan Lai, the director of the troupe.

"Why didn't you announce that Mo Mo-te would take part in the allegory?" the judge asked sharply.

Kuan smiled. "We often improvise a bit, sir," he said. "Mo Mo-te likes to show off his skill as a swordsman; therefore he assumed the role of Doubt, tormenting the erring soul."

"It comes too close to real torment to my taste," Judge Dee said curtly. "Look, he is attacking the dancer again!"

Now the girl evidently had difficulty in evading the vicious sword thrusts the warrior was aiming at her. Her breast was heaving and sweat streaked her made-up face. The judge thought there was something wrong with her left arm. He couldn't see it clearly because of the wide, swirling sleeve, but she seemed unable to use it, keeping it close to her body all the time. He said angrily to himself that if he was starting to see one-armed girls everywhere, he would have to take hold of himself. He sat up. A quick sword stroke cut off a corner from the dancer's fluttering left sleeve. A frightened cry sounded from the ladies' box.

The judge got up to shout to the warrior to stop. But at the same time the girl whistled, and now a huge black bear came ambling on to the stage. He turned his large head toward the warrior, who quickly retreated to a corner of the stage. Judge Dee sat down again.

The bear growled, then slowly went up to the girl, shaking its heavy head. The girl seemed in great fear. She covered her face with her right sleeve. The bear kept on advancing. The music had ceased; all was deadly quiet.

"The ugly brute will kill her!" the judge said angrily.

"It belongs to Miss Ou-yang, Your Honour," Kuan said reassuringly. "The chain on his collar is attached to that pillar at the back of the stage."

Judge Dee said nothing. He didn't like this at all. He noticed that Miss Pao had resumed her seat. She seemed to have lost interest in the show. But her face was still very pale.

The warrior made a few final feints with his sword, then disappeared. The bear was walking slowly around the girl who was now executing a quick dance, gyrating on the tips of her toes.

"Where is that fellow off to?" Judge Dee asked Kuan.

"He'll be going to our dressing room, sir," the director answered. "He'll be anxious to get rid of his make-up and his costume."

"Was he on the stage about one hour ago?" the judge asked again.

"He has been on ever since the interval," Kuan replied with a smile. "And he had to wear a heavy wooden mask all through. He was acting the part of the Spirit of Death, you know. Anyone else would have been tired out now, but he is an extraordinarily strong fellow. Just now he came on again because he couldn't resist the temptation to show off his skill."

Judge Dee hadn't heard his last words. His eyes were riveted on the stage, where the bear had now raised itself on its haunches. It was groping with its enormous paws for the girl, growling angrily. The girl drew back, but suddenly the bear was on her with amazing swiftness. The girl fell on the floor, and the animal stood over her, opening its huge jaws lined with long yellow teeth.

The judge suppressed a cry. Suddenly the girl crept out from under the hulking animal and came gracefully to her feet. She patted the bear on its head, then took it by its collar and made a deep bow. She led the animal off stage amid thunderous applause from the audience.

Judge Dee wiped the perspiration from his brow. In the excitement he had forgotten all about his cold, but now he realized again that he had a bad headache. He wanted to get up, but the abbot laid his hand on his arm and said: "Now Mr. Tsung Lee, the poet, will pronounce the epilogue!"

A young man with a shrewd, beardless face stood in the centre of the empty stage. He made a bow, then began in a sonorous, well-modulated voice:

> All you good men and women! Noble Excellencies!
> Monks and lay-brothers, and all you novices!
> To all of you who kindly watched our humble play
> Of the stirring story of that poor erring soul
> Losing her struggle with Doubt and Ignorance, I say:
> Never despair of reaching in the end your goal!
> However long the forces of Darkness scheme,
> The Truth of Tao shall all of you redeem.
> Hear now the Sublime Truth, expressed in clumsy verse:
> All wicked evil, Truth and Reason shall disperse,
> Defeat for ever the deadly shades of night,
> Dissolve the morning clouds in the Eternal Light!

He made another deep bow and left the stage. The orchestra struck up the finale.

Judge Dee looked questioningly at the abbot. Spoken in a monastery called Morning Cloud, the last line about "dissolving morning clouds" was most inauspicious, even rude. The abbot barked at the director: "Get me that poet here!" And to the judge: "The impudent rascal!"

When the young man was standing in front of them, the abbot addressed him harshly: "What made you add that last line, Mr. Tsung? It completely spoilt the auspicious atmosphere of this solemn occasion!"

The young man seemed quite at ease. He gave the abbot a quizzical look and replied with a smile: "The last line, Your Holiness? I had feared that the line before the last might perhaps be considered inappropriate. It's not always easy to find the right rhymes on the spot, you know!"

The abbot was about to make an angry retort, but Tsung continued placidly: "Short verses are easier, of course, Like this one, for instance:

> One abbot up in the hall,
> One abbot under the floor
> In all two abbots—
> One preaches to the monks,
> The other to the maggots."

The abbot angrily stamped his staff on the floor. His face was

A POET TAUNTS A TAOIST ABBOT

twitching. Judge Dee expected him to burst out in a fit of rage. But he succeeded in mastering himself. He said coldly: "You may go, Mr. Tsung."

He rose. The judge noticed that his hands were trembling. Judge Dee took leave of him with a few polite phrases.

As they were walking towards the exit, the judge said to Tao Gan: "We'll go now to the actors' dressing room. I must have a talk with that fellow Mo Mo-te. Do you know where it is?"

"Yes, Your Honour, on the same floor as mine, in a side corridor."

"I never saw such a rabbit warren!" Judge Dee muttered. "And what is all that nonsense about no ground plan being available? They are required by law to have one!"

"The almoner claims, sir, that the section higher up—that is, the part of the monastery beyond the temple—is closed to everybody except the abbot and the ordained monks. That forbidden part may not be charted or depicted. The almoner agreed that it was awkward not to have a plan, for this is a very large place. Even the monks themselves sometimes lose their way."

"A preposterous situation!" the judge said peevishly. "Just because the Palace has deigned to show interest in the Taoist creed, those people think they are above the law! And I hear that Buddhist influence is also growing at Court. I don't know which of the two is worse!"

He walked over to the office on the opposite side of the hall. He told the monk in charge there that after he had changed, he wanted a novice to take him to Master Sun's quarters. Tao Gan borrowed a lantern from the monk, then they waited a while in front of the office to let the throng of monks who were leaving the hall file past them.

"Look at all those able-bodied fellows!" Judge Dee said sourly. "They ought to do their duty to society, marry and raise children!"

He sneezed.

Tao Gan gave him a worried look. He had come to know the judge as a man of a remarkably equable temper; even if he was annoyed he rarely showed it so clearly. He asked: "Did that solemn abbot give a satisfactory explanation of those three deaths that occurred here?"

"He did not!" the judge said emphatically. "It is just as I thought; there are highly suspicious features. When we are back in Han-yuan, I shall first obtain from the families of the dead girls more details about their background, then we'll come back to this monastery with Sergeant Hoong, Ma Joong, Chiao Tai, the scribes and a dozen constables, and institute a thorough investigation. And I'll not announce that visit beforehand, mind you! That's the little surprise I have in store for our friend the abbot!"

VI

Tao Gan nodded contentedly. Then he said:

"The almoner told me the same story about the ghosts of the people who were killed here a hundred years ago. I now know why that novice was listening so keenly up there in the corridor!"

"Why?" Judge Dee asked wiping his moustache.

"It is said that those ghostly apparitions sometimes whisper one's name. That means that the person who hears them will die soon."

"Silly superstitions! Let's go upstairs to the dressing room of those actors."

When they arrived on the first landing, Judge Dee looked casually into the narrow, semi-dark corridor on their right. He halted. A slender girl in a white dress was hurrying along away from them.

"That's the girl with the bear!" the judge said quickly to Tao Gan. "I want to talk to her! What's her name again?"

"Miss Ou-yang, sir."

The judge went after the white figure. When he was close behind her, he said: "Wait a moment, Miss Ou-yang!"

She swung round with a frightened cry. The judge saw that her face was of a deadly pallor and her eyes wide with fear. It struck him again that she closely resembled Miss Pao. He said kindly: "You needn't be afraid, Miss Ou-yang. I only wanted to congratulate you on your performance. I must say that . . ."

"Thank you, sir!" the girl interrupted in a soft, cultured voice. "I must hurry along now, I must . . ."

She looked anxiously past the judge and made to turn around again.

"Don't run away!" Judge Dee ordered curtly. "I am the magistrate, and I want to talk with you. You seem quite upset. Is that actor Mo Mo-te perhaps bothering you?"

She impatiently shook her small head.

"I must go and feed my bear," she said quickly.

The judge saw that all the time she kept her left arm close to her body. He asked sharply: "What is wrong with your left arm? Did Mo wound you with his sword?"

"Oh no, a long time ago my bear scratched me there. Now I must really . . ."

"I fear that Your Honour didn't like my poetry," a cheerful voice spoke up behind them. Judge Dee turned around. He saw Tsung Lee, who was making an exaggerated bow.

"I did not, young man!" the judge said annoyed. "If I had been the abbot I would have had you thrown out then and there!"

He turned to the girl again. But she had disappeared.

"The abbot'll think twice before he has me thrown out, sir!" the young poet said smugly. "My late father, Dr. Tsung, was a patron of this monastery, and my family still regularly donates substantial sums to it."

Judge Dee looked him up and down.

"So you are a son of the retired Governor Tsung Fa-men," he said. "The Governor was a great scholar. I have read his handbook on provincial administration. He wouldn't have liked your clumsy doggerels!"

"I only wanted to rile the abbot a bit," Tsung said with an embarrassed air. "The fellow is such a self-important stick! My father didn't think much of him, sir."

"Even so," the judge said, "your poem was in extremely bad taste. And what on earth did you mean by that silly rhyme about two abbots?"

"Doesn't Your Honour know?" Tsung Lee asked astonished. "Two years ago Jade Mirror, the former abbot of this monastery, died—or was 'translated,' as the correct term is, I think. He was embalmed, and now sits enthroned in the crypt under the Founder's shrine, in the sanctum. Jade Mirror was a very holy man—both dead and alive."

Judge Dee made no comment. He had worries enough without going into the life-histories of the abbots of the Morning Cloud Monastery. He said: "I am on my way to the actors' dressing room, so I won't detain you here further."

"I was going there too, sir," the young man said respectfully. "May I show Your Honour the way?"

He took them around the corner into a long corridor lined by doors on both sides.

"Is Miss Ou-yang's room near here?" the judge asked.

"Somewhat further along," Tsung replied. "But I wouldn't go there without her, Your Honour! That bear is dangerous."

"She must be in her room," Judge Dee said. Didn't you see her when you came up to us, just now?"

"Of course I didn't see her!" the poet said, astonished. "How could she have been here? Just before coming up I had a talk with her, down in the hall. She's still there!"

The judge gave him a sharp look, then glanced at Tao Gan. His assistant shook his head, a perplexed expression on his long face.

Tsung Lee knocked on a door near the end of the corridor. They entered a large, untidy room. Kuan Lai and two women quickly rose from the round table where they were sitting and greeted the judge with low bows.

Kuan presented the nice-looking young girl as Miss Ting, the actress who had acted the part of the Queen of the Western Paradise. He added that her specialty was acrobatic dancing, and juggling. The dowdy middle-aged woman he presented as his wife.

Judge Dee said a few kind words about the performance. The director seemed overwhelmed by the interest shown in his troupe by this distinguished person. He didn't quite know whether he ought to ask the judge to sit down with them, or whether that would be too presumptuous. Judge Dee solved his quandary by sitting down uninvited. Tsung Lee took the seat opposite, where a wine-jug of coarse earthenware was standing. Tao Gan took up his position behind Judge Dee's chair. Then the judge asked: "Where are Miss Ou-yang and Mo Mo-te? I would like to offer them my compliments too. Mo is a fine swordsman, and Miss Ou-yang's performance with the bear made my hair stand on end!"

This kind address apparently failed to put the director at his ease. His hand trembled when he poured out a cup of wine for the judge, so that he spilt some of it on the table. He sat down awkwardly and said: "Mo Mo-te will have gone to the store-room to return his costume, sir." Pointing at the pile of crumpled, red-stained sheets of paper on the dressing table he added: "Apparently he has been in here already to remove the paint from his face. As to Miss Ou-yang, she told me downstairs that she would come here after she had fed her bear."

Judge Dee got up and walked over to the dressing table, pretending that he wanted to adjust his cap in front of the mirror there. He looked casually at the crumpled sheets of paper and the pots with ointments and paint. He reflected that the red stains on the paper might as well be blood. When he was resuming his seat, he noticed that Mrs. Kuan was looking apprehensively at him. He took a sip of his wine, and asked Kuan about the stage technique of historical plays.

The director set out on a long explanation. The judge only half listened; he was trying to follow at the same time the conversation the others had struck up.

"Why didn't you go help Miss Ou-yang to feed the bear?" Tsung Lee asked Miss Ting. "She'd have liked that, I am sure!"

"Mind your own business!" Miss Ting said curtly. "Keep to your roses, will you?"

Tsung Lee said with a sly grin:

"Well, Miss Pao is rather an attractive girl, so why shouldn't I make poems for her? I even made one for you, dear. Here it is:

> True love, false love,
> Love of tomorrow, of yesterday—
> Plus and minus
> Keep us gay
> Minus and minus,
> Heaven'll fine us!"

Judge Dee looked around. Miss Ting's face had grown scarlet. He heard Mrs. Kuan say: "You'd better mind your language, Mr. Tsung!"

"I only wanted to warn her," Tsung Lee said unperturbed. "Don't you know that popular song they are now singing in the capital?" He hummed a fetching tune, beating the measure with his forefinger, then sang the words in a low pleasant voice:

> Two times ten and still unwed,
> There's yet hope for a bright tomorrow.
> Three times eight and alone in bed,
> There's nothing ahead but cold and sorrow!

Miss Ting wanted to make an angry remark, but now Judge Dee intervened. He addressed the poet coldly: "You interrupt my conversation, Mr. Tsung. I must also inform you that I have but a feeble sense of humour. Reserve your witticisms for a more appreciative audience." And to Kuan: "I have to go up and change for the banquet. Don't bother to see me out!"

Motioning Tao Gan to follow him he went out, closing the door in the face of the disconcerted director. He said to his lieutenant: "Before I go up, I'll try to find Mo Mo-te. You stay here and drink a few more rounds with those people. I perceive all kinds of undercurrents. You must try to find out what's going on. By the way, what did that paltry poet mean with his plus and minus?"

Tao Gan looked embarrassed. He cleared his throat, then replied: "They are coarse terms used in the street, Your Honour. Plus means man and minus woman."

"I see. Well, when Miss Ou-yang turns up, try to verify how long she was downstairs. She can't have been in two places at the same time!"

"That poet may have lied about meeting her in the hall, sir! And again when he pretended that he hadn't seen her talking to us. It's true that the corridor is very narrow, and that we were standing in between, but he could hardly have missed seeing her!"

"If Tsung Lee spoke the truth," the judge remarked, "the girl we talked to in the corridor must have been Miss Pao, posing as Miss Ou-yang. But no, that's wrong! The girl we met kept her arm close to her body and Miss Pao used both her arms when she gripped the balustrade, frightened by Mo's swordplay on the stage. I can't make head or tail of it! Find out what you can, then come up to my room!"

He took the lantern from Tao Gan, and went to the stairs. Tao Gan went back into the actors' room.

Judge Dee thought he remembered the way to the store-room well enough. While climbing the staircase in the next building he noticed that his back and legs were aching. He wondered whether that was due to his cold or to the unaccustomed going up and down stairs all the time. He thought he rather liked Kuan, but Tsung Lee was the type of fresh youngster he had small use for. The poet seemed to be on very friendly terms with the actors. Apparently he was interested in Miss Pao, but since she was about to become a nun there seemed to be little hope for the poet there. His indelicate doggerel about Miss Ting suggested a relation between her and Miss Ou-yang. But the morals of those people were no concern of his. It was Mo Mo-te who interested him.

He heaved a sigh when at last he found himself on the draughty landing on the floor above the temple nave. Through the lattice-work he heard the monotonous chant of the monks coming up from the well, apparently performing vespers.

Upon entering the corridor on his right he was astonished to see that there was no light. But when he held his lantern high, he realized that he had taken the wrong passage. There were no windows on the wall on his right, and this passage was narrower than the one leading to the store-room. Cobwebs hung from the low rafters. He was about to turn around and retrace his steps, when he suddenly heard a murmur of voices.

He stood still and listened, wondering where the whispers might be coming from. The corridor was deserted, and at the end there was a heavy iron grille. He walked up to the entrance, but there the vague whispers were drowned by the chant of the monks. With a puzzled frown he walked back to the middle of the passage, looking for a door.

Here he heard the whispering again, but he couldn't make out one word of what was being said. Suddenly he caught his own name: Dee Jen-djieh.

Then everything was silent.

VII

The judge tugged angrily at his beard. The ghostly voice had disturbed him more than he cared to admit. Then he took hold of himself. Probably some monks were talking about him in another room or passage near there. Often the echo played queer tricks in such old buildings. He stood listening for a while, but did not hear anything. The whispers had ceased.

Shrugging his shoulders he walked back to the landing. He now saw that he had indeed taken a wrong turn. The passage leading to the store-room was on the other side. He quickly walked around the well, and now found the right corridor. He recognized the three narrow windows on his right. The door of the store-room was standing ajar. He heard voices coming from inside.

As he went in he saw to his disappointment that there were only two monks. They were busy with the lock of a large box of red-lacquered leather. He didn't see Mo Mo-te, but a quick glance at the wall on the left showed that the round iron helmet was now hanging in its place above the coat of mail, and that the long sword had been put back in the scabbard. He asked the elder man: "Have you seen the actor Mo Mo-te?"

"No, Your Honour," the monk answered. "But we have just come in. We must have missed him."

The man spoke politely enough, but the judge didn't like the surly look of the younger monk, a tall, broad-shouldered fellow who stared at him suspiciously.

"I wanted to compliment him on his skill in sword-fighting," Judge Dee said casually. Apparently the actor had returned to Kuan's room, and there Tao Gan would keep an eye on him.

He set out on the long way to his own quarters on the third floor of the east wing.

He felt very tired when at last he knocked on the door of the dressing room. One of the maids opened the door. The others were preparing the rice for the evening meal on the brazier in the corner.

In the bedroom Judge Dee found his three wives gathered around the tea table, engaged in a game of dominoes. As they rose to greet him, his First Lady said with satisfaction: "You are just in time for a game, before we start dinner."

The judge looked wistfully at the pieces on the table, for dominoes was his favourite game. He said: "Much to my regret I can't have dinner with you here. I have to take part in the banquet the abbot is giving downstairs. There's a former Imperial Tutor staying here, too. I couldn't possibly refuse."

"Good Heavens!" his First Lady exclaimed, "that means that I must pay a courtesy visit to his wife!"

"No, the Tutor is a widower. But I'll have to call on him before the banquet. Take my ceremonial robes out, will you?"

He blew his nose vigorously.

"I am glad that I won't have to get dressed!" she said with relief. "But it's a shame that you should be up and about. You certainly have a head-cold. Look, your eyes are watering!"

While she opened the clothes box and started to lay out Judge Dee's green brocade robe, his third wife said: "I'll make you a poultice of orange peel. If you keep that around your head, you'll feel much better tomorrow!"

"How can I attend the banquet with a bandage round my head!" the judge exclaimed aghast. "I'd look like a fool!"

"You can pull your cap down over it, can't you?" his First Lady said practically as she helped him change. "Nobody'll notice it!"

The judge mumbled some protests but his third wife had already taken a handful of dried orange rinds from their medicine chest and was putting them in a bowl of hot water. When they were well soaked, his second wife wrapped them up in a linen bandage and together they wound it tightly around his head. His First Lady pulled his velvet cap well down and said: "There you are, it doesn't show at all!"

Judge Dee thanked them. He promised that he would come up as soon as the banquet was over. When he was at the door, he turned round and added: "All kinds of people are about here tonight, so you'd better keep the door to the corridor locked and barred, and let nobody in before the maids have ascertained who it is."

He went into the dressing room, where Tao Gan stood waiting for him. The judge told the maids to go to the bedroom and serve tea to his wives. He sat down with Tao Gan at the corner table and asked in a low voice: "Did Mo Mo-te go to Kuan's room? I just missed him."

"No," Tao Gan replied. "He must be walking about somewhere. But soon after you had left, Miss Ou-yang came in. Without make-up she doesn't resemble Miss Pao, although she has the same regular, oval face. I think it was Miss Pao we met in the corridor, for you'll remember that she spoke in a soft, pleasant voice, and Miss Ou-yang's is rather harsh, and a bit hoarse. And although I don't claim to be a connoisseur of women, I think the girl we met was plumper than Miss Ou-yang, who is rather on the bony side."

"Yet the girl we met didn't use her left arm, exactly like Miss Ou-yang. What did she talk about?"

"She is rather a taciturn girl, it seems. She only became a bit more lively when I made her join a conversation with Miss Ting about acrobatic dances. I referred casually to Tsung Lee having met Miss Ou-yang in the hall. She only remarked sourly that he was a bore. Then I said that you hadn't liked the abrupt way of her disappearing in the midst of a talk with you. She gave me a sharp look, and said vaguely that her bear needed a lot of attention."

"Somebody is fooling us!" Judge Dee exclaimed, angrily tugging at his beard. Then he asked: "What did they say about Mo Mo-te?"

"It seems he is a man of rather erratic habits. He'll join the troupe for a month or so, then disappear again. He always acts the part of the villain, and Kuan maintains that that tends to make a man a bit touchy in the end. I gathered that Mo is rather fond of Miss Ting, but she won't have him. Therefore Mo is fearfully jealous of Miss Ou-yang; he suspects that the two girls are having a little affair of their own together, just as Tsung Lee suggested in his poem. Kuan agrees that Mo went a bit too far in frightening Miss Ou-yang with that sword dance, but he added that with that nasty bear of hers about she needn't fear anybody. The animal follows its mistress about and obeys her like a lapdog, but nobody else dares to come near the brute. It has a vicious temper."

"It's a vexing puzzle!" the judge muttered. "Suppose that Miss Ou-yang or Miss Pao was running away from Mo Mo-te when we met her in the corridor, and that he is a dangerous maniac. That would fit in with the weird scene I saw through the window. The man I saw must have been Mo Mo-te, but who was the girl he was assaulting? We must find out whether there are other women staying in this monastery besides the ones we know about."

"I didn't dare to inquire about a mutilated woman without your orders, sir," Tao Gan said. "But I don't think that there are any other women staying here besides Mrs. Kuan and the two actresses, and Mrs. Pao with her daughter, of course."

"Don't forget that we have seen only a very small part of this monastery," the judge said. "Heaven knows what goes on in the section forbidden to outsiders! And we don't even have a map of the place! Well, I'll go and call on Master Sun now. You go back to the actors. When the elusive Mo Mo-te turns up, you stick to him like a leech, and go to the banquet with him. I'll see you there later."

In the corridor a novice stood waiting for the judge.

"Do we have to go outside to reach the west tower?" Judge Dee asked. The rain was still clattering against the shutters, he didn't like to get his ceremonial robe wet.

"Oh no, sir!" the novice replied. "We'll go to the west wing by way of the passage over the temple hall."

"More stairs!" the judge muttered.

VIII

They made the now familiar journey to the landing over the temple-nave. The novice took the passage opposite the one that led to the store-room. It was a long, straight corridor, lit by only one broken lantern.

While walking behind the novice, Judge Dee suddenly had the uncomfortable feeling that someone was watching him from behind. He halted in his steps and looked over his shoulder. He saw something dark flit past the entrance at the far end of the passage. It could have been a man in a grey robe. As he walked on, he asked the novice:

"Do the monks often use this passage too?"

"Oh no, sir! I only took it because it saves us from going outside in the rain. All people who have business in the west tower go up there by the spiral staircase, near the portal in front of the refectory."

When they had arrived in the small square hall in the west side of the building, the judge stood still in order to orientate himself.

"Where does that lead to?" he asked, pointing at a narrow door on his right.

"It gives access to the Gallery of Horrors, sir, in the left wing of the central court, behind the temple. But we novices are not allowed to go in there."

"I would have thought that viewing that gallery would be a good deterrent to committing sins!" Judge Dee remarked. He knew that every larger Taoist monastery had a gallery where the punishments meted out to sinners in the Ten Taoist Hells were painted in lurid detail on the wall, or plastically represented by statues moulded in clay or sculpted in wood.

As they ascended a few steps on their left, the novice warned: "You'll have to be careful sir! The balustrade of the landing in front of the Master's room is being repaired. Please keep close to me!"

When he was standing on the platform in front of a high, red-lacquered door, Judge Dee saw that part of the balustrade was indeed missing. He looked down into the dark shaft of the staircase. It seemed very deep.

"These are the stairs I mentioned just now. They lead down to the west wing," the novice explained. "They come out in front of the refectory, three floors down."

Judge Dee gave him his large red visiting card. The novice knocked on the door.

A booming voice told them to come in.

In the brilliant light of four high silver candelabra a tall man sat reading at a huge desk, piled with books and papers. The novice bowed deeply and placed the visiting card on the table. Master Sun glanced at it, then quickly got up and came forward to meet the judge.

"So you are the magistrate of our district!" he said in a deep, sonorous voice. "Welcome to the Monastery of the Morning Clouds, Dee!"

Judge Dee bowed, his arms respectfully folded in his wide sleeves.

"This person had never dared to hope, sir," he said, "that a mishap on the road would provide the long looked-for opportunity of paying my respects to such an eminent person."

"Let's dispense with all empty formality, Dee!" Sun said jovially. "Sit down here in front of my desk while I put these papers in order." As he resumed his seat in the armchair behind his desk, he said to the novice who had poured out two cups of tea: "Thank you, my boy, you may go now. I'll look after the guest myself."

While sipping the fragrant jasmine tea the judge looked at his host as he was quickly sorting out the papers before him. He was as tall as the judge, but more heavily built. His thick neck was half buried in his broad, bulging shoulders. Judge Dee knew the Master must be nearly sixty, but his rosy, round face didn't show a single wrinkle. A short, grey ringbeard grew round his chin, his silvery grey hair was combed back straight from the broad forehead and plastered to his large, round head. Having assumed the status of Taoist recluse, the Master wore no cap. He wore his moustache trimmed short, but he had thick, tufted eyebrows. Everything about him indicated that this was a remarkable personality.

Judge Dee read some of the scrolls inscribed with Taoist texts that covered the walls. Then Sun pushed the sorted-out papers away. Fixing the judge with his piercing eyes he asked: "You referred to a mishap on the road. Nothing serious, I hope?"

"Oh no, sir! I stayed for two weeks in the capital, and early this morning left there to go back to Han-yuan, in a tilt cart. We had hoped to be home before the evening meal. But shortly after we had crossed the district frontier, the weather got worse, and when we were up in the mountains here, the axle broke. Therefore I had to ask for shelter in this monastery. We'll leave tomorrow morning. I am told these storms don't last long."

"Bad luck for you, good luck for me!" Sun said with a smile. "I always enjoy talking with capable young officials. You should have come here earlier, Dee! This monastery is within your jurisdiction."

"I have been very remiss, sir!" the judge said hastily. "The fact is that there was some trouble in Han-yuan, and . . ."

"I heard all about it!" Sun interrupted him. "You did good work there, Dee. Prevented a major disturbance of the peace, in fact."

The judge acknowledged the compliment with a bow. He said:

"I shall certainly come back here soon, in order to be further instructed by Your Excellency." Since this learned and experienced high official was apparently in a friendly mood, he thought he ought to try to settle at least

JUDGE DEE VISITS AN EXALTED PERSON

one aspect of the problem of the mutilated naked woman. After a momentary hesitation he resumed: "Might I take the liberty of consulting Your Excellency about a curious experience I had here just now?"

"By all means! What happened, and where?"

"As a matter of fact," Judge Dee said, somewhat embarrassed, "I don't know what happened exactly. When I went up to the quarters assigned to me, I saw for a brief moment a scene that must have happened more than a hundred years ago, when the soldiers slaughtered the rebels here. Are such things possible?"

Sun leaned back in his armchair. He said gravely: "I wouldn't call it impossible, Dee. Doesn't it often happen that upon entering an empty room you definitely know that someone had been there a few moments before? You can't explain that, it's just a feeling. It means that the person who was there before you left something of himself behind. Yet he did nothing special there, perhaps he just looked at a book or wrote a letter. Now suppose that the same man died a violent death in that room. It is only to be expected that the terrible emotion of that moment impregnated the atmosphere of that room, and so deeply, too, that it lingers on for years. If a hyper-sensitive person, or a person who has become hyper-sensitive because he is very tired, happens to enter there, he may well perceive that imprint. Don't you think that some such reasoning might explain what you saw, Dee?"

The judge nodded slowly. Evidently Sun had given much thought to such abstruse matters. The explanation did not convince him, but it was a possibility he would have to keep in mind. He said politely: "You are probably right, sir. I am indeed rather tired, and on top of that I caught a cold in the rain outside. In that condition . . ."

"A cold? I haven't had a cold for thirty years!" Sun cut him short. "But I live according to a strict discipline, you know, nurturing my vital essence."

"Do you believe in the Taoist theory about reaching immortality in this life, sir?" Judge Dee asked, somewhat disappointed.

"Of course not!" Sun replied disdainfully. "Every man is immortal, but only in so far that he lives on in his offspring. Heaven has limited human life to a few score years, and all attempts at prolonging it beyond that limit by artificial means are futile. What we should strive after is to pass our limited life with a healthy mind and body. And that can be achieved by living in a more natural manner than we are wont to, especially by improving our diet. Be careful with your diet, Dee!"

"I am a follower of Confucius," the judge said, "but I fully admit that Taoism also contains deep wisdom."

"Taoism continues where Confucius left off," Master Sun remarked.

"Confucianism explains how man should behave as a member of an ordered society. Taoism explains man's relations to the Universe—of which that social order is but one aspect."

Judge Dee was not exactly in the mood for an involved philosophical discussion. But he felt he should not take his leave before having tried to verify two points. After a suitable pause he asked: "Could it be that undesirable elements from outside are roaming about here, sir? Just now, when the novice was taking me here, I had the feeling that we were being followed. While passing the corridor that links the nave with this tower, to be precise."

Master Sun gave him a searching look. He thought for a while, then he asked suddenly:

"Are you fond of fish?"

"Yes, I am," the judge replied nonplussed.

"There you are! Fish clogs the system, my dear fellow. It makes the blood-circulation sluggish, and that affects the nerves. That's what makes you see and hear things that aren't there! Rhubarb is what you need, I think. It purifies the blood. I'll look it up. I have rather a fine collection of medical books. Remind me tomorrow morning. I'll draw up a detailed dieting schedule for you."

"Thank you, sir. I hate to trouble you, but I would be most grateful for your elucidation on another point that has often puzzled me. I have heard people say that some Taoists, under the pretext of religious motives, practise orgies in secret, and force young women to take part in those. Is there any truth in these allegations?"

"Utter nonsense, of course!" Master Sun exclaimed. "Heavens, Dee, how could we Taoists indulge in orgies, on our strict diet? Orgies, forsooth!" He rose and added: "Now we had better go downstairs. The banquet is about to start and the abbot'll be waiting for us. I must warn you that he's not a very profound scholar, but he means well, and he manages this monastery quite efficiently."

"That must be an onerous task," Judge Dee said as he rose also. "The monastery is like a small city! I would like to explore it a bit, but I was told that there doesn't exist a floor plan, and that anyway the part beyond the temple is closed to visitors."

"All that hocus-pocus! Only meant to impress the credulous crowd! I have told the abbot Heaven knows how many times that the monastery is required to have a floor plan; Article 28 of the Regulations of Officially-recognised Places of Worship. Look here, Dee, I can orientate you in a trice." Walking over to the side wall he pointed to a scroll hanging there and went on: "This is a diagram I drew myself. It is really quite simple. The people who built this place two hundred years ago wanted the ground plan to represent the universe, and at the same time Man, as a miniature replica of it. The outline of the whole complex is an oval, which represents the Original Beginning. It faces south, and is built on four levels against the mountain slope. All along the east side is a deep ravine. On the west is the forest.

"Now then! We start from the front court, a triangle, with around it the kitchens, stables, and the rooms of the lay brothers and novices. Then we have the temple court, flanked by two squares, which stand for two large, three-storied buildings. The west wing has the refectory on the ground floor, the library on the second, and the quarters of the prior, the almoner and the registrar on the third. The east wing has on the ground floor the large assembly hall where they are now staging the mystery plays, and the offices. The second and third floor are for lodging visitors from outside. You and your family have been accommodated there, I suppose?"

"Yes," the judge replied, "we are on the north-east corner of the third floor. Two large, comfortable rooms."

"Good. We go on. Behind the temple court is the temple itself—there are some fine antique statues, well worth seeing. Behind the temple is the central court, with a tower on each corner. You are here in the south-west tower, which was assigned to me. On the left of the court is the Gallery of Horrors—a concession to popular beliefs, Dee! On the right are the quarters of the ordained monks, and at the back, over the gate, the private residence of the abbot. Lastly we have a circular section, the Sanctum. To sum up, we have a triangle, two squares, one square, and a circle, in that order. Each of those shapes has a mystical meaning, but we'll skip that. The main thing is that now you know how to orientate yourself. There are, of course, hundreds of passages, corridors and staircases that connect all the buildings, but if you keep this diagram in mind, you can't go far wrong!"

"Thank you, sir!" Judge Dee said gratefully. "What buildings are there in the Sanctum?"

"Only a small pagoda which contains the urn with the ashes of the Founding Saint."

"Does anyone live in that part of the monastery?"

"Of course not! I visited the place myself. There is only that pagoda and the surrounding wall. But as it is considered the holiest part, I did not draw it in my diagram, so as not to offend our good abbot. I replaced it by the halved circle you see there on top, the Taoist symbol of the working of the universe. It represents the interaction of the two Primordial Forces, the eternal rhythm of nature, which we call Tao. You may call those two forces Light and Dark, Positive and Negative, Man and Woman, Sun and Moon—take your choice! The circle shows how, when Positive reaches its

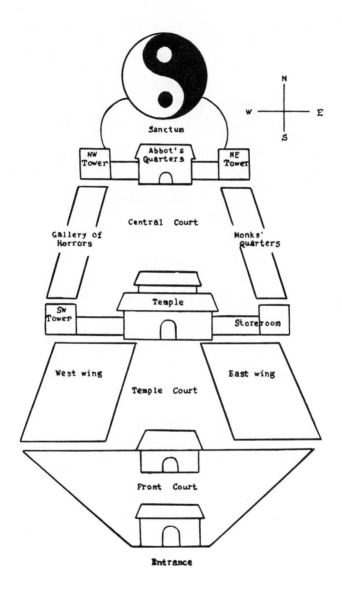

MASTER SUN'S DIAGRAM OF THE MONASTERY

lowest ebb, it merges with Negative, and how when Negative attains its zenith it naturally changes into Positive at its lowest point. The supreme doctrine of Tao, Dee, expressed in one simple symbol!"

"What is the meaning of the dot inside each half?" Judge Dee asked, interested despite himself.

"It means that Positive harbours the germ of Negative, and vice-versa. That applies to all natural phenomena, including man and woman. You know that every man has in his nature a feminine element, and every woman a masculine strain."

"That's quite true!" the judge said pensively. Then he added: "I seem to remember that somewhere I saw that circle also divided horizontally. Does that have a special significance?"

"Not that I know of. The dividing line ought to be vertical, as I drew it here. Well, let's not keep the abbot waiting. My old friend is rather a stickler for formality!" As they went outside Sun added quickly: "Mind your step now, the balustrade is broken here. The lay brothers were supposed to repair it, but they maintain that the preparations for the festival kept them too busy. They are a pack of lazybones, anyway! Here, I'll hold your arm, I don't suffer from any fear of heights!"

IX

They descended the winding staircase together. It was cold and damp in the stairwell. Judge Dee was glad when they entered the refectory on the ground floor, which was well heated by numerous braziers.

The small prior came to meet them, nervously blinking his eyes. He fell over his words in a frantic attempt to be exactly as polite to Master Sun as he was to Judge Dee. He conducted them to the main table in the rear of the refectory, where the abbot was waiting for them. Judge Dee wanted Master Sun to sit on the abbot's right side, but Sun protested that he was only a retired scholar without official rank, and that the judge as representative of the Imperial Government ought to sit in the place of honour. At last the judge had to give in, and the three men seated themselves. The prior, the almoner and Tsung Lee sat down at a smaller table next to theirs.

The abbot raised his cup and toasted his two distinguished table companions. This was the sign for the crowd of monks, seated at four long tables in front of them, to take up their chopsticks, which they did with alacrity. Judge Dee noticed that Kuan Lai, his wife, and the two actresses were sitting at a separate table near the entrance of the hall, where Tao Gan had joined them. Mo Mo-te was nowhere to be seen.

The judge stared dubiously at the cold, fried fish the abbot placed on his plate. The bowl of glutinous rice with raisins did not look very attractive either. He had no appetite at all. In order to conceal his lack of enthusiasm he remarked: "I thought that in Taoist monasteries no meat or fish were served."

"We do indeed strictly observe the monastic rules," the abbot said with a smile. "We abstain from all intoxicants—my wine cup is filled with tea. Not yours, though! We make an exception for our honoured guests in this one respect, but we keep strictly to a vegetarian diet. That fish is made of bean curd, and what looks like a roasted chicken over there is moulded from flour and sesame oil."

Judge Dee was dismayed. He was not a gourmet, but he liked at least to know what he ate. He forced himself to taste a small morsel of the bean curd fish, and nearly choked. Seeing the abbot's expectant look, he said quickly: "This is indeed delicious. You have excellent cooks!"

He quickly emptied his cup; the warm rice wine was not bad. The make-believe fish on his plate stared up at him mournfully with its one shriveled eye, which was in fact a small dried prune. Somehow or other it made Judge Dee think of the embalmed abbot. He said: "After the banquet I would like to see the temple. And also the crypt under the Sanctum, to offer a prayer for the soul of your predecessor."

The abbot put his rice bowl down and said slowly:

"This person shall be glad to show Your Honour the temple. But the crypt can unfortunately be opened only on certain days during the dry season. If we open it now, the air down there might get humid, and that would adversely affect the condition of the embalmed body. The intestines have been removed, of course, but some of the organs that remain are still susceptible to decay."

This technical information robbed the judge of the little appetite he had been able to muster. He quickly drank another cup of wine. The bandage around his head was lessening his throbbing headache, but his body was stiff and painful all over, and he felt slightly sick. He looked with envy at Sun Ming who was eating with a hearty appetite. When Sun had emptied his bowl, he wiped his mouth with the hot towel a novice handed to him, then said: "The late abbot, His Reverence Jade Mirror, was a talented man. He was completely familiar with all the most abstruse texts, wrote a beautiful hand, and he was also a good painter of animals and flowers."

"I would like to see his work," Judge Dee said politely. "I suppose the library here has many of his manuscripts and pictures?"

"No," the abbot said, "unfortunately not. It was his express instruction that all his paintings and writings were to be buried with him in the crypt."

"Commendable modesty!" Master Sun said with approval. "But listen, there's that last painting he did of his cat! It is hanging now in the side hall of the temple. I'll take you there after the meal, Dee!"

The judge didn't feel the slightest interest in the late abbot's cat, and the temple hall would doubtless be stone-cold. But he murmured that he would be delighted.

Sun and the abbot started with relish on a thick, brown broth. Judge Dee poked suspiciously with his chopsticks at the unidentified objects that floated on its surface. He could not muster sufficient courage for tasting the broth. He cudgelled his brain for some more conversation, and at last managed to formulate some intelligent questions about the internal organization of the Taoist church. But the abbot seemed ill at ease. He disposed of the subject with a few brief explanations.

The judge felt relieved when he saw the prior, the almoner, and Tsung Lee come to their table to offer a toast. Judge Dee rose and walked back with them to their table to return the courtesy. He sat down opposite the poet, who had apparently partaken liberally of the hot wine. His face was flushed and he seemed in high spirits. The prior informed the judge that two lay brothers had already replaced the broken axle. The grooms had rubbed down and fed the horses. Thus the distinguished guest would be able to continue his journey the next morning. Unless he decided, of course, to prolong his stay—which would delight the prior.

Judge Dee thanked him warmly. The prior muttered some self-deprecatory remarks, then rose and excused himself. He and the almoner had to make preparations for the evening service.

When he was alone with the poet, the judge remarked: "I don't see Mrs. Pao and her daughter here."

"Daughter?" Tsung Lee asked with a thick tongue. "Do you seriously sustain the thesis, sir, that such a refined and slender girl can be the daughter of such a vulgar, fat woman?"

"Well," Judge Dee said noncommitally, "the passing of the years sometimes effects astonishing changes."

The poet hiccoughed.

"Excuse me!" he said. "They are trying to poison me with their filthy food. It upsets my stomach. Let me tell you, Magistrate, that Mrs. Pao is no lady. The logical conclusion is that White Rose isn't her daughter." Shaking his forefinger at the judge he asked with a conspiratorial air:

"How do you know that the poor girl isn't being forced to become a nun?"

"I don't," the judge replied. "But I can ask her. Where would they be?"

"Probably taking their meal up in their room. Wise precaution too, for a decent girl shouldn't be exposed to the leers of those lewd monks. The fat woman acted wisely, for once!"

"She didn't prevent the girl from being exposed to your gaze, my friend!" Judge Dee remarked.

The poet righted himself, not without difficulty.

"My intentions, sir," he declared ponderously, "are strictly honourable!"

"I am glad to hear that!" the judge said dryly. "By the way, I would have liked to see the crypt you spoke of. But the abbot informed me just now that it can't be opened at this time of the year."

Tsung Lee gave the judge a long look from his bleary eyes. Then he said:

"So that's what he told you, eh?"

"Have you been down there yourself?"

The poet looked quickly at the abbot. Then he said in a low voice: "Not yet, but I am going to! I think the poor fellow was poisoned! Just as they are trying to poison you and me now! Mark my words!"

"You are drunk!" Judge Dee said contemptuously.

"I don't deny that!" Tsung said placidly. "It's the only way to stay sane in this mortuary! But let me assure you, sir, that the old abbot wasn't drunk when he wrote his letter to my father, the last one before he died—I beg your pardon, before he was translated."

The judge raised his eyebrows.

"Did the old abbot say in that letter that his life was in danger?" he asked.

Tsung Lee nodded. He drank deeply from his wine beaker.

"Who did he say was threatening him?" Judge Dee asked again.

The poet set down his beaker hard. He shook his head reprovingly and said: "You shouldn't try to tempt me to lay myself open to the charge of bringing a false accusation, Magistrate! I know the law!" Leaning over to the judge he whispered portentously: "Wait till I have collected proof!"

Judge Dee silently caressed his sidewhiskers. The youngster was a disgusting specimen, but his father had been a great man, widely respected in both official and scholarly circles. If the old abbot had indeed written such a letter to Dr. Tsung before he died, the matter deserved further investigation. He asked: "What is the present abbot's opinion?"

The poet smiled slyly. Looking at the judge with watery eyes he said:

"You ask him, Magistrate! Perhaps he won't lie to you!"

Judge Dee got up. The youngster was very drunk.

When he had returned to his own table, the abbot said bitterly: "I see that Mr. Tsung is drunk again. How different he is from his late father!"

"I gather that Dr. Tsung was a patron of this monastery," the judge remarked. He took a sip from the strong tea that indicated the end of the banquet.

"He was indeed," the abbot replied. "A remarkable family, Your Honour! The grandfather was a coolie in a village down south. He used to sit in the street under the window of the village school, and learned to write by tracing in the sand the characters the teacher wrote on the blackboard. After he had passed the village examination, a few shop-keepers collected the money for letting him pursue his studies, and he came out first in the provincial examinations. He was appointed magistrate, married a girl from an impoverished old family, and later died as a Prefect. Dr. Tsung was his eldest son. He passed all the examinations with honours, married the daughter of a wealthy tea merchant, and ended his career as Provincial Governor. He invested his money wisely, and founded the enormous family fortune."

"It is because every man of talent can rise to the highest functions, regardless of means or social position, that our great Empire will flourish for ever and ever," Judge Dee said with satisfaction. "To come back to your predecessor, what disease did he die of?"

The abbot put down his cup. He replied slowly: "His Holiness Jade Mirror did not die of a disease. He was translated; that is he chose to leave us because he felt that he had reached the limit set for his stay on earth. He departed for the Isles of the Blest in good health and in full possession of his mental powers. A most remarkable and awe-inspiring miracle that left a lasting impression on all of us who had the privilege of witnessing it."

"It certainly was a memorable experience, Dee!" Sun Ming added. "I was present at it, you know. The abbot summoned all the elders and, sitting on his high seat, delivered an inspired sermon of nearly two hours. Then he folded his arms, closed his eyes and passed away."

Judge Dee nodded. The dissolute youngster had evidently been indulging in drunken fantasies. Or perhaps he was repeating false rumours. He said: "Such a miracle is liable to excite the envy of other sects. One could imagine that the black-robed Buddhist crowd would use it for spreading malicious rumors."

"I certainly wouldn't put it past them!" the abbot said.

"Anyway," Judge Dee resumed, "if evil-minded persons ever made slanderous allegations, an autopsy would soon prove them unfounded.

Signs of violence can be detected, even on an embalmed body."

"Let's hope that it'll never come to that!" Sun said cheerfully. "Well, it's time I returned to my studies." Getting up he added to the judge: "I'll first show you that picture of the old abbot's cat, though! It's a relic of this temple, Dee!"

The judge suppressed a sigh. He thanked the abbot for the lavish entertainment, then followed Sun to the exit. While passing the actors' table he said quickly to Tao Gan:

"Wait for me in the portal here! I'll be back soon."

Master Sun walked with the judge through the side-corridor, and took him to the west hall of the temple.

Against the back wall stood a simple altar with four burning candles. Sun lifted one of them and let its light fall on a medium-sized scroll-painting suspended on the wall, mounted with a frame of antique brocade. It was a picture of a long-haired grey cat, lying on the edge of a table of carved ebony. Next to it was a woolen ball, behind it a bronze bowl with a piece of rock of interesting shape, and a few bamboos.

"That was the abbot's favourite cat, you know!" Sun explained in a low voice. "The old man painted it countless times. It's rather good, isn't it?"

Judge Dee thought it was very mediocre amateur's work, but he understood that its value lay in its association with the holy man. The side hall was very cold, just as he had feared. "A remarkable picture!" he said politely.

"It was the last picture he did," Sun said. "He painted it up in his room, on the afternoon of the day he died. The cat refused to eat and died a few days later. And then to think that people say that cats don't attach themselves to their masters! I advise you now to have a look at the statues of the Taoist Triad in the main hall; they are more than ten feet high—the work of a famous sculptor. I'll be off now. I hope to see you tomorrow morning before you leave."

Judge Dee respectfully conducted him to the gate of the front hall, then he went back to the refectory. Since the statues had been there for two hundred years, they would be standing there a little longer, he presumed. He could see them when he revisited the temple at some later date.

He found his assistant waiting for him in the portal. Tao Gan reported in a low voice: "Mo Mo-te is still missing, sir. Kuan told me that nobody can say when or where he'll turn up, for he likes to go his own way. The director and the others were garrulous enough at table, but they really know very little about what is going on here, and care less. It was a pleasant meal, though. The only discordant note was an altercation at the

SCROLL-PAINTING OF THE OLD ABBOT'S CAT

table of the lay brothers. The brother in charge of the refectory maintained that the others hadn't put enough covers on the table. One monk was complaining that he didn't have a bowl and chopsticks."

"You call it a pleasant meal?" Judge Dee asked sourly. "I only had a few cups of wine and some tea, the rest made my stomach turn!"

"I had a very satisfactory dinner," Tao Gan said contentedly. "And all that good food gratis, for nothing!"

Judge Dee smiled. He knew that Tao Gan was inclined to be parsimonious. The gaunt man resumed: "Kuan invited me to come up to his room for a few more drinks, but I think I ought to have a look around for our mysterious actor first."

"Do that!" the judge said. "I'll go now and pay a visit to Mrs. Pao and her daughter. Their relation to Miss Ou-yang puzzles me. Tsung Lee suggested that White Rose isn't Mrs. Pao's daughter, and that she is being forced to become a nun, against her will. But the fellow was drunk. He also maintained that the former abbot had been murdered, but I asked the abbot and Master Sun, and that proved pure nonsense. Do you know where Mrs. Pao's room is?"

"On the second floor, sir, the fifth door in the second corridor, I would say."

"Good. Let's meet again in Kuan's room. I'll join you there after my talk with Mrs. Pao. I don't hear the rain any more, so we can go to the east wing directly by crossing the courtyard."

But a drenched novice who just came in informed them that although the storm had abated somewhat, it was still raining. The judge and Tao Gan made the detour through the front hall of the temple, now crowded with monks. They parted in front of the assembly hall on the ground floor of the east wing.

Judge Dee found the second floor completely deserted. The narrow, cold corridors were scantily lit by an occasional lantern. It was very still; he only heard the rustling of his brocade robe.

He was just about to start counting doors when he thought he heard whispered voices. He stood still and listened. He heard a swishing of silk behind him and at the same time smelled a sweet, cloying perfume. He was about to turn around when suddenly a searing pain shot through his head and everything went black.

X

Judge Dee's first thought was that his cold must have suddenly taken a turn for the worse. His head was aching badly and he had a queer empty feeling in the pit of his stomach. He smelled a faint, feminine perfume. He opened his eyes.

He stared astonished at the blue silk curtains above his head. He was lying, fully dressed, in a strange bedstead. He raised his hand to his head and found that his cap and the bandage were gone. There was a large lump on the back of his head. He felt it with his fingertips, and winced.

"Try to take a sip of this!" a soft voice spoke up by his side.

Miss Ting bent over him, a teacup in her hand. She passed her left arm round his shoulders and helped him to sit up. Suddenly he felt dizzy. She steadied him, and after a few sips of the hot tea he felt somewhat better. Slowly he began to realize what had happened.

"I was knocked down from behind," he said looking sourly at her. "What do you know about that?"

Miss Ting sat down on the edge of the bed. She said placidly: "I heard a bump against my door. I went to open it and found you lying unconscious on the floor, your head against my doorjamb. Since I thought that signified that you had intended to pay me a visit, I dragged you inside and put you on the bed. Fortunately I am rather strong, for I can assure you that you are by no means a light burden. I wet your temples with cold water till you came to. That's all I know."

Judge Dee frowned. He asked curtly: "Whom did you see in the corridor?"

"Nobody at all!"

"Did you hear the sound of footsteps?"

"No!"

"Let me see your satchel with perfume!"

Miss Ting obediently loosened the small brocade satchel from her sash and gave it to the judge. He smelled it. It was a sweet perfume, but quite different from the cloying smell he had perceived just before he was attacked. He asked again: "How long have I been unconscious?"

"Quite some time. I would say two hours or so. It's nearly midnight now." Then she added, pouting: "Is the verdict guilty or not guilty?"

Judge Dee smiled wanly.

"I am sorry!" he said. "I was a bit confused. You were very kind, Miss Ting. If it hadn't been for you, the rascal who knocked me down would doubtless have finished me off then and there."

"It was the bandage under your cap that saved your life," Miss Ting remarked. "They must have hit you a vicious blow with something sharp, and if you hadn't been wearing that thick bandage filled with orange peel around your head, the blow would have cracked your skull."

"I ought to go up and thank my wives!" Judge Dee muttered. "It was they who insisted on my wearing the bandage. But I must first look into this treacherous attack!" He wanted to climb down from the bed, but a sudden attack of dizziness forced him to lie down again.

"Not so quick, Magistrate!" Miss Ting said. "It was a nasty blow. I'll help you get down and over to that arm-chair there."

When the judge was sitting at the rickety table, she dipped the bandage in the brass water basin on the dressing table. "I'll put this around your head again," she remarked, "it'll help to make the lump go down."

Sipping his tea Judge Dee looked thoughtfully at her pleasant, frank face. She was not particularly handsome, but decidedly attractive. He put her age at about twenty-five. The straight robe of black silk with the broad red sash set off her narrow waist and small, firm breasts. She had the lithe, supple body of the trained acrobat. After she had wound the bandage round his head and replaced his cap, the judge said: "Sit down and let's talk a little, while I am getting ready to go. Tell me, why did you, a nice-looking and capable young girl, choose this particular profession? I don't consider it dishonourable, mind you, but I'd have thought that a girl like you could easily have found a better way of life."

She shrugged her shoulders. Pouring out another cup of tea for the judge she answered: "Oh, I fear that I am a rather wayward and self-willed person. My father has a small pharmacy in the capital, and also five daughters, worse luck! I am the eldest, and father wanted to sell me as a concubine to the wholesale drug-dealer to whom he owed money. I thought the dealer was a nasty old man, but the alternative was a brothel and I didn't fancy that either. I had always been rather strong and fond of sports, so with my father's permission I joined Kuan's troup. Kuan advanced the money my father needed. I soon learned to act, and also to do acrobatic dances and juggling. After one year Kuan had the loan back, plus the interest. Kuan is a decent fellow. He never made passes at me or forced me to grant my favours to patrons of our show. So I stayed on." She wrinkled her nose as she went on: "I know that people say all actors are crooks and all actresses whores, but I can assure you that Kuan is scrupulously honest. And as regards myself, though I don't claim to lead a saintly life, I never sold my body and I never will."

Judge Dee nodded. He resumed: "You say that Kuan never bothered you, but what about Mo Mo-te?"

"Well, he did make a few passes at me in the beginning, but rather because he felt it was his duty as a man than because he really wanted me.

I could feel that immediately. Yet he took my refusal badly. It hurt his stupid pride. He has been unpleasant to me ever since, which I regret, for he is a superb swordsman and I would have liked to do an act with him."

"I didn't like the way he threatened Miss Ou-yang on the stage," the judge remarked. "Do you think Mo is the type of man who takes delight in inflicting pain on a woman?"

"Oh no! He has a violent temper, but he is not mean or nasty. You can take that from me, and I know a thing or two about men!"

"Did Miss Ou-yang reject him too?"

Miss Ting hesitated. She replied slowly: "Miss Ou-yang has joined our troupe only recently, you see, and . . ."

Her voice trailed off. She quickly emptied her teacup. Then she took a chopstick from the table, threw the saucer up in the air and caught it on its tip where she made the saucer whirl round expertly.

"Put that down!" the judge said annoyed. "It makes me dizzy all over again!" And when she had skillfully caught the saucer and put it back on the table he added: "Answer my question! Did Ou-yang reject Mo Mo-te?"

"You needn't shout at me!" Miss Ting said stiffly. "I was just coming to that. Miss Ou-yang is a bit too fond of me, you know. I don't go for that sort of thing, so I keep her at a distance. But Mo is convinced that we are having an affair. That's why he is jealous and hates her."

"I see. How long has Mo been with the show?"

"About one year. I don't think he is really an actor, but a vagabond who roams all over the Empire, making his living in various ways. At any rate I don't think Mo is his real name. I once saw a jacket of his marked with the name Liu, but he maintained he had bought it in a pawnshop. And another thing, he must have visited this monastery before."

"How do you know that?" the judge asked eagerly.

"On our first day here he already knew his way about quite well. We all think this a creepy place and keep to our own rooms as much as possible, but Mo wanders about all by himself most of the time and isn't at all afraid of getting lost in this rabbit warren."

"You'd better be careful with him," Judge Dee said gravely. "He may be a criminal, for all we know. I am also worrying about Miss Ou-yang."

"You don't think she might be a criminal too, do you?" Miss Ting asked quickly.

"No, but I feel I ought to know a little more about her."

He looked expectantly at the girl. She hesitated a few moments, then said: "I promised Kuan I wouldn't tell anybody, but after all you are the magistrate here, and that makes it different. Besides, I wouldn't like you to suspect Miss Ou-yang of some evil designs. She is not really an actress, and Ou-yang isn't her real name. I don't know who she is; I only know that she is from the capital, and a wealthy woman. She paid Kuan a large sum for offering his services to this monastery for the commemoration festival, and for letting her join his troupe during their stay here. She assured Kuan that her only purpose was to warn someone here, and that therefore she wanted to perform an act on the stage with her bear, and that she would choose her own make-up. Kuan didn't see any objection to that, and since it would mean a double profit for us, he agreed. After our arrival here she didn't take part in our sessions with the monks. She left it to Kuan, his wife and me to teach those blockheads how to move about on the stage. Mo wasn't a great help either, for that matter."

"Do you think Mo knew Miss Ou-yang before?" the judge asked quickly.

"That I don't know. When they are together, they are mostly quarreling with each other. Well, tonight we saw that she had made herself up so as to resemble Miss Pao, and later Kuan asked her about it, but she said only that she knew what she was doing. When you came unexpectedly to see Kuan, he got very frightened, because he thought that Miss Ou-yang had been up to something illegal, and that you had come to investigate. That's all, but please don't let Kuan or the others know that I told you."

Judge Dee nodded. He thought ruefully that this strange tale complicated matters still further. He got up from his chair but suddenly felt very ill. He motioned to Miss Ting that he wished to be left alone and stumbled to the night-commode in the corner. He vomited violently.

After he had washed his face in the basin on the dressing table, and combed his beard, he felt much better. He drank a cup of tea, then went to the door and called Miss Ting in. He found that he could walk steadily now, and his headache was gone. He said with a smile: "I'll be on my way now. Thanks again for your timely assistance. If ever I can do anything to help you, let me know. I am bad at forgetting!"

Miss Ting nodded. She lowered her eyes and played for a while with the ends of her red sash. Suddenly she looked up and said: "I'd like to ask your advice about . . . about a rather personal matter. It's a bit awkward, but as a judge you must hear many things people are not supposed to talk about. Anyway, to put it plainly, I didn't enjoy the few love affairs I had as much as a girl is supposed to do. But I must confess I do feel very much attracted to Miss Ou-yang, more than to any man I ever met. I keep telling myself that it's all nonsense and that it will pass. I purposely keep out of her way. But at the same time I am worrying whether perhaps I am by nature unfit for marriage. I would hate to make a man who married me unhappy, you know. What do you think I should do?"

Judge Dee began to scratch his head but a sharp pain made him desist hurriedly. He slowly tugged at his moustache instead. Then he said: "I would do nothing, for the time being. Maybe you didn't really like the men you associated with before, or maybe they didn't really like you. At any rate those temporary liaisons can never be compared with married life. Continued intimacy fosters mutual understanding, and that is the basis of a happy love-life. Moreover, Miss Ou-yang is a bit mysterious, and that together with the flattering attention she pays to you may also account for the attraction you feel. So go on keeping her at a distance, till you know more about your own feelings, and about her intentions. Don't rush into an adventure that may lessen your self-respect and warp your emotions, unless you are completely sure of yourself and of the other party. Speaking now as your magistrate, I can add only that since both of you are grown-up and free women, your love-life is no concern of mine. The law intervenes only when minors or dependents are involved. To let everybody arrange his private life as he likes, provided he doesn't injure others or prejudice legally defined relationships—that is the spirit of our society and the laws that govern it."

"That man Tsung Lee always makes unpleasant references to Miss Ou-yang and me!" Miss Ting said unhappily.

"Don't mind him, he is an irresponsible youngster. By the way, he has a theory that Miss Pao is being forced to become a nun."

"Nonsense!" Miss Ting exclaimed. "I had some talks with her alone, her room is on this same floor. She is very keen on entering a nunnery. She gave me to understand that she had an unhappy love-affair and that she therefore wished to retire from worldly life."

"I was on my way to Mrs. Pao when I was attacked," the judge said. "Now it is too late. I'll visit them tomorrow morning. Is Mo's room also on this floor?"

"Yes, it is." She counted on her fingers, then continued: "Mo's room is the fourth on your right, after you have turned the corner."

"Again many thanks!" Judge Dee said as he turned to the door. "And don't worry about yourself!"

She gave him a grateful smile, and he went outside.

XI

He quickly looked up and down the corridor. It seemed unlikely that his attacker would dare to lie in wait for a second attempt, but one never knew. However, all was silent as the grave. He walked down the corridor, deep in thought.

That rascal Mo Mo-te was tall and strong enough to have dealt him the blow. And as to motive, if Mo was a maniac who chose women as his victims, and if he had been the actor who had come barging into the reception room during his conversation with the abbot, Mo might well have feared that he, the judge, was about to investigate irregularities with girls in the monastery, and thus trace Mo's doings with that one-armed woman. If the scene he had witnessed hadn't been a hallucination! At any rate he ought to ask the abbot which actor had intruded on them during their talk in the reception room.

What Miss Ting had told him about Miss Ou-yang worried him also. The girl had evidently made herself up to resemble Miss Pao in order to warn her or her mother. But against what or whom? Probably Miss Ou-yang had lied to Kuan. It was a preposterous idea that a wealthy girl from the capital would keep an enormous bear as a pet. It was far more likely that Miss Ou-yang was a member of some travelling show, who had joined Kuan's troupe on the orders of a third person, as yet unknown. It was all very confusing.

Shaking his head disconsolately, Judge Dee rounded the corner. He halted in front of the fourth door on the left. He knocked, but as he had expected, there was no answer. He pushed against the door and found that it was not locked. This was the opportunity to search Mo Mo-te's personal effects.

When he had opened the door, he vaguely saw a table with a candle in front of a large cupboard, the door of which was open. He stepped inside and closed the door behind him, then walked over to the table feeling in his sleeve for his tinderbox. Suddenly he heard a deep growl behind him.

He swung round. By the door, close to the floor, a pair of green eyes was staring fixedly at him. They slowly rose, then the judge felt the floor boards tremble under a heavy tread.

His way to the door was cut off. He quickly felt his way around the table and frantically groped in the dark for the door of the cupboard he had seen. He found it and stepped inside, pulling the door shut behind him. He heard the growling very near, on the other side. There was a sound of scratching nails. Then the growling grew louder.

Judge Dee cursed his absentmindedness. He now remembered, too late, that Miss Ting had spoken about the fourth door on the right. He had entered by mistake the room opposite, evidently that of Miss Ou-yang. She was out, but that awful brute was there.

The scratching stopped. The planks under Judge Dee's feet shook as the bear lay down in front of the cupboard.

This was a most unpleasant situation. Presumably Miss Ou-yang would arrive before long, and he could shout at her through the door. But in the meantime he was at the mercy of that fearsome creature. He hadn't the slightest idea of the behaviour of bears. Would the animal presently try to smash the door? It seemed solid enough, but if the bear threw its enormous weight against it, he could doubtless easily smash the entire cupboard to pieces.

The cupboard was empty, but there wasn't much space. He had to stand half-bent, the ceiling boards pressed down painfully on the lump on the back of his head. And the air was getting very close. Soon it would become suffocating. He carefully opened the door at a narrow crack.

A waft of fresh air came inside, but at the same moment there was a commotion outside that made the cupboard shake. The bear growled ominously, and again began to scratch at the door. The judge closed it quickly, and kept both hands on the handle.

A cold fear gripped his heart. This was a situation he was utterly unable to cope with. Soon the stale air began to hurt his lungs; sweat broke out all over his body. If he put the door ajar again, would the bear push his paw inside and force it open?

Just when he had decided that he would have to risk it again, he heard someone enter the room. A voice said gruffly: "Are you after the mice again? Back to your corner, quick!"

The floor shook again under the bear's heavy tread. The judge opened the door very slightly and filled his lungs with fresh air. He saw Miss Ou-yang lighting the candle. Then she went up to the dressing table, took a handful of sugared fruit from a drawer and threw it to the bear.

"Well caught!" she said. The bear growled.

Judge Dee heaved a deep sigh of relief. He didn't relish the task ahead of announcing his presence from his undignified hide-out, but anything was better than being mauled by that fearful brute! He opened his mouth to speak, then saw to his embarrassment that Miss Ou-yang had untied her sash and was now impatiently tugging at her robe. He would have to wait until she had changed into her night-dress. He was about to pull the door shut again when he suddenly halted. He looked wide-eyed at the girl's bare arms. They were thin, but there was a rippling movement of well-developed muscles, and the upper arms were covered with black hair. There was a long red scar on the left arm. The robe fell down and revealed the bare torso of a young man.

The judge opened the door wider. He cleared his throat and said: "I am the magistrate. I entered here by mistake." As the bear lumbered forward with an angry growl he quickly added: "Keep that beast away from me!"

The young man at the dressing table looked dumbfounded at the figure in the cupboard. Then he barked an order at the bear. It went back to its corner by the window, still growling. Its neckhairs stood on end.

"You can come out!" the youngster said curtly. "He won't touch you."

Judge Dee stepped into the room and went to the chair by the table, eyeing the bear suspiciously.

"Sit down!" the other exclaimed impatiently. "I tell you it's safe!"

"Even so, I want you to put him on the chain!" the judge said curtly.

The youngster took off his wig, then went up to the bear and attached a heavy chain to its iron collar. The other end was fastened to a hook in the window sill. Judge Dee thought that the snap of the lock was one of the nicest sounds he had ever heard. He sat down on the bamboo chair.

The young man put on a loose jacket. He sat down, too, and said in a surly voice: "Well, now you have found me out, what are you going to do about it?"

"You are Miss Pao's brother, aren't you?" the judge asked.

"I am. But fortunately that woman Pao isn't my mother! How did you know?"

"When watching your act," Judge Dee replied, "it struck me that White Rose was very frightened when Mo Mo-te threatened you with his sword, while your scene with the bear left her completely unperturbed. That indicated that she knew everything about you and your bear. And when just now I saw your face, I noticed that there's a basic resemblance."

The young man nodded.

"Anyway," he said, "I have committed only the minor offence of posing as a member of the other sex. And in a good cause."

"You'd better tell me all about it. Who are you?"

"I am Kang-te, eldest son of Kang Woo, the well-known rice merchant in the capital. White Rose is my only sister. Half a year ago she fell in love with a young student, but my father disapproved of the match and refused to give his consent to the marriage. Soon after that the young fellow fell off his horse when returning drunk from a party. He broke his back and died on the spot. My sister was broken-hearted. She maintained that her sweetheart had become despondent because of my father's refusal, and that my parents were responsible for his taking to drink, and thus for his death. That was nonsense, because the fellow was a drunkard to begin with. But you try to reason with a girl in love! White Rose announced that she would enter religion. Father and mother did what they could to persuade her to give up that plan, but that only made her all the more stubborn. She threatened to kill herself if they didn't let her go. She entered the White Crane Nunnery in the capital as a novice."

Kang rubbed his upper lip where he had evidently worn a moustache, and continued unhappily: "I went there several times and tried to reason with her. I explained to her that the young man had been notorious for his dissolute life, and that father had been quite right in opposing the marriage. The only result was that she grew furious with me and refused to see me again. Last time I went there, the abbess told me that White Rose had left, and that she didn't know where she had gone. I bribed the gate-keeper, and he told me that a certain Mrs. Pao, a pious widow, had struck up a friendship with her, and taken her away. My parents were worried, and my father ordered me to make further inquiries. By dint of much effort I at last discovered that Mrs. Pao had taken my sister to this monastery, to be initiated as a nun. I decided to follow her in order to try again to persuade my sister to return home. Since I knew she would refuse to see me if I went as I was, I disguised myself as an actress. I am of rather slight build, and I have taken part in some amateur theatricals. As Miss Ou-yang I approached Kuan, and bribed him to offer his services to this monastery for the commemoration festival, and to let me join his troupe. The fellow acted in good faith. You shouldn't blame him, sir.

"The stratagem worked. Mo Mo-te unwittingly did me a service when he teased me during his sworddance. It frightened my sister and made her forget her resentment against me. After the show she slipped away from Mrs. Pao and hurriedly told me behind the stage that she was in an awful quandary. Mrs. Pao had been very kind to her. She had more or less adopted her as her daughter. Her one great aim in life was to see my sister properly ordained as a nun, for she was a very pious woman. However, in this monastery White Rose had met a young fellow, a certain Mr. Tsung. Though she didn't know him very well yet, her meeting him made her doubt whether after all she had taken the right decision. But on the other hand she could never disappoint Mrs. Pao who had gone to so much trouble for her, and who had consoled her when her own family had turned against her. Those were the words she used, 'turned against her.' I ask you, sir! Well, I said she had better come up to my room for a quiet talk about what she should do. I told her to take off her black dress. In her white undergarment people would take her for me. She did so and then went away, stuffing her folded black robe in her sleeve."

He scratched his head and resumed ruefully: "I was going to follow her upstairs but in the hall I ran into that fool Tsung. When I had got rid of him and gone up to my room, my sister wasn't there. I went to Mrs. Pao's room, but found nobody there. Then I had a few drinks with Kuan Lai. Just now I went to Mrs. Pao's room again, on the off-chance that one of them would still be up. But the lights were out and the door locked. Tomorrow I'll try again. That's all, sir."

Judge Dee slowly caressed his sidewhiskers. He had heard about Kang Woo. He was indeed a well known merchant in the capital. He said: "You would have done better if you had placed this matter in the hands of the proper authorities, Kang."

"I beg to differ, sir. White Rose is entering religion with my parents' consent, and Mrs. Pao is highly thought of in Taoist circles in the capital. And you know, sir, that the Taoists have much influence in government circles nowadays. My father is a Confucianist, but as a merchant he could not afford to become known as an anti-Taoist. It would be bad for his business."

"Anyway," Judge Dee said, "from now on you'll leave this matter to me. Tomorrow morning I'll speak personally with Mrs. Pao and your sister. I shall be glad to try to make her go back on her decision, and her interest in Mr. Tsung will probably help. I wouldn't choose him for my own son-in-law, but he has a good background and he may improve with the years. Anyway I hold that Heaven has assigned to woman the duty of marrying and bearing children. I don't hold with nuns, whether Taoist or Buddhist. Now tell me, how did you get this awful animal, and why did you bring him along here?"

"I am fond of hunting, sir. I caught him seven years ago up north, when he was still a small cub. He has been with me ever since. It has been very interesting to teach him dancing and other tricks. He is very fond of me, considers me as the father-bear or something! Only once he lacerated my left arm with his paw, but that was by mistake. It was meant as a caress! It healed well. It only gives me trouble in humid weather like we are having to-day, then the arm is a bit stiff. When I joined Kuan's troupe I took the bear along, in the first place because he only obeys me and at home no one else can look after him, and secondly because it gave me a good act in Kuan's show."

The judge nodded. All the pieces were falling into place now. On the stage Kang had made little use of his left arm because the scar was bothering him, and when he and Tao Gan had met White Rose in the corridor, she had kept her left arm close to her body because of the black dress tucked away in her sleeve. And she had been in a great hurry because she didn't want to meet Mrs. Pao. She must have met her around the corner, and decided to defer the talk with her brother till next day. He resumed: "I know next to nothing about bears. What would he have done if you hadn't come? Do you think he would have smashed the cupboard to get at me?"

"Oh no! They are cunning enough, but not very enterprising. They don't do things they have never attempted before, unless they are taught to do them. That's why I can leave him here in this room off the chain. He'll never try to get the door open. He would have sniffed and scratched at that cupboard from time to time to make sure that you were still there, then he would have curled up in front and waited till you came out. They have infinite patience."

Judge Dee shivered involuntarily.

"They don't devour people, do they?" he asked.

"Worse than that!" Kang said with a wry smile. "They'll knock a man down and maul him, then play with him as a cat plays with a mouse, till he is dead. I once saw the remains of a hunter who had been torn to pieces by a bear. It wasn't a pretty sight!"

"Good Heavens!" Judge Dee exclaimed. "What a nice playmate!"

Kang shrugged his shoulders.

"I never had any trouble with him," he said. "He also likes my sister, though he doesn't obey her as he does me. But he hates strangers. They make him nervous. He is quite funny that way, though. Some strangers he doesn't mind. He just gives them one look, then curls up in a corner and ignores them. Evidently you don't come into that category, sir! But I must say that he is in a bad temper now because he doesn't get enough exercise. Later, a couple of hours before dawn, the only time that this bee-hive here is quiet, I shall take him to the well between this building and the next. There are no doors or windows on the ground floor there, and the alley is closed by a solid gate. It was used formerly as a kind of prison for offending monks, I heard. There he can exercise a bit without danger to anybody."

Judge Dee nodded. Then he resumed: "By the way, have you perhaps seen Mo Mo-te while looking for Mrs. Pao and your sister?"

"I did not!" Kang said angrily. "That rascal is always bothering Miss Ting. I had to keep to my disguise, else I would have given him a thrashing he would remember! He may be taller and heavier than I, but I am a trained boxer and I'll lick him! Now I'll see to it that he keeps away from Miss Ting. That's a fine girl, sir, and good at sports, too. She can ride a horse, better indeed than many a man! If she married me I could take her with me on my hunting trips! I have no use for those delicate, pampered damsels my parents are always urging me to marry. But she is very independent. I doubt whether she would have me!"

Judge Dee rose.

"Ask her!" he said. "You'll find her a very outspoken girl. I must be going now. My assistant will be looking for me."

He tried a friendly nod at the bear, but the animal only glared at him with its small mean eyes.

XII

As soon as Mr. Kang had closed the door, Judge Dee stepped up to the one opposite. It was not locked. But when he had pushed it open, he saw that nobody was there. A spluttering candle stood on the bamboo table. It had nearly burned out. Except for a made-up bed and two chairs there was no other furniture. There were no boxes or bundles, and not a single garment hung on the wooden clothes rack. If it had not been for the burning candle one would not have thought that anyone was staying there.

The judge pulled the drawer out, but it contained nothing but dust. He went down on his knees and looked under the bed. There was nothing but a small mouse that scurried away.

He got up, dusted his knees and went out, making for Tao Gan's room. It was well past midnight. He supposed that his gaunt assistant would have grown tired of keeping the actors company.

He found Tao Gan sitting alone in his chilly, bare room, hunched over a brazier that contained only two or three glowing coals. Tao Gan hated spending more than absolutely necessary. His long, gloomy face lit up when he saw the judge enter. Rising he asked quickly: "What happened, Your Honour? I looked everwhere but . . ."

"Give me a cup of hot tea!" Judge Dee said curtly. "Do you happen to have anything to eat here?"

While Judge Dee sat down heavily at the small table, Tao Gan quickly rummaged through his travelling box and found two dried oil-cakes. He handed them to the judge saying dubiously: "I am sorry I have nothing else to . . ."

The judge took a quick bite.

"They are excellent!" he said contentedly. "No vegetarian nonsense about these, they have the nice flavour of pork fat!"

After he had munched the cakes and drunk three cups of tea, he yawned and remarked: "The only thing I want now is a good long sleep! But although some of our problems are solved, there are still a few things that need our urgent attention. Including an attempted murder!" He told Tao Gan what had happened, and gave him an outline of his talks with Miss Ting and with the pseudo Miss Ou-yang. "So you see," he concluded, "that the case of the pious maid, White Rose, is practically finished. Tomorrow morning, before we leave here, I shall have a talk with her and Mrs. Pao. There remains the problem of who hit me on the head and why!"

Tao Gan sat deep in thought, winding and unwinding on his forefinger the three long hairs that sprouted from his left cheek. At last he said:

"Miss Ting told you that Mo Mo-te is familiar with the monastery. Could he perhaps be really a vagrant Taoist monk? Those fellows roam all over the Empire, visiting famous Taoist sites and engaging in all kinds of mischief on the side. Since they don't shave their heads like the Buddhists, they can easily act the part of laymen. Mo Mo-te may have visited this monastery before. Probably he became involved in the deaths of one or more of the three girls. The one-armed woman you saw may be another of his victims. Suppose he now came back disguised as an actor, either to silence the one-armed girl, or to blackmail eventual accomplices here?"

"There's much to what you say, Tao Gan," Judge Dee said pensively. "It agrees with a vague theory I had been trying to formulate myself. It reminds me of your remark about one cover being missing at the banquet. That might mean that Mo has resumed his Taoist garb, and mixed with the monks. If he had an accomplice here, he could easily manage that. The inhabitants of the monastery saw him wearing a mask most of the time, or with his face painted. That would also explain why we can't find him, and why his room is completely empty, as I saw just now. And if it was he who overheard my talk with the abbot, he might well want me out of the way."

"But murdering a magistrate is no small undertaking!" Tao Gan remarked.

"That's exactly why Mo is our most likely suspect. I don't think that anyone living in this monastery would dare to do that. Everybody knows that the murder of an Imperial official sets our whole administrative machine into motion, and this monastery in no time would be swarming with investigators, police-officers and special agents who would literally leave no brick unturned to find the criminal. But Mo is an outsider. He'll disappear as soon as he has done whatever he came to do, and little does he care what happens afterwards to the monastery and its inmates!"

Tao Gan nodded his agreement. After a while he spoke: "We must also keep in mind another possibility, sir. You told me that at the banquet you made inquiries regarding the death of the former abbot. Now suppose there had really been something wrong about the old fellow's demise, and that someone who had been concerned in that crime overheard your questions. Isn't it then to be expected that he would want to prevent you at all cost from initiating an investigation?"

"Impossible! I tell you that more than a dozen people were present when the old abbot died. I said clearly to the abbot that I didn't believe that . . ." He suddenly broke off. Then he went on slowly: "Yes, you are perfectly right! I also said that signs of violence can often be detected even on an embalmed corpse. Someone may have heard that, and wrongly concluded that I was thinking of having an autopsy conducted." He paused. Then he hit his fist on the table and muttered: "Tsung must tell me all the details about the old abbot's death! Where can we find that confounded poet?"

"When I left Kuan Lai, they were still drinking happily. Probably Tsung Lee is still there. The office paid the actors their fee tonight, and these people like to keep late hours!"

"Good, let's go there." Getting up, the judge added: "Either that blow on my head, or the couple of hours of enforced rest after it, must have cured my cold! My head is clear now and I have got rid of that feverish feeling. What about you, though?"

"Oh," Tao Gan said with his thin smile, "I am all right! I never sleep much. I usually pass the night dozing a bit and thinking about this and that."

Judge Dee gave his assistant a curious look as the elderly man carefully doused the candle with his nimble fingers. During the year this strange, sad man had been working for him as one of his assistants he had grown rather fond of him. He wondered what he could be thinking of at night. He opened the door.

That same moment he heard the rustling of silk. A dark shape hurried away through the corridor.

"You guard the stairs!" he barked at Tao Gan. He rushed towards the corner round which the unknown listener had disappeared.

Tao Gan ran quickly to the staircase, taking a roll of black waxed thread from his sleeve. As he was stringing it across the stairs, a foot above the first step, he muttered with a sly smile: "Oh dear, oh dear! If our visitor comes rushing along here I am afraid he'll have a very bad fall!"

Just when he had fastened both ends to the bannister, the judge came back.

"No use!" he said bitterly. "There's a narrow staircase on the other side of the building!"

"What did he look like, sir?"

"I only caught a glimpse of him when I stepped outside. He was round the corner like a flash, and when I got there, he was nowhere to be seen. But it was the same villain who attacked me!"

"How does Your Honour know that?" Tao Gan asked eagerly.

"He left behind a whiff of that same sweet perfume I noticed just before I was knocked down," the judge replied. He tugged at his beard, then said angrily: "Look here, I am sick and tired of this game of hide and seek! We must do something quickly, because that rascal may have overheard everything we said just now. We'll first go to Kuan's room. If Tsung isn't there, I'll go straight to Master Sun and rouse him. We'll organize a posse to search every nook and cranny of this place, forbidden to visitors or not! Come along!"

Upon entering the actors' dressing room they found only the director and Tsung Lee. The table bore an impressive array of empty wine jars. Kuan had passed out. He was lying back in his armchair snoring loudly. Tsung Lee sat hunched over the table, aimlessly drawing figures with his forefinger in the spilt wine. He would have got up when he saw the judge enter, but the latter said curtly: "Remain seated!"

Taking the chair next to the young man he went on harshly: "Listen you! An attempt on my life was made. It may be connected with your talking about the former abbot's death. I refuse to be made to run around in circles any longer. I want to hear here and now everything you know about that affair. Speak up!"

Tsung Lee passed his hand over his face. The unexpected arrival of the judge and his man, and the harsh address, seemed to have sobered him somewhat. He looked unhappily at the judge, cleared his throat and said hesitantly:

"It's an old story, sir, I really don't know . . ."

"Stop beating about the bush!" Judge Dee barked. And to Tao Gan: "See whether these two tipplers have left anything in those jars and pour me a cup. It'll help me to stay awake!"

The poet looked wistfully at the cup Tao Gan was filling, but the thin man made no move to include him. He sighed and began: "You must know that my father was a close friend of Jade Mirror, the former abbot. He often visited this monastery, and they corresponded regularly with each other. In his last letter the abbot wrote that he didn't trust True Wisdom, the present abbot, who was then prior here. Jade Mirror hinted vaguely at irregularities with girls who had come to stay here to be initiated, and . . ."

"What kind of irregularities?" the judge interrupted sharply.

"He didn't express himself clearly, sir. It seems he suspected that monks tempted those girls to take part in some sort of secret rites, a kind of religious orgies, you know. And he thought apparently that the prior connived at those goings on. He also wrote that he had discovered that the prior secretly had planted nightshade in a hidden corner of the garden That made Jade Mirror suspect that he was planning to poison somebody."

Judge Dee sat down his wine beaker hard on the table. He asked angrily: "Why in Heaven's name weren't those things reported to the magistrate? How can we acquit ourselves of our duties when people keep things hidden from us or tell only half-truths?"

"My father was a very conscientious man, Your Honour," the poet said apologetically. "He wouldn't dream of taking any official steps before he had ascertained all the facts. Since during his visits to the monastery Jade Mirror had never referred to those matters, and since the abbot was over seventy, he reckoned with the possibility that the old man was perhaps seeing things that weren't there. His mind was none too clear, sometimes. My father thought nothing ought to be done before Jade Mirror's vague allegations had been verified. He didn't even want to consult Master Sun without tangible proof. Unfortunately my father fell ill just at that time, and he died before he could do anything about it. But on his death-bed he enjoined me to go and make discreet inquiries here."

Tsung Lee heaved a sigh, then went on: "After my father's demise I was fully occupied for several months with putting the family affairs in order. I am the eldest son, you know. Then there arose a complicated dispute about some land we own, and the law-suit dragged on for months. Thus one year passed by before I could come here and start my investigation. I have been at it now for two weeks, but I can't say I have made any progress. Three girls died here, but as you doubtless know, these deaths had a natural explanation. There's not the slightest indication that those young women were used for any unholy experiments. As regards the death of Jade Mirror, I was hampered in my work by the fact that the area north of the temple is closed to visitors. And I wanted especially to visit the crypt to have a look at the papers the dead abbot left. At last I decided I would try to frighten the abbot, in the forlorn hope that if he were guilty he would give himself away, or take some imprudent steps against me. Hence my poem about the 'deadly shades of night,' and about the two abbots. You'll have noticed, sir, that the abbot was very annoyed."

"So was I," Judge Dee remarked dryly, "and I haven't the murder of an abbot on my conscience. That doesn't mean anything." He thought for a moment, then resumed: "During the banquet True Wisdom gave me a brief account of the manner in which the old abbot died. Tell me all you know about that!"

Tsung Lee cast a longing look at the wine cup in Judge Dee's hand.

"Give him a cup!" the judge said sourly to Tao Gan. "The wick is dry, so the lamp needs oil, it seems."

The poet gratefully took a long draught, then continued: "Since Jade Mirror's death was considered a miraculous event, all details have been placed on record, to be incorporated in the history of this monastery. About one year ago, on the sixteenth day of the eighth moon, Jade Mirror stayed in his room all morning. He was alone, and presumably he had been reading the scriptures, as he often did in the morning. He took his noon meal in the refectory, together with True Wisdom, Sun Ming, and the other monks. Thereafter he returned to his own room, together with True Wisdom, for a cup of tea. Soon after that, True Wisdom came out and told the two monks who were standing in the corridor outside that the abbot wanted to devote the afternoon to painting a picture of his cat."

"Master Sun showed me that picture," Judge Dee said. "It is hanging now in the side hall of the temple."

"Yes, sir. The old abbot was very fond of cats, and he liked painting them. True Wisdom returned to the temple. The two monks knew that the old abbot didn't like to be disturbed when he was painting. Since they were on duty that day in the abbot's quarters, they remained waiting outside his door to be on hand if he should call them. For an hour or so they heard the abbot humming some of his favourite religious chants, as was his wont when he was painting and the work got on well. Then he began to speak loudly, as if he was engaged in a dispute with someone. As his voice grew louder and louder, the monks became worried and went inside. They found the abbot sitting in his armchair, an exalted look on his face. He had left the picture lying on his desk, nearly finished. He ordered the monks to summon Master Sun, the prior, the almoner and the twelve eldest monks. He said he had an important message for them.

"When all had assembled before the abbot, he smiled happily and announced that Heaven had revealed to him a new formulation of the Truth of Tao, and that he wanted to impart that to them. Sitting upright in his chair with his cat on his lap, he then delivered with flashing eyes a very mystic sermon, couched in strange, obscure language. Later the text was published together with an extensive commentary by the Chief Abbot from the capital, who elucidated all the obscure expressions and proved that this was indeed a masterly summing up of the deepest mysteries. Sermon and commentary are now used as a basic text in all the monasteries of this province.

"The abbot spoke for more than two hours. Then suddenly he closed his eyes and leaned back in his chair. His breathing became irregular, then ceased altogether. He was dead.

"All present were deeply moved. Seldom had there been so perfect an example of a Taoist adept of his own will peacefully translating himself from this world to the next. The Chief Abbot in the capital declared Jade Mirror a holy man. His body was embalmed and enshrined in the crypt with magnificent ceremonies that lasted three days and were attended by thousands of people.

"So you see, sir," Tsung Lee concluded dejectedly, "that there were more than a dozen witnesses who can attest that the old abbot died a natural death, and that he did not once refer to his life having been threatened, by True Wisdom or anybody else. I am more and more inclined to think that when the old man wrote his last letter, his mind was wandering. I told you that he was more than seventy years old, and it was known that he behaved a bit strangely, at times."

Judge Dee made no comment. He remained silent for a long while, playing with his sidewhiskers. It was very quiet in the room, the only sound heard was the soft snoring of the director. At last the judge spoke: "We must remember that the old abbot suggested in his letter that True Wisdom was planning to poison someone with the seeds of the nightshade. Now our medical books state that this poison will bring the victim into a state of extreme exaltation before the coma sets in and he dies. The behaviour of the abbot during his last hours could conceivably be interpreted from this angle. The old abbot might well have ascribed his exaltation to the inspiration of Heaven, and forgotten all about his suspicions of True Wisdom. The only objection to this theory is that the abbot, before summoning the others to hear his last sermon, had been quietly working an hour or so on that picture of his cat. We shall investigate this immediately. Do you know how to get to the crypt, Tsung?"

"I studied a sketch map my father once made, Your Honour. I know the way, but I also know that all doors in the corridors leading there are kept securely locked!"

"My assistant will take care of that," Judge Dee said rising. "Mr. Kuan won't miss us. Let's be on our way!"

"Who knows whether we might not find Mo Mo-te or the one-armed girl in that closed part of the monastery!" Tao Gan said hopefully.

He took the lantern from the corner table, and they went out. Kuan was still snoring peacefully.

XIII

At this late hour the monastery was deserted. They met no one on the ground floor, or on the stairs leading to the latticed landing over the temple hall.

Judge Dee had a quick look at the passage leading to the store-room but no one was there.

Tsung Lee took them in the opposite direction, through the long passage leading to the tower on the south-west corner, where Sun Ming had his quarters. When they arrived in the small hall that gave access to the landing in front of Sun's library, Tsung Lee pulled the narrow door on the right open and went down a flight of stairs. They found themselves before a spacious portal. Pointing to the pair of high, double doors, lavishly decorated with wood carving, the poet whispered:

"That's the entrance to the Gallery of Horrors. That big padlock looks rather formidable!"

"I have seen worse!" Tao Gan grunted. He took a leather folder with various instruments from his capacious sleeve, and set to work. Tsung Lee held the lantern for him.

"I was told that the gallery hadn't been opened for some months," the judge observed. "Yet there isn't a speck of dust on the cross bar!"

"They were in here yesterday, sir," the poet said. "A worm-eaten statue had to be repaired."

"There you are!" Tao Gan said contentedly. He opened the padlock and took the cross bar down. The judge and Tsung Lee went inside. Tao Gan pulled the door shut behind them. Tsung lifted the lantern high and Judge Dee surveyed the long, broad gallery. It was cold and damp in there. Pulling his robe closer he muttered: "Disgusting exhibition, as usual!"

"My father used to say that these galleries ought to be abolished, sir," Tsung remarked.

"He was right!" the judge said caustically.

Tao Gan surveyed the gallery too. He muttered with a sniff: "All these horrors are no use! People will still get themselves into mischief, horrors disregarding! They are just made that way."

The wall on their right was covered with scrolls bearing Taoist texts on sin and retribution. But all along the left wall stood a row of life-size statues which represented the torments inflicted on the souls of sinners in the Taoist Inferno. Here one saw gruesome devils sawing a writhing man in two, there a group of grinning goblins were boiling a man and a woman in an iron kettle. Further on, ox-headed and horse-headed devils were dragging men and women by their hair before the Black Judge of the Nether World, sculptured in relief but with a long beard of real hair. All the statues were vividly coloured. The light of Tsung's lantern shone on the leering masks of the demons, and the horribly distorted faces of their victims.

The three men walked on quickly, keeping close to the wall on the right so as not to come too near all the horrors. Judge Dee's eye was caught by a woman, stark naked, lying spreadeagled on her back against a large boulder, while a huge blue devil pressed the point of his spear against her breast. Her long hair hung over her face. Her hands and feet had been cut off, and her body of cracked plaster was loaded with heavy chains, but it showed all details with obscene clarity. The next scene was even worse. Two demons clad like ancient warriors, in blood-stained armour, were hacking a naked man and woman to pieces on a large chopping block, using battle-axes. Of the man only the rump was left, but the woman, lying on her face over the block, was just having her arms cut off.

Quickening his pace Judge Dee said crossly to Tao Gan: "I'll tell the abbot to have the statues of those women removed. All these scenes are sufficiently repulsive. They need not include women who are thus exposed. Such lurid representations are not allowed in an officially recognized place of worship."

The door at the end of the gallery was not locked. A steep flight of steps brought them to a large, square room.

"Here we must be on the first floor of the north-west tower," Tsung Lee said. "If I remember the plan correctly, the door over there gives access to the stairs leading down to the crypt, under the Sanctum."

Tao Gan began to work on the lock.

"This hasn't been opened for a long time," he remarked. "It's all rusty."

It took some time before a snapping sound announced that Tao Gan had sprung the lock. He pushed the heavy door open. A musty odour rose from the darkness below.

Judge Dee took the lantern from Tsung Lee and went carefully down the narrow, uneven steps. When he had counted thirty, the steps made a right turn. He counted again thirty steps, now hewn directly from the rock. He let the light of the lantern fall on the solid iron door that barred his way, fastened by a heavy chain with a padlock. He pressed himself against the damp wall to make room for Tao Gan.

When the gaunt man had also opened this lock and removed the chain, the judge stepped inside. A sound of flapping wings came from the darkness. He quickly drew back. A small black shape fluttered past his head.

"Bats!" he said disgustedly. He went inside and lifted the lantern high above his head. The two others remained standing behind him. Silently they surveyed the awe-inspiring scene.

In the centre of the small, octagonal crypt stood a dais of gilded wood. On it was throned a human figure, sitting in a high abbot's chair of carved red lacquer. It was dressed in full regalia; a robe of stiff gold brocade with a broad stole of red silk was draped round the narrow shoulders. Under the high tiara, glittering with gold, a brownish, sunken face stared at them with strange eyes that looked like shriveled slits. A ragged white beard hung from the chin. One strand had come loose. The left hand was hidden under the stole. The other held a long abbot's staff in thin, claw-like fingers.

Judge Dee made a bow. His two companions followed his example.

Then the judge took a step forward and let the light shine on the walls. The stone surface had been polished smooth, and Taoist texts were carved there in beautiful, large characters, filled in with gold lacquer. Against the back wall stood a large box of red leather, secured with a copper padlock.

There was no other furniture, but the floor was covered by a thick carpet, showing blue Taoist symbols woven into a gold-brown ground. The air was dry and crisp.

As they were walking around the dais, more small bats flew around the lantern. Judge Dee shooed them away.

"Where could they be coming from?" Tsung Lee asked in a hushed voice.

The judge pointed at two apertures in the ceiling.

"Those are airshafts," he said. "Your poem about the two abbots was all wrong. There are no maggots here. It's too dry. You should have said bats. But probably you couldn't have found a word rhyming with that anyway!"

"Cats!" the poet murmured.

"We are coming to them! The old abbot painted many of them. Open that box, Tao Gan! It must contain his pictures and manuscripts. I see no other place for storing them."

Judge Dee and Tsung Lee looked on while Tao Gan sprang the padlock. The box was tightly packed with rolls of paper and silk. Tao Gan unrolled a few from the top. Handing the judge two rolls he said: "Here are more pictures of that grey cat, Your Honour."

Judge Dee looked casually at them. One showed the cat playing on the floor with its woollen ball, the other while it was playing in the grass, trying to catch a butterfly with its raised paw. Suddenly he stiffened. He stood stock-still for a while, staring straight ahead of him. Then he put the two pictures back into the box. He said tensely: "Close the box. I need no further proof! The old abbot was indeed murdered!"

Tao Gan and Tsung wanted to ask questions, but the judge barked: "Hurry up with that box; we'll now go and charge the criminal with his foul murder!"

Tao Gan quickly replaced the scrolls, closed the box and ran after the judge. Judge Dee cast one last look at the sunken face of the figure on the dais. Then he bowed, and made for the stairs.

"Aren't the abbot's quarters in the building over the fourth gate?" he asked Tsung Lee while they were going up.

"Yes sir! If we go back to the west tower, we can take the passage that leads east, straight to the rooms of the gate-house of the Sanctum."

"You take me there. Tao Gan, you run back through the Gallery of Horrors to the temple, and take the picture of the cat that is hanging above the altar in the side hall. Then you rouse a novice and have him bring you to the abbot's quarters, along the usual way."

They completed the climb up to the north-west tower in silence. From there Tao Gan went straight on; Tsung Lee took the judge to the dark

JUDGE DEE AND HIS HELPERS INSPECT THE CRYPT

passage on their left. Through the shuttered windows they could again hear the wind and rain outside. There were sounds of earthenware breaking on the flagstones of the central courtyard below.

"The gale is blowing tiles from the roof," the poet remarked. "That will be the last of the storm; they usually begin and end with a violent gale."

The two men came to a halt in front of a solid-looking door. It was locked.

"As far as I remember from the plan, Your Honour," Tsung Lee said, "this is the back door of the abbot's bedroom."

Judge Dee rapped hard on it with his knuckles. He pressed his ear to the smooth surface. He thought he heard someone moving about inside. He repeated his knocking. At last there was the sound of a key, and the door was slowly opened a crack. The light of their lantern shone on a haggard face, distorted by fear.

XIV

When the abbot recognized the judge, he seemed greatly relieved, his tense features relaxed somewhat. He asked haltingly: "What . . . what gives this person the honour . . ."

"Let's go inside!" Judge Dee interrupted curtly. "There's an urgent matter I want to talk over with you."

The abbot took them through a simply furnished bedroom to the comfortable library adjoining it. Judge Dee noticed at once the queer, cloying smell. It came from a large antique incense-burner, standing on the side table. With a gesture the abbot invited the judge to sit down in the high-backed armchair next to his desk. He himself went to sit behind it, and motioned Tsung Lee to a chair by the window. He opened his mouth a few times, but apparently he didn't yet trust himself to speak. He evidently had received a bad shock.

The judge leaned back in his armchair. He studied the abbot's twitching face for a while, then said affably: "A thousand pardons for disturbing you so late in the night—or so early in the morning, rather! Fortunately I found you still up and about. I see that you are still fully dressed. Did you expect company?"

"No . . . I was taking a brief nap in the armchair in my bedroom," the abbot said with a wan smile. "In a few hours I'll have to conduct the matins; it . . . it didn't seem worth while to change. Why did Your Honour come by the back door? I thought that . . ."

"You didn't think that the old abbot had risen from the crypt, did you?" Judge Dee asked quietly. As he saw the sudden panic in True Wisdom's eyes he added: "He couldn't, because he is very dead. I can tell you, because I have just come from there."

The abbot had now mastered himself. He sat up and asked sharply: "Why did you go to the crypt? I told you that at this time of the year . . ."

"You did," the judge interrupted him. "But I felt it necessary to examine the papers left by your predecessor. Now I want to verify a few points about his death, while my memory of what I saw is still fresh. Hence my barging in here at this unusual hour. Let your thoughts go back to that last day of your predecessor's life. You had the noon meal together with him in the refectory. You hadn't seen him during the morning, had you?"

"Only during the matins. Thereafter His Holiness retired to his room, as a matter of fact to this very library. It has always been the private quarters of the abbots of this monastery."

"I see," Judge Dee said. He turned round in his chair and looked at the three high windows in the wall behind him. "Those give on to the central courtyard, I suppose?"

"They do," the abbot replied hurriedly. "During the day this room is very well lighted; that's why my predecessor liked it. Its bright light made it very suitable for painting, the only relaxation he ever indulged in."

"Very suitable indeed," the judge remarked. He thought a moment, then went on: "By the way, when I was talking with you in the reception room, an actor came in, and you commented on their careless behaviour. Did you see who it was before he shut the door again?"

The abbot, who had succeeded in taking hold of himself, again became ill at ease. He stammered: "No . . . that is to say, yes, I did. It was that swordsman, Mo Mo-te."

"Thank you." Judge Dee looked fixedly at the frightened man behind the desk, slowly stroking his long beard.

They sat in silence for a while. Tsung Lee started to shift impatiently in his chair. Judge Dee did not move; he listened to the rain against the shutters. It seemed less heavy than before.

There was a knock on the door. Tao Gan came in with a roll under his arm. After he had handed it to the judge, he remained standing by the door.

Judge Dee unrolled the picture and laid it on the desk before his host. He said: "I gather that this is the last painting Jade Mirror did."

"Yes. After the noon meal I had a cup of tea with him here. Then he dismissed me, saying that he wanted to devote the afternoon to doing a picture of his cat. The poor animal was sitting on that side-table of carved ebony over there. I left immediately, as I knew that His Holiness liked to be alone when he worked. The last I saw was that he was spreading a sheet of blank paper out on this desk, and . . ."

Suddenly the judge got up and hit his fist on the table.

"You are lying!" he barked.

The abbot shrank back in his chair. He opened his mouth, but the judge shouted: "Look at this painting, the last work of the great and good man whom you foully murdered by putting nightshade poison in his tea after the noon meal, here in this library!" He quickly bent over the table and pointed at the picture. "Do you mean to tell me that a man can paint such an intricate picture in the space of one hour? Look at the detailed treatment of the fur, the careful sketch of the carving of the table! It must have taken him at least two hours. You lie when you say that he began to paint it after you had left him. He must have done it in the morning, before the noon meal!"

"Don't dare to say that!" the abbot said angrily. "His Holiness was a skillful artist. Everybody knows that he worked very quickly. I won't . . ."

"You can't fool me!" Judge Dee snapped. "This cat, your victim's pet, did its master one last service! This cat proves clearly that you are lying. Here, look at its eyes! Don't you see that the pupils are wide open? If it had been painted at noontime, in summer, and in this brightly lit room, the pupils would have been just narrow slits!"

A long shudder shook the abbot's spare frame. He stared with wide eyes at the picture in front of him. Then he passed his hand over his face. He looked up into the blazing eyes of the judge, and said tonelessly: "I want to deliver a statement in front of Master Sun Ming."

"As you like!" Judge Dee replied coldly. He rolled the picture up again and put it in his bosom. The abbot led them down a broad stair-case. Below, he said in the same toneless voice: "The storm is over. We can go by the courtyard."

The four men crossed the wet, empty central courtyard, strewn with broken tiles. Judge Dee walked with the abbot in front, Tao Gan and Tsung Lee following close behind.

The abbot made for the building west of the temple, and pushed a door open in the corner of the yard. It gave access to a narrow passage that led them straight to the portal in front of the refectory. As they went to the spiral staircase leading up into the south-west tower, a deep voice spoke up: "What are you people doing here in the deep of night?"

Sun Ming was standing there, carrying a lighted lantern.

Judge Dee said gravely: "The abbot wants to make a statement, sir. He expressed the wish to do so in Your Excellency's presence."

Master Sun lifted the lantern and gave the abbot an astonished look. He said to him curtly: "Come up to my library, my friend. We can't engage in delivering statements here in this draughty portal!" Turning to the judge he asked: "Is the presence of those two other fellows necessary?"

"I am afraid it is, sir. They are important witnesses."

"In that case you better carry my lantern," Sun said handing it to the judge. "I know my way about."

He went up the stairs, followed by the abbot, with Judge Dee, Tao Gan and Tsung close behind him. The judge noticed that his legs felt as if they were made of lead. There seemed to be no end to the winding stairs.

At last they arrived at the top of the dark staircase. Judge Dee lifted his lantern and saw Sun Ming step on to the landing in front of his library. The abbot followed him. When Judge Dee's head was on a level with the platform, he heard Sun say: "Mind your step now!" Suddenly he shouted: "Hold on, man!"

At the same time there was a hoarse cry. Then a sickening thud from the darkness deep below them.

XV

Judge Dee stepped hastily onto the landing, holding the lantern high. Sun Ming grabbed his arm, his round face was of a deadly pallor. He said hoarsely: "The poor fellow grabbed for the balustrade that wasn't there!"

He let Judge Dee's arm go and wiped the perspiration from his face.

"Run down and have a look!" Judge Dee ordered Tao Gan. And to Sun Ming: "He won't have survived that fall. Let's go inside, sir."

The two men entered the library. Tsung Lee had followed Tao Gan downstairs.

"The poor wretch!" Sun said as he sat down behind his desk. "What was it all about, Dee?"

Judge Dee took the chair opposite; his legs were trembling from fatigue. He took the rolled-up picture from his bosom and placed it on the desk. Then he spoke: "I paid a visit to the crypt, sir, and there looked at a few pictures the old abbot Jade Mirror made of his cat. It struck me that he used to do those in great detail. On one painting the cat's pupils were just slits; it must have been done at noon. Then I remembered that on his last picture which you showed me in the temple, the pupils of the cat were wide open. That proved to me that the picture was painted in the morning, and not at noon, as True Wisdom had always said."

He unrolled the scroll and pointed to the cat's eyes.

"I can't understand what you are getting at, Dee!" Sun said annoyed. "What has all this to do with Jade Mirror's death? I was there myself, I tell you, the man died peacefully and . . ."

"Allow me to explain, sir," Judge Dee interrupted respectfully. He then told Sun about the reference to nightshades in the old abbot's letter to Dr. Tsung, and how the symptoms of nightshade poisoning accorded well with the old abbot's behaviour during his last hours. He added diffidently: "If I may say so, sir, it has often struck me that Taoist texts are always couched in a highly obscure and ambiguous language. One could imagine that the old abbot's last sermon was in fact a confused mixture of various religious passages he remembered. It needed the commentary of the Chief Abbot to make sense. I presume he chose some mystic terms from the abbot's sermon, and made those the theme for a lucid discussion, or he . . ." He broke off, giving Master Sun an anxious look.

But Sun was perplexed. He made no attempt to speak up in favour of Taoist texts. He just sat there, slowly shaking his large head. The judge went on: "True Wisdom put a large dose of the poison in Jade Mirror's tea when, after the noon meal, they were having a cup together in the library. The picture was nearly finished then. The abbot had spent the entire morning on it, first doing the cat itself, then painting in background and details. He had only to do the bamboo leaves when he interrupted his work for the noon meal. After he had drunk the poisoned tea, True Wisdom left and told the two monks who were waiting outside that the abbot should not be disturbed, because he was starting on a picture. The poison soon brought him into a state of mental excitement. He started to hum Taoist hymns, then began to talk to himself. There can be no doubt that he thought he was becoming inspired. It didn't enter his mind that he had been poisoned. You'll remember, sir, that he did not say one word about that being his last sermon, nor about wanting to depart from this world after he had finished. There was no reason to. He only wanted to pass on to his followers the revelation that Heaven had granted him. After that he leaned back in his chair, wanting to rest awhile after his lengthy speech. But then he passed away—a happy man."

"Almighty Heaven!" Sun now exclaimed. "You must be right, Dee! But why did the fool murder Jade Mirror? And why did he insist on making his confession in front of me?"

"I think," Judge Dee replied, "that True Wisdom had committed a sordid crime, and that he feared that the old abbot had discovered it and was planning to expose him. Jade Mirror wrote in his last letter to Dr. Tsung that he suspected that immoral acts were being committed with the girls who came here to be initiated and to be ordained as nuns. If this had come out, True Wisdom would, of course, have been finished."

Sun passed his hand over his eyes in a weary gesture.

"Immoral acts!" he muttered. "The fool must have been dabbling in black magic, involving rites with woman partners. August Heaven, I am responsible also, Dee! I shouldn't have kept myself shut up in my library all the time. I should have kept an eye on what was going on. And Jade Mirror is guilty too, in a way. Why didn't he at once tell me about his suspicions? I hadn't the faintest idea that . . ."

His voice trailed off. Judge Dee resumed: "I think that True Wisdom, together with a villain who now calls himself Mo Mo-te, was responsible for the fate of the three girls who died here last year. They must have been forced to take part in the unspeakable secret rites, just like those others who came here before the old abbot died. Mo Mo-te has now re-visited this monastery, in the guise of a member of Kuan's troupe. Mo probably threatened the abbot and tried to blackmail him. I noticed that the abbot was afraid of Mo. That, together with broad hints at the old abbot's having been murdered with deadly nightshade, made in public by Tsung Lee, must have made True Wisdom desperate. When at the end of the banquet he saw Tsung Lee talking with me, and when directly afterwards I told True Wisdom that I wanted to visit the crypt, he thought I was planning to institute an investigation. He became frantic, and tried to kill me. He dealt me a blow on my head from behind, but before I lost consciousness, I perceived the smell of a peculiar incense he burns in the bedroom. Ordinarily one doesn't smell it when one is near him, but I got a waft of it from the folds of his robe when he lifted his arm to hit me. Later he spied on me when I was talking with my assistant, and when he fled, I again noticed that particular smell. The man must have lost his head completely."

Sun Ming nodded forlornly. After a while he asked: "But why did the fellow insist on delivering a statement in front of me? If he had thought I would speak up in his favour, he must have been an even greater fool than I always thought he was!"

"Before I answer that question, sir," Judge Dee said, "I would like to ask you first whether True Wisdom was aware of the fact that the balustrade of the landing was broken?"

"Of course he was!" Sun replied. "I told him myself that I wanted to have it repaired. He was diligent enough, I must grant him that!"

"In that case," Judge Dee said gravely, "he committed suicide."

"Nonsense! I myself saw him grabbing for that balustrade, Dee!"

"He fooled both you and me," the judge said. "Remember that he couldn't have known that we would meet you at the bottom of the staircase leading up here. He thought that you would be in your library. He never intended to meet you, sir, let alone make a statement. He only wanted to come up here because he knew he was lost, and because the landing was the best place he could think of for committing suicide before I could arrest him. He pretended it was an accident in order to safeguard his reputation and the interests of his family. For now we shall never be able to say with absolute certainty what part he took in all that happened here. Your unexpected appearance did not materially change his scheme."

Tao Gan and Tsung Lee came in.

"He broke his neck, Your Honour," the former announced soberly. "He must have died instantly. I fetched the prior. They are now bringing the corpse to the side hall of the temple, to lie in state there pending the official burial. I explained that it had been an accident." Turning to Sun he added: "The prior wishes to speak to you, sir."

Judge Dee rose. He said to Sun: "For the time being we'd better keep to that theory of an accident. Perhaps Your Excellency will be so kind as to discuss with the prior the necessary measures to be taken. I suppose the Chief Abbot in the capital must be informed as soon as possible!"

"We'll send a messenger first thing tomorrow morning," Sun said. "We'll also have to ascertain the wishes of His Holiness regarding the succession. Pending his answer, the prior can take care of the routine administration here."

"I hope that tomorrow morning you'll kindly help me to draw up the official report about this, sir," the judge said. "I'll leave the picture of the cat here; it's an important piece of evidence."

Sun Ming nodded. He gave the judge an appraising look, then said: "You had better go and get a few hours sleep, Dee! You look a bit off colour!"

"I still have to arrest Mo, sir!" the judge replied dejectedly. "I am convinced that Mo is the real criminal, more guilty than the abbot. It must depend on Mo's testimony whether we report the abbot's death just now as suicide, or as death by misadventure. And now that the abbot is dead, Mo is the only one who can tell us what really happened to the three girls who died here."

"What does the fellow look like?" Sun asked. "You say he is an actor? I watched the entire mystery play, except for the last scene."

"Mo was on the stage all the time. He acted the part of the Spirit of Death. But you couldn't see his face, sir, because he wore one of those large wooden masks. I saw him in the last scene where he performed a sword dance, but then his face was painted. I suspect that now he is posing as one of the monks here. He is a tall, broad-shouldered fellow, and usually looks rather morose."

"Most of the monks do," Sun muttered. "Wrong diet, I suppose. How do you expect to find him, Dee?"

"That is what I must try to work out now, sir!" Judge Dee replied with a rueful smile. "I can't settle this case without Mo's full confession."

He took his leave with a deep bow. As he went to the door, with Tao Gan and Tsung Lee, the small prior came in, looking more nervous than ever.

XVI

When the three men entered the temple hall, they found the almoner, talking in a hushed voice to a small group of monks. Seeing Judge Dee he quickly came forward and led him silently to the side hall.

The abbot's corpse had been laid on a high bier, and covered with a piece of red brocade, embroidered in gold thread with Taoist symbols. The judge lifted one end. He looked for a while at the dead man's still face. As he let it drop again, the almoner whispered: "Four monks will be here all night reading prayers, Your Honour. The prior plans to announce the abbot's demise in a few hours, during matins."

Judge Dee expressed his condolence, then went back to the front hall where Tao Gan and Tsung Lee stood waiting for him. The poet asked diffidently: "May I invite Your Honour to have a cup of tea up in my room?"

"I refuse to climb any more steps!" Judge Dee replied firmly. "Tell one of those monks to bring a large pot of bitter tea to that room over there!"

He went to the small cabinet over on the other side of the front hall. It was apparently used as a reception room. Judge Dee sat down at the tea table, a beautiful antique piece of carved sandalwood. He motioned Tao Gan to take the chair opposite him. Silently the judge studied the painted portraits of Taoist Immortals, yellowed by age, that were suspended in gorgeous frames on the walls. Through the open-work carving in the wall above them he could vaguely see the heads of the large gilded statues on the altar in the dim temple hall.

Tsung Lee came in carrying a large teapot. He poured out three cups. The judge told him to be seated also.

While sipping their tea they listened to the monotonous chant that came drifting over to them from the side hall opposite. The monks by the abbot's bier had started intoning the prayers for the dead.

Judge Dee sat motionless, slumped back in his chair. He felt completely exhausted. His legs and his back were throbbing with a dull ache, and he had a queer, empty feeling in his head. He tried to review the circumstances that had led up to the old abbot's murder and True Wisdom's suicide. He had a vague feeling that some features still needed a further explanation; there were some isolated facts which would complete his mental picture of Mo Mo-te—if only he could find the correct interpretation. But his brain was numb; he couldn't think clearly. Mo Mo-te's helmet kept appearing before him. He had the distinct feeling that there was something wrong with that helmet. His thoughts became confused; he realized that the monotonous chant of the monks was lulling him to sleep.

He suppressed a yawn and sat up with an effort. Placing his elbows on the table he looked at his two companions. Tao Gan's thin face was as impassive as ever. Tsung Lee looked utterly tired; his face was sagging. The judge reflected that now that the poet's fatigue had made him drop his habitual insolent airs, he wasn't an unprepossessing youngster. Judge Dee emptied his teacup, then addressed him: "Now that you have executed your late father's command, Tsung Lee, you'd better settle down to a serious study of the Confucianist Classics, so as to prepare yourself for the literary examinations. You may yet prove yourself a worthy son of your distinguished father!" He gave the youngster a sour look, then he pushed his cap back from his forehead, and continued in a brisk voice: "We must now have a consultation about how we can catch Mo Mo-te, and save his most recent victim. He must tell us where he concealed that one-armed woman, and who she is."

"A one-armed woman?" Tsung Lee asked astonished.

"Yes," Judge Dee said giving him a sharp look. "Ever seen such a mutilated woman about here?"

Tsung Lee shook his head.

"No sir, I have been here now more than two weeks, but I never even heard about a one-armed woman. Unless," he added with a smile, "Your Honour would be referring to that statue in the Gallery of Horrors!"

"A statue?" Judge Dee asked. It was now his turn to be astonished.

"Yes, the one with all those chains, sir. Its left arm had become worm-eaten, and it fell off. They repaired it very quickly though, I must say." As Judge Dee looked fixedly at him he added: "You know, that naked woman being speared by a blue devil. I heard you remark to Tao Gan that you . . ."

Judge Dee hit his fist on the table.

"You utter fool!" he burst out. "Why didn't you tell me that earlier?"

"I thought . . . I told you about a statue being repaired, when we entered the gallery, sir. And . . ."

The judge had jumped up and grabbed the lantern.

"Come along quick, you two!" he barked and ran out into the temple hall.

He seemed to have forgotten his fatigue completely. He rushed up the stairs two at a time to the landing above the temple. Tao Gan and Tsung Lee had difficulty in keeping up with him.

Panting, the judge took them through the west passage to the tower, then ran down the steps that led to the entrance of the Gallery of Horrors. He kicked the door open and went inside. He halted in front of the blue devil and the naked woman spread-eagled against the boulder.

"Look, she is bleeding!" he muttered.

Tao Gan and Tsung Lee stared aghast at the thin stream of blood that trickled along the cracked plaster on the woman's breast, from the spot where the spearpoint had entered.

Judge Dee bent and carefully brushed aside the hair that covered the face.

"White Rose!" Tsung Lee gasped. "They've killed her!"

"No," Judge Dee said. "See, her fingers are twitching."

The body had been covered with a coat of white plaster, but the hands and feet had been painted black. A casual observer would not see them against the dark background.

The girl's eyelids fluttered. She gave them one glance from eyes half-crazed with pain and fear, then the bluish lids came down again. A strap of leather ran over the lower half of her face. While gagging her effectively, at the same time it kept her head fixed tightly to the wall.

Tsung Lee stretched out his hands to remove the gag, but the judge pushed him back roughly.

"Keep your hands off!" he ordered. "You might hurt her worse than she already is! Leave this to us!"

Tao Gan had taken off the chains that were wound round her waist, arms and legs. He said: "This ironware serves only to conceal the clamps that fix her limbs, sir!" He pointed to iron hooks round her ankles, thighs and upper and lower arms. Then he quickly took from his sleeve his folder with instruments.

"Wait!" Judge Dee ordered.

He closely examined the spearpoint. Then he carefully pressed down the flesh surrounding it till the point came free. Blood welled up and stained the coat of white plaster that covered the girl's body. It didn't seem more than a fleshwound. With his strong hands the judge bent the spear so that it pointed away from the girl's body, then broke the shaft with a quick twist. The hand of the wooden devil cracked and fell to the floor.

"Now you go ahead with the legs!" he snapped at Tao Gan. "Give me a pair of pincers!"

While Tao Gan began to loosen the iron clamps that secured the girl's legs, the judge set to work on the gag. When he had pulled out the nails that fixed the ends of the leather strap to the wall, he removed the wad of cotton wool from the girl's mouth, then started with infinite care on the clamps that had cut deep into the flesh of her arms.

"Expert workmanship!" Tao Gan muttered with grudging admiration. He was loosening the clamp that held her right thigh.

Tsung Lee had buried his face in his hands. He was sobbing convulsively. The judge barked at him: "Hey there! Support her head and shoulders!"

As Tsung Lee put his arm round her shoulders and held her limp body upright, Judge Dee helped Tao Gan to remove the last clamp that held her right arm. The three men lifted her from the boulder and laid her on the floormats. The judge took off his neckcloth and wrapped it around her waist. Tsung Lee squatted at her side, stroking her cheeks and whispering endearing words. But the girl was in a dead faint.

Judge Dee and Tao Gan wrenched two long spears from the hands of a pair of green devils further on. They laid the spears side by side on the floor. Tao Gan took off his upper robe and fastened it to the shafts so as to make a primitive stretcher. When they had laid the girl on it, Tao Gan and Tsung Lee took hold of the ends of the shafts.

"Take her to Miss Ting's room!" Judge Dee ordered.

XVII

Judge Dee had to knock for a long time before Miss Ting opened. She wore only a thin bed-robe. Looking the judge up and down with sleep-heavy eyes she said: "You could be my husband, using my room at all hours!"

"Shut up and get out of the way!" the judge said crossly. She stepped back and looked dumbfounded at the two men as they carried their burden inside. While they were putting the unconscious girl on Miss Ting's bed, Judge Dee said to her: "Fan the coals in that brazier and heat up this room. Prepare a large pot of hot tea and make her drink as much as possible. She was exposed naked for many hours in a cold and damp gallery, and although the coat of plaster on her body may have acted as a protection, she still may have got a dangerous chill. Then soak the plaster thoroughly with warm water and remove it with a towel. Be careful, the wound on her breast is only superficial, but the bruises on her arms and legs may be worse than they seem. Verify also whether her back is injured. As an acrobat you know all about sprained muscles and bone-setting, don't you?"

Miss Ting nodded. She cast a pitying glance at the still figure on the bed.

"I'll get some drugs and plasters now," the judge added. "These two men will stand guard outside the door. Set to work!"

Miss Ting asked no questions but immediately began to revive the coals in the brazier with a bamboo fan. Judge Dee took Tao Gan and Tsung Lee outside. He said: "Fetch Mr. Kang. If Mo should appear, arrest him. Not too gently!"

He rushed upstairs, to his own quarters on the third floor.

He roused the sleeping maids. When they had opened the door, he went into the bedroom, which was lighted only by two burned-down candles. Through the open bed curtains he saw that his three wives were sleeping peacefully, lying close together under the embroidered quilt.

He tiptoed to their medicine chest and rummaged about in its drawers till he had found the box with the oil-plasters and a few small boxes with salves and powders. As he turned around, he saw that his First Lady had awakened. She raised herself to a sitting position. Pulling her night robe up to cover her bare torso she looked at him with sleep-heavy eyes.

Judge Dee gave her a reassuring smile, then went out again.

Back in front of Miss Ting's room, Tao Gan reported that Kang I-te's room was empty. Neither he nor his bear were there. They had seen no one.

"Go to Mrs. Pao's room," the judge ordered, "and bring her here."

"Who was the fiend who tortured her, Your Honour?" Tsung Lee asked tensely. His face was distorted with anger and anxiety.

"We'll know soon!" the judge answered curtly.

Tao Gan came back. The door of Mrs. Pao's room had been locked. He had forced it open but nobody was there. He had found only a bundle of clothes belonging to White Rose. Mrs. Pao's luggage was missing, and neither of the two beds had been slept in.

Judge Dee made no comment. He started pacing up and down the corridor, his hands on his back.

After a long wait Miss Ting opened the door and beckoned the judge.

"I'll call you when I am ready," he said to the two men, and followed her inside.

He walked up to the bed. Miss Ting folded the covers back. While she held the candle close Judge Dee examined the bruises on the white body. The girl was still unconscious, but her lips twitched when the judge probed the deep cuts left by the clamps.

He righted himself and took a small box from his sleeve.

"Dissolve the contents in a cup of hot tea," he ordered. "It's a pain-stilling soporific."

Then he further examined the girl's body. He didn't like the heart-beat, but there seemed to be no internal lesions. She was a virgin, and there were no signs that she had been beaten except for a bluish spot on her left temple. He put salve on the bruises, then covered them with thick oil-plasters. He saw to his satisfaction that Miss Ting had pasted the membrane of an egg over the wound on her breast. The judge covered her up again. He took a pinch of white powder from another box he had brought and inserted it in White Rose's nostrils.

Miss Ting handed him the cup with the medicine. On a sign from the judge she raised the girl's head. The girl sneezed and opened her eyes. The judge made her drink the medicine, then let her lie back again. He sat down on the edge of the bed. The girl stared up at him with wide, uncomprehending eyes.

"Call the two men here!" Judge Dee ordered Miss Ting. "Soon she'll be able to talk, and I want them to be present as witnesses."

"Her condition isn't . . . dangerous?" Miss Ting asked anxiously.

"Not too bad," Judge Dee said. Giving her a quick smile he patted her on the shoulder and added: "You did very well. Now get those two fellows!"

As Tao Gan and Tsung Lee came in, the judge said softly to White Rose: "You are safe now, my dear. Presently you'll have a nice long sleep."

He didn't like the queer stare in the girl's eyes. "You talk to her!" he ordered Tsung Lee.

The poet bent over her and softly called her name. Suddenly the girl seemed to understand. She looked at him and asked in a barely audible voice: "What happened? Did I have a nightmare?"

Judge Dee made a peremptory sign to Tsung. The poet knelt down by the side of the bedstead and took the girl's hand in his, stroking it softly. The judge said to the girl reassuringly: "Whatever it was, it's all past and done with now!"

"But I still see it all before me!" she cried out. "All those horrible faces!"

"Tell me about it!" Judge Dee said encouragingly. "You know how it is with bad dreams, don't you? Once you have told them, they lose their power over you, and they are gone, gone forever. Who took you up to the gallery?"

White Rose heaved a deep sigh. Staring at the curtains above her she said slowly: "I remember that after watching the stage show I felt very

A YOUNG GIRL IN THE HANDS OF EVIL PERSONS

confused. I have always been close to my brother. I had been terribly
frightened when that man threatened him with his sword. I muttered some
excuse to Mrs. Pao, and joined my brother backstage. I told him that I was
in awful difficulties, and that I wanted to talk with him alone. He told me
to go up to his room, posing as him. He had disguised himself as an actress,
you know."

She gave the judge a questioning look.

"Yes, I know all about that," Judge Dee said. "What happened after
you met us up in the corridor?"

"When I had rounded the corner I ran into Mrs. Pao. She was very
angry; she cursed me soundly and practically dragged me to our room.
There she made some excuses. She said she was responsible for me, and
couldn't allow me to associate with an actress of dubious reputation. I was
angry because of her rude behaviour, and that gave me the courage to tell
her that I wasn't sure that I wanted to become a nun after all. I added that
I wanted to talk things over with Miss Ou-yang, whom I said I had known
well in the capital.

"Mrs. Pao took this information rather calmly. She said that the decision was of course up to me, but that the monastery would have started
preparations for my initiation, and that she would have to inform the
abbot immediately. When she came back, she told me that the abbot
wanted to see me."

Turning her eyes to Tsung Lee she continued: "Mrs. Pao took me over
to the temple. We went up the staircase on the right. After having gone up
and down a few flights of steps we entered a small dressing room. Mrs. Pao
said I would have to change into a nun's cowl, as that was the proper dress
in which to be received by the abbot. I suddenly realized that they were
going to try to force me to become a nun. I refused.

"Then Mrs. Pao flew into a rage. I didn't recognize her any more; she
called me awful names. She tore my clothes off. I was so stupefied by the
unbelievable change in her that I hardly resisted. She pushed me naked
into the next room."

She gave the judge a pitiable look. He quickly made her drink another
cup of tea. She went on in a low voice: "I saw a large, luxuriously appointed bedroom. A couch stood against the back wall; the yellow brocade
curtains were half drawn. A muffled voice spoke from there: 'Come here,
my bride, you shall now be properly initiated!' I knew at once that I had
fallen into a trap set by evil people, and that I must try to escape. I turned
round to the door, but the woman grabbed me and quickly bound my
hands behind my back. Then she started dragging me by my hair to the
couch. I kicked her and screamed for help as loud as I could. 'Leave her!'
the voice said. 'I want to have a good look at her!' Mrs. Pao forced me

down on my knees in front of the couch, then stepped back. I heard a chuckle from the bedstead. It sounded so horrible that I burst out crying. 'That's better!' Mrs. Pao said. 'Now be a good girl and do as he says!' I shouted at her that they would have to kill me first. 'Shall I get the whip?' the loathsome woman asked. But the voice said: 'No, it wouldn't do to break that nice skin. She needs a little time, to reflect. Put her to sleep!' Mrs. Pao stepped up to me and hit me a sharp blow on the side of my head. I fainted."

Tsung Lee wanted to say something, but Judge Dee raised his hand. After a brief pause White Rose went on: "An excruciating pain in my back made me regain my senses. I was half lying, half hanging over some hard thing. I couldn't see well because my hair was hanging over my face. I tried to open my mouth but I had been gagged. My arms and legs were held by clamps that cut into my flesh at the slightest attempt to move. My back was aching and my skin taut all over, I felt it was covered with a crust of something.

"I felt terrible, but I forgot all pain when I saw through the hair a horrible blue face leering at me. I thought I had died and that I was in the Nether World. I fainted from sheer terror. It was again the pain in my arms and legs that made me come to. By breathing hard through my nose I could blow the hairs apart a little. I realised that the devil pressing the spear to my breast was in fact a wooden statue. I understood that I had been made to replace one of the statues in the Gallery of Horrors and that my body had been painted over with a coat of plaster. My relief at still being alive was soon replaced by a new terror. Someone must be standing behind me with a candle. What new torture were they planning for me, lying there completely defenceless? Then the light went out. All was pitch-dark. I heard the sound of soft footsteps, moving away. I made a frantic attempt to open my mouth, anything was better than being left lying there alone in the dark. Soon the silence was broken by the sounds of rats scurrying about . . ."

She closed her eyes, a long shiver shook her body. Tsung Lee started to cry. His tears dropped on her hand. She looked up and continued wearily to the judge: "I don't know how long I was there; I was half crazed by pain and fear, and the damp cold seemed to penetrate to my very bones. At last I saw a light and heard voices. I recognized yours, sir, and did my utmost to give you a sign. I tried to move my feet and my fingers, but they were completely numb. I heard you make a remark on my unseemly exposure, but . . . but I did have a loincloth, at least?"

She gave him an embarrassed look.

"Certainly!" Judge Dee replied quickly. "The other statues hadn't, though. Hence my remark."

"I thought so!" she said relieved. "But I didn't know for certain, because of the layer of plaster, you see. Well, then . . . then you went on.

"I knew my only hope was to draw your attention when you passed again on your way back. I forced myself to think clearly. Suddenly it came to me that if I could move my breast in such a way that the spearpoint resting against it would cut into my flesh, the blood would show clearly on the white plaster and thus might catch your eye. With a supreme effort I succeeded in moving my torso a little. The pain of the spear entering my flesh was nothing compared to the agonizing pain in my back and arms. The plaster coat prevented me from feeling whether much blood had come out. But then I heard a drop fall on the floor. I knew I had succeeded, and that gave me courage.

"Soon I heard footsteps again. Someone came running through the gallery, he rushed past me without another look. I knew that you would come too, but it took a very long time, it seemed. At last you came . . ."

"You are a very brave girl!" Judge Dee said. "I have only two questions to ask you, then you must have a rest. You gave a general description of how Mrs. Pao took you to the room where that man was waiting for you. Could you give me some more details about the way you went?"

White Rose frowned, in an effort to remember.

"I am certain," she said, "that it was in one of the buildings east of the temple. But as to the rest . . . I had never been there before, and we made so many turns . . ."

"Did you pass perhaps a square landing, with a screen of lattice-work all around it?"

She shook her head forlornly.

"I really don't remember!" she replied.

"It doesn't matter. Tell me only whether you recognized the voice that came from the bedstead. Could it have been the abbot?"

Again she shook her head.

"I still hear that hateful voice in my ears, but it doesn't remind me of anyone I know. And I have good ears," she added with a faint smile. "I recognized Tsung Lee's voice when you entered the gallery the first time, though I only heard it in the distance. The relief when . . ."

"It was Tsung Lee who gave me the idea that you were in the gallery," Judge Dee remarked. "Without him I wouldn't have found you."

She turned her head and looked affectionately at the kneeling youngster. Then she lifted her head to the judge and said weakly: "I feel so peaceful and happy now! I can never repay you for . . ."

"You can!" Judge Dee said dryly. "Teach this fellow to make better poetry!"

As he rose, the girl smiled faintly. Her eyelids fluttered; the sleeping drug was taking effect. Turning to Miss Ting, the judge whispered: "As soon as she is asleep, throw that youngster out and rub her gently all over with this ointment here."

There was a knock on the door. Kang I-te came in, dressed as a man.

"I just put my bear outside," he said. "What is all this commotion?"

"Ask Miss Ting!" the judge said gruffly. "I have other things to do." He beckoned Tao Gan to follow him.

Miss Ting had been staring at Kang with wide eyes. Now she gasped: "You are a man!"

"That ought to solve your problem," Judge Dee remarked to her. Kang had eyes only for her; he had hardly noticed the poet and the still figure on the bed. The last Judge Dee saw him do was clasp Miss Ting in his arms.

XVIII

Outside, the judge said sourly to Tao Gan: "I'd better resign as magistrate and set up business as a professional matchmaker. I have brought together two young couples, but I can't find a dangerous maniac! Let's go to your room. We must devise a plan, and quick!"

While they were walking down the corridor, Tao Gan said sadly: "I am awfully sorry, sir, that when passing through the gallery to fetch the painting from the temple, I didn't pause to have a second look at that poor naked woman. Then I would have noticed the blood and . . ."

"You needn't be sorry," the judge remarked dryly. "It does you credit. Leave it to your colleague Ma Joong to gape at unclothed women!"

Seated in Tao Gan's small room, Judge Dee silently drank the tea his lieutenant made for him. Then he sighed and said: "Well, I know now that it was the armless wooden statue from the Gallery of Horrors that I saw Mo move about in that secret hide-out of his. So we have found the one-armed woman, but I still can't understand how I could have seen the original wooden statue through a window that isn't there! However, let's leave that problem for the time being, and concentrate on the new, concrete facts we learned. Mo must have used Mrs. Pao as a procuress, and the dead abbot must have connived at their sordid affairs. Mo must have planned to place Miss Kang in the Gallery of Horrors for some time. He had removed the wooden statue before we arrived here, and probably also prepared the clamps in the wall. The cheek of that villain to go on with his infernal scheme, right under my nose!" The judge tugged angrily at his beard. "When Mrs. Pao had informed Mo and the abbot that White Rose was thinking of giving up her plan of becoming a nun, and wanted to establish contact with Miss Ou-yang, they decided to act quickly. They knew I was scheduled to leave the monastery this morning, and if I should inquire after her, they could easily explain the girl's absence by saying that she had gone into retreat for a few days in the forbidden part of the monastery. Thereafter they would have cowed the poor girl so thoroughly by their infernal tortures that she wouldn't have dared to denounce them, and they would doubtless have found some way to explain things to Miss Ou-yang, or Kang I-te rather, and to Tsung Lee. By then she would have been raped, and she herself wouldn't have liked to see her brother or the poet again. Those unspeakable fiends!"

He knitted his thick eyebrows. Tao Gan quietly pulled at the three long hairs on his cheek. No human depravity could ever astonish him. The judge resumed: "The abbot escaped earthly justice, but we'll get Mo Mo-te, and he is the main criminal. I don't think the abbot had the pluck; he was a coward at heart. But Mo is a completely ruthless, perverted maniac. There's no time for half-measures now, Tao Gan! I'll go and rouse Master Sun. We'll have all the inmates assembled in the large hall and we'll let Kuan Lai and Kang I-te look them over. If Mo isn't found among them, we'll search the entire accursed place, as I had already planned."

Tao Gan looked doubtful.

"I am afraid, sir, that we can't have the whole monastery roused without Mo suspecting that the commotion has something to do with him. He will have fled before the check began. The storm is over, and Heaven knows how many exits this place has. Once he is in the mountains, it'll prove very difficult to catch him. It would be quite different, of course, if we had Ma Joong, Chiao Tai, and the rest of the staff here, with twenty constables or so. But with only the two of us . . ." He didn't complete the sentence.

Judge Dee nodded unhappily. He had to agree that his lieutenant was right. But what to do then? Absent-mindedly he took up a chopstick, and tried to balance the saucer of his teacup on its tip.

"It's a great pity that we haven't a plan of this monastery," Tao Gan resumed. "If we had one, we could probably make a good guess where that bedroom is to which Mrs. Pao took White Rose. It can't be far from the store-room where Your Honour saw Mo putting away the wooden statue of the naked woman from the gallery. And then we could also verify the thickness of the walls there."

"Master Sun showed me a diagram," Judge Dee said. "A kind of outline of the plan the monastery is built on." He kept his eyes on the saucer; he thought he had got it nearly balanced. "That was a great help for my general orientation. But of course it didn't give any details."

He let the saucer go and lifted the chopstick at the same time. The saucer fell and broke into pieces on the stone floor.

Tao Gan stooped and picked the broken pieces up. Trying to fit them together on the table he asked curiously:

"What were you trying to do, sir?"

"Oh," the judge replied a little self-consciously, "it's a trick Miss Ting did. You make the saucer whirl round on top of the chopstick, you see. It can't fly away because of the rim round the bottom. It's quite a neat trick. That whirling saucer reminded me of the round Taoist symbol Master Sun drew at the top of his diagram, the two primordial forces turning round and round in eternal interaction. Funny I let it drop. When I saw Miss Ting doing it, it looked very easy!"

"Most tricks look easy when they are done well!" Tao Gan remarked with his thin smile. "But as a matter of fact they call for very long practice! Good, there's no piece missing. Tomorrow I'll mend this saucer, then it can still be used for many more years!"

"What makes you so parsimonious, Tao Gan?" Judge Dee asked curiously. "I know that you have ample private means, and no family obligations. You needn't become a wastrel, even if you don't grudge every single copper!"

His thin lieutenant gave him a shy look. He said, rather diffidently: "Heaven has presented us with so many good things, sir, and gratis too! A roof to shelter us, food for our stomach, clothes for our body. I am always afraid that some day Heaven'll become angry, seeing that we take all those good things for granted, even spend them recklessly. Therefore I can't bear to throw away anything that can still be used in some way or another. Look, sir, there'll only remain that one bad crack, the one that cuts horizontally through the flower design. But that can't be helped!"

Judge Dee sat up in his chair. He stared fixedly at the re-assembled saucer that Tao Gan held together in his cupped hands.

Suddenly he jumped up and started to walk back and forth in the small room, muttering to himself. Tao Gan looked up, then stared again at the broken saucer in his hands. He wondered what the judge had seen there.

Judge Dee halted in front of Tao Gan. He exclaimed excitedly: "I am a fool, Tao Gan! I have let myself be led around by my nose, that's what I've done! There's no need to assemble all the inmates, I know now where to find our man! Come along. I'll go to Master Sun's library. You'll wait for me on the landing over the temple!"

He took the lantern and ran out, followed by Tao Gan.

The two men went down. They parted in the empty courtyard.

Judge Dee crossed over to the west wing, passed through the portal of the refectory, and ascended the stairs to Sun's quarters.

He knocked several times on the carved door, but there was no answer. He pushed, and found that the door wasn't locked. He went inside.

The library was in semi-darkness, the candles burning low. The judge went over to the narrow door behind the desk, which presumably led to Sun's bedroom. He knocked again. He pressed his ear against the door, but heard nothing. He tried to open it, but it was securely locked.

He turned round and pensively surveyed the room. Then he stepped up to the scroll with the diagram, and looked for a while intently at the round symbol of the two forces depicted at the top. He turned to the door and left. Giving the broken balustrade a brief look, he entered the passage leading east to the square landing over the temple hall.

The judge vaguely heard the murmur of prayers coming up from the temple-nave below. Tao Gan was nowhere to be seen. He shrugged his shoulders and took the corridor leading to the store-room. Its door was standing ajar.

He went inside and lifted his lantern high. The room was exactly as he had seen it the last time he was there looking for Mo Mo-te. But the double door of the antique cupboard in the farthest corner was standing open. He ran up to it, stepped inside and held his lantern close to the picture of the two dragons on the back wall. The round circle in between them was indeed the Taoist symbol of the two forces, but the dividing line was horizontal. When he had asked Sun about it, he had forgotten that it had been here that he had seen the circle thus divided. Tao Gan's remarks and the broken saucer had made him see the connection.

He now also saw what he hadn't noticed before, namely that there was a small dot in each half of the circle, the germ mentioned by Sun when he had explained the meaning of the symbol to him. Looking closer, the dots turned out to be in fact small holes, bored deeply into the wood. He tapped the circle with his knuckle. No, it wasn't wood, it was an iron disk. And a narrow groove separated it from the lacquered surface surrounding it.

He thought he knew what those two holes in a round metal disk meant. He lifted his cap and pulled the hairpin from his top-knot. Inserting its point into one of the holes, he tried to make the disk turn to the left. It didn't budge. Then he tried the opposite direction, holding the hairpin with two hands. Now the disk turned around. He could make it turn easily five times, then it seemed to get stuck. With some difficulty he succeeded in making it turn around four more times. The right half of the back wall of the cupboard started to move a little, like a door about to swing open. He heard vague sounds on the other side. He softly pushed the door shut again.

He stepped back into the room, ran out into the corridor and looked around on the landing. Tao Gan hadn't come yet. Well, he would have to do without a witness. He went back to the store-room, entered the cupboard, and pulled the door open.

He saw a narrow passage only three feet wide, running five feet or so to the right, parallel with the wall. With two quick strides he turned the corner. He looked into a small room, dimly lit by only one dust-covered oil lamp hanging from the low ceiling. A tall, broad-backed man stood bent over the bamboo couch that took up the back wall, rubbing it with a piece of cloth. On the floor the judge saw a kitchen chopper lying in a pool of blood.

XIX

The man righted himself and turned round. Seeing the judge standing there he said with a benign smile: "So you found this secret room all by yourself! You are a clever fellow, Dee! Sit down and tell me how you did it! You can sit there on the couch; I just cleaned it. But mind the blood on the floor!"

Judge Dee looked quickly at the life-size wooden statue of a naked woman that was standing in the corner. The plaster was peeling off, and where the left arm should have been there was only a ragged stump of worm-eaten wood. He sat down by the other's side and looked around. The room was scarcely six foot square, and contained no other furniture except the couch they were sitting on. In the wall in front of him was a round aperture, apparently an air-shaft. On his right he saw a dark niche. He said slowly: "I suspected there was a secret room here near the corner of the building, but judging by the depth of the window niches in the corridor, that was impossible. There didn't seem to be enough space for one."

"There isn't!" Sun said with a chuckle. "But a thick supporting wall is built on the outside against the corner of this building, and this snug little room is inside that wall. You can't see it from the other side of the ravine that runs along this side of the monastery, nor can you see it from the windows of the east wing opposite. The old builders knew their job, you see! What made you think there was a secret room here, Dee?"

"Only a lucky accident," the judge replied with a sigh. "Last night, shortly after my arrival here, a window blew open and I got a brief glimpse of this room. I saw you while you were moving that wooden statue which you had taken from the Gallery of Horrors. I only saw your back, and I mistook the smooth grey hair plastered to your head for a close-fitting helmet. And I thought the statue was a real woman. That was the hallucination I consulted you about."

"Well, well!" Sun said astonished. "So you consulted me about myself, so to speak!" He laughed heartily.

"That scene," Judge Dee continued with impassive face, "set me chasing after the actor Mo Mo-te, who wore such an antiquated helmet during his sword dance. I can't understand, though, why that window on the right there doesn't show on the outside. That is the window I must have seen."

"It is," Sun replied. "But it's a trick-window, you know. I can't claim any credit for it; it was there already when last year I discovered this useful little room. The shutters are, as you see, on the inside, and the panels of oiled paper on the outside are flush with the surface of the wall, and painted like bricks. Transparent paint was used, so that one can open the shutters at daytime and have light to see by, without any outside people noticing anything." He pensively caressed his short ringbeard and went on: "Yes, I remember now, last night I opened it to get some fresh air. The window is on the side away from the wind, you see. I didn't think it would do any harm, for I knew that the shutters of all the windows opposite were closed tightly because of the storm. When I heard one blow open, I quickly closed mine, but apparently I wasn't quick enough! I was a bit careless there, I fear!"

"You were even more careless when, during your explanation of the diagram in your library, you stated that the circle of the two forces is always divided vertically. I knew for certain that somewhere I had seen the circle with a horizontal dividing line, but at that moment I didn't remember where and when that had been. If you had then told me that the circle might be represented in varying positions, I would have dismissed the subject from my mind, and forgotten all about it."

Sun hit his hand on his knee. He said with a smile: "Yes, now I remember you asking about that. I must confess that I hadn't thought at all about the secret lock when I was giving you my explanation. You are an observant fellow, Dee! But how did you manage to turn the disk around? It screws a vertical bar up and down along the side of the door, and it doesn't turn easily. There's a special key for it, you know! He took from his bosom an iron hook with two protruding dents and a long handle. The judge saw that the dents would fit the two holes in the disk.

"I found that my hairpin did as well," he said. "It only takes more time, of course. But to come back to our subject I think you were careless a third time when you placed Miss Kang in the Gallery of Horrors. She couldn't move her head or body and the black paint on her hands and feet was a clever device, but with all those people about here, there was still a great risk that she would be discovered."

"No," Sun said reprovingly, "there you are completely wrong, Dee. Ordinarily there wouldn't have been any risk, the gallery is closed this time of the year. And it was a very original idea, don't you think? I presume the girl would have become quite amenable after passing one night there. I'll repeat the experiment, some day. Though painting her was quite a job, I'll tell you! But I like to do things well. You are an enterprising fellow, Dee. That deduction from the cat's eyes was quite clever of you. I had overlooked that clue when I suggested to our poor friend True Wisdom how he could eliminate the old abbot. True Wisdom, I regret to say, was really a mean person, only out for wealth and power, but lacking the initiative and will-power for acquiring all that by himself. When he was still the prior here, he once stole a large sum of money from the monastery treasury. He would have been done for if I had not helped him. Therefore he was obliged to help me with my own little pastimes! The old abbot now, that was another man for you! Clever as they make them! Fortunately he was getting on in years, and when he found out that something was going on with those girls here, he immediately suspected True Wisdom—that poor fish who didn't even know what a woman looks like! I found it safer to instruct True Wisdom to do away with old Jade Mirror, and I persuaded the Chief Abbot in the capital to appoint True Wisdom as successor."

Sun pensively pulled at his ragged eyebrows. Giving Judge Dee a shrewd look he went on: "True Wisdom had become rattled, of late. He kept worrying about the insinuations made by that rascally poet, and he also maintained that a strange monk had wormed his way into this monastery and was spying on him. It was a fellow with a morose face. True Wisdom thought he had seen him before somewhere. Presumably the same fellow you were after, Dee! All nonsense, of course. Just before your arrival I had to take True Wisdom up to my attic and give him a good talking to. But it didn't help, apparently. He was steadily losing his head; that's why the fool tried to kill you. He badly bungled that—I am glad to say."

The judge remained silent. He thought for a while, then said: "No, True Wisdom's fears of that morose monk were well-founded. Where did you find that girl called Liu who died here while you were treating her for a lingering disease?"

"Lingering disease is a most appropriate term!" Sun said with a chuckle. "Well, Miss Liu was something quite special, Dee. A strong, well-developed girl, and lots of spirit! She was a member of a band of vagabonds, and got arrested while stealing chickens from a farm outside the capital. My good Mrs. Pao got her by bribing the prison guards."

"I see. That morose monk, as you call him, was Miss Liu's brother. I was told that his real name might be Liu. At times he went about as a vagrant Taoist monk, and in that role he had visited this monastery before. He suspected that his sister had been murdered here. He came back in the guise of the actor Mo Mo-te, in order to find the murderer and to avenge her death. The abbot was quite right in worrying about Mo; he is a splendid swordsman, and you know how particular those gangs are with regard to settling blood-feuds."

"Well," Sun said indifferently, "the abbot is dead and gone, and we'll blame everything on him, so your bellicose Mr. Mo will be satisfied. My friend True Wisdom made a sad mistake, though, when at the last moment he wanted to denounce me to you, hoping thereby to save his own skin."

Judge Dee nodded. He said: "The abbot didn't commit suicide, of course. I ought to have suspected that at once. You pushed him from the landing, didn't you?"

"That's true!" Sun said happily. "I thought I showed great presence of mind on that occasion! I was quite impressed by your reasoning, Dee! It was so logical that I nearly began to believe that he had committed suicide myself! Listen, I am sorry I can't offer you a cup of tea. That is unfortunately not included in the facilities of this cosy little room!"

"Did you have other helpers here besides the abbot and Mrs. Pao?"

"Of course not! As an experienced magistrate you'll know very well, Dee, that if you want to keep something secret, you shouldn't rope in all the world and his wife!"

"I suppose you killed Mrs. Pao here?" the judge asked looking at the blood-stained chopper on the floor.

"Yes, I could take no chances with her, after I had found the gallery open and Miss Kang gone. Killing her presented no problem of course, but I had to do some hard work to get her remains through that air-shaft over there, she was a portly woman, you know. But her pieces will rest in peace, if you'll allow me a feeble pun! At the bottom of the ravine is a cleft; nobody has yet succeeded in exploring its depths. I somewhat regret the loss of Mrs. Pao, though, for she made herself quite useful, and I had built up an excellent reputation for her in the capital. But the pious widow had to go, for she was the only one who could testify against me after you had wrecked my plans with little Miss Kang." He added with a quick smile: "Don't think I hold that against you, Dee! I enjoy a battle of wits with a clever opponent like you. You are doubtless a fine chess player. Let's have a game tomorrow. You do play chess, don't you?"

"Hardly," Judge Dee replied. "My favourite game is dominoes."

"Dominoes, eh?" Sun said, disappointed. "Well, I won't quarrel with another man's tastes. As regards Mrs. Pao, I'll soon find another woman who'll continue her pious work."

"Mrs. Pao was indeed an important witness," the judge said slowly. He caressed his sidewhiskers, looking pensively at his host. Then he resumed: "Tell me, why did you leave the capital and settle down in this lonely monastery?"

A reminiscent smile curved Sun's thin lips. He patted the silvery locks on his large round head and replied: "When I had the signal honour of explaining to His Majesty the Taoist creed, a few courtiers and Palace ladies became interested in the secret rites. I found the daughter of a certain chamberlain rather attractive, and she was so enthusiastic! Unfortunately the stupid wrench killed herself. It was all hushed up, of course, but I had to leave the Palace. I found this monastery a suitable place for continuing my studies. Mrs. Pao got three girls to keep me company during the past year, quite satisfactory ones. Unfortunately all of them died, as you doubtless know."

"What did really happen to the girl who fell from the tower above us here—by accident, as it was said?"

"She didn't go up to the tower at all! At least not on the day she died. She had been to my special room up there, of course. You should see it, Dee, it's all draped with yellow brocade! Miss Kang was quite impressed, I think. But to come back to the other one, Miss Gao, as she was called. She went the same way as Mrs. Pao just now, but of her own free will, mind you. I had put her in this room here, and chose to forget about her for a day or so, to teach her a lesson. She succeeded in wriggling through that narrow air-shaft there. She was quite a slender girl, you see."

"If you confess as readily in my tribunal as you do now," Judge Dee said dryly, "you'll make things very easy for me."

Sun raised his tufted eyebrows.

"In the tribunal?" he asked, astonished. "What on earth are you talking about, Dee?"

"Well," the judge replied, "You committed five murders, not to speak of rape and abduction. You weren't thinking I would let you get away with that, did you?"

"My dear fellow!" Sun exclaimed. "Of course you'll let me get away with it—if you insist on using that vulgar expression. Your only witnesses against me were our good abbot and Mrs. Pao—and neither of them is with us any more. After the instructive experiences I had with the two girls in the old abbot's time, I never showed myself before the girls were completely under control. All the blame for the treatment Miss Kang underwent will go to True Wisdom and Mrs. Pao." As Judge Dee shook his head emphatically, Sun exclaimed: "Come now, Dee, I think you are a clever man, don't disappoint me! Of course you could never initiate a case against me. What would the higher authorities think if you accused me, the famous Taoist sage and former Imperial Tutor Sun Ming, of a string of fantastic crimes, and that without a shred of proof? Everybody would think you had gone raving mad, Dee. It would break your career! And I would be genuinely sorry for that, for I really like you, you know!"

"And if, in order to substantiate my case, I referred to that unsavoury affair in the Palace you just told me about?"

Sun Ming laughed heartily.

"My dear Dee, don't you realize that the said little mishap is a closely guarded Palace secret, involving most illustrious names? As soon as you breathed one word about that, you would find yourself demoted and sent to a far-away place—if they didn't put you in jail, in solitary confinement for the rest of your life!"

Judge Dee thought for a while, slowly stroking his beard.

"Yes," he said with a sigh, "I am afraid that you are quite right."

"Of course I am right! I quite enjoyed this conversation, it's nice to be able to discuss one's hobbies with such an understanding person as you. But I must ask you to forget all about this, Dee. You'll return to Han-yuan with the personal satisfaction that you solved for yourself some knotty problems, and got the better of me in the case of little Miss Kang. And I'll continue my peaceful life here in the monastery. Of course you won't try to restrain either directly or indirectly my future activities. You are much too clever for that—you are doubtless aware of the fact that I still have considerable influence in the capital. You have now learned the valuable lesson, Dee, that law and custom are only there for the common people; they don't apply to exalted persons like me. I belong to that small group of chosen people, Dee, who because of their superior knowledge and talents are far above ordinary human rules and limitations. We have advanced beyond such conventional notions as 'good' and 'bad.' If the storm destroys a house and kills all the inmates, you don't summon the storm to your tribunal, do you? Well, this lesson you'll find very useful later, Dee, when you have been appointed to a high post in the capital, as doubtless you will be. Then you'll remember this conversation, and you'll be grateful to me!" He rose and clapped the judge on his shoulder. "We'll go down to the hall now," he added briskly. "The monks'll be starting the preparations for breakfast by and by. This mess here I'll clean up later. First of all we need a good meal. Both of us had rather a strenuous night, I dare say!"

Judge Dee also got up.

"Yes," he said wearily, "let's go down." Noticing that Sun was going to take his wide cloak he said politely: "Allow me to carry that for you, sir. The weather has cleared."

"Thank you!" Sun said, handing him the cloak. "Yes, it's funny with these mountain storms; they'll start suddenly, rage for a time with incredible vehemence, then as suddenly subside. I don't complain, though, as they occur only at this time of the year. Generally the climate here suits me very well."

Judge Dee took up the lantern. They passed through the cupboard. As Sun turned the disk to close the secret door he said over his shoulder: "I don't think I need to change this lock, Dee! There aren't many persons like you who are observant enough to notice that the design of the Two Forces is in an unusual position!"

Silently they walked through the corridor, then descended a steep flight of steps that brought them to the portal of the temple. Sun looked outside and said with satisfaction: "Yes, it is indeed dry now and the wind has gone down. We can walk to the refectory across the courtyard."

When they were descending the steps leading down into the paved court, grey in the morning twilight, Judge Dee said: "What did you use that other secret room for, sir? Up there, above the store-room? I saw a small round window there, barely visible. Or shouldn't I ask that?

Sun halted in his steps.

"You don't say!" he exclaimed astonished. "I never knew about that one! Those ancient architects were up to all kinds of tricks! You are a useful fellow to have around, Dee! Show me where you saw that window!"

Judge Dee took him over to the high gate that closed the space between the east wing and the building of the store-room. He put the lantern and the cloak on the ground, lifted the heavy crossbeam from the iron hooks, and pulled the door open. When Sun had gone inside, Judge Dee stepped back and closed the door. As he replaced the crossbar, he heard Sun knocking on the panel of the peephole. Judge Dee took up the lantern and opened it. The light shone on Sun's astonished face.

"What do you mean by that, Dee?" he asked perplexed.

"It means that you shall be judged inside there, Sun Ming. Unfortunately you were right when you explained to me that I could never initiate a case against you in my tribunal. I therefore now leave the decision to a Higher Tribunal. Heaven shall decide whether five foul murders shall be avenged, or whether I shall perish. You have two chances, Sun, whereas your victims had none. It is quite possible that your presence there shall be ignored. Or, if you are attacked, you may be able to draw the attention of the one man that can save you."

Sun's face grew purple with rage.

"One man you say, you conceited fool? In an hour or so there'll be scores of monks about in the yard, they'll set me free at once!"

"They'll certainly do so—if you are then still alive," the judge said gravely. "There is something with you in there."

Sun looked round. Indistinct sounds came from the darkness.

He grabbed the bars of the peephole. Pressing his distorted face close to them he shouted frantically: "What is that, Dee?"

"You'll find out," the judge said. He shut the panel.

As he entered the temple building again, a scream of terror rent the air.

XX

Judge Dee slowly climbed the stairs to the landing over the temple. There was still no sign of Tao Gan. He went into the corridor leading to the store-room, and opened the second window on his right. Deep down below he heard weak moans, mixed with angry growling. Then there were dry, snapping sounds as of dead branches breaking. He raised his eyes to the windows in the guest-building opposite. All of them remained as they were, the shutters securely closed. He heaved a deep sigh. The case had been decided.

He laid Sun's cloak on the low window sill, then quickly turned away. After breakfast he would draw up the document about Sun's accidental death, which occurred when he leaned too far out of the low window while watching the bear down below.

With a sigh he retraced his steps to the landing. He heard quick foot-steps, then saw Tao Gan who came rushing round the corner. His lieuten-ant said with a contented smile: "I was just going to look for you, sir! You needn't search for Mo Mo-te. I have got him!"

He took the judge to the next corridor. A powerfully-built man clad in a monk's cowl was lying unconscious on the floor, with hands and feet securely tied. Judge Dee stooped and held his lantern close. He recognized the morose face. This was the tall, sullen man he had met in the store-room, together with the elder monk whom he had asked whether Mo had been there.

"Where did you find him?" he asked.

"Soon after Your Honour had gone up to Master Sun's library, I saw him sneaking up here. I followed him, but he is a wily customer. It took me quite some time before I could come up behind him close enough to throw my thin noose of waxed thread over his head. I pulled it tight till he passed out, then trussed him up neatly."

"You'd better untruss him again!" Judge Dee said wryly. "He's not our man. I was wrong about him all along. His real name is Liu, he and his sister were members of a gang of vagabonds. But he also works on his own, sometimes as a Taoist mendicant monk, sometimes as an actor. He is probably a rough-and-ready rascal, but he came here for a laudable purpose, namely to avenge the murder of his sister. When you have freed him, come and sit down with me on the landing. I am tired."

He turned round and walked back to the landing, leaving Tao Gan standing there dumbfounded. Judge Dee sat down on the wooden bench and let his head lean back against the wall.

When Tao Gan came, the Judge pointed to the place by his side. Sitting there together in the semi-darkness, he told Tao Gan about his discovery of the secret room and his conversation with Sun Ming. He said in conclusion: "I don't blame myself for not realizing earlier that I had mistaken Sun's round head with smooth silvery hair for that of a soldier wearing a close-fitting iron helmet. There was no reason for connecting a man of Sun's eminence and supposed integrity with such sordid crimes. But I ought to have begun suspecting him as soon as True Wisdom admitted his guilt, and thereby confirmed that there had indeed been irregularities with women in this monastery."

Tao Gan looked puzzled. After a while he asked: "Why should that have aroused suspicions regarding Master Sun, sir?"

"I ought then to have realized, Tao Gan, that a man of Sun's intelligence and experience could not have failed to notice that queer things were going on here. I should have suspected him all the more since, when I talked with him just after True Wisdom's death, Sun stressed that he always stayed in his library and used to keep himself aloof from all that went on in the monastery. I should have remembered then that True Wisdom had assured me during our first interview that Sun, on the contrary, had always shown a lively interest in all the affairs of the monastery. And that should have suggested to me at once that Sun was implicated in the murders, and that the abbot wanted to denounce him as an accomplice. And that, therefore, Sun pushed him from the landing. When directly thereafter we were drinking tea with Tsung Lee in the temple hall, I had a vague feeling that there was something wrong somewhere, but I failed to discover the truth. I needed a broken saucer to see all the facts in their proper connection!"

The judge heaved a deep sigh, and slowly shook his head. Then he yawned and continued: "Taoism penetrates deep into the mysteries of life and death, but its abstruse knowledge may inspire that evil, inhuman pride that turns a man into a cruel fiend. And its profound philosophy about balancing the male and female elements may degenerate to those unspeakable rites with women. The question is, Tao Gan, whether we are meant to discover the mystery of life, and whether that discovery would make us happier. Taoism has many elevated thoughts; it teaches us to requite good with good, and bad also with good. But the instruction to requite bad with good belongs to a better age than we are living in now, Tao Gan! It's a dream of the future, a beautiful dream—yet only a dream. I prefer to keep to the practical wisdom of our Master Confucius, who teaches us our simple, everyday duties to our fellow-men and to our society. And to requite good with good, and bad with justice!" After a while he resumed: "Of course it would be foolish to ignore entirely the existence of mysterious, supernatural phenomena. Yet most occurrences which we consider as such prove in the end to have a perfectly natural explanation. When I was in the passage where you have now deposited Mo, I heard my name whispered. I remembered the weird story about the ghosts of the slaughtered people, and thought that it was a warning that I was about to die. However, when thereafter I entered the store-room, I found there Mo Mo-te and another monk, a confederate of his, who apparently had helped him to change from his warrior's costume into an old monk's cowl they had taken from a box there. I now realize that those two must have been talking about me, and a queer effect of the echo made me overhear them in the next corridor."

"That's right!" a hoarse voice spoke up. "My friend said I should report my sister's murder to you. But I know better. You smug officials won't lift a finger for us, the common people!"

The hulking shape of Mo Mo-te stood before them.

Judge Dee looked up at the threatening figure.

"You ought to have followed your friend's advice," he said evenly. "You would have saved yourself much trouble. And me too."

Mo scowled at him, fingering the red weal round his throat. Then he stepped up close to the judge. Bending over him he growled: "Who killed my sister?"

"I found the murderer," Judge Dee replied curtly. "He confessed, and I sentenced him to death. Your sister has been avenged. That's all you need to know."

Quick as lightning Mo pulled a long knife from his bosom. Keeping it poised expertly at Judge Dee's throat, he hissed: "Tell me or you are done for! It's me who shall kill her murderer! I am her brother. And what are you, eh?"

Judge Dee folded his arms in his sleeves. Looking up at Mo with his burning eyes he said slowly: "I represent the law, Mo. It's I who take vengeance." Lowering his gaze he added in a voice that was suddenly utterly tired: "And it is I who shall answer for it."

He closed his eyes and leaned his head against the wall again.

Mo glared at Judge Dee's pale, impassive face. His large hand tightened on the hilt of the knife until the knuckles stood out white. Sweat began to pearl on his low forehead; his breathing came heavily. Tao Gan looked tensely at the hand with the knife.

Then Mo averted his blazing eyes. He gave Tao Gan a sombre glance, put the knife back in his bosom and said suddenly: "Then I have nothing to seek here any more."

He turned around and walked unsteadily to the stairs.

After a while Judge Dee opened his eyes. He said in a toneless voice: "Forget all I told you about Sun Ming and his crimes, Tao Gan. We shall keep to the story that it was the abbot and Mrs. Pao who maltreated and killed those three girls and tortured Miss Kang. Sun died by an unfortunate accident. He is survived by three sons and we must not wantonly destroy other people's lives. Too many already do their utmost to destroy their own, all by themselves!"

For a long time the judge and his lieutenant sat there together, silently listening to the chant that came up to them from the temple hall below, punctuated by beats on a wooden gong. The monks at the abbot's bier were still reciting the prayers for the dead. Judge Dee could make out the words of the refrain, repeated with monotonous insistence:

> To die is to return home
> Returning home to one's father's house,
> The drop that regains the stream,
> The large stream that flows on for ever.

At last Judge Dee rose. He said: "Go now to the store-room and fix the secret lock so that it can't work. The secret room contains the old statue of the naked woman, and I shall forbid having naked woman exposed in the Gallery of Horrors, anyway. That secret room shall never again tempt anyone to commit deeds of evil! We'll meet after breakfast!"

He went with Tao Gan as far as the first window in the corridor, where he had deposited Sun's cloak as evidence of the accident. While Tao Gan went on, he opened the shutters wide.

All was quiet deep down below. Suddenly a dark shape swooped down into the space between the two buildings, followed by another. The mountain vultures had discovered prey.

Judge Dee went back to the landing and descended the stairs leading down to the temple hall. When he stepped out on the open platform in front of the temple gate, he looked up. The red rays of dawn were streaking the grey sky.

He went down the broad steps, then headed for the main entrance of the east wing. While passing the high gate that closed off the well between the east wing and the building he had just left, he suddenly stood still. He

JUDGE DEE AND HIS THREE WIVES

stared at a hand that held on to the top of the gate with blood-stained, broken fingers. For one brief moment he thought that Sun was hanging there on the other side, in a last frantic attempt to escape. But then a vulture came down, picked up the hand and flew away towards the mountains.

Slowly the judge climbed the stairs leading up to the third floor. Every step hurt him and his back was aching. He had to rest a while on each landing. When at last he knocked on the door of his own quarters, he was swaying on his feet.

In the dressing room the maids were busy fanning the coals in the brazier, heating the morning rice.

When he entered the bedroom, he found that his three wives had just risen. The window curtains were still drawn, and in the dim light of the candles the room was cosy and warm. The First Lady sat with bare torso by the dressing table and the two others, still in their bed-robes, were helping her to do her hair.

Judge Dee sat down heavily at the small tea table. He took off his cap, removed the bandage and felt the bruised spot. As he carefully replaced his cap, his third wife gave him a searching look and asked anxiously: "I hope that my bandage helped?"

"It most certainly did!" the judge replied with feeling.

"I knew it would!" she said happily. Handing him a cup of steaming tea she added: "I'll draw the curtains and open the shutters. I hope the storm has blown over."

Slowly sipping his tea, the judge followed his First Lady's graceful movements as she combed her long tresses, looking intently into the round mirror of polished silver that his second wife held up for her. He passed his hand over his eyes. In these peaceful surroundings the horrors of the past night suddenly seemed nothing but a weird nightmare.

His First Lady gave her hair a final pat. She thanked the other who had been assisting her. Pulling her bed-robe up round her bare shoulders she came over to the tea table and wished the judge a good morning. Noticing his haggard face she exclaimed: "You look all done in! What on earth have you been at all night? I saw you come in once to take things from our medicine chest. Has there been an accident?"

"A person fell ill," Judge Dee replied vaguely, "and we needed some drugs. Then there were a few odds and ends that had to be attended to. Now everything has been straightened out."

"You shouldn't have been gadding about all night, and that with your cold!" she said reprovingly. "Well, I'll quickly make you a nice bowl of hot gruel, that'll do you good!" Passing by the open window she looked out and added briskly: "We'll have a pleasant trip back to Han-yuan. It's going to be a beautiful day!"

COLOPHON

JUDGE DEE was a historical person who lived from 630 to 700 A.D. In the earlier part of his career when he served as magistrate in various country districts, he earned fame as a detector of crimes, and later, after he had been appointed at Court, he proved to be a brilliant statesman who greatly influenced the internal and foreign policies of the T'ang Empire. The adventures related here, however, are entirely fictitious, although many features were suggested by original old Chinese sources. The clue of the cat's eyes, for instance, I borrowed from an anecdote told about the Sung scholar and artist Ou-yang Hsiu (1007-1072 A.D.); he possessed an old painting of a cat among peonies, and pointed out that it must have been painted at noon, because the flowers were wilting, and the cat's pupils mere slits.

The Chinese professed three creeds, Confucianism, Taoism and Buddhism, the last having been introduced from India in the first century A.D. Since old Chinese detective and crime stories were written in the main by Confucianist scholars, that literature evinces a pronounced partiality to Confucianism, a feature which I adopted in my Judge Dee novels. The characterization of Confucianist and Taoist ideals given in the present novel is based on authentic Chinese texts.

The plates I drew in the style of 16th century Chinese illustrated block-prints, especially the fine Ming edition of the *Lieh-nü-chuan* (Biographies of Illustrious Women). Those plates represent, therefore, costumes and customs of the Ming period, rather than those of the T'ang dynasty. Note that in Judge Dee's time the Chinese did not wear pigtails; that custom was imposed on them after 1644 A.D. when the Manchus had conquered China. The men did their long hair up in a top-knot, and wore caps both inside and outside the house. Tobacco and opium were introduced into China many centuries later.

7 - vii - 1961   *Robert Van Gulik*

THE CHINESE MAZE MURDERS

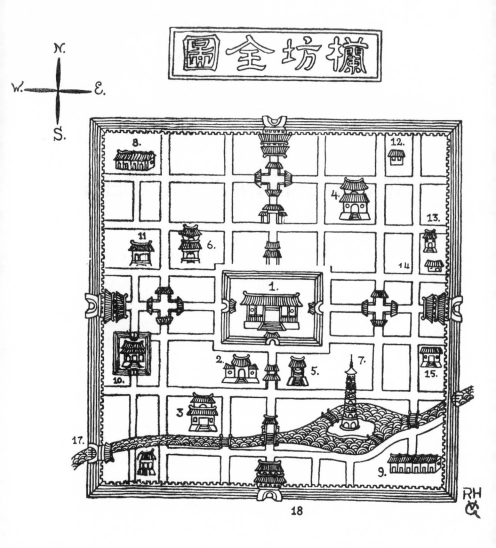

SKETCH MAP OF LAN-FANG

1. *Tribunal*
2. *Temple of the City God*
3. *Temple of Confucius*
4. *Temple of the War God*
5. *Bell Tower*
6. *Drum Tower*
7. *Pagoda*
8. *Northern Row*
9. *Southern Row*
10. *Chien Mow's Mansion*
11. *General Ding's Mansion*
12. *Eternal Spring Wineshop*
13. *Hermitage of the Three Treasures*
14. *Mrs. Lee's House*
15. *Former Yoo Mansion*
16. *Yoo Kee's Mansion*
17. *Watergate*
18. *Execution Ground*

FOREWORD

After the appearance of my translation of the old Chinese detective novel *Dee Goong An,** I was asked to search for other Chinese novels of that kind. However, such books are now rather scarce and moreover it proved difficult to find one that appeals equally to modern Chinese and Western taste. As a matter of fact, *Dee Goong An* is an exception. As a rule style and contents of ancient Chinese crime and mystery stories differ so much from modern ones that they are of slight interest to the present-day Oriental reader, and even less to the Westerner.

On the other hand old Chinese crime stories contain many clever plots and much material relating to the detection of crime. I thought, therefore, that it would be an interesting experiment to write a Chinese-style detective story myself, utilizing plots found in Chinese stories from bygone times.

I engaged upon this experiment mainly in order to prove to present-day Chinese and Japanese authors that it is possible to write a detective novel in traditional Chinese style that yet appeals to the modern Oriental reader. I thought this all the more worthwhile since at present the book-market in China and Japan is flooded with bad translations of third-rate foreign thrillers, while their own ancient crime novels are practically forgotten. When I had completed my English manuscript of *The Chinese Maze Murders* it was translated into Japanese by Professor Ogaeri Yukio, and published in 1951 by the Kodan-sha in Tokyo, under the title *Meiro-no-satsujin*, with a preface by the well-known Japanese mystery writer Edogawa Rampo. Then I myself prepared a Chinese version, which was published in 1953 by the Nanyang Press in Singapore under the title *Ti-jen-chieh-chi-an.* Both editions were favourably received in the Chinese and Japanese press. Encouraged by this success I wrote two more "Judge

*Dee Goong An, Three Murder Cases Solved by Judge Dee. An old Chinese detective novel translated from the original Chinese with an introduction and notes, by R. H. van Gulik, Litt.D.; one illustrated vol. publ. Tokyo, 1949. (Reprinted by Dover Publications, Inc., in 1976 under the title *Celebrated Cases of Judge Dee.*)

Dee" novels, *The Chinese Bell Murders* and *The Chinese Lake Murders*, of which Chinese and Japanese versions are now in preparation.

Having thus attained my main object, it occurred to me that Western readers also might perhaps be interested in this new type of crime novel. Therefore I decided to publish my English text of *The Chinese Maze Murders*, an additional motive being that the Chinese element has been introduced so often by Western writers of detective stories that I thought that the reader might be interested in seeing how it looks in genuine Chinese garb.

For information on the background of the present novel and the Chinese sources utilized, the reader is referred to my Postscript at the end of the book. Here it may suffice to say that I borrowed three plots from ancient Chinese sources, rewriting them as one continuous story centering round the famous ancient Chinese master-detective Judge Dee. I retained the typical feature of old Chinese detective novels, such as the prologue which gives some idea of the main events of the story itself, the chapter heading in two parallel lines, the peculiar Chinese device of letting the detective solve a number of cases simultaneously, etc., and in general tried to preserve as much as possible Chinese style and atmosphere.

The scene of my story is laid in Lan-fang, an imaginary border town of China during the 7th century A.D. The reader will find a Chinese map of that city on page 110 of the present edition. The plates were drawn by me in the style of book-illustrations of the Ming Dynasty.

All the credit of what may be found satisfactory in this novel must go to the ancient Chinese writers who evolved the plots. All its shortcomings must be blamed on the present author.

The Hague, Spring 1956

Robert Van Gulik

DRAMATIS PERSONAE

It should be noted that in Chinese the surname,
here printed in capitals, precedes the personal name.

Main Characters:

DEE Jen-djieh, newly appointed magistrate of Lan-fang, a town district on the Northwest border of the Chinese Empire. Referred to as Judge Dee, or the judge.

HOONG Liang, Judge Dee's confidential adviser and sergeant over the constables of the tribunal. Referred to as Sergeant Hoong, or the sergeant.

MA Joong
TAO Gan } the three trusted lieutenants of Judge Dee
CHIAO Tai

Persons connected with "The Case of the Murder in the Sealed Room":

DING Hoo-gwo, a retired general living in Lan-fang. Found murdered in his own library.

DING Yee, a Junior Candidate of Literature, his only son. Referred to as Candidate Ding, or Young Ding.

WOO Feng, son of Commander Woo of the Board of Military Affairs in the capital. A Junior Candidate of Literature and amateur painter.

Persons connected with "The Case of the Hidden Testament":

YOO Shou-chien, an ex-Governor who died while living retired in Lan-Fang.

Mrs. YOO, *née* Mei, the Governor's young second wife.

Mrs. LEE, a painter, friend of Mrs. Yoo.

YOO Kee, the Governor's eldest son by his first wife.

YOO Shan, infant son of Mrs. Yoo.

Persons connected with "The Case of the Girl with the Severed Head":

FANG, a blacksmith. Later appointed headman of the constables of the tribunal, and hence referred to as Headman Fang or the headman.

White Orchid, his eldest daughter.

Dark Orchid, his second daughter.

His son.

Others:

CHIEN Mow, the local tyrant who usurped power in Lan-fang.

LIU Wan-fang, his eldest counsellor.

Corporal LING, a deserter from the regular army, reinstated by Judge Dee.

Orolakchee, an Uigur chieftain. His real name is Prince Ooljin. His false name, Orolakchee, means *agent* or *representative.*

The Hunter, accomplice of Orolakchee.

Tulbee, an Uigur girl.

Occurs in Chapter XIX only:

Master Crane Robe, an old recluse.

First Chapter

A STRANGE MEETING TAKES PLACE ON A LOTUS LAKE;
JUDGE DEE IS ATTACKED ON HIS WAY TO LAN-FANG

Heaven created an immutable pattern for ten thousand ages,
Regulating sun and stars above, mountains and rivers below;
Thereafter the sages of old did model our sacred social order,
Taking Heavenly Justice as warp, and man-made Law as woof.

A wise and honest judge is Heaven's unerring instrument,
The people's father and mother, both compassionate and stern;
In his court the oppressed obtain redress of all their wrongs,
No criminal there escapes, despite base fraud and guile.

Under the present illustrious Ming dynasty, in the Yoong-lo era, our Empire is at peace, crops are plentiful, there are neither droughts nor floods, and the people are prosperous and content. This fortunate state of affairs is due entirely to the August Virtue of His Imperial Majesty. Naturally, in this blessed time of peace crimes are few, so that the present provides scant material for the study of crime and detection. Rather than the present one must turn to the past for accounts of baffling crimes, and their marvellous solution by perspicacious magistrates.

Finding myself with ample leisure for the pursuit of my favourite study, I diligently search old records and dusty archives for famous ancient criminal cases, and I have made it a habit always to listen carefully to my friends and acquaintances when, gathered in the tea house, they start discoursing on the astounding crimes solved by famous judges of past centuries.

The other day, late in the afternoon, I strolled through the Western Park to admire the lotus flowers that were in full bloom. I crossed the carved marble bridge that leads to the island in the center of the lotus pond, and found myself an empty corner table on the open terrace of the restaurant there.

Sipping my tea and nibbling dried melon seeds I enjoyed the beautiful

view over the lake all covered with lotus flowers. I observed the motley
crowd and, as I often do, amused myself by trying to deduce from the
appearance of some passers-by their personality and background.

My eye fell on two remarkably beautiful girls who passed by walking
hand in hand. Their strong resemblance suggested at once that they were
sisters. But evidently their characters were entirely different. The younger
one was gay and vivacious, who talked all the time. The elder, on the
contrary, was reserved and shy, who hardly answered the other. Her face
bore an expression of deep sadness. I felt sure that somewhere there was a
deep tragedy in her life.

As the two girls disappeared among the crowd, I noticed that they were
followed by an elderly woman; she had a slight limp, walked with a cane
and seemed intent on overtaking the girls. I took her to be their duenna.
But as she passed in front of the terrace I saw such an evil leer on her face
that I hastily transferred my attention to a handsome young couple that
came walking along.

The young man wore the cap of a Candidate of Literature, the girl was
dressed demurely as a housewife. They walked apart but from the fond
looks they gave each other it was clear that they belonged together. I
concluded from their furtive air that theirs must be an illicit love affair.
Just when they were passing in front of me the girl made to take the
young man's hand, but he hastily withdrew his and shook his head with a
frown.

Letting my eyes rove over the guests assembled on the terrace I noticed
a plump, neatly clad man who was sitting alone just like myself. He had a
round, pleasant face; I placed him as a member of the landed gentry. Since
he seemed the talkative type I hastily averted my eyes fearing that he
would mistake my intent gaze as an invitation to strike up an acquain-
tance. I preferred to be left alone with my own thoughts, all the more so
since I had seen a glint in his eyes that made me wary. I reflected that a
man with a cold, calculating look that so belied his friendly face might
well be capable of committing a dark, premeditated deed of evil.

After a while I saw an old gentleman with a flowing white beard slowly
come up the steps of the terrace. He was clad in a brown robe with wide
sleeves seamed with black velvet, and a high cap of black gauze on his
head. Although he wore no insignia of rank, he had a most distinguished
appearance. He stood for a moment leaning on his crooked staff, surveying
the crowded terrace with piercing eyes from under bushy white eyebrows.

Since a person of such venerable age cannot be left standing, I hastily
rose and offered the newcomer a place at my table. He accepted with a
courteous bow. While drinking our tea we exchanged the usual polite
inquiries and it transpired that his family name was Dee and that he was a
retired prefect.

Soon we were engaged in an agreeable conversation. My guest proved to be a man of wide learning and elegant taste; time passed unnoticed while we discoursed on prose and poetry, in between looking at the gay crowd that milled along the waterfront.

I had noticed that my guest spoke with the accent of Shansi Province. So during a lull in the conversation I asked whether by any chance his family was related to the old Dee clan of Tai-yuan, the capital of that province, which centuries ago, during the Tang dynasty, had produced the great statesman Dee Jen-djieh.

Suddenly the old gentleman's eyes blazed. He angrily tugged at his long beard.

"Ha!" he exclaimed, "my family is indeed a branch of the Dee clan from which issued the great Judge Dee, and I am very proud to count him among my ancestors. Yet at the same time this fact is a source of continuous vexation. Whenever I am eating my bowl of rice in a restaurant or sipping the fragrant brew in a tea house, as often as not I will hear the other guests tell each other stories about my illustrious ancestor. It is true that what they say about Dee Jen-djieh's brilliant career at the Imperial Court is usually substantially correct; moreover such facts can be verified by referring to the official annals of the Tang dynasty. Mostly, however, those ignorant persons will bandy about bizarre tales about the earlier part of Dee Jen-djieh's career when he was serving as district magistrate in the provinces, and as 'Judge Dee' became famous for having solved many a mysterious criminal case. In our family the truthful account of most of those cases has been faithfully transmitted over untold generations. It greatly annoys me to have to listen to all those spurious stories told in the tea house, and I usually leave without finishing my meal."

The old gentleman shook his head and angrily stamped his staff on the stone flags.

I was delighted to learn that my guest was indeed a descendant of the famous Judge Dee. I rose and bowed deeply in front of him to show my deference for his distinguished family. Then I spoke thus: "Venerable Sir, know that I am a keen student of true accounts describing the feats of detection performed by the eminent judges of our glorious national past. Far from being an idle gossip, however, I delight in a careful analysis of those ancient records. For do they not serve as a mirror for us who live in this late age, warning us by showing our own foibles and defects? Those accounts not only improve the morals and ameliorate the customs, they also act as a powerful deterrent for all wicked people. Nowhere can be found more eloquent proof of how closely the net of Heavenly justice is woven, and of how, in the long run, no evil-doer ever succeeds in slipping through its mazes.

"Now, in my opinion antiquity has no detective that can compare with Judge Dee. For many years I have been sedulously collecting notes about the cases solved by his brilliant mind. Now that a propitious fate has granted me this meeting with you, Sir, who are a fount of information on this subject, I wonder whether it would be presuming on your kindness if I humbly requested you to give me the benefit of hearing a few lesser-known cases from your own lips."

The old gentleman readily agreed, and I invited him to join me in a simple supper.

Twilight was falling and the guests had left the terrace for the restaurant inside where the servants had lighted candles and coloured paper lanterns.

I avoided the main hall with the chattering dining crowd and led my guest to a small side room overlooking the lake, now bathed in the red glow of sunset.

I ordered two dinners of four courses and a pot of warm wine.

When we had tasted the dishes and drunk a few rounds, the old gentleman stroked his long whiskers and said: "I shall relate to you three astonishing criminal cases which my revered ancestor Judge Dee solved under most unusual circumstances. At that time he was serving as magistrate of Lan-fang, a far-away district on the northwestern border of our Empire."

He then set out on a long and complicated narrative.

Although what he told was not without interest, he proved much given to lengthy digressions and his voice was as indistinct and monotonous as the humming of a bumblebee. After a while I found my attention flagging. I emptied three cups in succession to clear my mind, but the amber liquid only made me still more drowsy. While the voice of my guest droned on and on, I seemed to hear the spirit of sleep rustle in the close air.

When I woke up, I found myself alone in the chilly room, bent over the table with my head resting on my folded arms.

A surly waiter was standing over me and told me that the first night-watch had been sounded; did I perchance mistake this restaurant for a hostel where people stay overnight at will?

My head was heavy and I did not immediately find the right phrase to put the boorish yokel in his place. Instead I inquired after my guest, describing his appearance in some detail.

The waiter answered that earlier in the evening he had been serving another section of the restaurant, and anyway did I think that he had time to look every single guest up and down? Presently he produced a bill for two six-course dinners and eight pots of wine. I could do nothing but pay, although by then I greatly doubted whether my encounter with the old gentleman had not been a dream, and whether that rascal of a waiter was not taking advantage of my confusion to overcharge me grossly.

I left feeling I had been ill-used and walked home through the deserted streets. My page was fast asleep, huddled in a corner of my library. I did not wake him but tiptoed to the bookshelves. I took down the annals of the Tang dynasty, the Imperial Gazetteer and my own notes on Judge Dee. Poring over these volumes I found that although the general features of the old gentleman's story accorded well enough with historical fact, there existed no such place as Lan-fang on the northwestern border. I thought that possibly I had misheard the name and resolved to visit the old gentleman next day to ask him for further elucidation. Then I found to my dismay that although I clearly remembered every word of the story he told me, try as I might I could not recollect one single personal detail concerning him; I had forgotten both his full name and his present place of residence.

I shook my head, moistened my brush, and that very night committed to writing the entire story he told me, laying down my brush only when the cock started crowing.

The next day I made exhaustive enquiries among my friends, but no one had ever heard about a retired prefect by the name of Dee living in our town; neither did subsequent investigations as to his whereabouts bring to light more information. Still, this fact did not dissolve my doubts. The old gentleman might well have been only passing through, or he might be living somewhere in the countryside.

Thus I now make bold to offer this story as it is, leaving it to the better judgment of the discerning reader to decide whether my encounter on the lotus lake was dream or reality. If this tale of three mysterious crimes should distract the reader for a few moments from the cares and anxieties of daily life, I shall not grudge the coppers extorted from me. For no matter what actually happened, that waiter evidently was a mean rascal; it is quite inconceivable that one, or even two gentlemen of refined taste ever should consume eight pots of wine at one single sitting.

Four horse carts were slowly wending their way through the mountains east of the city of Lan-fang.

In the first cart Judge Dee, the new magistrate of Lan-fang, had made himself as comfortable as was possible on such an arduous journey. He was sitting on a bed roll, and leaned his back against a large package with books. His faithful assistant, old Sergeant Hoong, was sitting opposite him on a bale of cloth. The road was rough and these precautions provided scant protection from the continual bumps.

The judge and the sergeant both felt tired, for they had been on the road for several days on end.

After them followed a large tilt cart with silk curtains. Here Judge Dee's three wives, his children and the maids were trying to snatch some sleep, curled up among pillows and padded quilts.

The two other carts were loaded with luggage. Some of the servants were perched precariously on top of the bales and boxes; others preferred to walk by the side of the horses, which were covered with sweat.

Before dawn they had left the last village. Thereafter the road had led through a desolate mountain region. The only people they had met were a few wood gatherers. In the afternoon their progress had been retarded for two hours by a broken wheel and now dusk was falling, making the mountains seem even more forbidding.

Two tall fellows rode at the head of the procession. Broad swords hung down their backs, each had a bow fastened to the pommel of his saddle, and arrows rattled in their quivers. These two were Ma Joong and Chiao Tai, two of Judge Dee's loyal lieutenants. They acted as the armed escort of the group. Another of Judge Dee's lieutenants, a lean man with a slight stoop, called Tao Gan, brought up the rear together with the old house steward.

When he reached the top of the mountain ridge, Ma Joong reined in his horse. The road ahead descended into a wooded valley. Another steep mountain rose up on the opposite side.

Ma Joong turned round in his saddle, and called out to the coachman: "An hour ago you said that we were approaching Lan-fang, you dogshead! And here is another mountain to cross!"

The coachman grumbled something about fellows from the city always being in a hurry, then said sullenly: "Don't worry, from the next ridge you will see Lan-fang lying at the foot of the slope."

"I have heard that bastard speak about a 'next ridge' before," Ma Joong observed to Chiao Tai. "How awkward that we arrive in Lan-fang at so late an hour! The departing magistrate must have been waiting for us since noon. And what about the other dignitaries of the district administration and their welcome banquet? By now their bellies must be as empty as mine!"

"Not to speak of a dry throat!" Chiao Tai added. He turned his horse around and rode up to the judge's cart.

"There still is one valley to be crossed, Your Honour," he reported, "but then we shall at last reach Lan-fang."

Sergeant Hoong suppressed a sigh. "It is a great pity," he remarked, "that Your Honour was ordered to leave Poo-yang so soon. Although two major criminal cases came up directly after our arrival there, all in all it was a pleasant district."

Judge Dee smiled wryly and tried to settle his back more comfortably against the book package.

"It would seem," he said, "that in the capital the remnants of the Buddhist clique joined forces with friends of the Cantonese merchants, and effected my transfer long before my term of office in Poo-yang had expired. Yet it will be most instructive to serve as magistrate in such an outlying district as Lan-fang. Doubtless we shall find there interesting special problems that one will never meet with in the larger cities of the interior."

The sergeant agreed that that was so, but he remained gloomy. He was over sixty years old, and the discomforts of the long journey had worn him out. Since his early childhood he had been a retainer of Judge Dee's family. When Judge Dee had entered official life, he had made him his confidential adviser, and at every post where the judge had served he had appointed him sergeant over the constables of the tribunal.

The coachmen cracked their whips. The cortège passed over the top of the ridge and descended into the valley along a narrow winding road.

Soon they found themselves down in the valley, where the road was darkened by high cedar trees that rose from the thick undergrowth on both sides.

Judge Dee was just thinking of ordering his servants to light the torches, when he heard confused shouting ahead and behind.

A number of men, their faces covered with scarves of black cloth, had suddenly emerged from the wood.

Two men took hold of Ma Joong's right leg and dragged him from his horse before he had time to draw his sword. A third jumped from behind on Chiao Tai's horse, and pulled him down to the ground by a stranglehold on his neck. At the end of the cortège two other robbers were attacking Tao Gan and the steward.

The coachman jumped down and disappeared in the wood. Judge Dee's servants ran away as fast as they could.

Two masked faces appeared before the window of Judge Dee's cart. Sergeant Hoong was knocked unconscious by a blow on his head. The judge just barely dodged a spear that was thrust inside. He quickly gripped the shaft with both hands. The other pulled from outside to wrench it loose. The judge first held on tight, then suddenly pushed it in the direction of the pulling man. His assailant tumbled backwards. Judge Dee pulled the spear from his hands and jumped out of the window. He kept his two attackers at a distance by whirling the spear round and round. The robber who had hit Sergeant Hoong was armed with a club. The man with the spear had now drawn a long sword. Both attacked the judge fiercely, and he reflected that he would not be able to hold out long against these two determined opponents.

The two ruffians who had dragged Ma Joong from his horse were ready

to cut him down with their swords while he was scrambling up. Unfortunately for them, however, they were up against a formidable fighter, who only a few years back had himself been a famous highwayman. Until Judge Dee had caused their reform, both Ma Joong and Chiao Tai had been "brothers of the green woods." Thus there were very few things about street fighting that Ma Joong did not know. Instead of trying to get up he twisted his body around, gripped the ankle of one attacker and jerked him off his balance. At the same time Ma Joong placed a vicious kick on the other man's knee. This double move gave him time to jump up. He felled the stumbling man with a terrible fist blow on his head. Turning round like lightning he gave the man who was clasping his crushed knee a kick in the face that made his head snap back and nearly broke his neck.

Drawing his sword Ma Joong rushed over to Chiao Tai who lay on the ground wrestling desperately with a man clinging to his back. Two others stood ready with long knives to stab Chiao Tai as soon as they got the chance. Ma Joong ran his sword right through the chest of one robber. Without taking the time to withdraw his sword he went on to the second and gave him a kick in his groin that doubled him up on the ground. Picking up the robber's long knife Ma Joong thrust it under the left shoulder of the man fighting with Chiao Tai.

Just when he was helping Chiao Tai up, Ma Joong heard Judge Dee call out: "Look out!"

Ma Joong swiftly turned round, and thus the club of Judge Dee's assailant who had run up to help his comrades, missed Ma Joong's head. It landed with a thud on his left shoulder. He sank down with a curse. The robber lifted his club to brain Chiao Tai. The latter had drawn his knife. He dived under the robber's raised arm and plunged his knife to the hilt in the other's heart.

Judge Dee, now faced with only the swordsman, made quick work of him. He made a feint with his spear at his attacker who raised his sword to parry the blow. Then Judge Dee suddenly practised the fencer's trick known as "the tumbling flag pole;" he turned the spear round in the air and knocked his opponent unconscious with the shaft.

Leaving it to Chiao Tai to truss up the robbers, Judge Dee ran on to the luggage carts. One robber was sprawling on the ground, clutching frantically at his neck. The other, with a knobstick in his hand, was looking under the cart. The judge laid him out by hitting him over the head with the flat of his spear point.

Tao Gan came crawling out from under the cart, with a thin rope in his hand.

"What is happening here?" the judge inquired.

Tao Gan answered with a grin: "One of these yokels knocked down the

JUDGE DEE ATTACKED BY TWO ROBBERS

steward. The other hit me a glancing blow on my head. I let myself fall down with a horrible gasp, and did not move. They thought that I was laid out and started to tear down the luggage. I rose and from behind slipped my thin noose over the head of the nearest ruffian. Then I dived under the cart, pulling the cord as tight as I could. The other robber could not follow me there without exposing himself, and his club was of no use. He was just debating with himself what to do, when Your Honour solved his dilemma for him."

Judge Dee smiled, then hurried back to where he heard Ma Joong cursing roundly. Tao Gan took a length of catgut from his sleeve and securely bound the hands and feet of the two robbers. Then he loosened the noose round the neck of the man who by now was nearly suffocated.

These two robbers had been deceived by Tao Gan's inoffensive appearance. Tao Gan was of middle age, not much of a fighter, but an extremely wily person, who for many years had earned his living as a professional swindler. Once, Judge Dee had extricated him from an ugly situation, and made him one of his lieutenants. Owing to his intimate knowledge of the ways and by-ways of the underworld he had proved very useful for tracking down criminals and collecting evidence. And, as the robber with the blue face had good reason to know, Tao Gan was full of unexpected tricks.

When he came to the head of the cortège, Judge Dee found Chiao Tai in a hand-to-hand fight with one of Ma Joong's first attackers who had recovered from the blow on his head. Ma Joong himself was crouching on the ground, his left arm lamed by the blow on his shoulder. With his right he was trying to fight off the attacks of a little robber, who danced round him with amazing agility, brandishing a short dagger.

The judge raised his spear. Just then Ma Joong succeeded in catching his opponent's wrist. He twisted his arm in an iron grip till the robber let the dagger drop. Then Ma Joong forced him down and put his knee on his stomach.

The robber let out a pitiful cry.

Ma Joong rose to his feet with difficulty, while his captive hammered his head and shoulders with punches from his free hand. These, however, did not seem to bother Ma Joong. He said panting to the judge: "Would you remove the mask, Your Honour?"

Judge Dee pulled down the scarf. Ma Joong exclaimed: "May Heaven preserve us! It's a wench!"

They looked into the blazing eyes of a young girl. Ma Joong let go her arm in sheer astonishment.

Judge Dee hastily pinned her arms behind her back and said sourly: "Well, on occasion one will find an abandoned woman among these robber bands. Tie her up like the others!"

Ma Joong called out to Chiao Tai who by now had subdued and trussed up his opponent. Ma Joong remained standing there scratching his head in perplexity while Chiao Tai bound the girl's hands behind her back. She did not say a word.

Judge Dee went to the tilt cart with the women. His First Lady was crouching in the window with a dagger in her hand. The others were cowering under the quilts in a dead fright.

The judge told them that the fight was over.

Judge Dee's servants and the coachmen had emerged from their hiding places. They hastily set to work to light torches.

In the flickering light Judge Dee surveyed the results of the battle.

On their own side there was little damage. Sergeant Hoong had regained consciousness, and had his head bandaged by Tao Gan. The old steward had suffered more from fright than from the robber's blow. Ma Joong was sitting on a tree trunk stripped to the waist. His left shoulder was purple and swollen, and Chiao Tai was massaging it with medicinal oil.

Ma Joong had killed two robbers, Chiao Tai one. The six others were all more or less the worse for wear. Only the girl was entirely unhurt.

The judge ordered his servants to tie the robbers on top of one luggage cart, and the dead bodies on the other. The girl would have to walk.

Tao Gan produced a padded basket, and the judge and his lieutenants drank a cup of hot tea.

Ma Joong rinsed his mouth, spat contemptuously and said to Chiao Tai: "All in all, it was an amateurish attack. I don't think that these fellows are professional highwaymen."

"Yes," Chiao Tai agreed; "with ten men they could have done a better job."

"They did well enough for my taste," Judge Dee remarked dryly.

They silently drank another cup of tea. All were exhausted and no one felt inclined to say much. One only heard the whispering voices of the servants, and the groans of the wounded robbers.

After a brief rest the cortège set into motion again. Two servants with lighted torches led the way.

It took them well over an hour to cross the last mountain ridge. Then the road came out on a broad highway, and soon they saw the battlements of the northern city gate of Lan-fang silhouetted against the evening sky.

Second Chapter

JUDGE DEE OPENS THE FIRST SESSION OF THE TRIBUNAL;
HE DISCOVERS IN THE ARCHIVES AN UNSOLVED PROBLEM

Chiao Tai looked amazed at the formidable gate surmounted by a high gate tower. Then he remembered that Lan-fang was a border town where one had to reckon with sudden attacks from the barbarian hordes of the western plains.

He knocked with the hilt of his sword on the iron-studded gate.

After considerable time the shutters of a small window in the gate tower opened. A gruff voice called out from above: "The gate is closed for the night. Come back tomorrow morning!"

Chiao Tai gave a thunderous knock on the gate. He shouted: "Open up! The magistrate has arrived!"

"What magistrate?" the voice asked.

"His Excellency Dee, the new magistrate of Lan-fang. Open the gate, you fathead!"

The shutters slammed shut.

Ma Joong rode up to Chiao Tai. He asked: "What is all this delay?"

"The lazy dogs were asleep!" Chiao Tai said disgustedly. As he spoke he again let his sword rattle on the door.

They heard the clanking of chains. At last the heavy doors opened a few feet.

Chiao Tai forced his horse through, and nearly trampled down two slovenly clad soldiers wearing rusty helmets.

"Throw the gates wide open, lazy dogs!" Chiao Tai barked.

The soldiers looked impudently at the two horsemen. One opened his mouth to say something, but seeing the fierce look on Chiao Tai's face he thought better of it. Together with his colleague he pushed open the gate.

The cortège passed through and moved south along the dark main street.

The town presented a desolate appearance. Although the first night-watch had not yet sounded, most of the shops were closed for the night with solid wooden shutters.

Here and there small groups of people clustered round the oil lamps of the street vendors. When the cortège passed by, they turned round and looked for a moment indifferently at the horse wagons, then turned again to their noodle bowls.

No one came to meet the new magistrate and there were no signs of welcome.

The cortège passed under a high ornamental archway that spanned the street. Here the main street divided to left and right, running along a high wall. Ma Joong and Chiao Tai took this to be the rear wall of the tribunal compound.

They turned east and followed the wall till they came to a large gate. Over its archway there hung a weather-beaten wooden board with an engraved inscription reading: "The Tribunal of Lan-fang."

Chiao Tai jumped from his horse and started to knock on the door with all his might.

A squat man clad in a patched robe opened the door. His ragged beard was dirty with grease and he had a horrible squint. Lifting up a paper lantern he surveyed Chiao Tai. Then he snarled: "Don't you know that the tribunal is closed, soldier?"

This was too much for Chiao Tai. He gripped the man by his beard and violently shook his head; it bumped against the doorpost with dull thuds. Chiao Tai only released him when the man started crying for mercy.

Chiao Tai said peremptorily: "His Excellency Magistrate Dee has arrived. Open the door and call the personnel of the tribunal!"

The man hurriedly pushed the double doors open. The cortège passed through and came to a halt in the main courtyard, in front of the large reception hall.

Judge Dee descended from his cart and looked around. The high, six-fold doors of the reception hall were barred and locked, the windows of the chancery opposite shuttered. Everything was dark and deserted.

Folding his hands in his sleeves Judge Dee ordered Chiao Tai to bring the gate keeper before him.

Chiao Tai dragged him along by his collar. The squat man hastily knelt.

Judge Dee asked curtly: "Who are you, and where is the outgoing magistrate, His Excellency Kwang?"

"This insignificant person," the man stammered, "is the warden of the jail. His Excellency Kwang left early this morning by the southern city gate."

"Where are the seals of office?"

"They must be somewhere in the chancery," the warden answered in a quavering voice.

Judge Dee's patience gave out. He stamped his foot on the ground and shouted: "Where are the guards, where are the constables? Where are the scribes, where are the clerks, where is everybody in this accursed tribunal?"

"The headman of the constables left last month. The senior scribe has been on sick leave for the last three weeks, and . . ."

"So there is nobody but you," the judge interrupted him. Turning to Chiao Tai he continued: "Throw this warden in his own jail. I shall find out for myself what is wrong here!"

The warden started to protest but Chiao Tai boxed his ears and bound his hands behind his back. He turned the warden around, gave him a kick and barked: "Lead us to your jail!"

In the left wing of the compound, behind the empty quarters of the guards, they found quite a capacious jail. Evidently the cells had not been used for a long time; but the doors looked solid enough and the windows had iron grates.

Chiao Tai pushed the warden into a small cell and locked the door.

Judge Dee said: "Let us now have a look at the court hall and the chancery!"

Chiao Tai took up his paper lantern. They found the double gate of the court hall without difficulty. As Chiao Tai gave the door a push it swung open with a creaking of rusty hinges. He lifted his lantern.

They saw a large, empty hall. A thick layer of dust and dirt covered the stone flags and cobwebs hung from the walls. Judge Dee walked up to the dais and looked at the faded and torn red cloth that covered the bench. A large rat scurried away.

The judge beckoned Chiao Tai. Then he stepped up onto the dais, walked round the bench and pulled aside the screen that covered the door opening leading to the magistrate's private office, behind the court hall. A cloud of dust descended on the judge.

The office was empty but for a bare, ramshackle desk, an armchair with a broken back, and three wooden footstools.

Chiao Tai opened the door in the wall opposite. A dank smell assailed them. The walls were covered with shelves supporting rows of leather document boxes, green with mould.

Judge Dee shook his head.

"What fine archives!" he murmured.

He kicked open the door to the corridor and silently walked back to the main courtyard, Chiao Tai with his lantern leading the way.

Ma Joong and Tao Gan had locked their prisoners in the jail. The three dead robbers had been deposited in the quarters of the guards. Judge Dee's servants were busy unloading the luggage under supervision of the house steward. The latter informed the judge that the magistrate's living quarters in the back of the compound were in excellent condition. The departing magistrate had left everything there in good order; the rooms had been swept, the furniture was clean and in a good state of repair. Judge Dee's cook was lighting the kitchen fire.

Judge Dee heaved a sigh of relief; at least his family had shelter.

He ordered Sergeant Hoong and Ma Joong to retire. They could spread their bed rolls in a side room of his own quarters. Then the judge beckoned Chiao Tai and Tao Gan to follow him, and went back to his deserted private office.

Tao Gan placed two lighted candles on the desk.

Judge Dee lowered himself gingerly into the rickety armchair. His two lieutenants blew the dust off the footstools and sat down.

The judge folded his arms on the desk. For a while no one spoke.

They presented a queer spectacle together. All three were still clad in their brown traveling robes, torn and muddy from the fight with the robbers. Their faces were drawn and haggard in the uncertain light of the candles.

Then the judge spoke: "Well, my friends, the hour is late and we are tired and hungry. Yet I would like to have a consultation with you about this queer state of affairs we have found here."

Tao Gan and Chiao Tai nodded eagerly.

"This town," Judge Dee continued, "baffles me completely. Although my predecessor was in residence here for three years and kept his living quarters in excellent condition, he apparently never used the court hall, and sent home the entire personnel of the tribunal. Although a courier must have duly informed him of my arrival scheduled for this afternoon, he went away without even leaving a message for me, entrusting the seals of office to that scoundrel of a warden. The other officials of the district administration simply ignored our arrival. How do you explain all this?"

"Could it be, Your Honour," Chiao Tai asked, "that the people here are planning to rebel against the central government?"

Judge Dee shook his head.

"It is true," he replied, "that the streets are deserted and the shops closed at an unusually early hour. But I did not notice any sign of unrest and there were no barricades or other military preparations. The attitude of the people in the street was not antagonistic; they were just indifferent."

Tao Gan pensively pulled at the three long hairs that sprouted from a mole on his left cheek.

"For a moment," he remarked, "I thought that maybe the plague or some other dangerous epidemic disease had ravaged this district. That, however, does not tally with the fact that there were no signs of panic, and the people were partaking freely from the food at the street stalls."

Judge Dee combed with his fingers some dry leaves from his long side whiskers. After a while he said: "I would rather not ask that warden for elucidation. The fellow has all the marks of a consummate rascal!"

The steward entered followed by two of Judge Dee's servants. One carried a platter with bowls of rice and soup and the other a large tea pot.

The judge ordered the steward to have bowls of rice brought to the jail for the prisoners.

They ate in silence.

When they had finished the scratch meal and drunk a cup of hot tea, Chiao Tai sat for a while in deep thought, twisting his small moustache. Then he spoke: "I fully agree with Ma Joong, Your Honour, when out there in the mountains he said that the robbers who attacked us were no professional highwaymen. How about questioning our prisoners about what is going on here?"

"An excellent idea!" the judge exclaimed. "Find out who their leader is and bring him here!"

After a while Chiao Tai came back, leading by a chain none other than the robber who had tried to stab Judge Dee with his spear. The judge gave him a sharp look. He saw a strongly built man with a regular, open face; he seemed more like a small shopkeeper or a tradesman than a highway robber.

As he knelt in front of the desk, Judge Dee ordered curtly: "State your name and profession!"

"This person," the man said respectfully, "is called Fang. Until recently I was a blacksmith in this city of Lan-fang, where my family has been living for several generations."

"Why," Judge Dee inquired, "did you, engaged in an old and honourable trade, prefer the despicable life of a highwayman?"

Fang lowered his head and said in a dull voice: "I am guilty of assault with murderous intent. I fully realize that the death penalty awaits me. I confess my guilt which needs no further proof. Why should Your Honour bother to make further inquiries?"

Deep despair rang from his words. Judge Dee said quietly: "I never sentence a criminal until I have heard his full story. Speak up and answer my question!"

"This person," Fang began, "has been a blacksmith for over thirty years, having learned the trade from his father. I and my wife, one son and two daughters were strong and healthy; we had our daily bowl of rice, and now and then even a slice of pork. I considered myself a happy man.

"Then, one unfortunate day, Chien's men saw that my son was a sturdy young fellow, and they pressed him into their service."

"Who is this Chien?" the Judge interrupted him.

"What," Fang replied bitterly, "is Chien not? For more than eight years he has usurped all power in this district. He owns half the land and nearly one-fourth of the shops and houses in this town. He is magistrate, judge, and military commander, all in one. He regularly sends bribes to the officials of the prefecture, five days on horseback from here. He has convinced them that if it were not for him, the barbarian hordes from over the border would long have overrun this district."

"Did my predecessors acquiesce in this irregular state of affairs?" Judge Dee inquired.

Fang shrugged his shoulders. He answered: "The magistrates appointed here soon found out that it was easier and much safer to be satisfied with a shadow existence, leaving all real power in the hands of Chien. As long as they acted as his puppets, Chien gave them rich presents every month. They lived in peace and comfort while we of the people suffered."

"Your story," Judge Dee said coldly, "sounds absurd to me. Unfortunately it is true that occasionally a local tyrant usurps power in an outlying district. And sadder still, sometimes a weak magistrate will accept such an unlawful situation. But you cannot make me believe, my man, that for eight years every magistrate who was appointed here submitted to the man Chien."

Fang said with a sneer: "Then we of Lan-fang were just unlucky! There was but one magistrate who, four years ago, turned against Chien. After two weeks his body was found on the river bank, his throat cut from ear to ear."

Judge Dee suddenly leaned forward. He asked: "Was that magistrate's name by any chance Pan?"

Fang nodded.

"Magistrate Pan," Judge Dee continued, "was reported to the central authorities as having fallen in a skirmish with invading Uigur hordes. I was in the capital at that time. I remember that his body was forwarded there with military honours and that he was posthumously promoted to the rank of prefect."

"That was how Chien covered up his murder," Fang said indifferently. "I know the truth. I myself saw the body."

"Proceed with your story!" Judge Dee said.

"Thus," Fang went on, "my only son was forced to join the band of ruffians that Chien keeps as his private guards, and I never saw him again.

"Then a wretched old crone who acts as procuress for Chien came to see me. She said that Chien offered ten silver pieces for White Orchid, my eldest daughter. I refused. Three days later my daughter went to the market, and never came back. Time and again I went to Chien's mansion and begged to be allowed to see her, but every time I was cruelly beaten and chased away.

"Having lost her only son and her eldest daughter my wife began ailing. She died two weeks ago. I took my father's sword and went to Chien's mansion. I was intercepted by the guards. They fell on me with their clubs, and left me for dead in the street. One week ago a band of ruffians set fire to my shop. I left the city with Dark Orchid, my youngest daughter, who was also caught tonight, and joined a band of other desperate men out in the mountains. Tonight we made our first attempt at holding up travellers."

Deep silence reigned. The judge was going to lean back in his armchair but remembered in time that the back was broken. He hastily placed his elbows on the desk again. Then he spoke: "Your story has a very familiar ring. It usually is some such tale of woe that robbers dish out in the tribunal when they have been caught in the act. If you lied, your head will fall on the execution ground. If it turns out that you have spoken the truth, I shall reserve my verdict."

"For me," the blacksmith said dejectedly, "there is no hope left. If Your Honour does not have my head chopped off, Chien will certainly kill me. The same goes for my comrades, who are all victims of Chien's cruel oppression."

Judge Dee gave a sign to Chiao Tai. He rose and led Fang back to the jail.

The judge left his armchair and began to pace the floor. When Chiao Tai had come back, Judge Dee stood still and said pensively: "That man Fang evidently told the truth. This district is in the power of a local tyrant; magistrates are nothing but powerless figureheads here. That explains the queer attitude of the local population."

Chiao Tai struck his large fist on his knee.

"Must we," he exclaimed angrily, "bow to that scoundrel Chien?"

The judge smiled his thin smile. "The hour is late," he said, "you two had better retire and have a good night's rest. Tomorrow I shall have much work for you. I shall stay here for an hour or so and have a glance at those old archives."

Tao Gan and Chiao Tai offered to stay up to assist the judge but he firmly refused.

As soon as they had left, Judge Dee took up a candle and entered the next room. With the sleeve of his dirty travelling robe he rubbed the mould from the labels of the document boxes. He found that the most recent file was dated eight years earlier.

The judge carried this box into his office and spread out the contents on his desk.

It took his experienced eye but little time to verify that they were mostly documents relating to the routine of the district administration. On the bottom of the box, however, he found a small roll, marked "The Case Yoo versus Yoo." Judge Dee sat down. He unrolled the document and glanced through it.

He saw that it was a law suit concerning the inheritance of Yoo Shou-chien, a provincial governor who, nine years before, had died whilst living in retirement in Lan-fang.

Judge Dee closed his eyes and cast his thoughts back fifteen years, when he was serving in the capital as a junior secretary. At that time the name Yoo Shou-chien had been famous all over the Empire. He had been an exceptionally able and scrupulously honest official; devoted to the state and the people, he had earned fame both as a benevolent administrator and a wise statesman. Then, when the Throne appointed him Grand Secretary of State, Yoo Shou-chien suddenly resigned from all his offices; pleading poor health he had buried himself in some obscure border district. The Emperor himself had urged him to reconsider his decision, but Yoo Shou-chien had steadfastly refused. Judge Dee remembered that at that time this sudden resignation had created quite a sensation in the capital.

So Lan-fang had been the place where Yoo Shou-chien lived his last years.

Slowly Judge Dee unrolled the document once more, and read it carefully from beginning to end.

He found that when Yoo Shou-chien settled down to a life of retirement in Lan-fang, he was a widower of over sixty. He had an only son called Yoo Kee, then thirty years old. Shortly after his arrival in Lan-fang the old governor had remarried. He chose as his bride a young peasant girl of barely eighteen, of the surname Mei. Out of this unequal marriage there was born a second son, called Yoo Shan.

When the old governor fell ill and felt that his end was drawing near, he called his son Yoo Kee and his young wife with her infant son to his deathbed. He told them that he bequeathed a scroll picture he had painted himself to his wife and his second son, Yoo Shan; all the rest of his possessions were to go to Yoo Kee. He added that he trusted that Yoo Kee would see to it that his stepmother and his half-brother would receive what was due to them. Having made this statement the old governor breathed his last.

Judge Dee looked at the date of the document and reflected that now Yoo Kee must be about forty, the widow nearly thirty, and her son twelve years old.

The document stated that as soon as his father had been buried, Yoo Kee expelled his stepmother and Yoo Shan from his house. He had said that the last words of his father evidently implied that Yoo Shan was an illegitimate child and that he was not bound to do anything either for him or for his adulterous mother.

Thereupon the widow had filed a complaint with the tribunal contesting the oral will, and claiming half of the property for her son, on the basis of common law.

At that time Chien had just established himself as the ruler of Lan-fang. It seemed that the tribunal had done nothing to settle this suit.

Judge Dee rolled up the document. He reflected that at first sight the widow did not have a strong case. The last words of the old governor together with the disparity in age between him and his second wife seemed to suggest that Mrs. Mei had indeed been unfaithful to her husband.

On the other hand it was curious that a man of such high ethical standards as the great Yoo Shou-chien had chosen this peculiar way of proclaiming that Yoo Shan was not his son. If he had really discovered that his young wife deceived him, one would have expected that he would have quietly divorced her, and sent her and her son away to live in some distant place, thus protecting the honour of himself and of his distinguished family. And why this queer bequest of the picture?

It also seemed strange that Yoo Shou-chien had not left a written testament. A man of his long official experience ought to have known that oral testaments nearly always engender bitter family quarrels.

This case had several angles that deserved a careful investigation. Perhaps it might also bring to light the key to the mystery of Yoo Shou-chien's sudden resignation.

Judge Dee rummaged through the documents but he could find nothing else that had a bearing on the case Yoo versus Yoo. Neither did he find any material that might be used against Chien.

The judge replaced the documents in the box. He remained sitting in deep thought for a long time. He pondered ways and means to oust the tyrant Chien, but time and again his thoughts reverted to the old governor and his curious bequest.

One candle spluttered and went out. With a sigh Judge Dee took up the other one and walked to his own quarters.

Third Chapter

THE JUDGE WITNESSES A QUARREL ON THE MARKET;
A YOUNG MAN PREDICTS HIS FATHER'S MURDER

The next morning Judge Dee found to his dismay that he was late. He had a hurried breakfast and then went immediately to his private office.

He saw that the room had been thoroughly cleaned. His armchair had been repaired and the desk polished. On its top all Judge Dee's favourite writing implements had been laid out with a care in which the judge recognized the hand of Sergeant Hoong.

The judge found the sergeant in the archives room. Together with Tao Gan he had swept and aired the dank place; now it smelled pleasantly of the wax they had used for polishing the red leather document boxes.

Judge Dee nodded contentedly. As he sat down behind his desk, he ordered Tao Gan to fetch Ma Joong and Chiao Tai.

When all his four lieutenants were assembled before him, the judge first inquired how Sergeant Hoong and Ma Joong were doing. Both said that they were none the worse for the fight of the night before. The sergeant had replaced the bandage on his head by a plaster of oil paper and Ma Joong could move his left arm again although it was still somewhat stiff.

Ma Joong reported that early that morning he and Chiao Tai had inspected the armoury of the tribunal. They had found a good collection of pikes, halberds, swords, helmets, armor and leather jackets, but that everything was old and dirty and needed a thorough polishing.

Judge Dee said slowly: "Fang's story offers a plausible explanation for the strange situation here. If all he said is true, we must act quickly before Chien finds out that I am going to turn against him and steals the first move. We must attack before he knows what is happening. As our old proverb says: 'A dangerous dog bites without first baring its teeth'!"

"What shall we do with that warden?" Sergeant Hoong inquired.

"For the time being we shall leave him where he is," the judge replied. "It was a lucky inspiration that made me lock that rascal up. Evidently he is one of Chien's men. He would have run immediately to his master to tell him all about us."

Ma Joong opened his mouth to ask something but Judge Dee raised his hand. He continued: "Tao Gan, you will now go out and collect all information you can get about Chien and his men. At the same time you will make inquiries about a wealthy citizen called Yoo Kee. He is the son of the famous Governor Yoo Shou-chien who about eight years ago died here in Lan-fang.

"I myself shall now go out with Ma Joong to obtain a general impression of this town. Sergeant Hoong shall supervise affairs here in the tribunal together with Chiao Tai. The gates shall remain locked and no one is to leave or enter during my absence except for my house steward. He will go out alone to buy food.

"Let us meet here again at noon!"

The judge rose and put on a small black cap. In his simple blue robe he looked like a scholarly gentleman of leisure.

He left the tribunal with Ma Joong walking by his side.

First they strolled south and had a look at the famous pagoda of Lan-fang. It stood on a small island in the middle of a lotus lake. The willow trees along its banks were waving in the morning breeze. Then they walked north and mingled with the crowd.

There was the usual coming and going of an early morning and the shops along the main street did a fair amount of business. But one heard little laughter, and people often talked in a low voice, quickly looking right and left before they spoke.

When they had reached the double arch north of the tribunal, Judge Dee and Ma Joong turned left and strolled to the market place in front of the Drum Tower. This market presented an interesting scene. Vendors from over the border clad in quaint gaudy costumes praised their wares in raucous voices, and here and there an Indian monk lifted up his almsbowl.

A group of idlers had gathered round a fish dealer who was having a violent quarrel with a neatly dressed young man. The latter apparently was being overcharged. Finally he threw a handful of coppers into the fishmonger's basket, shouting angrily: "If this were a decently administered town you would not dare thus to deceive people in broad daylight!"

Suddenly a broad-shouldered man stepped forward. He jerked the young man around and hit him on the mouth.

"That will teach you to slander the Honourable Chien!" he growled.

Ma Joong was going to intervene but the judge laid a restraining hand on his arm.

The spectators hurriedly dispersed. The young man did not say a word. He wiped the blood from his mouth and went his way.

Judge Dee gave Ma Joong a sign. Together they followed the young man.

When he had entered a quiet side alley, the judge overtook him. He said: "Excuse my intrusion. I happened to see that ruffian maltreat you. Why don't you report him to the tribunal?"

The young man stood still. He gave Judge Dee and his stalwart companion a suspicious look.

"If you are agents of Chien," he said coldly, "you can wait long before I incriminate myself!"

Judge Dee looked up and down the alley. They were alone.

"You are greatly mistaken, young man," he said quietly. "I am Dee Jen-djieh, the new magistrate of this district."

The young man's face turned ashen; he looked as if he had seen a ghost. Then he passed his hand over his forehead and mastered his emotion. He heaved a deep sigh and his face lit up in a broad smile. He bowed deeply, saying respectfully: "This person is the Junior Candidate Ding, the son of General Ding Hoo-gwo, from the capital. Your Honour's name is quite familiar to me. At long last this district has a real magistrate!"

The judge inclined his head slightly to acknowledge the compliment.

He remembered that many years ago General Ding had fought against the barbarians across the northern border. But when he had returned to the capital the general had been compelled to resign. Judge Dee wondered how the general's son came to be in this distant place. He said to the young man: "There is something very wrong in this town. I would like you to tell me more about the situation here."

Candidate Ding did not answer immediately. He remained in thought for a few moments. Then he spoke: "These things had better not be discussed in public. Might I have the honour of offering the gentlemen a cup of tea?"

Judge Dee assented. They went to the tea house on the corner of the alley and sat down at a table somewhat apart from the other guests.

When the waiter had brought the tea, young Ding said in a whisper: "A ruthless man called Chien Mow has all the power in his hands. There is nobody here who dares to oppose him. Chien keeps about one hundred ruffians in his mansion. They have nothing to do but loaf about this town and intimidate the people."

"How are they armed?" Ma Joong asked.

"Out in the street these rascals have only clubs and swords with them, but I would not be astonished if in Chien's mansion they kept quite an arsenal."

Judge Dee asked: "Do you often see barbarians from over the border in this town?"

Candidate Ding shook his head emphatically.

"I have never seen a single Uigur here," he replied.

"Those attacks Chien reported to the government," Judge Dee observed to Ma Joong, "are evidently but an invention of his, to convince the authorities that he and his men are indispensable here."

Ma Joong asked: "Have you ever been inside Chien's mansion?"

"Heaven forbid!" the young man exclaimed. "I always avoid that entire neighbourhood. Chien has surrounded his mansion with a double wall, with watchtowers on the four corners."

"How did he seize power here?" Judge Dee inquired.

"He inherited great wealth from his father," young Ding replied, "but none of his eminent qualities. His father was a native of this town, an honest and diligent man who became rich as a tea merchant. Until a few years ago the main route to Khotan and the other tributary kingdoms of the west ran through Lan-fang and this town was quite an important emporium. Then three oases along the desert route dried up and it shifted a hundred miles to the north. Chien then collected a band of ruffians around him and one day proclaimed himself master of this city.

"He is a clever and determined man who could easily have been successful in an official military career. But he will obey no one. He prefers to govern this district as the undisputed ruler, responsible to no one in the Empire."

"A most unfortunate situation," Judge Dee commented. He emptied his tea cup and rose to go.

Candidate Ding hurriedly leaned forward and begged the judge to stay a little longer.

The judge hesitated, but the young man looked so unhappy that at last he sat down again. Candidate Ding busied himself with refilling the tea cups. He seemed at a loss how to begin.

"If there is anything on your mind, young man," Judge Dee said, "don't hesitate to speak!"

"To tell Your Honour the truth," young Ding finally said, "there is a matter that weighs heavily on my mind. It has nothing to do with the tyrant Chien. It concerns my own family."

Here he paused. Ma Joong shifted impatiently on his chair.

Candidate Ding made an effort and continued: "Your Honour, my old father is going to be murdered!"

Judge Dee raised his eyebrows.

"If you know that in advance," he observed, "it should not be difficult to prevent the crime!"

The young man shook his head.

"Allow me to tell the whole story. Your Honour may have heard that my poor old father was slandered by one of his subordinates, the wicked Commander Woo. He was jealous of my father's great victory in the north and although he could never prove his false accusation, the Board of Military Affairs ordered my father to resign."

"Yes, I remember that affair," Judge Dee said. "Is your father also living here?"

"My father," young Ding replied, "came to this distant place partly because my late mother was a native of Lan-fang, and partly because he wished to avoid the larger cities where he might be embarrassed by meeting former colleagues. We thought that here we would be able to live in peace.

"One month ago, however, I began to notice that suspicious looking men often loitered in our neighbourhood. Last week I secretly followed one of them. He went to a small wine shop called 'Eternal Spring' in the northwest corner of the city. Who can describe my astonishment when I learned from another shop in that street that Woo Feng, the eldest son of Commander Woo, is living over that wine shop!"

Judge Dee looked doubtful.

"Why," he asked, "should Commander Woo send his son here to annoy your father? The commander has ruined your father's career. Any further action would only land him into trouble."

"I know what his plans are!" Candidate Ding exclaimed excitedly. "Woo knows that my father's friends in the capital have discovered evidence that the commander's accusation was pure slander. He sent his son here to kill my father and thus save his own wretched life! Your Honour does not know that man Woo Feng. He is a confirmed drunkard, a most dissolute person who likes nothing better than indulging in acts of violence. He has hired ruffians to spy on us and he will strike as soon as he sees the chance."

"Even so," Judge Dee remarked, "I don't see how I could intervene. I can only advise you to keep an eye on Woo's movements and at the same time to take a few simple precautions in your own mansion. Is there any indication that Woo is in contact with Chien Mow?"

"No," the young man answered. "Woo apparently has made no attempt at enlisting the support of Chien. As regards precautions, my poor father has been receiving threatening letters ever since he resigned from the service. He rarely goes out and the gates of our mansion are locked and barred day and night. Moreover my father has had all doors and windows of his library walled up save one. That door has only one key which my father always keeps with him. When he is inside, he pushes a bar across the door. It is in that library that my father spends most of his time, compiling a history of the border wars."

Judge Dee told Ma Joong to note down the address of the Ding mansion. It was located not far from there, beyond the Drum Tower.

As he rose to go, the judge said: "Don't fail to report to the tribunal if there are any new developments. I have to go now. You will realize that

my own position in this town is not too comfortable. As soon as I have
settled with Chien, I shall make a further study of your problem."

Candidate Ding thanked the judge and conducted his guests to the door
of the tea shop. There he took his leave with a deep bow.

Judge Dee and Ma Joong walked back to the main street.

"That young fellow," Ma Joong observed, "reminds me of the man who
insisted on wearing an iron helmet day and night because he was in constant fear that the vault of Heaven would crash down on his head!"

The judge shook his head.

"It is a very queer affair," he said pensively. "I don't like it at all."

Fourth Chapter

TAO GAN REPORTS ON A MYSTERIOUS OLD MANSION;
AN INGENIOUS TRAP IS SET IN THE DARK TRIBUNAL

Ma Joong looked astonished, but Judge Dee vouchsafed no further comment. Silently they strolled back to the tribunal. Chiao Tai opened the
gate for them and informed the judge that Tao Gan was waiting for him in
his private office.

Judge Dee had Sergeant Hoong called in. As his four lieutenants seated
themselves in front of his desk the judge gave a brief account of his
encounter with Candidate Ding. Then he ordered Tao Gan to report.

Tao Gan's face was even longer than usual as he began: "Matters don't
look too good for us, Your Honour. That man Chien has established
himself in a powerful position. He has drained the district of its wealth but
he has been careful to leave alone members of influential families who
came here from the capital, in order to prevent them from sending unfa-
vourable reports about him to the central authorities. This applies to General Ding whose son Your Honour just met, and to Yoo Kee, the son of
Governor Yoo Shou-chien.

"Chien Mow has been clever enough not to turn the screws too tightly.
He takes a generous percentage of all business conducted in this district,
but leaves the merchants a reasonable margin of profit. After a fashion he
also maintains the public peace; if a man is caught stealing or brawling he
is beaten half to death on the spot by Chien's henchmen. It is true that

these men eat and drink in restaurants and inns without paying a copper. On the other hand Chien spends money freely and many of the large shops have good customers in him and his men. It is the small shopkeepers and tradesmen that suffer most from his tyranny. On the whole, however, the people of Lan-fang are resigned to their fate and reason that it could easily be worse."

"Are Chien's men loyal to him?" the judge interrupted.

"Why should they not be?" Tao Gan asked. "Those ruffians, about one hundred in all, spend their time drinking and gambling. Chien recruited them from the scum of the city and picked up quite a number of deserters from the regular army. Chien's mansion, by the way, looks like a fortress. It stands near the western city gate. The high outer wall has iron spikes all along its top and the main entrance is guarded day and night by four men who are armed to the teeth."

Judge Dee remained silent for some time, slowly caressing his side whiskers. Then he asked: "Now what did you learn about Yoo Kee?"

"Yoo Kee," Tao Gan replied, "lives near the Watergate. He seems to be a man of retiring habits who lives very quietly. But people tell many stories about his father, the late Governor Yoo Shou-chien. He was an eccentric old man who spent most of his time on his large country estate at the foot of the mountain slope, outside the eastern city gate. That country mansion is a dark old house surrounded by a dense forest. People say that it was built more than two centuries ago. At the back the governor constructed a maze that covers several acres. The path is bordered by thick undergrowth and large boulders which form an impenetrable wall. They say that this maze abounds in poisonous reptiles; others aver that the Governor laid many a weird man-trap along the path. Anyway this maze is so perfect that no one except the old Governor himself has ever ventured to enter it. He, however, used to go there nearly every day and would stay inside for hours on end."

Judge Dee had followed Tao Gan's words with great interest.

"What a curious tale!" he exclaimed. "Does Yoo Kee often visit the country mansion?"

Tao Gan shook his head.

"No," he replied. "Yoo Kee left there as soon as the old Governor had been buried. He has never gone back there since. The mansion is empty but for an aged gate keeper and his wife. People say that the place is haunted and that the ghost of the old Governor walks about there at night. All give the estate a wide berth, even in broad daylight.

"The Governor's town mansion was located just inside the eastern city gate. But Yoo Kee sold it soon after his father's death and bought his present house, right at the other end of the city. It stands on an empty plot of ground in the southwest corner, near the river. I had no time to go there myself, but people say that it is quite an imposing mansion, surrounded by a high wall."

Judge Dee rose and started pacing the floor.

After a while he said impatiently: "The overthrow of Chien Mow resolves itself into a purely military problem and I for one find but small interest in such problems. They resemble too much a game of chess; the opponent and all his resources are known right from the beginning; there are no unknown factors. I am greatly intrigued, on the other hand, by two most interesting problems, namely the ambiguous last will of old Governor Yoo, and the murder of General Ding that has been announced in advance. I would like to concentrate on these two matters which I find of absorbing interest. Instead I must first dispose of this miserable local tyrant! What an annoying situation!"

The judge tugged angrily at his beard. Then he rose and said: "Well, I suppose that it can't be helped. I shall now have my noon meal. Afterwards I shall open the first session of this tribunal."

Judge Dee left his office. His four lieutenants walked over to the empty guard house, where the judge's steward had prepared a simple meal for them.

As they were entering, Chiao Tai gave a sign to Ma Joong. The two remained standing together for a moment in the corridor outside.

Chiao Tai whispered to Ma Joong: "I fear that His Excellency underrates the problem we are up against. You and I have had military experience, we know that we have not got a chance. Chien Mow has one hundred well-trained men, the only fighters we have are, except for our judge himself, just you and me. The nearest military post is three days on horseback from here. Shouldn't we warn our judge not to act too rashly?"

Ma Joong twisted his short moustache.

"Our judge," he replied in a low voice, "has all the data we have. I take it that he has evolved a scheme to deal with the situation."

"The most clever scheme," Chiao Tai observed, "is of no avail against such superior strength. It does not matter for us, but what about our judge's wives and his children? Chien will have no mercy on them. I think it is our duty to propose to the judge that we first pretend to submit to Chien and afterwards work out some plan for attacking him. We could have a regiment of our army here in two weeks."

Ma Joong shook his head.

"Unbidden advice is never welcome," he said. "Let us wait a while and see what happens. I for one know of no better death than to fall in a really good fight."

"All right," Chiao Tai said, "if it comes to an open conflict I shall take care of at least four of those ruffians. Let us now join the others. Don't say a word about this; it is no use alarming the sergeant and Tao Gan."

Ma Joong nodded.

They entered the guard house and fell to their meal with gusto.

When they had eaten their rice, Tao Gan wiped his chin and said: "I have served more than six years under our judge and I thought I had come to understand him fairly well. But now it baffles me how he can be so preoccupied with an old lawsuit and a murder that will probably never take place, at a time when we are confronted with so difficult and urgent a problem as the overthrow of Chien Mow. You, Sergeant, have known His Excellency all your life. What do you say?"

Sergeant Hoong was busy swallowing the last of his soup, lifting his moustache with his left hand. He quietly put the bowl down. Then he said with a smile: "In all these years I have learned but one thing about understanding our judge. That is, to give up trying to!"

All laughed. They rose and went back to the judge's private office.

As Sergeant Hoong was assisting Judge Dee in changing into his ceremonial robes, Judge Dee said curtly: "Since I lack all the court personnel, today the four of you must take their places."

So speaking Judge Dee pulled aside the screen that separated his office from the court hall, and ascended the dais.

When he was seated behind the bench, the judge ordered Sergeant Hoong and Tao Gan to stand by his side and act as scribes, taking notes of the proceedings. Ma Joong and Chiao Tai were to stand below, in front of the dais, as constables.

As he took up his position, Ma Joong shot Chiao Tai a bewildered look. They wondered why the judge insisted on keeping up the semblance of a real session of the tribunal. Looking at the empty court hall Chiao Tai thought to himself that it rather reminded him of a theatrical performance.

Judge Dee hit his gavel on the bench. He said solemnly: "I, the magistrate, open the first session of this tribunal. Chiao Tai, bring the prisoners before me!"

Soon Chiao Tai came back leading the six robbers and the girl; he had shackled them together on a long chain.

As they approached the dais, the prisoners looked amazed at the judge sitting in full ceremonial dress behind the shabby bench in the deserted court hall.

With an impassive face Judge Dee ordered Tao Gan to note down the full name and former profession of each of the prisoners.

Then Judge Dee spoke: "You men have committed the crime of assault with murderous intent on the public road. The law prescribes for you death by decapitation, confiscation of all your property, and your heads exposed for three days, nailed to the city gate, as a warning to others.

"However, in view of the fact that none of your victims was killed and none suffered grievous bodily harm, and because of the special reasons that drove you to this desperate deed, I, the magistrate, decide that in this particular case mercy shall prevail over justice. I shall let you go free on one condition.

"This condition is that all of you shall serve for an indefinite time as constables of this tribunal under Fang as your headman, binding yourselves loyally to serve the state and the people until I shall release you."

The prisoners looked dumbfounded.

"Your Honour," Fang spoke up, "these persons are profoundly grateful for the leniency shown to us. Yet this only means that our death sentence is deferred for a few days. Your Honour does not yet know Chien Mow's vindictive spirit, and . . ."

The judge hit his gavel on the table. He called out in a thunderous voice: "Look up at your magistrate! Observe carefully these insignia of the power that has been vested in me. Know that on this very day, this very hour, all over the Empire thousands of men wearing these same insignia are dispensing justice in the name of the state and the people. Since time immemorial they have stood as a symbol of the social order decided upon in the wise counsels of your ancestors, and perpetuated by the mandate of Heaven and the free will of the uncounted millions of our black-haired people.

"Have you not sometimes seen people trying to plant a stick in a gushing mountain stream? It will stand for a moment or so, then it is carried away by the mighty stream that flows on for ever. Thus occasionally wicked or ignorant men will rise and endeavour to disrupt the sacred pattern of our society. Is it not crystal clear that such attempts can never end in anything but miserable failure?

"Let us never lose faith in these tokens, lest we lose faith in ourselves.

"Stand up, and be freed of your chains!"

The prisoners had not followed all the implications of Judge Dee's words. But they were deeply impressed by his utter sincerity and carried away by his supreme confidence. Judge Dee's lieutenants, however, had fully understood and they knew that his words had been meant as much for them as for the prisoners. Ma Joong and Chiao Tai bent their heads and hurriedly loosened the chains.

Judge Dee then addressed the robbers: "Afterwards each of you will report to Tao Gan and Sergeant Hoong what wrongs he suffered at the hands of Chien Mow. In due time each single case shall be heard in this tribunal. At present, however, there are more pressing affairs. The six of you will go immediately to the main courtyard and clean the weapons and the old uniforms of the constables. My two lieutenants Ma Joong and Chiao Tai shall instruct you in military drill. Fang's daughter shall report to my house steward for work as a maid in my mansion.

"The first session of the tribunal is closed!"

The judge rose and returned to his private office.

He changed into a comfortable informal robe. Just as he was going to sort out some more documents, Headman Fang came in. After he had bowed, he said respectfully: "Your Honour, beyond the valley where the attack took place there live more than thirty other men in an improvised camp. They had to flee the city because of Chien Mow's iniquities. I know them all. Five or six are scoundrels; the rest are honest people whom I'll answer for. It occurred to me that one of these days I might go out there and enlist the best of them for service in the tribunal."

"An excellent idea!" the judge exclaimed. "You will take a horse and go there at once. Select those men you deem suitable. Let them come back to the city at dusk, in groups of two or three and by different routes!"

Headman Fang hurriedly took his leave.

Late that afternoon the main courtyard of the tribunal resembled a military encampment.

Ten men wearing the black lacquered helmets and the leather jackets with red sash that are the regular uniform of constables, were engaged in a drill led by Headman Fang. Ten others clad in light mail coats and decked with shining helmets were practising pike fencing under the supervision of Ma Joong. Chiao Tai was instructing ten more in the secrets of sword fighting.

The gate of the tribunal was closed. Sergeant Hoong and Tao Gan stood on guard.

Later that night, Judge Dee ordered all the men to assemble in the court hall.

By the light of a single candle the judge issued his instructions. When he had finished he cautioned them all to maintain complete silence for a while. Then he snuffed out the candle.

Tao Gan left the court hall. He closed the door carefully behind him and walked through the dark corridors, lighting his way with a small paper lantern.

He went to the jail and unlocked the warden's cell.

Tao Gan loosened the chain with which the warden had been attached to a ring in the wall. He said in a surly voice: "The judge has decided to dismiss you from his service because of gross negligence. You failed to take proper care of the seals of the tribunal that were entrusted to you. In the coming days our judge shall recruit new personnel for the tribunal, and the first criminal to be kneeling in chains before his dais will be that self-styled tyrant Chien Mow!"

The warden only scowled.

Tao Gan led him through the dark, empty corridors and across the deserted main courtyard. They passed the empty quarters of the guards. Everything was dark and silent.

Tao Gan opened the gate. He gave the warden a push.

"Get out!" he growled. "Never show your ugly face here again!"

The warden looked contemptuously at Tao Gan. He said with a sneer: "I shall be back sooner than you think, you dogshead!"

Then he disappeared into the dark street.

Fifth Chapter

TWENTY RUFFIANS ATTACK IN THE DEAD OF NIGHT;
JUDGE DEE SETS OUT ON A DANGEROUS EXCURSION

Shortly after midnight loud sounds shattered the silence in the dark tribunal.

Hoarse voices shouted orders, weapons clattered. A ram was applied to the main gate; its dull thuds reverberated in the still night air.

But inside the tribunal nothing stirred.

The wood of the gate splintered; heavy wooden boards crashed to the ground. Twenty ruffians swinging clubs and brandishing spears and swords rushed inside. A huge fellow with a lighted torch led the way.

They poured into the first courtyard, shouting: "Where is that dog-official? Where is that wretched magistrate?"

The big fellow kicked open the gate of the main courtyard and stood aside to let the others pass while he drew his sword.

The ruffians halted inside, for the place was pitch dark.

Suddenly all six doors of the large reception hall swung open. The courtyard was brilliantly lighted by dozens of large candles and lanterns that stood arranged in double rows inside.

The invaders, their eyes blinking from this sudden change from dark to light, vaguely saw soldiers lined up on left and right. The light shone on their helmets and the long points of their pikes, leveled for action. At the

CHIEN MOW'S MEN INVADE THE TRIBUNAL

bottom of the stairs they saw a row of constables with drawn swords.

On top of the stairs there stood an imposing figure clad in full ceremonial dress of shimmering brocade, the winged judge's cap on his head.

By his side there stood two tall men in the uniform of cavalry captains. Their breast and armplates glittered and coloured pennants fluttered from their pointed helmets. One held a heavy bow ready with an arrow on the string.

The judge called out in a thunderous voice: "Here is the magistrate of Lan-fang! Surrender your arms!"

The huge ruffian with the naked sword was the first to recover from his surprise.

"Fight your way out!" he yelled to the others.

As he lifted his sword, he fell backwards with a horrible gasp. Chiao Tai's arrow had pierced his throat.

At the same time a hoarse command rang out from the hall.

"Right about . . . turn!"

Immediately there was a loud clanking of iron and the tramping of heavy feet.

The ruffians looked at each other in consternation. One of them leaped forward. He shouted at the others: "Brothers, we are done for! The army is here!"

So speaking he threw down his pike in front of the stairs. As he unbuckled his sword belt he said: "Well, it took me six years to become a corporal. I suppose I shall have to start as a private again!"

Ma Joong barked: "Who calls himself a corporal here?"

The man stood automatically at attention.

"Corporal Ling, Sixth Detachment Foot Soldiers, Thirty-third Army of the Left Wing. At your orders, Captain!"

"All deserters out in front!" Ma Joong shouted.

Five men lined themselves up behind the corporal and awkwardly stood at attention.

Ma Joong said curtly: "You men shall appear before the military tribunal."

In the meantime the other ruffians had handed their arms to the constables. They bound each man's hands behind his back.

The judge spoke: "Captain, ask how many other deserters there are around this town."

Ma Joong bellowed the question at the ex-corporal.

"About forty, Sir!"

Judge Dee stroked his beard.

"When you people have gone on to inspect the other border districts," he said to Ma Joong, "I would like to have some soldiers here on guard duty. You will propose to the Commander, Captain, that those deserters are re-enlisted."

Ma Joong barked immediately: "Corporal Ling and five privates, go back wherever you came from; get rid of those civilian rags; present yourselves here tomorrow at noon sharp, uniform and equipment as per regulation!"

The six men shouted "We obey!" and marched off.

Judge Dee gave a sign. The constables led the prisoners to the jail where Tao Gan was waiting for them.

Tao Gan noted down their names. The fifteenth and last was none other than the dismissed warden. Tao Gan's face lit up in a broad grin.

"You were quite right, you bastard! You are indeed back here earlier than I thought!"

So speaking Tao Gan turned him around and sent him back into his former cell with an accurately placed kick.

In the main courtyard, the newly made soldiers recruited by Fang had shouldered their pikes, and marched off to the quarters of the guards.

Judge Dee saw that they marched in good order. He said with a smile to Ma Joong: "That is not bad for one afternoon's drill!"

The judge came down the steps. Two constables closed the doors of the reception hall. Sergeant Hoong emerged loaded with old pans, kettles and rusty chains.

Judge Dee remarked: "You have a fine commanding voice, Sergeant!"

Early next morning when the sun had just risen, three men left the tribunal on horseback.

Judge Dee rode in the middle, clad in hunting dress. Ma Joong and Chiao Tai, resplendent in their uniforms as cavalry captains, rode by his side.

As they headed west, the judge turned around in his saddle and looked at the large yellow banner that was waving from the roof of the tribunal. It bore an inscription in red letters: "Military Headquarters."

"My ladies worked on that banner till deep in the night!" Judge Dee said with a smile to his companions.

They rode straight to Chien Mow's mansion.

Four stalwart figures armed with halberds stood in front of the gate.

Ma Joong reined in his horse right in front of them. He pointed with his riding whip at the door, and ordered: "Open up!"

Evidently the deserters who had been sent back the night before had spread the news about the arrival of the soldiers. The guards hesitated for but one moment. Then they threw open the gate and Judge Dee and his lieutenants rode through.

In the first courtyard a few dozen men stood about in groups talking excitedly. They immediately fell silent and cast an apprehensive glance at the three horsemen. Those who carried swords hurriedly tried to conceal these weapons in the folds of their robes.

The three rode on without looking right or left.

Ma Joong forced his horse up the four steps that led to the second courtyard, followed by the judge and Chiao Tai.

Corporal Ling was supervising about thirty men who were busily engaged in polishing swords and spears and oiling leather jackets.

Without stopping Ma Joong called out to the corporal: "Follow with ten privates!"

The third courtyard was deserted but for a few servants who scurried away when they saw the three horsemen.

Ma Joong rode up to the large building at the back, the hoofs of his horse clattering on the flagstones. The beautifully carved, red-lacquered doors indicated that this was the main hall of the mansion.

They dismounted and threw the reins to three of the corporal's men.

Ma Joong kicked open the central door with his iron boot and stepped inside followed by his two companions.

Evidently they had interrupted an urgent conference. Three men were sitting close together in the centre of the hall. In the middle, a tall broad-shouldered man sat in a large armchair covered with a tiger skin. He had a heavy-jowled, imperious face, with a thin moustache and a short black beard. He seemed to have just left his bed; he still wore a night robe of white silk, and over it a loose house robe of purple brocade. His head was covered with a small black cap. The two others, both elderly men, were sitting opposite him on footstools of carved ebony. They also apparently had dressed in a hurry.

The hall had a most warlike appearance. It resembled an armoury rather than a reception hall. The walls were decorated with spears, pikes and shields; the floor was covered with the skins of wild animals.

The three men looked up at the intruders in speechless amazement. Judge Dee did not say a word. He walked straight to an empty armchair and sat down. Ma Joong and Chiao Tai planted themselves right in front of Chien Mow and gave him a baleful look.

Chien's two counsellors hastily left their footstools and retreated behind their master's armchair.

The judge addressed Ma Joong in a casual voice: "Captain, the town is under martial law. So I leave it to you to deal with these rascals!"

Ma Joong turned round.

"Corporal Ling!" he bellowed.

The corporal hurriedly stepped over the threshold, followed by four of

MA JOONG AND CHIAO TAI ARREST A CRIMINAL

his men. Ma Joong asked: "Which of these criminals is the traitor Chien Mow?"

The corporal pointed to the man in the armchair.

Ma Joong snapped; "Chien Mow, you are arrested on the charge of sedition!"

Chien jumped up. He stood facing Ma Joong and shouted in a voice that yielded nothing to Ma Joong's in harshness: "Who is giving orders in my own house? Guards, cut them down!"

As he spoke, Ma Joong struck him with his mailed fist full in the face. Chien fell down, upsetting an elegant tea table that crashed to the floor together with a costly porcelain tea set.

Six fierce looking ruffians came rushing from behind the large screen in the back of the hall. They carried long swords and their leader brandished a double axe.

They suddenly halted when they saw Ma Joong and Chiao Tai in their full armour. Ma Joong folded his arms. He gruffly addressed the body guards: "Give up your arms! Our commander will decide later whether you underlings are guilty or not."

Chien's nose had been broken; a stream of blood stained his robe. He lifted his head and called out: "Don't listen to that bastard, men! Have you not eaten my rice for ten years? First kill that dog-official there!"

The leader of the body guard sprang over to the judge raising his axe.

Judge Dee did not move. He slowly caressed his side whiskers, staring contemptuously at his attacker.

"Wait, brother Wang!" Corporal Ling shouted; "did I not tell you that the whole town is swarming with soldiers? We have not got a chance. The army has taken over!"

The man with the axe hesitated.

Chiao Tai stamped his foot impatiently on the floor.

"Let us get a move on!" he cried. "We have better things to do than picking up these few rascals!"

He turned around and made as if to step outside.

Chien Mow had lost consciousness. Ma Joong, completely ignoring the body guards, stooped down and started to bind up Chien.

Judge Dee rose from his chair. As he straightened his robes, he said coldly to the man with the axe: "Put that dangerous instrument down, my man!"

He turned his back on him and looked hard at the two counsellors. They had stood there silently throughout the proceedings. Evidently they did not want to commit themselves either way before the issue was decided.

"Who might you two be?" the judge asked haughtily.

The elder one bowed deeply.

"Your Honour," he replied, "this person has been compelled to serve this man Chien as a counsellor. Allow me to assure Your Honour that . . ."

"You will tell your tale in the tribunal!" Judge Dee interrupted him. To Ma Joong he said: "Let us hurry back to the tribunal. We shall take only this man Chien Mow and his two counsellors. We shall deal later with the rest of them." Ma Joong said promptly: "As you order, Magistrate!"

He gave a sign to Corporal Ling. The four soldiers bound the two counsellors securely. Chiao Tai unwound a thin chain from his waist. He made a loop at either end and threw the nooses over the heads of the two prisoners. He dragged them outside. As he fastened the chain to his saddle bow Chiao Tai said curtly: "If you don't want to strangle yourselves, you had better walk fast!"

Chiao Tai mounted his horse and Judge Dee followed his example. Ma Joong slung the unconscious Chien Mow over his saddle. He called out to Corporal Ling: "Divide your soldiers into four groups of twelve. Each group is responsible for ten of Chien's men. Go to the city gates and lock your prisoners in the towers. At noon an officer shall inspect the four gates!"

"I obey!" the corporal shouted.

The three rode across the courtyard, the two counsellors trotting behind Chiao Tai's horse.

In the second courtyard an elderly man with a grey goatee was waiting for them. He fell on his knees and knocked his head on the stoneflags.

Judge Dee halted his horse. He said curtly: "Rise and state your name!"

The other hastily scrambled up. He replied with a bow: "This unworthy person is the steward of this mansion."

Judge Dee ordered: "You will be fully responsible for this mansion and everything in it, including the servants and the womenfolk, till officers from the tribunal come to take over!"

Then the judge rode on.

Ma Joong bent over in his saddle and asked the steward in a conversational tone: "Have you ever seen how in the army they sometimes flog a criminal slowly to death with a thin rattan? It usually takes about six hours."

The bewildered steward respectfully replied that he had not yet had that advantage.

"That is exactly what will happen to you if you don't execute His Excellency's orders to the letter!" Ma Joong said casually. He spurred on his horse, leaving the steward standing there trembling, his face ashen.

As the three horsemen passed through the main gate of Chien's mansion, the four guards presented arms.

Sixth Chapter

FOUR GUILDMASTERS ARE RECEIVED IN THE MAIN HALL;
MRS. YOO VISITS THE TRIBUNAL WITH AN OLD PICTURE

Once back at the tribunal, Ma Joong and Chiao Tai delivered the still unconscious Chien Mow and his two panting counsellors to Headman Fang. Then they went to Judge Dee's private office. Sergeant Hoong was assisting the judge to change into his informal dress.

Ma Joong pushed back his iron helmet and wiped the perspiration from his brow. He looked with admiration at the judge, exclaiming: "If that was not the most colossal bluff I have ever seen!"

The judge smiled bleakly.

"It would never have done," he explained, "to fight it out with Chien. Even if we had really had some two hundred soldiers at our disposal, it would have been a bloody battle. Chien Mow is a rascal but he is by no means a coward and the men under him would have put up a stiff fight.

"From the beginning I had planned to bluff them, impressing upon Chien and his men that all was over and done with and our victory a foregone conclusion. My original plan was to pose as a provincial governor or an Imperial censor on a border inspection tour.

"As soon as Tao Gan informed me that there were many deserters from the regular army among Chien's men, I changed my plan accordingly."

"Was it not taking a risk to let that corporal and five men return to Chien's mansion after the attack on the tribunal?" Chiao Tai asked. "They might have started making inquiries and found out that we were bluffing."

"That," Judge Dee replied, "was exactly what decided the issue. No one in his senses would have let six good men march back to their master unless he had overwhelmingly superior numbers behind him. It never occurred to Corporal Ling to check. Chien is a shrewd man, but even he did not doubt the presence of the regular army. He decided to die in a last desperate fight, but his followers thought better of it, especially when we suggested that we might let them go free."

"Now that we have created this imaginary regiment," Sergeant Hoong asked, "how do we get rid of it again?"

"If I am not greatly mistaken in my estimation of the course a rumour will take," Judge Dee said calmly, "this regiment will first wax in popular imagination till it has become a full-fledged army, and then evaporate again without any effort on our part.

"Now about business. First I must organize this tribunal. Then Chien Mow's affairs must be disentangled.

"Tao Gan will go out now and summon the wardens of all the quarters of this city to appear before me immediately. He will also invite the masters of the most important guilds to pay me a visit at noon.

"Sergeant Hoong, you will go to Chien's mansion with Headman Fang and ten constables. The womenfolk and the servants will remain confined to their quarters until further orders. You will check with the steward all valuables, place them in the strong room and seal the door. Headman Fang will make a search for his son and his eldest daughter, White Orchid.

"Ma Joong and Chiao Tai will make the rounds of the four city gates and verify whether Corporal Ling has duly posted his men and whether the forty henchmen of Chien who did not belong to the army have been put under lock and key in the gate towers. If everything is found in order, you will inform Ling that he is re-enlisted without loss of rank.

"Take your time and find out the antecedents of the ex-soldiers. Those who did not desert in battle or flee because of some major offense can be re-enlisted. This afternoon I shall draw up a report to the Board of Military Affairs to have their position regularized. At the same time I shall apply for a hundred soldiers to be sent out here."

Having thus spoken the judge ordered Sergeant Hoong to bring him a large pot of hot tea.

It did not take Tao Gan long to round up the wardens. They did not look very happy when they were shown into Judge Dee's private office.

It was they who, being recruited locally to act as links between the tribunal and the population, were responsible for the reporting of births, deaths and marriages and many other affairs which had been completely neglected under Chien Mow's rule. As members of the district administration, the wardens should have been present in the tribunal to bid welcome to the new magistrate. They expected a severe scolding.

That was exactly what they got, and with a vengeance. They emerged from Judge Dee's office trembling and pale and scurried away as fast as they could.

Judge Dee then walked over to the large reception hall of the tribunal and there received the masters of the guilds of the goldsmiths, the carpenters, the rice dealers and the silk merchants. The judge politely inquired their names, and the steward served refreshments.

The guildmasters congratulated the judge on the speedy arrest of Chien Mow and expressed their joy that now the district would return to normal. They were somewhat disturbed, however, over such a large number of soldiers occupying the city.

Judge Dee raised his eyebrows.

"The only soldiers here," he remarked, "are a few dozen deserters whom I have re-enlisted for guard duty."

The master of the goldsmiths' guild gave his colleagues a knowing look. He said with a smile: "We fully understand, Your Honour, that your lips are sealed. But the guards of the northern gate said that when Your Honour entered the city they were nearly trampled down by a squadron of cavalry. Last night a goldsmith saw a column of two hundred soldiers march through the main street with straw wrapped around their boots."

The master of the guild of silk merchants added: "My own cousin saw a convoy of ten horsecarts pass by, loaded with army supplies. However, Your Honour can fully trust us. We realize that a military inspection tour of the border districts must be kept secret lest the barbarian hordes across the river hear about it. The news shall not spread outside the city. Would it not be better, however, if the Commander did not display his flag over the tribunal? If the spies of the barbarian tribes see this flag, they will know that the army is here."

"That flag," Judge Dee answered, "I put up myself. It only means that I, the magistrate, have temporarily placed this district under martial law, as I am entitled to do in a state of emergency."

The guildmasters smiled and bowed deeply.

"We perfectly understand Your Honour's discretion!" the eldest said gravely.

Judge Dee did not comment further on this but broached quite a different subject. He requested the masters to send him that very afternoon three elderly men qualified and willing to serve in the tribunal respectively as senior scribe, head of the archives, and warden of the jail; and a dozen dependable youngsters to serve as clerks. The judge further requested them to lend the tribunal two thousand silver pieces to pay for elementary repairs of the court hall and for the salaries of the personnel; this sum would be paid back as soon as the case against Chien Mow had been concluded and his property confiscated.

The guildmasters readily agreed.

Finally Judge Dee informed them that the next morning he would open the case against Chien Mow, and asked them to make this fact known throughout the district.

When the guildmasters had taken their leave, the judge went back to his private office. There he found Headman Fang waiting for him together with a good-looking young man.

Both knelt before the judge. The young man knocked his head on the floor three times in succession.

"Your Honour," Fang said, "allow me to present my son. He was kidnapped by Chien's henchmen and compelled to work as a servant in his mansion."

"He shall serve under you as a constable," Judge Dee said. "Did you find your eldest daughter?"

"Alas," Fang replied with a sigh, "my son has never seen her and the most diligent search did not produce any trace of her. I closely questioned the steward of Chien's mansion. He remembers that at one time Chien Mow expressed the desire to acquire White Orchid for his harem, but maintains that his master dropped the matter when I refused to sell my daughter. I do not know what to think."

Judge Dee said pensively: "It is your assumption that Chien Mow kidnapped her, and you may yet be proved right. It is not unusual for a man like Chien to keep a secret love nest outside his mansion. On the other hand we must also reckon with the possibility that he had really nothing to do with her disappearance. I shall question Chien on this subject and institute a thorough investigation. Do not give up hope too soon!"

As the judge was speaking, Ma Joong and Chiao Tai came in.

They reported that Corporal Ling had executed his orders to the letter. Ten soldiers were stationed at each of the four city gates and a dozen of Chien's men were locked in each gate tower. The number of prisoners had been increased by five ex-soldiers who had deserted to escape punishment for real crimes. Corporal Ling had demoted to water carriers the loafers who had been guarding the gates before.

Ma Joong added that Ling had all the qualities of a good military man; he had deserted because of a quarrel with a dishonest captain and was overjoyed at once more being in the regular army.

Judge Dee nodded and said: "I shall propose that Ling is made a sergeant. For the time being we shall leave the forty men stationed at the gates. If their morale remains good, I propose to quarter them all together in Chien's mansion. In course of time I shall designate that as garrison headquarters. You, Chiao Tai, will remain commanding officer of those forty men and the twenty we trained here in the tribunal, till the soldiers I shall send for have arrived."

Having thus spoken the judge dismissed his lieutenants. He took up his brush and drafted an urgent letter to the far-away prefect describing the events of the past two days. The judge added a list of the men he wanted re-enlisted and a proposal that Corporal Ling be promoted to sergeant. Finally he requested that one hundred soldiers be sent to Lan-fang as permanent garrison.

As he was sealing this letter, the headman came in. He reported that a Mrs. Yoo had come to see the judge. She was waiting at the gate of the tribunal.

Judge Dee looked pleased.

"Bring her in!" he ordered.

As the headman was showing the lady into Judge Dee's office, the judge gave her an appraising look. She was about thirty years old and still a remarkably beautiful woman. She was not made up and was very simply dressed.

Kneeling before the desk she said timidly: "Mrs. Yoo *née* Mei respectfully greets Your Honour."

"We are not in the tribunal, Madam," Judge Dee said kindly, "so there is no need for formality. Please rise and be seated!"

Mrs. Yoo rose slowly and sat down on one of the footstools in front of the desk. She hesitated to speak.

"I have always," Judge Dee said, "greatly admired your late husband, Governor Yoo. I consider him one of the greatest statesmen of our age."

Mrs. Yoo bowed. She said in a low voice: "He was a great and a good man, Your Honour. I would not have dared to intrude upon Your Honour's valuable time were it not that it is my duty to execute my late husband's instructions."

Judge Dee leaned forward.

"Pray proceed, Madam!" he said intently.

Mrs. Yoo put her hand in her sleeve and took out an oblong package. She rose and placed it on the desk.

"On his deathbed," she began, "the Governor handed me this scroll picture which he had painted himself. He said that this was the inheritance he bequeathed to me and my son. The rest was to go to my stepson, Yoo Kee.

"Upon that the Governor started coughing and Yoo Kee left the room to order a new bowl of medicine. As soon as he had gone, the Governor suddenly said to me: 'Should you ever be in difficulties, you will take this picture to the tribunal and show it to the magistrate. If he does not understand its meaning, you will show it to his successor, until in due time a wise judge shall discover its secret.' Then Yoo Kee came in. The Governor looked at the three of us. He laid his emaciated hand on the head of my small son, smiled and passed away without saying another word."

Mrs. Yoo broke down sobbing.

Judge Dee waited until she was calmer. Then he said: "Every detail of that last day is important, Madam. Tell me what happened after that."

"My stepson, Yoo Kee," Mrs. Yoo continued, "took the picture from my hands, saying that he would keep it for me. He was not unkind then. It was only after the funeral that he changed. He told me harshly to leave the house immediately with my son. He accused me of having deceived his father and forbade me and my son ever to set a foot in his house again. Then he threw this scroll picture on the table and said with a sneer that I was welcome to my inheritance."

GOVERNOR YOO'S PICTURE

roked his beard.

overnor was a man of great wisdom, Madam, there must be
meaning in this picture. I shall study it carefully. It is my duty
to warn you, however, that I am keeping an open mind about its secret
message. It may either be in your favour or prove that you have been
guilty of the crime of adultery. In either case I shall take appropriate steps
and justice shall take its course. I leave it to you, Madam, to decide
whether you want me to keep this scroll or whether you prefer to take it
back with you and withdraw your claim."

Mrs. Yoo rose. She said with quiet dignity: "I beg Your Honour to keep
this scroll for study. I pray to Merciful Heaven that it will grant you to
solve its riddle."

Then she bowed deeply and took her leave.

Sergeant Hoong and Tao Gan had been waiting outside in the corridor.
Now they came in and greeted the judge. Tao Gan was carrying an armful
of document rolls.

The sergeant reported that they had inventoried Chien Mow's property.
They had found several hundred gold bars and a large amount of silver.
This money they had locked in the strongroom together with a number of
utensils of solid gold. The women and the house servants had been confined to the third courtyard. Six constables of the tribunal and ten soldiers
had been quartered in the second courtyard under supervision of Chiao
Tai, to guard the mansion.

With a contented smile Tao Gan placed his load of documents on the
desk. He said: "These, Your Honour, are the inventories we made, and all
the deeds and accounts that we found in Chien Mow's strongroom."

Judge Dee leaned back in his chair and looked at the pile with undis-
guised distaste.

"The disentangling of Chien Mow's affairs," he said, "will be a long and
tedious task. I shall entrust this work to you, Sergeant, and Tao Gan. I
don't expect that this material will contain anything more important than
evidence of unlawful appropriation of land and houses and petty extortion. The guildmasters have promised to send me suitable persons this
afternoon to take up the duties of the clerical personnel, including an
archivist. They should be useful in working out these problems."

"They are waiting in the main courtyard, Your Honour," Sergeant
Hoong remarked.

"Well," the judge said, "you and Tao Gan will instruct them in their
duties. Tonight the archivist will assist you in sorting out these documents.
I leave it to you to draft for me an extensive report with suggestions as to
how Chien Mow's affairs should be dealt with. You will keep apart, however, any document that has a bearing on the murder of my late colleague,
Magistrate Pan.

"I myself wish to concentrate on this problem here."

As he spoke, the judge took up the package that Mrs. Yoo had left with him. He unwrapped it and unrolled the scroll picture on his desk.

Sergeant Hoong and Tao Gan stepped forward and together with the judge they looked intently at the picture.

It was a medium-sized picture painted on silk, representing an imaginary mountain landscape done in full colours. White clouds drifted among the cliffs. Here and there houses appeared amidst clusters of trees, and on the right a mountain river flowed down. There was not a single human figure.

On top of the picture the Governor had written the title in archaic characters. It read:

BOWERS OF EMPTY ILLUSION

The Governor had not signed this inscription; there was only an impression of his seal in vermilion.

The picture was mounted on all four sides with borders of heavy brocade. Below there had been added a wooden roller and on top a thin stave with a suspension loop. This is the usual mounting of scroll pictures meant to be hung on the wall.

Sergeant Hoong pensively pulled his beard.

"The title would seem to suggest," he remarked, "that this picture represents some Taoist paradise or an abode of immortals."

Judge Dee nodded.

"This picture," he said, "requires careful study. Hang it on the wall opposite my desk so that I can look at it whenever I like!"

When Tao Gan had suspended the picture on the wall between the door and the window, the judge rose and walked over to the main courtyard.

He saw that the prospective members of his clerical staff were decent looking men. The judge addressed them briefly, and concluded: "My two lieutenants will now instruct you. Listen carefully, for tomorrow you will have to start your duties when I hold the morning session of this tribunal."

Seventh Chapter

THREE ROGUISH MONKS RECEIVE THEIR JUST PUNISHMENT;
A CANDIDATE OF LITERATURE REPORTS A CRUEL MURDER

The next morning, before the break of dawn, the citizens of Lan-fang began trooping to the tribunal. When the hour of the morning session approached, a dense crowd filled the street in front of the main gate.

The large bronze gong was sounded three times. The constables threw the double gate open and the crowd poured into the court hall. Soon there was not a single standing place left.

The constables ranged themselves in two rows to right and left in front of the dais.

Then the screen at the back was pulled aside. Judge Dee ascended the dais clad in full ceremonial dress. As he seated himself behind the bench, his four lieutenants took up their position by his side. The senior scribe and his assistants stood next to the bench, now covered with a new cloth of scarlet silk.

A deep silence reigned as the judge took up his vermilion brush and filled out a slip for the warden of the jail.

Headman Fang took it respectfully with two hands and left the court hall with two constables.

They came back with the elder of Chien's two counsellors. He knelt in front of the dais.

Judge Dee ordered: "State your name and profession!"

"This insignificant person," the man spoke humbly, "is called Liu Wan-fang. Until ten years ago I was the house steward of Chien Mow's late father. After the latter's death Chien kept me as his adviser. I assure Your Honour that I have always on every possible occasion urged Chien to mend his ways!"

The judge observed with a cold smile: "I can say only that your attempts had a remarkably small result! The tribunal is collecting and sifting the evidence of your master's crimes; doubtless this material will prove your complicity in many of Chien's misdeeds. However, at present I am not concerned with the minor crimes you and your master committed. For the present I wish to confine myself to the major issues. Speak up, what murders did Chien Mow commit?"

Liu answered: "Your Honour, it is true that my master appropriated unlawfully people's land and houses and he often had persons severely beaten up. But to the best of my knowledge Chien never wilfully killed anyone."

"Liar!" Judge Dee shouted. "What about Magistrate Pan who was dastardly murdered here?"

"That murder," Liu replied, "surprised my master as much as myself!"

The judge shot him an incredulous stare.

"Of course we knew," Liu continued hurriedly "that His Excellency Pan was evolving plans to oust my master from his position. Since Judge Pan had no one with him but one assistant, my master did not act for a few days. He wished to wait and see what course of action Judge Pan would take. Then one morning two of our men came running to our mansion. They reported that Judge Pan's body had been found on the river bank.

"My master was greatly vexed because he knew that people would say that he was responsible for this murder. He hurriedly drew up a false report to the prefect stating that Judge Pan and six militia had ventured across the river to apprehend a rebel Uigur chieftain, and that the judge had been slain in the ensuing fight. Six of Chien's men signed as witnesses, and . . ."

Judge Dee hit his gavel on the bench.

"I have never," he exclaimed angrily, "heard such a string of outrageous lies! Give that dogshead twenty-five lashes with the whip!"

Liu started to protest, but the headman promptly hit him in his face. The constables tore Liu's robe from his back, threw him on the floor, and the whip swished through the air.

The thin thong cut deeply into the flesh. Liu screamed desperately that he was telling the truth.

After the fifteenth blow the judge raised his hand. He knew that there was no reason for Liu to shield his fallen master and that Liu would realize that the testimony of the other prisoners would soon expose him if he tried to lie. Judge Dee wished to confuse him so that he would tell all he knew, reflecting that fifteen lashes with the whip was probably but a fraction of the punishment that this scoundrel deserved.

The headman gave Liu a cup of bitter tea. Then Judge Dee continued the interrogation.

"If what you say is true, why then did Chien Mow not try to discover the real murderer?"

"That," Liu replied, "was unnecessary since my master knew who had committed that foul deed."

Judge Dee raised his eyebrows.

"Your tale," he remarked dryly, "becomes increasingly absurd. If your master knew the murderer's identity, why did he not arrest him and forward him to the prefect? That would have gained Chien the confidence of the authorities."

Liu shook his head dejectedly.

"That question, Your Honour, can only be answered by Chien himself. Although my master consulted us in minor matters, he never told us one word about things of real importance. I know that in all major issues my master let himself be directed by a man whose identity we have never been able to guess."

"I thought," Judge Dee observed, "that Chien was perfectly capable of conducting his affairs himself. Why should he need to employ some mysterious adviser?"

"My master," Liu replied, "is a clever and brave man, expert in all martial arts. But after all, he was born and brought up in this small border town. What do we of Lan-fang know about the handling of a prefect and how to deal with the central authorities? It was always after a visit of the stranger that my master made one of the many clever moves that prevented the prefect from intervening in affairs here."

Judge Dee leaned forward in his chair. He asked curtly: "Who was that secret adviser?"

"For the last four years," Liu said, "my master used to receive regularly secret visits from him. Late at night my master would send me to the side gate of our mansion and inform the guards that he expected a guest who was to be conveyed immediately to his library. This visitor always came on foot, clad in a monk's cloak, with a black scarf wrapped round his head. None of us ever saw his face. My master used to be closeted with him for hours on end. Then he would depart as silently as he had come. My master never gave us any explanation of these visits. But they were always the prelude to some major undertaking.

"I am convinced that this man had Judge Pan murdered without my master's previous knowledge. He came that same night. He must have had a violent quarrel with my master; outside in the corridor we heard them shout at each other although we could not distinguish any words. After that interview my master was in a bad temper for several days."

The judge said impatiently: "I have heard enough of this mysterious tale. What about Chien's kidnapping the son and the eldest daughter of the blacksmith Fang?"

"It is about affairs such as these," Liu said, "that I and my colleagues can give Your Honour full particulars. Fang's son was indeed taken by Chien's men. The mansion was short of coolies and Chien sent out his henchmen to collect a few strong young men in the street. They brought in four. Three were later returned when their parents paid ransom. The blacksmith made trouble with the guards so Chien decided to keep his son to teach the blacksmith a lesson.

"As to the girl, I know that my master happened to see her when he passed her father's shop in his palanquin. He took a fancy to her and made an offer to buy her. When the blacksmith refused, my master soon forgot all about it. Then the blacksmith came to our mansion and accused us of having kidnapped her. My master was angry and sent his men to burn the blacksmith's house."

Judge Dee leaned back in his chair and slowly stroked his long beard. He reflected that Liu was evidently speaking the truth. His master had had nothing to do with the disappearance of Fang's eldest daughter. Quick measures should be taken to arrest Chien's secret adviser. If at least it was not too late for that already.

Then he ordered: "Tell me what happened after my arrival here two days ago!"

"One week ago," Liu replied, "Magistrate Kwang reported to my master Your Honour's scheduled arrival. He asked leave to depart early in the morning since he thought it awkward to meet Your Honour. My master agreed. He ordered that no one should take the slightest notice of Your Honour's arrival in order 'to show the new magistrate his place,' as he put it.

"My master then waited for the old jail warden to report. He failed to show up on the first day. He came the next evening and told my master that Your Honour was determined to attack him. He added that there were only three or four men in the tribunal but he described them as exceedingly fierce and rough men."

Here Tao Gan smiled proudly. It was not often that he heard such a flattering description of himself.

"My master," Liu continued, "ordered twenty of his men to enter the tribunal that very night, capture the magistrate and give all others a thorough beating. When Ling and five men came back with the alarming news that a regiment of the regular army had quietly occupied the city, my master was asleep and nobody dared to disturb him. Early yesterday morning I myself brought Ling to my master's bedroom. He ordered a small black flag to be hoisted immediately over the main gate and then rushed to the main hall. When we were consulting about what to do, Your Honour came with the officers and arrested us."

"What was the meaning of that black flag?" the judge inquired.

"We understand that that was the summons for the mysterious visitor. Every time the flag was hoisted, he used to come that same night."

Judge Dee gave a sign to the headman. Liu Wan-fang was led away.

Then the judge filled out another slip for the warden of the jail and handed it to the headman.

After a while Chien Mow was brought in and led before the dais.

A murmur rose from the crowd as they saw the man who had ruled them with an iron hand for the past eight years.

Chien certainly was an imposing figure. He was well over six feet tall. His broad shoulders and his thick neck showed his great strength.

He made no move to kneel. First Chien looked haughtily at the judge, then turned round and with a sneer surveyed the gaping crowd.

"Kneel before your magistrate, you insolent dog!" the headman barked.

Chien Mow grew purple with rage. Thick veins stood out like whipcords on his forehead. He opened his mouth to speak. Then suddenly a stream of blood gushed from his broken nose. He tottered on his feet for a moment, then collapsed on the floor in a heap.

At a sign from the judge the headman stooped down and wiped the blood off Chien's face. He was unconscious.

The headman sent a constable for a bucket of cold water. They loosened Chien's robe and bathed his forehead and breast. But all was in vain. Chien did not regain consciousness.

Judge Dee was greatly annoyed. He ordered the headman to recall Liu Wan-fang.

As soon as he was kneeling before the bench, the judge asked: "Was your master suffering from any disease?"

Liu looked in consternation at the prone figure of Chien. The constables were still trying to revive him.

Liu shook his head.

"Although my master has an extraordinarily strong body," he said, "he suffers from a chronic disease of the brain. He has been consulting doctors for years but no medicine has been of any avail. When he flew in a rage, he would often collapse like this and remain unconscious for several hours. The doctors said that the only way to cure him was to open his skull and let out the poisonous air inside. But no doctor in Lan-fang possessed that particular skill."

Liu Wan-fang was led away. Four constables carried the limp form of Chien Mow back to the jail.

"Let the warden report to me as soon as this man recovers!" Judge Dee ordered the headman.

The judge reflected that this collapse of Chien Mow was extremely unfortunate. It was of utmost importance to learn from Chien the identity of his mysterious visitor. Every hour's delay gave that shadowy figure in the background a better chance to make good his escape. The judge regretted deeply that he had failed to question Chien directly after his arrest. But who could have foreseen that he had this unknown accomplice?

With a sigh Judge Dee straightened himself in his chair. He hit his gavel on the bench. In a clear voice he spoke: "For eight years the criminal Chien Mow has usurped the privilege of our Imperial Government. From now on law and order are re-established in Lan-fang. The good will be protected, the wicked relentlessly persecuted and punished according to the laws of the land.

"The criminal Chien Mow has been guilty of sedition and shall receive his just punishment. In addition to the crime of sedition he has committed a number of other criminal acts. Everyone who has a complaint against Chien Mow shall file this with the tribunal. Every case shall be investigated and compensation given wherever possible. It is my duty to warn you that the settling of all those cases will take time. You can rest assured, however, that in due time your wrongs will be righted and justice done."

The crowd of spectators burst out in loud cheers. It took the constables some time before order was restored in the court hall.

In a corner three Buddhist monks had not taken part in the general excitement. They stood huddled together in a whispered consultation.

Now they pressed forward through the crowd, shouting at the top of their voices that they were suffering under a terrible wrong.

As they approached the dais Judge Dee noticed that none of the three looked very prepossessing. They had coarse, sensuous faces and shifty eyes.

When they were kneeling in front of the dais Judge Dee ordered: "Let the eldest of you state his name and his complaint!"

"Your Honour," the monk in the middle spoke, "this ignorant monk is called 'Pillar of the Doctrine.' I live with my two colleagues here in a small temple in the southern quarter of this town. We pass our days in devout prayer and self-examination.

"Our poor temple has but one valuable possession, to wit a golden statue of our Gracious Lady Kwan Yin, Amen! Two months ago that villain Chien Mow came to our temple and took the holy statue away. In the Nether World he will be boiled in oil for this awful sacrilege. In the meantime, however, we humbly pray Your Honour to have the holy treasure returned to us or, should that scoundrel have had it melted, to grant us compensation in gold or silver!"

Having thus spoken the monk knocked his head three times on the floor.

Judge Dee slowly caressed his side whiskers. After a while he asked in a conversational tone: "Since this statue is the only treasure your temple possesses, I suppose that you looked after it with due care and devotion?"

"Indeed, Your Honour," the monk answered hurriedly, "every morning I personally dusted it with a silk whisk, reciting prayers all the while!"

"I trust," the judge continued, "that your two colleagues were equally diligent in serving the goddess?"

"This insignificant person," the monk on the right said, "has for several years every morning and night burned incense in front of our Gracious Lady, and reverently contemplated her merciful features, Amen!"

"This ignorant monk," the third added, "every day spent enraptured hours in front of our Gracious Lady, Amen!"

Judge Dee nodded with a satisfied smile. Turning to the senior scribe he said curtly: "Give each of the complainants a piece of charcoal and a sheet of white paper!"

As these implements were handed to the astonished monks the judge ordered: "You there on the left walk to the left side of the dais. The monk on the right goes to stand on the right. You, Pillar of the Doctrine, turn round and face the audience!"

The monks shuffled to the positions indicated.

Then Judge Dee said peremptorily: "Kneel and draw me a sketch of that golden statue!"

A murmur rose from the crowd.

"Silence!" shouted the constables.

The three monks were quite some time over their work. From time to time they scratched their bald heads. They perspired freely.

At last Judge Dee ordered Headman Fang: "Show me those sketches!"

When the judge had seen the three sheets, he pushed them disdainfully over the edge of the bench.

As they fluttered to the floor everyone could see that they were completely different. One showed the goddess with four arms and three faces, the second with eight arms, and the third was an attempt to depict her in the familiar two-armed form with a small child by her side.

Judge Dee called out in a thunderous voice: "These scoundrels filed a false accusation! Give them twenty blows with the bamboo!"

The constables threw the three monks with their faces on the floor. They turned up their robes and pulled down their loincloths. The bamboo sticks swished through the air.

The monks screamed and cursed as the bamboo tore their flesh. But the constables did not release them until they had had the full number of strokes.

They could not walk. A few helpful spectators dragged them away.

The judge announced: "Before these crooked monks came forward, I was just going to issue a warning that no one should try to gain illegal profit by filing trumped-up claims against Chien Mow. Let the fate of these three monks be a warning example!

"I wish to add that since this morning this district is no longer under martial law."

Having thus spoken Judge Dee turned to Sergeant Hoong and whispered something. The sergeant hurriedly left the hall.

THREE MONKS REPORT A THEFT TO THE TRIBUNAL

As he came back he shook his head.

"Order the warden of the jail," the judge said in a low voice, "to call me as soon as Chien Mow regains consciousness, even if it should be in the middle of the night!"

Then Judge Dee lifted his gavel. He was about to close the session when he noticed a commotion at the entrance of the court hall.

A young man was making frantic efforts to push through the packed crowd.

The judge ordered two constables to lead the newcomer before him.

As he sank panting to his knees before the dais, Judge Dee recognized Candidate Ding, the young man with whom he had drunk tea two days before.

"Your Honour!" Candidate Ding cried out, "that fiend Woo has foully murdered my old father!"

Eighth Chapter

AN OLD GENERAL IS MURDERED IN HIS OWN LIBRARY; JUDGE DEE GOES TO VISIT THE SCENE OF THE CRIME

Judge Dee leaned back in his chair.

He slowly folded his hands in his wide sleeves and said: "State when and how the murder was discovered!"

"Last night," Candidate Ding began, "we celebrated my father's six-tieth birthday. The entire family had gathered round the festive dish in the main hall of our mansion and everyone was in high spirits. It was near midnight when my father rose and left the table. He said he would retire to his library and on this auspicious day write the preface to his history of the border wars. I myself conducted him to the door of the library. I knelt and wished him good night. My father closed the door and I heard him push the crossbar in its place.

"Alas, that was the last time I saw my revered father alive. This morn-ing our steward knocked on the library door to apprise my father that breakfast was ready. When he received no answer despite repeated knock-ing, the steward called me. Fearing that my father had fallen ill during the night, we forced the door by beating in a panel with an axe.

"My father was lying slumped over his desk. I thought he was asleep and lightly touched his shoulder. Then I knew he was dead. I saw the hilt of a small dagger protruding from his throat.

"I rushed to this tribunal to report that Woo has dastardly done to death my defenseless old father. I beseech Your Honour to avenge this terrible wrong!"

Candidate Ding burst out sobbing and knocked his head on the floor several times.

Judge Dee remained silent for a while, his thick eyebrows knitted in a deep frown. Then he spoke: "Compose yourself, Candidate Ding! This tribunal shall open the investigation without delay. As soon as my suite is ready, I shall proceed to the scene of the crime. Rest assured that justice shall be done!"

The judge hit his gavel on the bench and announced the session closed. He rose and disappeared behind the screen of his private office.

The constables had some difficulty in clearing the court hall. The spectators were eagerly discussing the exciting events. Everyone was full of praise for the new magistrate and admired his shrewdness in exposing the fraud of the three greedy monks.

Corporal Ling had followed the proceedings accompanied by two young soldiers. As he tightened his belt to go he remarked: "That judge is an imposing magistrate, although he lacks, of course, the fine bearing of our two captains, Ma and Chiao. That can be acquired only by long years of military service."

One of the soldiers, a shrewd young fellow, asked: "The judge announced that the martial law has been ended. That means that the army units that were here left during the night. But I have not seen one single soldier except our own!"

The corporal gave him a condescending look. He said sternly: "Privates should not concern themselves with high strategy. Since, however, you are a keen youngster, I shall go so far as to disclose to you that the regiment passed through here on an inspection tour of the entire border. This is an important military secret. One word about it and I'll have your head chopped off!"

The soldier asked: "But how could they leave without anybody seeing them, Corporal?"

"Soldier," the corporal replied proudly, "nothing is impossible for our Imperial army! Did I never tell you about the crossing of the Yellow River? There was no bridge or ferry, and our General wished to cross. So two thousand of us jumped in the water holding each other's hands so as to form two rows. One thousand soldiers stood themselves in between holding their shields over their heads. The General galloped on his horse over this iron bridge!"

The young soldier thought to himself that this was the most incredible story he had ever heard. But knowing the Corporal's short temper he said respectfully, "Yes, Sir!" They left the court hall together with the last spectators.

In the main courtyard the official palanquin of the judge had been put in readiness. Six constables were standing in front and six behind. Two soldiers were holding the horses of Sergeant Hoong and Tao Gan by the reins.

Judge Dee emerged from his office, still clad in his ceremonial dress. Sergeant Hoong assisted him to ascend the palanquin.

Then the sergeant and Tao Gan mounted their horses. The cortège moved out into the street. Two constables ran in front carrying long poles with placards bearing the inscription "The Tribunal of Lan-fang" in large letters. Two others beating copper hand-gongs headed the procession. They shouted: "Make way! Make way! His Excellency the Magistrate is approaching!"

The crowd stood respectfully aside. When they saw Judge Dee's palanquin they broke out in loud cheers, shouting, "Long live our Magistrate!"

Sergeant Hoong who was riding by the side of the judge's palanquin bent over to the window and remarked happily: "This is quite different from three days ago, Your Honour!"

Judge Dee smiled bleakly.

The Ding mansion proved to be an imposing building.

Young Ding came out into the first courtyard to welcome the judge. As Judge Dee descended from his palanquin, an old man with a shaggy grey beard came forward and presented himself as the coroner. In daily life he was the proprietor of a well-known medicine shop.

Judge Dee announced that he would proceed directly to the scene of the murder. Headman Fang and six constables would go to the main hall and there set up a temporary tribunal and make the necessary preparations for the autopsy.

Candidate Ding invited the judge and his assistants to follow him.

He led them along a winding corridor to the back courtyard. They saw a charming landscape garden with artificial rocks and a large goldfish pond in the middle. The doors of the main hall stood wide open. The servants were busy clearing away the furniture.

Candidate Ding opened a small door on the left and led them through a dark, covered corridor to a small yard eight feet square, enclosed on three sides by a high wall. The wall opposite showed a narrow door of solid wood. One panel had been battered in. Young Ding pushed this door open and stood aside to let the judge pass.

A smell of stale candles hung in the air.

Judge Dee stepped over the threshold and looked around.

It was a fairly large room of octagonal shape. High up on the wall there were four small windows with panes of coloured glass that filled the room with a soft, diffused light. Above the windows there were two grated openings, each about two feet square. This was the only ventilation; except for the door through which they had entered there were no other openings in the wall.

A spare figure clad in a house robe of dark green brocade was slumped over the huge writing desk of carved ebony standing in the centre of the room, facing the door. The head leaned on the crooked left arm, the right hand was stretched out on the desk still holding a writing brush of red lacquer. A small skull cap of black silk had dropped to the floor exposing the victim's long grey hair.

The desk showed the usual array of writing implements. A blue porcelain vase with wilted flowers stood on a corner. On either side of the dead man there stood a copper candle stick; the candles had burned down entirely.

Judge Dee looked at the walls covered with bookshelves as high as a man could reach. He said to Tao Gan: "Examine those walls for a secret panel. Inspect the windows and those openings there!"

As Tao Gan took off his outer robe preparatory to climbing on the bookshelves, the judge ordered the coroner to inspect the body.

The coroner felt the shoulders and arms. Then he tried to lift the head. The body had grown stiff. He had to turn it over backwards in the armchair in order to expose the dead man's face.

The unseeing eyes of the old general stared at the ceiling. He had a lean, wrinkled face, frozen in an expression of surprise. From his scraggy throat there emerged an inch of a thin blade, not thicker than half a finger. It had a curious hilt made of plain wood, not much thicker than the blade and only half an inch long.

Judge Dee folded his arms and looked down on the body. After a while he said to the coroner: "Pull that knife out!"

The coroner had difficulty in getting a hold on the diminutive hilt. When he had it between his thumb and forefinger, however, it came out easily. It had not penetrated deeper than about a quarter of an inch.

As the coroner carefully wrapped up the short weapon in a sheet of oil paper, he observed: "The blood has thickened and the body is entirely stiff. Death must have ensued late last night."

The judge nodded. He mused: "After the victim had barred the door, he took off his ceremonial robe and cap that are hanging there next to the door, and changed into his house dress. Then he sat down behind the desk, rubbed ink and moistened his brush. The murderer must have struck shortly after, for the general had written only two lines when he was interrupted.

"The curious fact is that there cannot have been more than a few moments between his seeing the murderer and the dagger being stuck in his throat. He did not even lay down his brush."

"Your Honour," Tao Gan interrupted, "there is one fact which is still more curious. I cannot see how the murderer entered this room, let alone how he left it!"

Judge Dee raised his eyebrows.

"The only way by which a person can enter this room," Tao Gan continued, "is by that door. I have examined the walls, the small windows above the bookshelves and the grated openings. Finally I examined the door itself for a secret panel. But there are no hidden entrances of any description!"

Tugging at his moustache Judge Dee asked Candidate Ding: "Could the murderer not have slipped in shortly before or after your father entered here?"

Candidate Ding, who had been standing with a glazed stare by the door, now took hold of himself and replied: "Impossible, Your Honour! When my father came here, he unlocked the door. He stood for a moment in the entrance while I knelt. Our steward stood behind me. Then I rose and my father closed the door. No one could have entered then or earlier. My father always keeps that door locked and he had the only key."

Sergeant Hoong bent over to the judge and whispered in his ear: "We shall have to hear the steward, Your Honour. Yet even if we assume that the murderer somehow or other slipped in here unobserved, I cannot see how he went out again. This door was found barred on the inside!"

Judge Dee nodded. To Candidate Ding he said: "You assume that this murder was committed by Woo. Can you point out anything that proves that he was in this room?"

Ding slowly looked round. He sadly shook his head and said: "Woo is a clever man, Your Honour; he would not leave any traces. But I am convinced that a further investigation will bring to light clear proof of his guilt!"

"We shall have the body removed to the main hall," Judge Dee said. "You will now go there, Candidate Ding, and see that everything is ready for the autopsy!"

Ninth Chapter

JUDGE DEE PONDERS ALONE IN A DEAD MAN'S ROOM;
THE AUTOPSY BRINGS TO LIGHT THE CAUSE OF DEATH

As soon as Candidate Ding had left Judge Dee ordered Sergeant Hoong:
"Search the victim's clothes!"

The sergeant felt through the sleeves of the robe. He took from the
right sleeve a handkerchief and a small set consisting of toothpick and
earcleaner in a brocade cover. He found in the left sleeve a large key of
intricate design and a cardboard box. Then he felt in the dead man's girdle,
but found only another handkerchief.

Judge Dee opened the cardboard box. It contained nine crystallised
plums, neatly arranged in three rows of three. These sweet plums are a
delicacy for which Lan-fang is famous. The cover of the box bore a strip of
red paper with an inscription: "With respectful congratulations."

The judge sighed and put the box down on the desk. The coroner
removed the writing brush from the stiff fingers of the body. Two constables entered, and the dead General was carried away on a stretcher of
bamboo poles.

Judge Dee sat down in the victim's armchair.

"You will all go to the main hall," he ordered. "I shall stay here for a
while."

When the others had gone, the judge leaned back in the chair and
looked pensively at the bookshelves loaded with books and documents.
The only empty wall space was on both sides of the door. The door was
flanked by scroll paintings, and above it there hung a horizontal board
with the engraved inscription: "Studio of Self-examination." This evidently was the name that old General Ding had bestowed on his library.

Then Judge Dee looked at the set of writing materials neatly arranged
on the desk. The stone slab for rubbing the ink was a beautiful specimen,
and the bamboo brush holder by its side was delicately carved. Next to the
ink slab stood a red porcelain water container for moistening it. It was
marked in blue letters, "Studio of Self-examination"; evidently it had been
made specially for General Ding. A cake of ink was lying on a diminutive
stand of carved jade.

On the left the judge saw two bronze paper weights. They too bore an
engraved inscription: "The willow trees borrow their shape from the spring
breeze; the rippling waves derive their grace from the autumn moon." This

poetical couplet was signed: "The Recluse of the Bamboo Grove." Judge
Dee assumed that this was the pen name of one of the General's friends,
who had had these paper weights made for him.

He took up the brush that the dead man had been using. It was a very
elaborate one with a long tip of wolf's hair. The shaft was of carved red
lacquer and bore the inscription: "Reward of the Evening of Life." Alongside there was engraved in very small, elegant characters: "With respectful
congratulations on the completion of six cycles. 'The Abode of Tranquillity.' " Thus this brush was an anniversary gift from another friend.

The judge laid the brush down and had a closer look at the sheet of
paper the dead man had been writing on. There were only two lines,
written in a bold hand:

Preface. Historical records go back till the distant past. Many are the
illustrious men who have preserved the events of former dynasties for
posterity.

Judge Dee reflected that this was a complete sentence. Thus the General had not been interrupted in the midst of his writing. Probably he had
been pondering over the next sentence when the murderer struck.

The judge took up once more the red lacquer brush and idly looked at
its intricate carved design of clouds and dragons. It struck him how quiet
this secluded library was. Not a sound from outside penetrated here.

He suddenly felt a vague fear assail him. He was sitting in the dead
man's chair, in exactly the same position as the General had been when he
died.

The judge quickly looked up. He noticed with a shock that the scroll
painting by the door was hanging askew. He felt a sudden panic. Was it
from a secret panel behind that scroll that the murderer had stepped into
the room and thrust his dagger into the General's throat? It flashed
through his mind that if that were so, he himself was now at the murderer's mercy. He stared fixedly at the scroll, expecting it to move aside
and reveal the menacing shape.

With an effort the judge mastered his emotion. He reasoned that Tao
Gan would never have overlooked so obvious a place for a secret door. Tao
Gan must have left the scroll hanging askew when he had examined the
wall behind it.

Judge Dee wiped the cold perspiration from his forehead. His fright had
passed, but he still could not rid himself of the uncanny feeling that he
was very close to the murderer.

He moistened the brush in the water jar and bent forward over the desk
to try how it wrote. He noticed that the candlestick on his right was in the
way. The judge was just going to push it aside when he suddenly arrested
his movement.

JUDGE DEE IN GENERAL DING'S LIBRARY

He leaned back in the armchair and looked pensively at the candle. After the murdered man had written down the first two lines, he had apparently paused a moment to draw the candle nearer. Not for seeing better what he was writing, for then he would have pushed the candle to the left. His eye must have fallen on something he wished to observe closely under the light. At that very moment the murderer had struck.

Judge Dee frowned. He put the writing brush down and took the candlestick in his hand. He scrutinized it carefully but could not discover anything extraordinary about it. He put it back where it had stood before.

The judge shook his head in doubt. Then he rose abruptly and left the library.

As he passed the two constables standing on guard in the corridor, he ordered them to watch the library closely and let no one come near it until the broken panel was repaired and the door sealed.

In the main hall everything had been put in readiness.

Judge Dee seated himself behind the temporary bench. On the floor in front, the General's body was lying stretched out on reed mats.

When Candidate Ding had duly testified that it was the body of his father, Judge Dee ordered the coroner to proceed with the autopsy.

The coroner carefully took off all the dead man's garments. The poor emaciated body now was lying there fully exposed.

Candidate Ding had covered his face with the sleeve of his robe. The scribes and the other court personnel looked on in silence.

The coroner squatted by its side and examined the body inch by inch. He paid special attention to all the vital spots and felt the skull. He broke open the mouth with a silver lamella and inspected the tongue and the throat.

Finally the coroner stood up and reported: "The victim was apparently in good health and without physical defects. On the arms and legs there appear discoloured spots the size of a copper cash. The tongue is covered with a thick grey film. The wound in the throat was not lethal. Death was caused by a virulent poison administered by means of the thin blade stuck in the victim's throat."

The audience gasped. Candidate Ding lowered his arm and looked at the body with a horrified expression.

The coroner unwrapped the dagger and placed it on the bench.

"Your Honour will please notice," he said, "that beside the dried blood, the point shows some alien substance. That is the poison."

Judge Dee took the small dagger up by its hilt. He scrutinized the dark brown stains on the point.

"Do you know," he asked the coroner, "what poison this is?"

The coroner shook his head. He said with a smile: "We have no means,

Your Honour, to determine the nature of a poison that is administered externally. Those used internally are well known to us and we are familiar with the symptoms they produce, but those used to poison daggers are very rare. I will only go as far as to say that the colour and shape of the spots on the body suggest that it consisted of the venom of some poisonous reptile."

The judge made no further comment. He entered the coroner's statement on an official form and ordered him to read it and affix his thumbmark to it.

Then Judge Dee spoke: "The body can now be dressed and encoffined. Bring the house steward before me!"

As the constables covered the body with a shroud and placed it on the stretcher, the house steward entered the hall and knelt before the bench.

Judge Dee addressed him: "You are responsible for the routine of this household. Tell me exactly what happened last night. Begin with the dinner party."

"The anniversary dinner for His Excellency," the steward began, "was held in this very hall. The General presided over the table here in the middle.

"Gathered round it were the General's Second, Third and Fourth Ladies, young master Ding and his wife, and two young cousins of the General's First Lady who died ten years ago. A hired band of musicians played on the terrace outside. They left two hours before the General retired.

"When the hour of midnight was approaching, the young master proposed a final toast. Then the General rose, saying that he would retire to his library. The young master accompanied the General. I followed behind with a lighted candle.

"The General unlocked the door. I stepped inside and lighted the two candles on the desk with the one I had in my hand. I can testify that the room was completely empty. When I stepped out again the young master was kneeling before the General and bidding him good night. He rose. The General put the key in his left sleeve, went inside and closed the door. Both the young master and I heard him push the crossbar in its place. This is the complete truth!"

The judge gave a sign to the senior scribe. He read out his notes to the steward's statement. The latter agreed that that was what he had said, and affixed his thumbmark.

Judge Dee dismissed the steward. He asked Candidate Ding: "What did you do after that?"

Candidate Ding looked uncomfortable and hesitated to speak.

"Answer my question!" the judge barked.

"As a matter of fact," Ding said reluctantly, "I got involved in a violent quarrel with my wife. I went straight to my own quarters and my wife accused me of not having shown her proper respect during dinner. She averred that I had made her lose face before the other ladies. I felt tired after the feast and did not say much in return. Sitting on the bed I drank a cup of tea while two maids helped my wife to undress. Then my wife complained of a headache and made one of the maids massage her shoulders for half an hour or so. Then we went to bed."

Judge Dee rolled up the paper where he had jotted down his own notes. He said in a casual voice: "I have found no evidence linking this crime with Woo."

"I beseech Your Honour," Candidate Ding cried, "to put the question to that murderer under torture! Then he will confess how he committed this foul crime!"

The judge rose and announced that the preliminary investigation was closed.

He walked back to the front courtyard without saying a word. As he ascended his palanquin, Candidate Ding bowed deeply.

Once back at the tribunal Judge Dee went straight to the jail. The warden informed him that Chien Mow was still unconscious.

The judge ordered him to have a physician called. He was to do all he could to revive Chien Mow. Then Judge Dee took Tao Gan and Sergeant Hoong to his private office.

As he sat down behind his desk, the judge took from his sleeve the murderer's dagger. He told the clerk to bring a pot of hot tea.

When they had drunk a cup, the judge leaned back in his chair. Slowly stroking his beard he said: "This is a most extraordinary murder. Apart from the motive and the murderer's identity we are faced with two practical problems. First, how did the murderer enter and leave the sealed room? Second, how did he manage to thrust this queer weapon into his victim's throat?

Sergeant Hoong shook his head in perplexity. Tao Gan looked intently at the small dagger. Letting the three long hairs sprouting from his left cheek glide through his fingers he said slowly: "For a moment, Your Honour, I thought that I had solved the problem. When I was roaming through the southern provinces, I heard people tell stories about the savages that live in the mountains; they hunt with long blow pipes. I thought that this small blade with its weird tubular handle might have been shot from such a blow pipe, and reasoned that the murderer could have aimed it from outside through the grates in the wall.

"Then, however, I found that the angle at which this weapon entered the victim's throat is wholly irreconcilable with this theory, unless the murderer had been sitting under the table! Moreover I found that right opposite the back-wall of the library there is another high, blind wall. Nobody could have placed a ladder there."

Judge Dee slowly sipped his tea. "I agree," he said after a while, "that the blow-pipe theory is untenable. Yet I also agree with your point that this dagger was not stuck directly in the victim's throat. The hilt is so small that even a child could not hold it.

"I further draw your attention to the unusual shape of the blade. It is concave and resembles a gouge rather than a dagger. In the present stage of our investigation I would not like to make even a guess at how it was used. You, Tao Gan, will fashion for me an exact replica of this dagger in wood, so that I can safely experiment with it. But be careful while handling this thing; Heaven knows what deadly poison was smeared on its tip!"

"It is clear, Your Honour," Sergeant Hoong observed, "that we must also investigate further the background of this murder. Shouldn't we summon Woo for an interrogation here?"

The judge nodded.

"I was just going to propose," he said, "that we go to visit Woo now. I always prefer to see a suspect in his own surroundings. I shall go there incognito and you, Sergeant, shall accompany me."

Judge Dee rose.

Suddenly the warden of the jail came bursting into the office.

"Your Honour!" he cried, "Chien Mow has regained consciousness. But I fear that he is dying!"

The judge hurriedly ran after him, followed by Sergeant Hoong and Tao Gan.

They found Chien Mow stretched out on the wooden couch in his cell. The warden had placed a piece of cloth dipped in cold water on his forehead. His eyes were closed and his breath came in gasps.

Judge Dee bent over him.

Chien opened his eyes and looked up at the judge.

"Chien Mow," Judge Dee asked intently, "who killed Magistrate Pan?"

Chien stared at the judge with burning eyes. He moved his lips but no sound came from his mouth. With a tremendous effort he finally brought out one indistinct sound. Then his voice trailed away.

Suddenly his large frame shook in a convulsive shudder. He closed his eyes and stretched his body as if to find a more comfortable position. Then he lay quite still.

Chien Mow was dead.

Sergeant Hoong exclaimed excitedly: "He started to say 'You . . .' but could not continue the sentence!"

Judge Dee straightened himself. He nodded slowly and said: "Chien

Mow died before he could give us the information we need so badly!"

Looking down on the still body he added in a forlorn voice: "Now we shall never know who murdered Magistrate Pan!"

Putting his hands in his wide sleeves the judge walked back to his private office.

Tenth Chapter

JUDGE DEE PAYS A VISIT TO AN ECCENTRIC YOUNG MAN;
HE PRESIDES OVER AN ARTISTIC MEETING IN THE TRIBUNAL

Judge Dee and Sergeant Hoong had some difficulty in locating Woo's dwelling place. They asked in several shops behind the Temple of the War God, but no one had heard of a man called Woo Feng.

Then the judge remembered that he lived over a wine shop called "Eternal Spring." This proved to be a well-known establishment, famous for the superior quality of its wines. A street urchin took them into a side alley where they saw a red cloth banner marked "Eternal Spring" fluttering in the wind.

The shop was open in front; a high counter separated it from the street. Along the walls inside, a number of large earthenware wine jars were standing on wooden shelves. Red labels pasted on their side proclaimed the excellent quality of the contents.

The proprietor, a pleasant looking round-faced man, stood behind the counter idly looking out in the street while picking his teeth.

The judge and Sergeant Hoong walked round the counter and sat down at the square table inside. Judge Dee ordered a small jar of good wine. As the proprietor was wiping the table, Judge Dee inquired how his business was doing.

The proprietor shrugged his shoulders.

"Nothing to boast of," he replied, "but fairly steady. And, as I always say, just enough is better than too little!"

"Have you no one to help you in the shop?" the judge asked.

The proprietor turned around to ladle some pickled vegetables from a jar in the corner. He put them in the platter on the table and said: "I could do with some help, but unfortunately there always goes a hungry mouth with two helping hands. No, I prefer to look after things myself. And what might you two gentlemen be doing in this town?"

"We are just passing through," the judge replied. "We are silk merchants from the capital."

"Well, well!" the other exclaimed, "then you must meet my lodger, a Mr. Woo Feng, who is also from the capital."

"Is this Mr. Woo a silk merchant too?" asked the sergeant.

"No," the proprietor answered. "He is a kind of painter. I don't claim to be a judge in these matters, but I have heard people say that he is quite good. And I would say that he is bound to be, for he is at it from morning till night!" Walking over to the stairway he called up: "Master Woo, here are two gentlemen with the latest news from the capital!"

A voice shouted from upstairs: "I can't leave my work just now. Let them come up!"

The wine merchant was visibly disappointed. The judge consoled him by leaving a generous tip on the table.

They climbed the wooden stairs.

The second floor consisted of one large room lighted by a row of broad lattice windows in front and at the back, pasted over with fine white paper.

A young man clad in outlandish garb was working on a picture representing the Black Judge of the Nether World. He wore a gaudy jacket and his head was covered by a high turban of coloured silk such as is worn by some barbarian tribes over the border.

The painter had spread the silk canvas out on the huge table that stood in the middle of the room. The wall space between the windows was covered entirely by a great number of finished pictures, provisionally mounted on paper scrolls. A bamboo couch stood against the back wall.

"Sit for a while on that couch, gentlemen!" the young man said without looking up from his work. "I am putting in some blue paint here and if I stop, the colour will not dry evenly."

Sergeant Hoong sat down on the couch. Judge Dee remained standing and looked with interest at the young man as he was deftly handling his brush. He noticed that the picture, though expertly drawn, showed a number of unfamiliar features, especially in the treatment of the folds in the dresses and of the faces of the persons represented. Looking round at the pictures hanging on the wall the judge found that all of them showed these same foreign features.

The young man added a last stroke, then straightened himself and started washing his brush in a porcelain bowl. As he did so, he gave the judge a penetrating look. Slowly moving the brush round in the bowl he said: "So Your Honour is the new magistrate. Since evidently you are here incognito, I shall not embarrass you with the usual formalities!"

Judge Dee was quite taken back by this sudden statement.

"What makes you think that I am a magistrate?" he asked.

The young man smiled condescendingly. He left the brush in the jar. Folding his arms he leaned back against the table so that he faced Judge Dee and remarked: "I fancy myself a portrait painter. Now you, Sir, are the very prototype of a judge. Pray observe this Infernal Judge on this picture here! You could have sat as the model for it, though I admit it is by no means a flattering portrait!"

The judge could not forbear smiling. He realized that it was no use to try to fool this clever young man. So he said: "You are not mistaken, I am indeed Dee Jen-djieh, the new magistrate of Lan-fang, and this is my lieutenant."

Woo nodded slowly. Looking straight at the judge he said: "Your name is well known in the capital, Sir. Now, to what am I indebted for the honour of this visit? I don't think you have come to arrest me. That job you would have left to your constables."

"What," Judge Dee inquired, "makes you think that you might be arrested?"

Woo pushed his turban back.

"Sir, please forgive me for skipping all the usual polite preliminaries. Let me save your time and mine. This morning the news spread that old General Ding had been murdered. That, by the way, is just what the hypocritical scoundrel deserved. Now that sneaking son of his has been passing the word around that I, the son of Commander Woo, who is known to be the General's arch-enemy, intended to kill him. Young Ding has been snooping in this neighbourhood for more than a month, trying to worm information about me out of the proprietor of the shop here, at the same time telling all kinds of slanderous tales.

"Doubtless young Ding has now accused me of having killed his father. An ordinary magistrate would have sent out his constables to arrest me immediately. But you, Sir, are known as a man of unusual perspicacity. So you thought you would first come around here yourself and see what I looked like."

Sergeant Hoong had been listening with mounting anger to this nonchalant statement. Now he jumped up exclaiming: "Your Honour, the insolence of this dogshead is unbearable!"

Judge Dee raised his hand. He said with a thin smile: "Mr. Woo and I understand each other perfectly, Sergeant! I for one find him rather refreshing!"

As the sergeant sat down again, the judge continued: "You are right, my friend. Now I shall be as direct as yourself: why did you, the son of a

JUDGE DEE IN WOO FENG'S STUDIO

well-known military commander in the Board of Military Affairs, settle down all alone in this out-of-the-way place?"

Woo looked round at his pictures on the wall.

"Five years ago," he replied, "I passed the examination for Junior Candidate. To the disappointment of my father I then resolved to break off my studies and devote myself to painting. I worked under two famous masters in the capital but was not satisfied with their style.

"Two years ago I happened to meet a monk who had come all the way from Khotan, the tributary kingdom in the far west. That man showed me his style of painting, full of life and exciting colours. I realized that our Chinese artists ought to study that style in order to renew our national art. I thought that I might become the pioneer and resolved to travel to Khotan myself."

"Personally," the judge remarked dryly, "I find our national art perfectly satisfactory and I fail to see what a barbarian foreign nation could ever teach us. But I don't pretend to be a connoisseur. Pray proceed!"

"So I wangled travelling funds from my good father," Woo went on. "He let me go in the hope that this was youthful extravagance, and that some day I would return as a sedate young official. Until two years ago the route to the western kingdoms led via Lan-fang; thus I came here. Then I found that this route had been abandoned for the northern one. Now the plains to the west of this town are inhabited only by roaming Uigur hordes, people without art or culture."

"That being so," Judge Dee interrupted him, "why did you not leave this district at once and travel north to continue your journey?"

The young man smiled.

"That, Sir, is not so easy to make you understand. You must know that I am a lazy man and much given to moods. Somehow or other I felt comfortable here and thought that I might as well stay on for a while and practise. Moreover I took a liking to this house. I am mighty fond of wine and it suits me to have my dealer right under the same roof. That man has an uncanny intuition for a good wine and his stock can compare with the best shops in the capital. So I just stayed on here."

The judge did not comment on this statement. He said: "Now I come to my second question. Where were you last night, say from the first to the third night-watch."

"Here!" the young man replied immediately.

"Have you witnesses who can testify to that?"

Woo sadly shook his head.

"No," he replied. "It so happened that I did not know that the General was going to be murdered last night!"

Judge Dee went to the stairway and shouted for the proprietor.

When his round face appeared at the bottom of the stairs the judge called out: "Just to settle a friendly argument. Did you notice whether Master Woo went out last night?"

The man scratched his head, then said with a grin: "I am sorry I can't oblige, Sir! Last night there was much coming and going here. I really could not say whether Master Woo went out or not!"

Judge Dee nodded. He stroked his beard for some time, then said: "Candidate Ding reported that you have hired men to spy on his mansion!"

Woo burst out laughing.

"What a ridiculous lie!" he exclaimed. "I studiously ignore that fake general. I would not spend one copper to know what he was doing!"

"What," the judge asked, "did your father accuse General Ding of?"

Woo's face grew serious.

"That old scoundrel," he said bitterly, "sacrificed the lives of a battalion of the Imperial army, eight hundred good men in all, to extricate himself from a difficult position. Every single man was hacked to pieces by the barbarians. General Ding would have been beheaded were it not for the fact that at that time there was widespread discontent among the troops. Therefore the authorities did not want the General's foul deed to become common knowledge. He was ordered to tender his resignation."

Judge Dee said nothing.

He walked along the walls and examined Woo's work. They were all pictures of Buddhist saints and deities. The goddess Kwan Yin was very well represented, sometimes alone, sometimes with a group of attendant deities.

The judge turned round.

"If I may end a frank conversation with a frank statement," he remarked, "allow me to observe that I don't think that your so-called new style is an improvement. Maybe one must get accustomed to it. You might give me one of those pictures so that I can study your work at leisure."

Woo gave the judge a doubtful look. After a moment of hesitation he took down a medium-size picture showing the goddess Kwan Yin accompanied by four other deities. He spread it out on the table and picked up his seal, an intricately carved small block of white jade. It stood on a diminutive blackwood stand. Woo pressed the seal on a vermilion seal pad and then stamped it in a corner of the picture. The impression showed a quaint, archaic form of the character Feng, his personal name. Then he rolled the picture up and presented it to the judge.

"Am I under arrest?" he asked.

"A feeling of guilt seems to weigh heavily on your mind," the judge remarked dryly. "No, you are not under arrest. But you will not leave this house until further notice. Good day, and thanks for the picture!"

Judge Dee gave a sign to Sergeant Hoong. They went down the stairway. Woo bowed his farewell. He did not bother to conduct them to the door.

As they were walking down the main street, Sergeant Hoong burst out: "That insolent yokel would talk quite differently if he was lying in the screws before Your Honour's dais!"

The judge smiled.

"Woo is an extremely clever young man," he commented, "but he has already made his first bad mistake!"

Tao Gan and Chiao Tai were waiting in the judge's private office.

They had spent the afternoon in Chien's mansion and collected evidence relating to a few cases of extortion. Tao Gan confirmed Liu Wanfang's statement in court that Chien Mow had personally directed most affairs; his two counsellors seemed to be just hangers-on who said "Yes!" to their master whenever required.

Judge Dee drank the cup of tea that Sergeant Hoong offered him.

Then he unrolled Woo's picture and said: "Let us now start our artistic studies! Tao Gan, hang this picture on the wall, next to Governor Yoo's landscape!"

The judge settled back in his armchair and looked for some time at the two paintings.

"These two pictures," he said at last, "contain the key to the Governor's last will, and to the murder of General Ding!"

Sergeant Hoong, Tao Gan and Chiao Tai turned their footstools around so that they faced the paintings.

Ma Joong came in. He looked astonished at this unusual scene.

"Sit down, Ma Joong!" the judge ordered, "and join this gathering of connoisseurs!"

Tao Gan rose and stood with his hands on his back in front of the Governor's landscape. After a while he turned round and shook his head.

"For a moment," he said, "I thought that some inscription in very small letters might be hidden among the leaves of the trees or in the outlines of the rocks. But I cannot discover as much as a single character!"

Judge Dee pensively tugged at his whiskers.

"Last night," he spoke, "I pondered over that landscape for several hours and early this morning I again scrutinized it inch by inch. I must confess that this painting baffles me."

Tao Gan stroked his ragged moustache. He asked: "Could it be, Your Honour, that a sheet of paper has been concealed at the back of the picture, within the lining?"

"I thought of that possibility too," the judge answered, "and therefore I examined the picture against a strong light. If a sheet of paper had been pasted within the lining, it should have shown."

"When I was living in Canton," Tao Gan said, "I learned the art of mounting pictures. Shall I remove the lining entirely and also investigate the space covered by the brocade frame? At the same time I could verify whether the wooden rollers at top and bottom of the scroll are solid; it is not unthinkable that the old Governor concealed a tightly rolled piece of paper inside."

"If thereafter you can restore the scroll to its original form," the judge answered, "by all means try. Although I must confess that such a hiding place seems rather crude to me and unworthy of the Governor's brilliant mind. But we cannot afford to pass over the slightest chance for solving this riddle.

"This Buddhist picture by our friend Woo is quite another proposition. It contains a definite clue."

Sergeant Hoong asked astonished: "How can that be, Your Honour? Woo selected that picture for you himself!"

Judge Dee smiled his thin smile.

"That is because Woo did not realize how he had betrayed himself," he answered. "Woo may have no high opinion of my artistic sense, but I saw something in his picture that he himself had overlooked."

Judge Dee sipped his tea. Then he ordered Ma Joong to call Headman Fang.

When Fang was standing in front of the desk, Judge Dee looked at him gravely for a while. Then he said kindly: "Your daughter Dark Orchid is doing well. My First Lady informs me that she is an industrious and intelligent worker."

The headman bowed deeply.

"I am rather reluctant," the judge continued, "to take your daughter from her present safe surroundings, all the more so since there is as yet no news about the fate of your eldest daughter, White Orchid. On the other hand, Dark Orchid is the most suitable person to gather information for me in the Ding household. With the General's impending funeral the house will be in great confusion and they will need extra servants. If Dark Orchid could get herself a position there as temporary maid, she could find out much inside information from the other servants. I do not wish to do anything, however, without the consent of you, her father."

"Your Honour," the headman answered quietly, "I and my family consider ourselves your slaves. Moreover my youngest daughter is an independent and enterprising girl. She would enjoy executing such an order."

Ma Joong had been shifting uneasily on his chair. Now he interrupted:

"Is that not rather a job for Tao Gan, Your Honour?"

The judge shot a shrewd glance at Ma Joong. He replied: "There is no better source of information on what is going on in a household than the tittle-tattle of the maids. Instruct your daughter, Headman, to go to the Ding mansion straight away!

"As to our friend Woo, I want a double watch on him. You, Ma Joong, will go there tonight as the open watcher. You should make it appear as if you are trying to remain unobserved, but in such a way that Woo will know that you are a man from the tribunal sent to watch him. You will give him every opportunity to leave the house unobserved. Put all your skill and experience in this job, Ma Joong. This Woo is an extraordinarily clever young fellow!

"Tao Gan will be the real watcher. He should take good care to remain hidden. As soon as Woo has eluded Ma Joong, Tao Gan will follow Woo secretly and find out where he goes and what he does. If he tries to leave the city, you can come out in the open and arrest him."

Tao Gan looked pleased. He said: "Ma Joong and I have practised this trick of the double watch before, Your Honour! I shall now first take the Governor's painting and moisten it so that the lining can soak loose during the night. Then I shall start out with Ma Joong."

When Tao Gan and Ma Joong had taken their leave, the judge consulted with Chiao Tai and Headman Fang about the affairs of the Chien mansion.

He decided that Chien Mow's wives and concubines could be sent back to their respective families. The house servants should be released with one month salary advanced by the tribunal. Only the steward was to be detained for further questioning.

Chiao Tai reported that he was very satisfied with the discipline of the soldiers. Every morning and afternoon he took them through a strenuous military drill. He added that they stood in deadly fear of Corporal Ling.

When the headman and Chiao Tai had left, Judge Dee leaned back in his armchair.

He reflected that after all these years of working together he really knew very little about Chiao Tai. He had been Ma Joong's companion in "the green woods," but about his earlier life the judge knew nothing. Judge Dee had heard Ma Joong's entire story, and several episodes of it even twice. But Chiao Tai had always been very reticent. He seemed to take so much pleasure in his military duties in Lan-fang that Judge Dee wondered whether Chiao Tai had not been originally a career officer. He promised himself that he would try to find out in the near future.

But there were many more pressing affairs. With a sigh the judge started to study the documents relating to Chien Mow's misdeeds that Tao Gan had placed on his desk.

Eleventh Chapter

TAO GAN HAS AN ADVENTURE IN AN OLD TEMPLE;
MA JOONG MEETS HIS MATCH IN A DRINKING BOUT

Ma Joong thought it unnecessary to disguise himself. He only changed the black cap that marked him as an officer of the tribunal for a pointed bonnet such as is worn by people of the working class. Tao Gan replaced his cap by a collapsible one of black, thin gauze.

Before leaving, the two held a brief consultation in the quarters of the guards.

"It is easy enough," Ma Joong remarked, "to make myself conspicuous and give Woo to understand that I am stationed there to watch that he does not leave his quarters. But we don't know how that bastard will react. What if he goes out and tries to shake me off on the way?"

Tao Gan shook his head.

"He won't do that," he replied. "The point is that Woo does not know what your instructions are. He won't dare to go out and risk your arresting him on the spot, for that would be construed by the tribunal as a suspicious move. No, my only worry is that Woo won't try to elude you at all and will decide to stay at home as ordered. But if he slips out, you can be sure that I'll pick him up!"

Then they left the tribunal. Ma Joong walked ahead and Tao Gan followed him at some distance.

Sergeant Hoong had explained the location to Ma Joong. He found the Eternal Spring wine shop without difficulty.

Its interior looked most inviting. The light of two coloured paper lanterns shone on the red labels of the wine jars. The proprietor was measuring a pint of wine. Two loafers were leaning on the counter in front, leisurely picking pieces of salted fish from a platter.

Ma Joong saw that opposite the shop stood a middle-class dwelling house. He went to stand on the raised porch with his back against the black-lacquered door.

On the second floor of the wine shop several candles had been lighted. Ma Joong saw a shadow move across the paper of the lattice windows. Apparently Woo was hard at work.

Ma Joong bent forward and looked up and down the dark street. There was no sign of Tao Gan. He folded his arms and prepared himself for a long wait.

When the two happy drinkers had finished their pint of wine, the door behind Ma Joong suddenly swung open. An elderly gentleman was shown out by the gatekeeper. As he saw Ma Joong he asked: "Did you wish to see me?"

"Not me!" said Ma Joong curtly. He turned round and leaned against the doorpost.

"Now listen!" the gentleman said angrily, "this happens to be my house. Since you admit that you have no business here, I would thank you to walk on!"

"This street," Ma Joong growled, "is public property. No one can prohibit me from standing here!"

"You make yourself scarce quickly, my man!" the gentleman called out, "or I shall call the nightwatch!"

"If you don't like me to stand here, you bastard," Ma Joong shouted, "you just try and push me!"

The two loafers had turned round to follow the altercation. Leaning their backs against the counter they contentedly folded their arms to watch the fight.

A window on the second floor was pushed open. Woo looked out and shouted encouragingly to no one in particular: "Hit him on the head!"

"Shall I call the other servants, Master?" the gatekeeper asked.

"Call all the bastards together!" Ma Joong barked. "I am ready for them!"

The gentleman, seeing his bellicose attitude, thought better of it.

"I won't have fisticuffs in front of my door," he snapped. "Let that yokel stand there till his bones rot!"

Then he walked away, muttering angrily.

The gatekeeper slammed the door shut. Ma Joong heard a crossbar being pushed into position.

Woo, disappointed, closed his window.

Ma Joong sauntered over to the wine shop. The two loafers hurriedly made room for him along the counter.

Ma Joong gave them a baleful look and said sourly: "I hope that you two don't belong to that pleasant household over there."

"No, we are from the next street," replied one. "That fellow who lives opposite is a schoolmaster, and always grumpy."

"We don't come here to recite our lessons," the other loafer added, "but for a snack and a drink at this hospitable counter!"

Ma Joong guffawed. He put a handful of coppers on the counter and called out to the proprietor: "One pint of the best!"

The proprietor came forward hurriedly. He filled the cups to the brim and placed a new platter with dried fish and salted vegetables in front of them. He asked cheerfully: "Where might you be coming from, stranger?"

Ma Joong drained his cup in one gulp and waited till the proprietor had refilled it. Then he said: "I am the coachman of Mr. Wang, the big tea dealer from the capital. We arrived here this afternoon with three carts of tea cakes to be sold over the border. The master gave me three good silver pieces and told me to go and amuse myself. I meant to find myself a handsome wench. But I must have come to the wrong quarter!"

"Yes, in that case you are surely a long way from your destination," the proprietor answered. "The barbarian beauties from over the border are located in the Northern Row, nearly an hour's walk from here. The Chinese ladies live in the Southern Row, beyond the lotus lake in the southeastern corner of the city." Then he added ingratiatingly: "But the women here won't seem any good to a refined gentleman from the capital like you. Now yours must be a very lively profession. Why don't you come in and tell us a few of your adventures on the road?"

As he spoke he pushed the coppers back to Ma Joong and said: "That first round was on the house!"

The two loafers, looking forward to a free drinking bout, were immediately full of enthusiasm.

"A hefty fellow like you," one said to Ma Joong, "certainly has knocked out many a dangerous robber in his day!"

Ma Joong let himself be persuaded. They entered the shop and sat down at the square table. Ma Joong chose the seat facing the stairs.

The proprietor joined them and soon the cups were passing round with amazing swiftness.

After Ma Joong had told a few hair-raising stories, he saw Woo coming down the stairs.

Woo stopped halfway and shot Ma Joong a penetrating look.

"Won't you join us, Master Woo?" the proprietor called out. "This gentleman tells the most remarkable stories!"

"I am busy just now," Woo replied, "but I shall come down later in the evening. See that there is something left for me!"

So speaking he went up again.

"That is my lodger, a jovial fellow," the proprietor remarked. "You will enjoy talking with him. Don't leave before he comes down!"

And he poured out another round.

In the mean time Tao Gan had been busy.

As soon as he had seen Ma Joong take up his position opposite the wine shop, Tao Gan entered a dark alley. He quickly took off his robe, and put it on again inside out.

Now this robe was specially made. Its outside was good brown silk and looked very dignified. But the lining consisted of rough hemp-cloth with dirty spots and several clumsy patches. Tao Gan gave a pat to his cap; it flattened out and became a bonnet such as is often worn by beggars.

In this disreputable attire he entered the narrow space that divided the row of houses in Woo's street from the backwalls of those in the next.

Between the walls it was very dark, the ground was covered with refuse. Tao Gan had to pick his way carefully. He halted when he thought that he was at the back of the wine shop. Tao Gan stood on his toes and found that he could just reach the top of the wall. He pulled himself up and looked over the wall.

The back of the shop itself was dark. On the floor above, however, all windows were lighted. The backyard was full of empty winejars neatly stacked in double rows. There was no doubt that this was the rear of Woo's house.

Tao Gan let himself down again. He rummaged about till he had found a broken wine jar. He rolled it to the foot of the wall. Standing on top of it he could place his elbows on the wall. He laid his chin on his arms and leisurely surveyed the situation.

A narrow balcony ran all along the rear of Woo's atelier. The painter had placed there a row of potted plants. Below there was the plastered backwall of the wine shop. A narrow door stood ajar. Next to it Tao Gan saw a small outhouse that he took to be the kitchen. He reflected that it would be easy for Woo to leave his room by climbing down from the balcony.

He waited patiently.

After about half an hour one of Woo's windows was slowly pushed open. Woo looked out.

Tao Gan did not move. He knew that he was invisible against the darkness behind him.

Woo stepped over the window sill. He walked as sure-footed as a cat along the narrow balcony till he was above the outhouse. Then he climbed over the balustrade and let himself down on the sloping roof. For a moment he crouched on the tiles, apparently looking for an empty space among the winejars below. Then he jumped down neatly between two stacks and quickly made for the narrow passage that separated the wine shop from the house next door.

Tao Gan left his observation post. He ran out of the alley as fast as he could. He nearly broke a leg when he stumbled over an old wooden box. When he turned the corner of the alley he collided with Woo.

Tao Gan uttered a low-class oath. But Woo hurried on without looking back, making for the main street.

Tao Gan followed him at some distance.

There was a large crowd about in the street and Tao Gan did not have to be careful to keep in the shadows. Woo was easy to follow because of his outlandish turban that bobbed over the black caps of the crowd.

Woo kept walking on in a southerly direction. Suddenly he turned into a side street.

Here there were fewer people about. Without stopping in his brisk walk, Tao Gan pulled up the button in the middle of his cap till it had become the pointed bonnet of a commoner. He took from his sleeve a bamboo tube about one foot long. This was one of Tao Gan's many clever devices. It was a trick tube that contained six others of decreasing size. He pulled it out and it became a bamboo staff. Tao Gan changed his gait into the more sedate walk of an elderly householder.

He walked on till he was quite near Woo.

The painter turned into another alley and Tao Gan walked on behind him. They were now in a quiet area, Tao Gan reflected that they could not be far from the eastern city wall. Woo seemed to be quite familiar with this neighbourhood. He entered a narrow side street that seemed completely deserted.

Tao Gan looked round the corner before he followed Woo. He saw that it was a blind street that ended in the archway of a small Buddhist temple. It had apparently been abandoned, for the wooden gate had been demolished and no light showed within. There was no one about.

Woo walked straight on and climbed the crumbling stone steps leading up to the archway. There he stood still and turned round. Tao Gan hastily drew his head back.

When he looked again, Woo had disappeared into the temple.

Tao Gan waited a while, then emerged in the open and calmly sauntered to the temple. Over the archway he could faintly see three characters composed of weather-beaten coloured tiles inlaid among the bricks. They read: "Hermitage of the Three Treasures."

Tao Gan went up the steps and entered.

The temple seemed to have been deserted many years ago. All the furniture was gone and the place where the altar had stood was empty. He saw nothing but bare stone walls. Here and there the roof had caved in and he could see stars in the evening sky.

Tao Gan explored its interior, walking on tiptoe. But there was no trace of Woo.

Finally he looked out of the back door. He hastily withdrew behind the doorpost.

There was a small walled-in garden with a fishpond in the middle. On its bank stood an old stone bench. Woo was sitting there alone.

He had cupped his chin in his hands and seemed to find the old pond of absorbing interest.

"This must be a secret trysting place!" Tao Gan said to himself.

He found a window niche where he could sit down and keep an eye on Woo, while at the same time he remained hidden to any newcomers.

Having established himself there Tao Gan folded his arms and closed his eyes, straining his ears for any sound. He did not dare to look at Woo too often for he knew that many people are sensitive to a hidden stare.

He sat there for quite some time. Nothing happened.

Woo occasionally would change his posture. Once or twice he picked up a few pebbles and amused himself by throwing them into the pond. Finally he rose and started pacing up and down the yard, apparently lost in deep thought.

Another half hour passed.

Then suddenly Woo made as if to leave.

Tao Gan shrank back in his niche, flattening himself against the damp stone wall.

Woo walked back home at a brisk pace, looking neither left nor right.

Returned to his own alley, he stood still on the corner and looked out. Evidently he wanted to see whether Ma Joong was out in the street. Then he swiftly walked on and disappeared into the narrow passage between the wine shop and its neighbour.

Tao Gan sighed resignedly and strolled back to the tribunal.

In the wine shop all were in high spirits.

After Ma Joong's fund of stories had become exhausted, the proprietor had told quite a number of his own. The two loafers were a grateful audience. They vigorously clapped their hands after every story and were fully prepared to keep this up for hours on end.

Finally Woo came downstairs and joined the party.

Ma Joong had drunk more rounds of wine than he cared to remember. But he had a tremendous capacity and his head was still clear. He thought that if he could make Woo drunk, he might elicit some useful information from him.

Thus he hailed Woo boisterously as a fellow-citizen of the capital, and offered him a toast.

That was the beginning of a drinking bout that was talked about in that quarter for many months afterwards.

Woo complained that he was far behind the others. He emptied half a jar of strong white liquor in a rice bowl, and drank it down in one gulp. The wine had as little effect on him as if it had been water.

Then he shared a pint with Ma Joong, and told a long but very amusing story.

Ma Joong began to notice the influence of the wine. He racked his brain and told a rowdy tale. With some difficulty he reached the end of his narration.

THE DRINKING BOUT IN THE "ETERNAL SPRING"
WINESHOP

Woo shouted his approval. He emptied three cups in rapid succession. Then he pushed his turban back from his forehead, placed his elbows on the table and started to tell a string of queer stories about events in the capital, pausing only to drink some more. This he did with great relish, always emptying his cup in one draught.

Ma Joong kept him faithful company. He thought vaguely that Woo was a very companionable man. He remembered that he wanted to ask him something, but could not think what it was. Ma Joong proposed another round.

The two loafers were the first to pass out. The proprietor had them carried home by some friends in the neighbourhood. Ma Joong concluded that he was getting very drunk. He started to tell a spicy story but somehow or other he got mixed up when he approached the end. Woo emptied another cup and told a ribald joke that made the proprietor howl with mirth. The point of the tale had escaped Ma Joong but he still thought it a remarkably funny one and laughed loudly. He drank another toast to Woo.

Woo's face had turned red and perspiration trickled down his brow. He took off his turban and threw it in a corner.

From that moment on the conversation was very confused. Ma Joong and Woo both talked at the same time. They paused only for clapping their hands and drinking more.

It was past midnight when Woo announced that he wanted to go to bed. He rose with difficulty from his chair and succeeded in reaching the bottom of the stairs, all the time haranguing Ma Joong about their eternal friendship.

As the proprietor helped Woo to climb up, Ma Joong reflected that the wine shop was a very pleasant and hospitable place. He quietly slid to the floor and immediately started to snore uproariously.

Twelfth Chapter

JUDGE DEE DISCUSSES THE SECRETS OF TWO PICTURES; A YOUNG GIRL DISCOVERS PASSIONATE LOVE LETTERS

The next morning when Tao Gan was crossing the main courtyard on his way to the judge's private office, he saw Ma Joong sitting hunched on a stone seat, his head in his hands.

Tao Gan stood still and looked for a moment at this silent figure. Then he asked: "What is wrong with you, my friend?"

Ma Joong made a vague gesture with his right hand. Without looking up he said in a hoarse voice: "Go away, brother, I am resting. Last night I had a few drinks with Woo. Since it had grown late I decided to stay overnight in that wine shop, hoping that I would learn more about Woo's activities. I walked back here half an hour ago."

Tao Gan gave him a doubtful look. Then he said impatiently: "Come along! You must hear my report to His Excellency and see what I have brought here!"

As he spoke, he showed Ma Joong a small package wrapped up in oil paper.

Ma Joong reluctantly rose from his seat. They left the courtyard and entered Judge Dee's private office.

The judge was sitting behind his desk absorbed in a document. Sergeant Hoong was sitting in a corner sipping his morning tea. Judge Dee looked up from his papers.

"Well, my friends," he said, "did our painter go out last night?"

Ma Joong rubbed his big hand over his forehead.

"Your Honour," he said unhappily, "my head feels as if it were full of stones. Tao Gan will be able to present our report!"

Judge Dee shot a searching look at Ma Joong's gaunt features. Then he turned to listen to Tao Gan.

Tao Gan related in detail how he had followed Woo to the "Hermitage of the Three Treasures," and about his curious behaviour there.

When he had finished, Judge Dee remained silent for a while, a deep frown furrowing his brow. Then he exclaimed: "So the girl did not turn up!"

Sergeant Hoong and Tao Gan looked astonished and even Ma Joong evinced some interest.

The judge took the picture that Woo had given him. He rose and unrolled it on the desk, placing a paper weight on either end.

Then Judge Dee took a few sheets of writing paper and covered the picture up in such a way that only the face of the goddess Kwan Yin was visible.

"Look carefully at this face!" he ordered.

Tao Gan and the sergeant rose. They bent their heads over the picture. Ma Joong was going to leave his footstool also but he sat down again quickly with a look of pain.

Tao Gan said slowly: "This certainly is an unusual face for a goddess, Your Honour! Buddhist female deities are always depicted with a serene, quite impersonal face. This, however, seems to be the portrait of a living young girl!"

Judge Dee looked pleased.

"That is exactly what it is!" he exclaimed. "Yesterday when I looked over Woo's pictures it struck me that all his paintings of Kwan Yin show the same, very human face.

"I concluded that Woo must be deeply in love with a certain girl. Her image is continually in his mind. Thus whenever he paints a female deity, he gives it the features of this girl, probably without realizing it himself. Since Woo undoubtedly is a great artist, this picture must be a good portrait of that mysterious girl. It shows a definite personality.

"I am convinced that this girl is the explanation why Woo did not leave Lan-fang. She may provide the clue that links him with the murder of General Ding!"

"It should not be too difficult to trace this girl," Sergeant Hoong observed. "We might have a look around in the neighbourhood of that Buddhist temple."

"That," Judge Dee said, "is a very good idea. All three of you will imprint this picture on your memory!"

Ma Joong rose with a groan and had a look at the picture, too.

He pressed his hands against his temples and closed his eyes.

"What ails our wine bibber?" Tao Gan inquired nastily.

Ma Joong opened his eyes.

"I am sure," he said slowly, "that I have met that girl once. Somehow or other her face is familiar to me. But try as I may, I cannot remember when and where I saw her!"

Judge Dee rolled the scroll up again.

"Well," he said, "when your head is clear it may come to your mind. Now what have you brought there, Tao Gan?"

Tao Gan opened the package with great care. It contained a wooden board with a small square sheet of paper pasted on its surface.

He put it in front of the judge saying: "Your Honour, please be careful!

The thin paper is still moist and will easily tear. Early this morning as I was peeling off the lining of the Governor's painting, I discovered this sheet pasted behind the lining of the brocade mounting. This is the testament of Governor Yoo!"

The judge bent forward over the small writing.

Then his face fell. He leaned back in his chair and angrily tugged at his whiskers.

Tao Gan shrugged his shoulders.

"Yes, Your Honour, appearances often prove deceptive. Mrs. Yoo has been trying to fool us."

The judge pushed the board over to Tao Gan.

"Read it aloud!" he ordered curtly.

Tao Gan read:

I, Yoo Shou-chien, feeling the end of my days drawing near, hereunder state my last will and testament.

Since my second wife Mei has been guilty of adultery and the son she has given birth to is not my flesh and blood, all my possessions shall go to my eldest son, Yoo Kee, who shall continue the tradition of our ancient house.

Signed and sealed: Yoo Shou-chien.

After a slight pause Tao Gan remarked: "Of course I compared the seal impressed on this document with the Governor's seal on the painting itself. They are perfectly identical."

A deep silence reigned.

Then Judge Dee leaned forward and crashed his fist on the table.

"Everything is completely wrong!" he exclaimed.

Tao Gan gave Sergeant Hoong a doubtful look. The sergeant imperceptibly shook his head. Ma Joong goggled at the judge.

Judge Dee said with a sigh: "I shall explain to you why I am certain that there is something fundamentally wrong here.

"I start from the premise that Yoo Shou-chien was a wise and far-sighted man. He fully realized that his eldest son Yoo Kee had a wicked character and that he was violently jealous of his young half-brother; until Yoo Shan was born, Yoo Kee had for years considered himself as the only heir. When the Governor's end drew near, his last thoughts were how to protect his young widow and his infant son against the wiles of Yoo Kee.

"The Governor knew that if he divided the property equally between his two sons, not to speak of disinheriting Yoo Kee, the latter would certainly harm his infant half-brother and perhaps even kill him to appropriate his part of the inheritance. Therefore the Governor made it appear as if he disinherited Yoo Shan."

Sergeant Hoong nodded and gave Tao Gan a significant look.

"At the same time," the judge went on, "he concealed in this picture the proof that half or the greater part of his property should go to Yoo Shan. This is evident from the curious formula which the old Governor employed when he expressed his last will. He said clearly that the scroll should go to Yoo Shan, and 'the rest' to Yoo Kee; he carefully refrained from defining this 'rest.'

"The Governor's idea was through this hidden testament to protect his infant son until he would have grown into a young man and could take possession of his inheritance. He hoped that after ten years or so a wise magistrate would discover the hidden message of the scroll and restore to Yoo Shan his rightful inheritance. It is for this reason that he instructed his widow to show the scroll to every new magistrate that would be appointed to this district."

"That instruction, Your Honour," Tao Gan interrupted, "may never have been given. We have only Mrs. Yoo's word for it. In my opinion this document proves clearly that Yoo Shan is an illegitimate child. The Governor was a kind and forbearing man. He wished to prevent Yoo Kee from avenging the wrong done to his father. At the same time he wished to make sure that in due time the truth could be established beyond doubt. This is why he concealed the document in this scroll. When a clever magistrate would have discovered it, he would be able to dismiss any claim that Mrs. Yoo might try to file against Yoo Kee."

The judge had listened carefully to this argument. He asked: "How then do you explain that Mrs. Yoo is so eager that the riddle of this scroll is solved?"

"Women," Tao Gan replied, "are liable to overrate the influence they have on the man who loves them. I am convinced that Mrs. Yoo hopes that the old Governor in his benevolence has concealed in the scroll a money draft or directions how to find a hidden sum of money, to compensate her for losing part of the property."

The judge shook his head.

"What you say," he remarked, "is quite logical, but it does not accord with the old Governor's character. I am convinced that this document here is a forgery produced by Yoo Kee. It is my theory that the Governor hid some unimportant document in this scroll in order to lead Yoo Kee on to a false trail. As I said before, this is too crude a device for Governor Yoo to have used for concealing something of real importance. Besides this false clue, the picture must contain a real message concealed in a much more ingenious manner.

"Since the Governor feared that Yoo Kee would suspect that this scroll contained something valuable and would have it destroyed, he inserted some document in the lining for Yoo Kee to find. Thus he made sure that Yoo Kee, having found that, would not search further for the real clue.

"Mrs. Yoo told me that Yoo Kee kept the scroll for over a week. That would have given him sufficient time for discovering the document. Whatever it was, he replaced it with this spurious testament, so that he would be safe no matter what Mrs. Yoo would do with the scroll."

Tao Gan nodded. He said: "I admit, Your Honour, that that is also a very attractive theory. But I still think that mine is the simpler one."

"It should not be too difficult," Sergeant Hoong remarked, "to find a specimen of Governor Yoo's handwriting. Unfortunately he used archaic script for his inscription on this landscape painting."

Judge Dee said pensively: "I had planned to visit Yoo Kee in any case. I shall go there this afternoon and try to secure a good specimen of the Governor's regular handwriting and of his signature. You will go there now with my namecard, Sergeant, and announce my visit."

The sergeant and his colleagues rose and took their leave.

As they were crossing the courtyard the sergeant said: "Ma Joong, what you need is a large pot of hot, bitter tea. Let us sit down in the guard house for a while. I would not like to leave the tribunal before we cheered you up a bit!"

Ma Joong agreed.

In the guard house they found Headman Fang sitting at the square table talking earnestly with his son. The latter rose hastily when he saw the three men enter and offered them seats.

They all sat down and the sergeant ordered the constable on duty to bring a pot of bitter tea.

After some desultory talk Headman Fang said: "When you people came in I was just discussing with my son where we should search for my eldest daughter."

Sergeant Hoong sipped his tea. Then he said slowly: "I don't wish to mention a subject that must be painful to you, Headman. Yet I feel that we should not ignore the possibility that White Orchid had a secret lover and eloped with him."

Fang shook his head emphatically.

"That girl," he said, "is quite different from my youngest daughter. Dark Orchid is headstrong; she has a very independent character. She has known exactly what she wanted ever since she was as high as my knee, and usually knew how to get it, too. Dark Orchid should have been born a boy. My eldest, on the contrary, was always quiet and obedient. She has a soft, pliable character. I can assure you that she never even thought of having a lover, let alone eloping with one!"

"That being so," Tao Gan remarked, "I fear that we must be prepared for the worst. Could not some low ruffian have kidnapped her and sold her to a brothel?"

Fang sadly nodded his head.

"Yes," he said with a sigh, "you are quite right. I, too, think that we should check the licensed quarters. You know that there are two of that kind in this town. One, called the Northern Row, is located in the north-west corner of the city wall. The girls there are mostly from over the border. That quarter prospered greatly during the time when the route to the west still led through Lan-fang. Now that Northern Row has fallen on bad times, it is a favourite haunt for the scum of this city.

"The other one, known as Southern Row, consists of high-class estab-lishments only. The girls there are all Chinese, and some are quite edu-cated. They are not unlike the courtesans and singing girls of the larger cities."

Tao Gan pulled at the three hairs on his left cheek.

"I would say," he observed, "that we should start with the Northern Row. I gather from what you say that the houses of the Southern Row would not dare to kidnap girls. High class establishments like those are always careful not to offend against the law; they buy their girls in the regular way."

Ma Joong laid his big hand on the headman's shoulder: "As soon as our judge has cleared up the murder of General Ding," he said, "I shall request that the job of locating your eldest daughter is entrusted to Tao Gan and me. If there is any man who can find her, it is this wily old trickster, especially when I am at hand to do the rough work for him!"

Fang thanked Ma Joong with tears in his eyes.

At that moment Dark Orchid entered the gate, demurely dressed as a housemaid.

"How do you like the work, my girl?" Ma Joong called out.

Dark Orchid ignored him completely. She bowed deeply to her father and said: "I would like to report to His Excellency, father. Would you kindly take me there?"

Fang rose and excused himself. Sergeant Hoong went out to transmit Judge Dee's message to Yoo Kee, and the headman crossed the courtyard followed by his daughter.

They found Judge Dee sitting alone in his office, his chin cupped in his hands. He was deep in thought.

As he looked up and saw Fang and his daughter, his face brightened. He acknowledged their bows with a friendly nod and then said eagerly: "Take your time, my child, and tell me all about your experiences in the Ding household!"

"There can be no doubt, Your Honour," Dark Orchid began, "that the old General was in great fear for his life. The maids in the Ding mansion told me that all the food had first to be fed to a dog in order to prove that it had not been poisoned. The front and side gates had to be kept locked day and night, which is a great nuisance for the servants as they have to unlock the door for every visitor or tradesman who comes to the house. The servants don't like working there. Everyone in his turn has been the object of the old General's suspicion, and closely questioned by the young master. They don't stay longer there than a few months."

"Describe the members of the household!" the judge ordered.

"The General's First Lady died some years ago and now the Second Lady directs the household. She is in continual fear lest the others shouldn't treat her with sufficient respect, and she is not an easy mistress to work for. The Third Lady is quite an uneducated person, fat and lazy, but not hard to please. The Fourth Lady is very young; the General acquired her here in Lan-fang. I suppose that she is of the kind that men find attractive. But while she was dressing this morning, I noticed that she has an ugly mole on her left breast. She spends the greater part of the day in front of her mirror, if she is not trying to wangle some money from the Second Lady.

"Young Master Ding lives with his wife in a small, separate courtyard. They have no children. She is not very good-looking and is a few years older than her husband. But they say that she is quite accomplished and has read many books. The young master has occasionally brought up the question of taking a second wife, but she would never allow it. He now tries to make up to the young maidservants, but without much success. Nobody likes to work in that household and the maids don't care whether they offend the young master or not.

"This morning when I was cleaning young Master Ding's room, I rummaged a bit in his private papers."

"That was not what I ordered you," the judge remarked dryly.

Fang gave his daughter an angry look.

Dark Orchid blushed and went on quickly: "I found in the back of a drawer a package of poems and letters written by young Master Ding. The literary style was too difficult for me, but I gathered from the few sentences I was able to understand that the contents are very peculiar. I brought the package with me to show to Your Honour."

As she spoke she put her slender hand in her sleeve and took out a bundle of papers. She handed them to the judge with a respectful bow.

Judge Dee shot a quizzical look at the indignant Fang, then rapidly glanced through the papers.

He put them down and said: "These poems speak of a forbidden love affair, and in such a passionate language that it is all to the good that you could not understand them. The letters are of similar content, and all signed, 'Your slave Ding.' Apparently young Ding wrote them to give vent to his passion, for they were apparently never sent to their destination."

"The young master would hardly have written such things for the blue-stocking that his wife is!" Dark Orchid remarked.

Her father soundly boxed her ears, shouting: "Don't you dare to speak if you are not asked to, you forward hussy!" Turning to the judge he added apologetically: "It is all because my good wife is not here to edu-cate her, Your Honour!"

Judge Dee smiled.

"When we are through with this murder case, Headman," he said, "I shall arrange a suitable marriage for your daughter. There is nothing better for a headstrong young girl than to settle down to a regular household routine."

Fang respectfully thanked the judge. Dark Orchid looked furious, but she did not dare to speak.

Tapping the package with his forefinger, Judge Dee said: "I shall have these copied out immediately. This afternoon you will put the originals back where you found them. You did not do badly, young woman! Keep your ears and eyes open, but be careful not to pry into closed drawers and cupboards. Report to me again tomorrow."

As Fang and his daughter took their leave, the judge had Tao Gan called in.

"I have here a collection of letters and poems," he said. "You will copy them out carefully and try to deduce from all these passionate effusions some clue as to the identity of the lady to whom they are addressed."

Tao Gan glanced the poems through. His eyebrows shot up.

Thirteenth Chapter

YOO KEE ENTERTAINS A DISTINGUISHED GUEST AT TEA;
JUDGE DEE DECIDES TO REVISIT THE GENERAL'S STUDIO

The judge went to Yoo Kee's mansion accompanied only by Sergeant Hoong and four constables.

As his palanquin was being carried over the ornamental marble bridge, he looked with appreciation at the nine-storied pagoda that rose up from the lotus lake on the left.

Then they turned west and followed the river till they came to the deserted southwest corner of the city.

Yoo Kee's mansion stood apart on a stretch of waste-land. The judge noted that it was surrounded by quite a formidable wall. He reflected that this property was near the Watergate; people would like to have solid houses here in case of raids on the city by the barbarians from across the river.

As soon as the sergeant had knocked on the main gate, the double doors swung open. Two doorkeepers bowed deeply while Judge Dee's palanquin was carried into the main courtyard.

When the judge descended, a plump man of medium height hurriedly came down the steps of the reception hall. He had a large, round face with a short, pointed moustache. His small eyes darted to and fro under thin eyebrows, matching his quick movements and his hurried speech.

Bowing respectfully he said: "This person is the landowner Yoo Kee. Your Excellency's visit is a signal honour for my poor hovel. Please deign to enter!"

Yoo Kee led the judge up the stairs and through the high door of the reception hall. He offered his guest the seat of honour in front of the large, altar-like table against the back wall.

Judge Dee saw at a glance that the hall was furnished in a quiet, refined style. He assumed that the solid antique chairs and tables, and the fine paintings on the walls came from the collection of old Governor Yoo.

While a servant was pouring out the tea in a set of choice antique porcelain, the judge began: "I have always made it a habit to visit the prominent citizens of the district where I am appointed magistrate. In your case this is all the more pleasant since I had been looking forward to meeting the son of so distinguished a statesman as the late Governor Yoo Shou-chien."

Yoo Kee jumped from his chair. He bowed quickly three times in succession before the judge. As he sat down again, he rattled on: "Ten thousand thanks for Your Honour's kind words! Yes, my late father was a most remarkable man, most remarkable indeed! How unfortunate that this person is so unworthy a son of so great a father! Alas, real talent is bestowed by Heaven. It can be further cultivated through assiduous study. If, however, as in my own case, Your Honour, the foundation is not there, study from morning till night will be of no avail. But I hope I can claim at least that I realize my own limitations. I am not a gifted man, Your Honour, therefore I never dared to aspire to any high office. I merely pass my days quietly, supervising my houses and my land!"

He smiled ingratiatingly, rubbing his plump hands. Judge Dee opened his mouth to speak, but Yoo Kee went on: "I am ashamed that I am so unworthy of conversing with a man of Your Honour's learning. Most vexing, for I feel immensely honoured that so famous a magistrate condescends to visit my poor house. I humbly congratulate Your Honour on the quick arrest of that scoundrel Chien Mow. What a brilliant achievement! Former magistrates here just submitted to Chien. Most regrettable! I well remember that my revered father often commented unfavourably on the low moral standard of the younger officials. Ahem, Your Honour is of course an exception. I mean to say, as is well known . . ."

Yoo Kee hesitated a moment. Judge Dee quickly interrupted: "The late Governor must have left you quite some property."

"Yes indeed!" the other replied, "and what a misfortune that I am so stupid! It takes practically all my time to look after the administration of the land. And the tenants, Your Honour, the tenants! Quite honest people of course, of the best, I dare say, but always those arrears in the rent! And the local servants here, what a difference from the people in the capital! I always say . . ."

"I gather," Judge Dee said firmly, "that you have a beautiful country estate outside the east gate."

"Oh yes," Yoo Kee replied, "yes, that is a fine piece of land."

Then, for once, he stopped of his own account.

"Some day," Judge Dee said, "I should like to see the famous maze out there."

"An honour! An honour!" Yoo Kee exclaimed excitedly. "Unfortunately the place is in a bad state. I would have liked to rebuild the mansion but my revered father was so fond of it and even gave special instructions that nothing should be touched. Yes, Your Honour, I am a stupid man, yet not deficient in filial piety, I fondly hope. My father left an old couple in charge, faithful old retainers, but quite incapable of keeping up the estate. But you know how it is with those old servants; it is more or less understood that they should not be bothered. I have never gone out there. As a matter of fact, Your Honour will understand, the old couple might think . . ."

"I am particularly interested in that maze," Judge Dee said patiently. "I hear that it is a most ingenious one. Have you ever been inside?"

Yoo Kee's small eyes flashed with an uneasy glint.

"No, that is to say . . . No, I have never ventured inside. To tell Your Honour the truth, my father was very particular about the maze. He alone knew the secret . . ."

"I suppose," Judge Dee remarked casually, "that the late Governor's widow knew the secret of the maze?"

"A sad thing!" Yoo Kee cried, "Your Honour must know that my mother died when I was still very young. What a misfortune that was! And after a long, painful illness too!"

"As a matter of fact," Judge Dee observed, "I rather referred to the Governor's second wife, your stepmother."

Yoo Kee again jumped from his chair with amazing agility. As he walked up and down in front of the judge he exclaimed: "That distressing affair! How unfortunate that we must speak about that! Your Honour will realize how painful it is for a devoted son to be compelled to admit that his revered father ever made a mistake. A most human mistake, I should add, and one inspired only by his lofty, generous nature.

"Alas, Your Honour, my father let himself be deceived by a clever, wicked woman. She succeeded in exciting his pity, and he married her. Ah, these women! Instead of being grateful, she deceived him with Heaven knows what young rascal. Adultery, Your Honour, a black, abominable crime! My father knew, but he suffered in silence. Not even to me, his own son, did he communicate his sorrow. It was only on his deathbed, in his last words, that at last he revealed this awful wrong!"

Judge Dee tried to say something, but Yoo Kee went on: "I know what Your Honour is going to say: I should have accused that woman in the tribunal. But I could not bear the thought that my old father's private affairs would be dragged out in the tribunal before the vulgar crowd. I could not bear it!"

Yoo Kee covered his face with his hands.

"To my great regret," the judge said dryly, "this affair will have to be discussed in the tribunal. Your stepmother has filed a complaint against you, contesting the oral will and claiming half of the property."

"The ingrate!" Yoo Kee cried, "the unspeakable woman! She must be an evil fox-spirit, Your Honour! No human being could sink so low!"

He burst out in sobs.

Judge Dee slowly emptied his teacup. He waited till Yoo Kee had sat down and composed himself. Then he said in a conversational tone: "I always regret that it has never been given to me to meet your late father. But a man leaves his spirit behind him in his handwriting. Would it be importunate to ask you whether I might see some specimens of his calligraphy? The late Governor was famous for his original hand."

"Ah!" Yoo Kee exclaimed, "another misfortune! How embarrassing that I am unable to obey Your Honour's orders! This was another of my father's unexpected traits. No, let me put it correctly, another proof of his great modesty. When he felt his end approaching, he gave me strict orders to burn all his writings. He observed that there was no specimen of his brushwork that deserved being preserved for posterity. What a sublime character!"

Judge Dee murmured a suitable comment. Then he asked: "Since the Governor was such a famous man, I suppose that many people here in Lan-fang cultivated his friendship?"

Yoo Kee smiled disdainfully.

"This border place," he replied, "has not one single man with whom my late father would have cared to converse. Barring, of course, Your Honour! How my revered father would have enjoyed talking with Your Honour! He always was so interested in administrative affairs . . . No, my father was greatly occupied by his own literary studies and spent all his spare time supervising the work of the peasants on his land. That is why that woman was able to make up to him . . . Well, well, how I am chattering away!"

Yoo Kee clapped his hands and ordered more tea.

Judge Dee silently stroked his beard. He reflected that his host was an extremely astute man. He said so much that he said practically nothing.

While Yoo Kee prattled on and on about the inclement climate of Lan-fang, Judge Dee slowly sipped his tea.

Suddenly he asked: "Where did your father paint his pictures?"

Yoo Kee gave his guest a bewildered look. He did not reply for a few moments. He scratched his chin. Then he answered: "Well, not being much of an artist myself . . . Let me see now. Yes, my father did his painting in a pavilion behind the country mansion. Lovely place, right at the back of the garden, near the entrance of the maze. I believe that the large table my father used to work on is still there. At least if the old doorkeeper has taken proper care of it. Your Honour knows, those old servants . . ."

Judge Dee rose.

Yoo Kee insisted that he should stay a little longer. He set out on another confused story.

It was not without difficulty that the judge at last succeeded in taking leave of his host.

Sergeant Hoong was waiting for his master in the gatekeeper's lodge. They returned to the tribunal.

As Judge Dee sat down behind his desk, he heaved a deep sigh.

"What a tiring man that Yoo Kee is!" he remarked to Sergeant Hoong.

"Did Your Honour discover new data?" the sergeant asked eagerly.

"No," the judge replied, "but Yoo Kee said one or two things that may perhaps prove to be important. I did not succeed in securing a specimen of the Governor's handwriting to compare with the testament Tao Gan found inside the scroll. Yoo Kee claims that his father ordered him to destroy all his writings after his death. I thought that perhaps the Governor's friends here in Lan-fang might possess some, but Yoo Kee avers that his father had not one single friend. What is your impression of that mansion, Sergeant?"

"While I was waiting in the gatekeeper's lodge," Sergeant Hoong re-plied, "I had a long talk with the two doormen. They think that their master is a bit queer in the head. He is as eccentric as his father, but he lacks the Governor's brilliant mind.

"Although Yoo Kee himself is far from an athlete, he has a great love of boxing, wrestling and swordfighting. Most of the servants in that mansion have been selected for their physical prowess. Yoo Kee likes nothing better than to see them practise. He has made the second courtyard into a kind of arena and he will sit there for hours, shouting encouragement to the fighters and giving prizes to the winners."

Judge Dee slowly nodded his head.

"Weak men," he observed, "will often have an exaggerated veneration for physical strength."

"The servants say," the sergeant continued, "that Yoo Kee once lured the best fencing master of Chien Mow's mansion away by offering him a huge bribe. Chien was very angry. Yoo Kee is not a brave man, he expects every day that the barbarians will come and raid the city. That is the reason why he insists that his servants must be good fighters. He has even hired two Uigur warriors from over the river to instruct his servants in Uigur fighting methods!"

"Did the servants say anything about the old Governor's attitude to Yoo Kee?" inquired Judge Dee.

"Yoo Kee must have stood in deadly fear of his father," Sergeant Hoong replied. "Even the old Governor's death did not alter this. After his burial Yoo Kee sent all the old servants away because they reminded him too much of the awful presence of the old Governor. Yoo Kee has exe-cuted all his father's last instructions to the letter, including the one that everything on the country estate had to be left exactly as it was. Yoo Kee has never gone there since his father's death. The servants say that he changes colour if one as much as mentions that place!"

Judge Dee stroked his beard.

"One of these days," he said pensively, "I shall visit that country man-sion and have a look at the famous maze. In the meantime you will inquire where Mrs. Yoo and her son are living and invite them to come and see me. Perhaps Mrs. Yoo has kept some specimens of the old Governor's hand-writing. Then I can also verify Yoo Kee's statement that his father had no friends here in Lan-fang.

"As to the murder of Magistrate Pan, I have not yet given up hope entirely of obtaining a clue to that mysterious visitor of Chien Mow's. I instructed Chiao Tai to question all the former guards of Chien's mansion, and Headman Fang should interrogate Chien's second counsellor in jail. I am also considering whether to send Ma Joong to investigate the haunts where the low-class criminals of this city gather. If it was that mysterious man in the background who murdered Magistrate Pan, he must have had accomplices."

"And at the same time, Your Honour," the sergeant remarked, "Ma Joong might make inquiries there about the headman's eldest daughter, White Orchid. We talked it over with Fang this morning and he admits that very likely she was kidnapped and sold to a brothel."

The judge said with a sigh: "Yes, I fear that that is indeed what happened to the poor girl."

After a while Judge Dee continued: "As yet we have made very little progress with General Ding's murder. I shall order Tao Gan to go tonight to the Temple of the Three Treasures and see whether Woo or that unknown woman he is so fond of depicting shows up there."

The judge took a document from the pile that Tao Gan had brought during his absence. Sergeant Hoong, however, seemed reluctant to go. After some hesitation he said: "Your Honour, I cannot get it off my mind that we overlooked something in General Ding's library. The more I think about it the more I am convinced that the clue to the riddle is to be found there!"

Judge Dee put the document down and looked intently at the sergeant.

He opened a small lacquer box and took out the replica of the small dagger that Tao Gan had made for him. While he let it rest on his palm he said slowly: "Sergeant, you know that I have no secrets from you. Although I am considering various vague theories about the background of General Ding's murder, I must state frankly that I have not the faintest idea how this dagger was used, or how the murderer entered and escaped!"

Both were silent for some time.

Suddenly the judge made a decision.

"Tomorrow morning, Sergeant, we shall again go to the Ding mansion and search the library. Perhaps you are right and it is there that we must look for the solution of this crime!"

Fourteenth Chapter

A STRANGE CLUE IS FOUND IN A DEAD MAN'S ROOM; JUDGE DEE SENDS HIS MEN TO ARREST A CRIMINAL

The next morning the weather was fine. It promised to be a clear and sunny day.

After he had had his breakfast, Judge Dee informed Sergeant Hoong that he planned to go to the Ding mansion on foot.

"I shall also take Tao Gan," the judge added. "A little exercise will do him good!"

They left the tribunal by the western gate.

The judge had not informed Candidate Ding in advance of his intended visit. They found the mansion in the midst of preparations for the burial.

The steward led the judge and his two companions to a side room. The main hall had been converted into a mortuary, and there the body of the General was lying in state in an enormous coffin of lacquered wood before which twelve Buddhist priests were reading sutras aloud. Their monotonous chanting and the beating of wooden gongs resounded through the mansion, and the smell of incense hung heavily in the air.

Judge Dee noticed in the corridor a side table loaded with piles of anniversary gifts, all wrapped in red paper with congratulatory messages attached.

The steward saw the judge's astonished look and hastened to apologize. He said that these presents which now seemed so macabre would have been cleared away long since, were it not that all the servants were wholly occupied in making the preparations for the General's burial.

Young Ding came rushing into the room clad in a mourning robe of white hemp cloth. He started to apologize profusely for the disorder in his house.

Judge Dee cut short his explanations.

"Today or tomorrow," he said, "I shall hear your case in the tribunal. Since there are two or three points I wished to verify, I resolved to pay you this quite informal visit.

"I shall now proceed once more to your late father's library. You need not bother to accompany us."

They found two constables on guard in the dark corridor that led to the library. They reported that no one had even approached the place.

Judge Dee broke the seal and opened the door.

He hastily stepped backward, covering his face with his long sleeve.

A nauseating smell assailed their nostrils.

"There is something dead in there," the judge said. "Go to the main hall, Tao Gan, and ask those priests for a few sticks of Indian incense!"

Tao Gan hurried away.

He came back with three lighted incense sticks in each hand. They made a dense smoke with a penetrating smell.

The judge took them and once more entered the library waving the sticks so that he was enveloped in a cloud of blue smoke.

The sergeant and Tao Gan waited outside.

After a while Judge Dee emerged. He was carrying a thin forked stick that is used for suspending scroll pictures on the wall. On its end rested the half decayed body of a mouse.

He handed the stick to Tao Gan and ordered: "Have the constables put this dead animal in a sealed box!"

Judge Dee remained standing in front of the open door. He had placed the sticks of incense in the brush holder on the desk inside. Clouds of smoke wafted out of the door.

As they were waiting for the stench to disappear, Sergeant Hoong remarked with a smile: "That little animal gave me quite a fright, Your Honour!"

Judge Dee's face was impassive.

"You will not laugh, Sergeant, after you have entered that room. It is full of the spirit of violent death!"

When Tao Gan had come back, all three of them entered the library.

Judge Dee pointed to a small cardboard box that was lying on the floor.

"The other day," he said, "I left that box on the desk, next to the ink slab. It is the box with the sweet plums that we found in the General's sleeve. A mouse smelled them. See, its little feet are clearly visible in the dust that gathered on the desk."

The judge stooped and picked up the box carefully with two fingers. He laid it on the desk.

They saw that a corner of the cover had been gnawed away.

The judge opened the box. One plum of the nine was missing.

"This was the murderer's second weapon," Judge Dee said gravely. "These plums are poisoned!"

He ordered Tao Gan: "Search the floor for that plum. Don't touch it!"

Tao Gan went down on his knees. He found the plum, half eaten, under one of the bookshelves.

Judge Dee took a toothpick from the seam of his robe and stuck it in the plum. He put it back in the box and replaced the cover.

"Wrap this box up in a sheet of oilpaper," he said to Sergeant Hoong.

"We shall take it to the tribunal for further investigation."

The judge looked around. Then he shook his head.

"Let us return to the tribunal," he said. "Tao Gan will seal this door again, and the two constables shall remain on guard outside."

They walked back in silence.

As he entered his private office, the judge called out to the clerks to bring a pot of hot tea.

He sat down behind his desk. Tao Gan and the sergeant sat down on their customary footstools.

Silently they drank a cup of tea.

Then Judge Dee spoke: "Sergeant, let one of the runners go out and call that old coroner here!"

When the sergeant had gone, the judge said to Tao Gan: "This murder becomes more and more complicated. Before we have even determined how the murderer struck, we find that he kept a second weapon in reserve. As soon as we find out that the accused Woo has a mysterious girl friend, we learn that also the complainant Ding has a secret lover!"

"Could not it be, Your Honour," Tao Gan said slyly, "that it is one and the same girl? If Woo and Ding are rivals in love, that would throw an entirely new light on the latter's accusation!"

Judge Dee looked pleased.

"That," he said, "is a very interesting suggestion!"

After a pause Tao Gan resumed: "I still can't understand how the murderer succeeded in making General Ding accept that box with poisoned plums! The murderer must have handed it to him personally. We saw the pile of anniversary gifts on the table in the corridor. He would not have put it there, for how could he be sure that the General would pick up that particular box? It might as well have been taken by Candidate Ding or another member of the household."

"And then," the sergeant remarked, "we also have this problem: why didn't the murderer remove this box from the General's sleeve after he had killed him? Why leave this piece of evidence on the scene of the crime?"

Tao Gan shook his head perplexedly. After a while he said: "Seldom have we been confronted with so many difficult problems at the same time. Apart from this murder we have the hidden message in that landscape painting there on the wall, and all the while Chien Mow's mysterious visitor is still roaming about freely and planning Heaven knows what new mischief. Is there no clue to his identity at all?"

Judge Dee smiled bleakly.

"Nothing at all," he replied. "Last night Chiao Tai told me that he had interrogated Chien's former guards and his counsellors. None of them could supply any information. The mysterious stranger always came late at night and his long cloak concealed his build. He never spoke a word. The lower part of his face was covered by his neckcloth, the upper part concealed by the shadow of his hood. He did not even show his hands; he always kept them inside his sleeves!"

They drank another cup of tea.

Then a clerk announced that the coroner had arrived.

Judge Dee gave the old drug dealer a sharp look.

"The other day when you performed the autopsy on the General's body," he said to him, "you stated that most poisons used internally can be identified. Now I have here a box with sweet plums. A mouse ate one and died on the spot. You will examine these plums in my presence and try to determine what poison they contain. If necessary you can also examine the dead mouse."

Judge Dee handed the cardboard box to the coroner.

The old man opened the small bundle he had brought and took out a leather folder. It contained a set of thin knives with short blades and long handles. He selected one that had a fine, hair-sharp blade.

Then he took a square pad of white paper from his sleeve and put it on the corner of the desk. He picked up with a pair of pincers the plum the mouse had eaten from and laid it on the pad. With remarkable dexterity he cut from its flesh a slice as thin as the thinnest tissue paper.

The judge and his two lieutenants eagerly followed his every movement.

The coroner smoothed out the slice on the pad using the blade of the knife. He peered intently at it. Then he looked up and asked for a cup of boiled water, an unused writing brush, and a candle.

When a clerk had brought the required materials, the coroner moistened the brush and soaked the thin slice in water. Then he took a small square piece of very white, glazed paper, spread it out over the slice and pressed it with the palm of his hand.

The coroner lighted the candle. He took up the glazed paper and showed it to the judge; it bore the wet imprint of the slice. The coroner held it over the flame till it had dried.

He took the paper over to the window and scrutinized it for some time, softly running his forefinger over it. Tao Gan left his chair and looked over the coroner's shoulder.

The coroner turned round and handed the paper to the judge. He said: "I beg to report that this plum contains a large dose of a poisonous dye called gamboge. It was introduced by means of a hollow needle."

Judge Dee slowly caressed his whiskers. After a glance at the paper he asked: "How do you prove that?"

"This method," the coroner said with a smile, "has been used in our trade for many centuries. The alien matter in the juice of the plum is recognized by its colour and granulation. If Your Honour observes this imprint, a yellow tinge will be clearly recognisable. The difference in granulation can be noticed only by the sensitive fingers of an experienced drug dealer. Since the slice shows a number of small round spots I conclude that the gamboge was introduced by means of a hollow needle."

"Excellent work!" the judge said approvingly. "You will now examine the other plums."

As the coroner set to work Judge Dee idly played with the empty cardboard box. He pried loose the folded white paper that covered its bottom. Suddenly he bent over it and peered intently at a faint red mark on the edge of the paper.

"Well, well," he remarked, "what a careless thing to do!"

Sergeant Hoong and Tao Gan rose and eagerly bent their heads over the paper. Judge Dee pointed with his forefinger at the red mark.

"That is half of Woo's seal!" the sergeant exclaimed. "The same seal as the one he impressed on the picture the other day!"

The judge leaned back in his armchair.

"Thus two clues point straight to our painter," he said. "First, the poison used. Gamboge is used by all painters as a yellow pigment and they are familiar with the fact that it is dangerous poison. Second, this sheet of paper employed as filling for the box. I suppose that Woo once used it as a support for impressing his seal on a picture; inadvertently half of the seal impression was transferred on this paper underneath."

"This is the sort of thing we have been waiting for!" Tao Gan exclaimed excitedly.

The judge did not comment. He waited silently till the coroner had completed his examination of the other plums.

Finally the old man reported:

"Every one of these contains a lethal dose of gamboge, Your Honour!"

The judge selected a sheet of the official writing paper on his desk and pushed it over to the coroner.

"Please record your testimony on this paper!" he ordered, "and affix your thumbmark to it!"

The old coroner moistened his brush and filled out the document. After he had affixed his thumbmark to it the judge dismissed him with a few kind words. Then he ordered a clerk to call Headman Fang.

When the headman came in Judge Dee ordered curtly: "Take four constables and arrest the painter Woo Feng!"

Fifteenth Chapter

PAINTER WOO REVEALS HIS SECRET IN THE TRIBUNAL;
JUDGE DEE ORDERS A SEARCH OF THE EASTERN CITY

Three beats of the large bronze gong resounded through the tribunal announcing the opening of the afternoon session.

A fair crowd of spectators had assembled in the court hall. The old General Ding had been a well-known resident of Lan-fang.

Judge Dee ascended the dais. He ordered Candidate Ding to come forward.

As he was kneeling in front of the bench, Judge Dee spoke: "The other day you appeared before this tribunal and accused Woo Feng of having murdered your father. I have made a painstaking investigation and assembled evidence that warranted Woo's arrest. Yet there are not a few points that need clarification.

"I shall now hear the accused and you will listen carefully. If any point should come up concerning which you can supply additional information, you shall not fail to speak!"

Judge Dee filled out a slip for the warden of the jail. Soon two constables led Woo into the court hall. As he approached the dais, Judge Dee noticed that he looked quite unperturbed.

Woo knelt and waited respectfully till the judge addressed him.

"State your name and profession!" the judge said curtly.

"This insignificant person," Woo replied, "is called Woo Feng. I am a Junior Candidate by profession and a painter by preference."

"You," said the judge sternly, "are accused of having murdered General Ding Hoo-gwo. Speak the truth!"

"Your Honour," Woo said calmly, "I emphatically deny the accusation. I am familiar with the victim's name and the crime for which he was dismissed from military service, because I often heard my father speak about that disgraceful affair. But I beg to state that I have never met the General. I did not even know that he was living in Lan-fang until his son started to spread malicious rumours about me. Those rumours I totally ignored since they were so ridiculous as to make refutation quite unnecessary."

"If that is so," Judge Dee said coldly, "why then did the General stand in constant fear of you? Why did he keep the gates of his mansion closed day and night and confine himself to his locked library? And if you did not plan some foul scheme against the General, why did you hire ruffians to spy on his mansion?"

"As to Your Honour's first two questions," Woo replied, "they concern the internal affairs of the Ding mansion. Since I am completely ignorant of such things, I am in no position to express any opinion. As regards the last query, I deny ever having hired any people to spy on the Ding family. I challenge my accuser to produce one of those men I allegedly hired and confront him with me!"

"Don't be too sure, young man!" the judge said sternly. "As a matter of fact I have already apprehended one of those ruffians. You will be confronted with him in due time!"

Woo shouted angrily: "That scoundrel Ding bribed him to give false testimony!"

When he saw that at last Woo had lost his temper, Judge Dee thought to himself that this was the right moment to spring another surprise on the accused.

He leaned forward in his chair and said sharply: "I, the magistrate, shall tell you why you hated the Ding family! Not because of the feud between your father and General Ding. No, you had a quite personal and despicable motive. Look at this woman here!"

While he was saying this, the judge had taken from his sleeve a section cut out of Woo's painting showing only the face of the goddess Kwan Yin.

As he handed it to Headman Fang to pass it on to Woo, Judge Dee kept his eye on both the accused and Candidate Ding. He noticed that as soon as he had referred to a woman in the case both young men had turned pale. Ding's eyes widened in sudden fear.

Judge Dee heard a stifled cry by his side.

Headman Fang stood there with the picture still in his hand. His face had turned ashen. He looked as if he had seen a ghost.

"Your Honour!" he cried out, "this is my eldest daughter, White Orchid!"

A murmur rose from the crowd at this unexpected revelation.

"Silence!" the judge shouted in a thunderous voice.

He did not betray his own utter amazement, but said quietly: "Headman, give that picture to the accused!"

Judge Dee had not failed to observe that while Woo was greatly perturbed by the headman's identification, Candidate Ding looked relieved. That young man heaved a deep sigh and the colour came back to his cheeks.

Woo looked at the picture with a fixed stare.

"Speak up!" the judge barked. "What are your relations with this girl?"

Woo was deadly pale. But his voice was steady as he replied: "I refuse to answer!"

The judge leaned back in his chair. He said coldly: "The accused seems to forget that he is in the tribunal. I order you to answer my question!"

"You can torture me to death," Woo replied in a clear voice, "but you will never succeed in making me answer that question!"

Judge Dee sighed. He said: "You are guilty of contempt of court!"

At a sign from the judge, two constables tore down Woo's robe. Two others grabbed his arms and pressed him forward till his face touched the floor. Then they looked expectantly at Headman Fang, who was standing there with the heavy whip in his hand.

The headman looked up at the judge with a tortured expression on his face.

Judge Dee understood. Fang was a just man. He feared that in his anger he would flog Woo to death. The judge pointed at a sturdy constable.

He took over the whip from the headman. He raised his muscular arm and the thin thong descended on Woo's bare back.

Woo groaned as welt after welt rose on his flesh. After the tenth blow the blood streamed from his torn back. But he gave no sign that he would speak.

After the twentieth blow his body grew limp.

The constable reported that he had fainted. Judge Dee gave a sign and two constables jerked Woo to his knees. They burned vinegar under his nose till he regained consciousness.

"Look at your magistrate!" Judge Dee ordered.

A constable gripped Woo by his hair and pulled his head back.

The Judge leaned forward and looked intently at his contorted face.

Woo's lips moved convulsively. Then he said in a toneless voice: "I shall not speak!"

The constable with the whip was going to strike Woo in his face with the heavy handle. But Judge Dee raised his hand. He addressed Woo in a conversational tone: "Woo, you are an intelligent youngster. You must realize how utterly foolish your attitude is. Let me tell you that I know more about your relations with that poor misguided girl than you think!"

Woo only shook his head.

"I know," the judge continued calmly, "all about your meeting White Orchid in the 'Hermitage of the Three Treasures,' near the east gate, and . . ."

Suddenly Woo jumped up. He tottered on his feet and a constable had to grip his arm to steady him. Woo did not notice it. He lifted his bare right arm, streaked with blood. Shaking his fist at the judge he cried in a strident voice: "Now she is lost! It is you, you dog-official, who have murdered her!"

Loud exclamations rose from the crowd. Headman Fang stepped forward and stammered incoherent questions. The constables did not know what to do.

Judge Dee hammered his gavel on the bench. He shouted in a stentorian voice: "Silence and order!"

The murmur died out.

"If I have to issue one more warning," Judge Dee said sternly, "I shall have the hall cleared! Everyone stand in his appointed place!"

Woo had collapsed on the floor. His body shook with sobs. Headman Fang stood stiffly at attention. He bit his lips till the blood trickled from his chin.

Judge Dee slowly stroked his beard.

Then his deep voice broke the uneasy silence.

"Junior Candidate Woo, you will realize that there is nothing left but to tell the entire story. If, as I gather from your last remark, I have endangered White Orchid's life by mentioning your meeting her in the deserted temple, it is you who are responsible for her plight. You had ample opportunity to warn me."

The judge gave a sign to the constables. They offered Woo a cup of strong tea. He gulped it down. Then he said in a forlorn voice: "Her secret is now known to the entire town! She cannot be saved!"

Judge Dee observed dryly: "Leave it to this tribunal to decide whether she can be saved or not! I repeat, tell the entire story!"

Woo mastered himself. He began in a low voice: "Near the East Gate there stands a small Buddhist temple, called the 'Hermitage of the Three Treasures.' Many years ago, when the route to the west still passed through this city, monks from Khotan built the hermitage. Later they left. The temple fell into decay, people of the neighbourhood took away the doors and other woodwork for firewood. But the magnificent wall paintings by the monks remained.

"I discovered those murals by accident when I was roaming over the city in search of Buddhist works of art. I often went there and made copies of the murals. I took a liking to the small secluded garden behind the temple. I used to stroll out there at night to enjoy the moon.

"One evening, about three weeks ago, I had been drinking heavily. I resolved to walk to the temple to let my head cool in the garden there.

"When I was sitting on the stone bench, I suddenly saw a girl enter the garden."

Woo bent his head further down. Deep silence reigned in the court hall.

Woo looked up with unseeing eyes. He went on: "She seemed to me our Lady Kwan Yin descended upon earth. She was clad in a single thin robe of white silk. A white silk shawl covered her head. Her lovely face bore an expression of deep, unutterable sadness, tears glistened on her pale

WOO FENG'S STRANGE ENCOUNTER IN THE
TEMPLE GARDEN

cheeks. Those heavenly features are engraved on my mind. I shall remember them as long as I live!"

He covered his face with his hands. Then he let his arms drop listlessly.

"I rushed to her, stammering I know not what confused words. She shrank back in fright and whispered: 'Don't speak, go away! I am afraid!' I sank to my knees in front of her and implored her to trust me.

"She drew her robe closer round her and said in a low voice: 'I have orders never to leave the house, but tonight I slipped away. I must go back now, else I shall be killed! Tell no one. I shall come again!'

"Then a cloud obscured the moon. In the darkness I faintly heard her quick footsteps.

"That night I searched the temple and its neighbourhood for hours. But I could find no trace of her."

Woo paused. Judge Dee gave a sign to offer him another cup of tea. Woo impatiently shook his head and continued: "Since that unforgettable evening I have gone to that temple nearly every night. But she never came. It is clear that she is kept a prisoner. Now that her secret visit to the temple is known, the fiend that keeps her will kill her!"

Woo broke out in sobs.

After a short pause Judge Dee spoke: "Now you see for yourself how dangerous it is not to tell the complete truth. The tribunal shall do all that is possible to locate that girl. You, meanwhile, had better confess how you murdered General Ding!"

Woo cried: "I shall confess anything you like! But not now. I beseech Your Honour to send out your men now to save that girl! It may not be too late yet!"

Judge Dee shrugged his shoulders. He nodded to the constables. They dragged Woo to his feet and led him back to the jail.

"Candidate Ding," the judge spoke, "this is quite an unexpected development. Evidently it has nothing to do with Woo's murdering your father. It is clear, however, that the accused is in no condition to be interrogated further.

"I here break off the hearing of your case. It will be continued in due time."

The judge let his gavel descend on the bench. Then he rose and left the dais.

The crowd of spectators slowly filed out of the court hall, busily discussing among themselves the exciting new developments.

While Judge Dee changed into his informal robe, he ordered Sergeant Hoong to call Headman Fang.

Ma Joong and Tao Gan sat down on footstools by the side of the judge's desk.

When the headman had entered Judge Dee said: "Headman, this is a great shock for you. It is unfortunate that I did not show you that picture earlier, but I could not have guessed that it was in any way connected with your eldest daughter. However, this is the first definite indication of her whereabouts."

While speaking the judge had taken up his vermilion brush and filled out three official forms.

"You will now," he continued, "collect twenty armed constables and go immediately to the 'Hermitage of the Three Treasures.' Ma Joong and Tao Gan shall direct you. They are the two best men I have, with great experience in such work. These warrants will authorize you to enter and search every house in that quarter!"

The judge impressed the large seal of the tribunal on the documents and handed them to Ma Joong.

Ma Joong hastily stuffed them in his sleeve. Then all three rushed away.

Judge Dee ordered the clerk to bring a pot of hot tea. When he had drunk a cup, he said to Sergeant Hoong: "I am glad that the headman has at least some information about his missing daughter. Now it has come out that it was she who is depicted on Woo's paintings, I realize that there is some resemblance to Fang's youngest daughter, Dark Orchid. I ought to have noticed that immediately!"

"The only one who did see some resemblance, Your Honour," the sergeant said slyly, "was our brave fighter Ma Joong!"

The judge smiled thinly.

"It would seem," he said, "that Ma Joong observed Dark Orchid with more attention than you or I!"

Then the judge's face set again in its usual stern mien. He said slowly: "Heaven knows in what condition they will find that poor girl, if at all. If one translates the poetic description of our excitable artistic friend into everyday language, it is clear that on her visit to the temple White Orchid wore a common night robe. That means that she was kept imprisoned in a house quite near that temple, probably by some degenerate lecher. When he discovered that she had secretly left the house, he may well have become afraid and killed her. Some day her body will be discovered in a dry well . . ."

"In the meantime," Sergeant Hoong observed, "this does not bring us much nearer to the solution of the General's murder. I fear that we shall have to put the question to Woo under torture."

The judge did not react to the sergeant's second remark. He said: "I noticed one interesting fact. When during the session I mentioned a woman in the case both Woo and Ding turned pale; the latter was definitely afraid. As soon as Ding heard that it was the headman's daughter, he was visibly relieved. This means that there is also a woman connected with the General's murder. Evidently the same person as the one Ding wrote his passionate poetry to."

A soft knock sounded on the door.

Sergeant Hoong rose and opened. Dark Orchid came in.

She bowed deeply before the judge and said: "I could not find my father, Your Honour, so I made bold to come here alone to present my report."

"You are most welcome, young woman!" Judge Dee said eagerly. "We were just discussing the Ding mansion. Tell me, do you know whether young master Ding spends much of his time outside?"

Dark Orchid emphatically shook her small head.

"No, Your Honour," she replied. "The servants wish he would go out more. He hangs about in the house practically the entire day, snooping around and trying to catch them out in some mistake or omission. Once one of the maids even saw him late at night walking stealthily down a corridor. Probably he was checking up on whether the servants were gambling!"

"What was the reaction to my unexpected visit this morning?" the judge asked.

"I was in the young master's room when a servant reported Your Honour's arrival. He was sitting there drawing up an estimate of the costs of the funeral with his wife. The young master was very pleased that Your Honour had come again. He said to his wife: 'Did I not tell you that the first investigation of father's library was very superficial? I am glad that the judge has come back, I feel certain that they overlooked many clues!' His wife remarked sourly that he should not think that he was more clever than a magistrate and he hastily went out to welcome Your Honour."

The judge silently sipped his tea. Then he said: "Well, I am grateful to you for the work you have done. You have sharp ears and eyes! It is not necessary that you return to the Ding mansion. This afternoon we obtained some information about your elder sister, and your father has gone to search for her. Go to your quarters now; I hope sincerely that when your father comes back he will have good news!"

Dark Orchid hastily took her leave.

"It is curious," Sergeant Hoong remarked, "that Candidate Ding did not often go out at night. One would expect that he had some secret love-nest where he met the unknown woman!"

Judge Dee nodded.

"On the other hand," he said, "it may be an old affair that is long over and done with. Sentimental people have an unfortunate habit of keeping souvenirs of past affairs. Yet the originals that Dark Orchid showed me

DARK ORCHID REPORTS TO JUDGE DEE

seemed written very recently. Did Tao Gan find any clue to the woman's identity in those papers he copied out?"

"No," Sergeant Hoong replied, "but Tao Gan certainly enjoyed that work! He copied the texts out in his best calligraphy, chuckling all the time."

Judge Dee smiled indulgently. He rummaged among the piles of documents on his desk till he found Tao Gan's copies, neatly written out on ornamental letter paper.

Leaning back in his armchair the judge started reading. After a while he said: "Well, it is all about the same subject, expressed in different ways. Candidate Ding was deeply enamoured. As if poetry could serve no better purpose! Listen:

> The studded door is locked, the bed curtains drawn close,
> Embroidered coverlets are a soft home of love;
> Who thinks of Rites and Proper Conduct in this trance?
> Empassioned lovers care not what the Codes impose.
> Her feet like lotus buds, her lips like pomegranate,
> Her rounded thighs, her breasts like fresh-fallen snow —
> Who ever deems the full moon marred by its spots?
> It's the blemish that completes the beauty of agate.
> Who praises perfumes rare of the far-distant West?
> The fragrance of her limbs bemuses the enraptured mind
> He is a fool who with such beauty right before his eyes,
> Still travels far and wide, a useless quest . . .

The judge threw the paper disdainfully on his desk.

"It rhymes," he remarked dryly. "That is about all that can be said for it!" He slowly smoothed his long beard.

Suddenly the judge stiffened. He picked up the sheet which he had been reading aloud and eagerly scanned it.

Sergeant Hoong knew that Judge Dee had made a discovery. He rose and looked over the judge's shoulder.

Judge Dee crashed his fist on the table.

"Get me the testimony of the house steward, delivered during the preliminary hearing in the Ding mansion!" he ordered.

Sergeant Hoong fetched the leather box that contained the file of General Ding's murder. He extricated a sealed document.

Judge Dee read it through from beginning to end.

Then he put it back in the box. He left his armchair and started pacing the floor.

"What incredible fools people in love are!" the judge suddenly exclaimed. "I have now found the solution of half the General's murder. What a foul, despicable crime!"

Sixteenth Chapter

MA JOONG INVESTIGATES THE LICENSED QUARTER;
HE IS MADE A PARTNER IN A NEFARIOUS SCHEME

The first nightwatch had sounded when Ma Joong, Tao Gan and Headman Fang gathered in the house of the warden of the eastern quarter. Their faces were tired and drawn in the light of the candles. They sat down silently at the square table.

They had combed out the entire quarter, in vain.

Ma Joong had divided the constables into three groups of seven. One group was headed by Tao Gan, one by Headman Fang, and the third by Ma Joong himself. They had entered the quarter in inconspicuous groups of two or three and by different ways. Under various pretexts these groups had made inquiries in shops and other public places, then they had entered private houses and conducted a thorough search.

The headman's group broke up a secret meeting of thieves. Ma Joong dispersed a gambling party, and Tao Gan disturbed two frightened couples in a clandestine house of assignation. But not one trace of White Orchid was discovered.

Tao Gan closely questioned the woman who kept the house of assignation. He knew that if a girl is kidnapped and kept captive somewhere, such a woman will sooner or later come to know about it. However, half an hour of skillful questioning convinced Tao Gan that she knew nothing about White Orchid; he only learned two or three queer facts about certain leading citizens.

Finally they had to come out in the open and make a systematic search of every household, checking the inhabitants with the census register kept by the warden. But now they had to admit that the search had been a failure.

After a while Tao Gan said: "There is but one possibility left, namely that the girl was held only for a few days in a house near here. When her captor discovered that she had made a secret trip to the temple, he became alarmed and moved her either to a secret assignation house elsewhere in the city, or placed her in a brothel."

Headman Fang shook his head dejectedly.

"I don't believe," he said, "that they would have sold her to a brothel. We have lived here all our lives and they would run the risk that some visitor to the establishment would recognize her and inform me.

"A clandestine assignation house is the most likely place. But to check all those would take many days!"

"Did I not hear," Ma Joong remarked, "that the so-called Northern Row, the licensed quarter in the northwest corner of the town, is rarely visited by Chinese?"

The headman nodded.

"That is a low-class place," he replied, "used only by Uigurs, Turks and other barbarians from over the border. The girls are a motley crowd, left over from the prosperous days when this town was full of wealthy barbarian chieftains and traders from the western tributary kingdoms."

Ma Joong rose and tightened his belt.

"I shall go there now," he said curtly. "To avoid rousing suspicion, I shall go alone. I'll meet you later tonight in the tribunal!"

Tao Gan had been tugging at the three hairs on his left cheek.

"That is a good idea," he said pensively. "We had better act quickly, for by tomorrow the news of this raid will be all over the town. I shall now go to the Southern Row and have a talk with the owners of the houses there. I am not very hopeful, but we cannot afford to neglect even that possibility!"

The headman insisted that he should accompany Ma Joong.

"The scum of the city gathers in the Northern Row," he said. "To go out there alone is asking to be murdered on the spot!"

"Don't worry!" Ma Joong said. "I know how to handle those rascals!"

He threw his cap to Tao Gan and bound up his hair with a dirty strip of cloth. Then he tucked the slips of his robe in his girdle and rolled up his sleeves.

Cutting short the headman's protestations, Ma Joong walked out into the street.

In the main street there were still many people about. But Ma Joong made quick progress. All passers-by hastily made way when they saw the huge ruffian approaching.

When he had crossed the market of the Drum Tower he found himself in the quarter of the poor. Rows of low, tumble-down houses lined the narrow streets. Here and there a street vendor had lighted his oil lamp. The wares on sale were cheap flour cakes and dregs of wine.

As he approached the Northern Row, the scene became more lively. People in queer foreign attire were loitering about the wine shops, talking loudly in raucous, strange languages. They gave Ma Joong but a casual look. Here such a disreputable figure was a common sight.

Turning a corner he saw a row of houses garishly lighted by coloured lanterns of oil paper. He heard barbarian guitars being strummed and farther on the strident tones of a flute tore the air.

Suddenly a thin man clad in a ragged gown detached himself from the shadows. He said in broken Chinese: "Would the master like an Uigur princess?"

Ma Joong stood still and looked the fellow up and down. The man smirked ingratiatingly, showing his broken teeth.

"If I should beat your face to pulp," Ma Joong said sourly, "I could not possibly make you uglier! Run ahead and lead me to a good place. But cheap, mind you!"

As he spoke he jerked the man round and gave him a well-aimed kick.

"Yah, yah!" the other cried. He quickly led Ma Joong into a sidestreet.

On both sides stood one-storied houses. Once their façades had been gaily decorated with reliefs in plaster work. But wind and rain had washed off the colours and nobody had bothered to repair them.

Greasy, patched curtains screened the door openings. As they approached, heavily made-up girls clad in garish rags pulled aside the screens and invited them in in a mixture of Chinese and foreign languages.

The guide took Ma Joong to a house that looked slightly better than the others. Two large paper lanterns hung over the door.

"Here you are, master!" the guide said. "All Uigur princesses of the blood!" He added an obscene remark, then held out his dirty palm.

Ma Joong gripped him by the throat and bumped his head against the ramshackle door.

"That will serve to announce my arrival!" he said. "Your commission you get from the house. Don't try to earn a double fee, you bastard!"

The door swung open and a tall fellow with naked torso appeared. His bare head was closely shaved. He looked at Ma Joong with one baleful eye. The place of the other eye was taken by an ugly red scar.

"This dogshead," Ma Joong said gruffly, "wants to extract an extra tip from me!"

The other turned savagely on the guide.

"Get away!" he barked. "You can come back later for your commission!" And to Ma Joong, sullenly: "Come in, stranger!"

A nauseating smell of burned lambsgrease hung in the room. It was stiflingly hot. In the middle of the stamped-earth floor stood a large iron brazier with glowing coals. Half a dozen people were sitting round it on low wooden benches. They were roasting pieces of lambfat stuck on copper pins. There were three men. They had stripped to their baggy trousers; the light of a coloured paper lantern shone on their perspiring faces. The women that accompanied them wore wide pleated red and green muslin skirts and sleeveless short jackets. Their hair was done up in thick rolls mixed with red woollen cords. Their jackets hung open, displaying their naked breasts.

The doorkeeper gave Ma Joong a suspicious look.

"Fifty cash for a meal and a woman, to be paid in advance!" he said.

Ma Joong muttered something and started fumbling in his sleeve. He produced a string of money, and loosened the knot laboriously. Then he slowly counted out fifty coppers on the dirty counter.

The other stretched out his hand. But Ma Joong quickly gripped his wrist and pressed his hand down on the counter before he could scoop up the money.

"Don't you serve a drink with the meal?" he growled.

The man grimaced as Ma Joong tightened his grip.

"No!" he snarled.

Ma Joong let go and roughly pushed him back. He started to gather up the money saying: "Nothing doing! There are other places besides yours!"

The other looked greedily at the disappearing heap of coppers.

"All right!" he said, "you can have one jug of wine!"

"That is better!" Ma Joong said.

He turned around and prepared to join the company around the brazier. Adapting himself to the style of the establishment, he first slipped his right then his left arm out of his robe, and knotted the empty sleeves round his waist. He let himself down on the empty bench.

The others looked thoughtfully at his heavy torso, covered with scars.

Ma Joong pulled a stick with lambsfat from the fire. He was something of a gourmet and the rancid smell made his stomach turn. But he ripped off a piece with his teeth and ate it.

One of the three Uigurs was very drunk. He had put his arm round the waist of the girl next to him and rocked to and fro softly humming a queer little tune. Perspiration streamed down his head and shoulders.

The two others were sober. They were spare men, but Ma Joong knew that their flat, wiry muscles were not to be despised. They spoke rapidly together in their own tongue.

The owner placed a small earthenware jug on the floor by Ma Joong's side.

One of the girls rose and walked over to the counter. She took a three-stringed guitar from one of the shelves. Leaning against the wall she started to sing, accompanying herself on the guitar. Her voice was hoarse but the chant had a lilt that was not unpleasing. Ma Joong noticed that the wide muslin skirts of the girls were so thin that one could see right through.

From the door opening in the back emerged a fourth girl, not unattractive in a vulgar way. She was barefoot and dressed only in a loose pleated skirt of faded silk. Her naked torso was shapely but her breasts and arms were smeared with soot. Apparently she had been helping in the kitchen.

MA JOONG MEETS TULBEE

A faint smile appeared on her round face as she sat down next to Ma Joong.

He put the jug to his lips and swallowed a draught of the fiery liquor. Then he spat in the fire and asked: "What is your name, beauty?"

The girl smiled and shook her head. She did not understand Chinese.

"Fortunately my business with this wench does not include conversation!" Ma Joong remarked to the two men opposite.

The taller of the two men guffawed. He asked in atrocious Chinese: "What is your name, stranger?"

"My name is Yoong Bao," Ma Joong replied. "What is yours?"

"I am called The Hunter," the other answered. "Your girl's nickname is Tulbee. What brought you here?"

Ma Joong gave him a meaningful look. He laid his hand on the thigh of the girl by his side.

"You need not come all the way out here for that!" The Hunter said with a sneer.

Ma Joong scowled angrily. He rose. The girl tried to pull him down but he roughly pushed her back. He walked around the brazier and jerked The Hunter up by his arm. Swinging him round he barked: "What do you mean by interrogating me, you dirty dogshead?"

The Hunter looked at the others. The second Uigur concentrated on a piece of roasted fat. The owner stood leaning on the counter picking his teeth. They made no sign to come to his assistance. The Hunter said sullenly: "Don't take offence, Yoong Bao! I just asked because Chinese rarely come here."

Ma Joong let him go and returned to his seat. The girl put her arm round him and he fondled her for a while. Then he emptied his jug in one gulp.

Wiping his mouth with the back of his hand he said: "Well, since we are gathered here as old friends, I don't mind answering your question. A few weeks ago I had a friendly argument with a fellow in the military post three days away from here. I patted him on the head and the fellow's skull broke. Since the authorities often misunderstand such incidents, I thought I had better do some travelling. Now I am here, and my funds have dwindled to practically nothing. If there is any job to be done with money in it, I am your man!"

The Hunter rapidly translated for the other man, a squat fellow with a bullet-shaped head. They gave Ma Joong an appraising look.

"There is not much going on just now, brother!" The Hunter said cautiously.

"Well," Ma Joong said, "what about kidnapping a girl? That is a commodity that is always in demand!"

"Not in this town, brother!" the other answered. "All the houses have enough and to spare. A few years ago, when all the traffic went through this town, yes, then one could get good silver for a girl. But not now!"

"Are there no Chinese girls in this quarter?" Ma Joong inquired.

The Hunter shook his head.

"Not one," he replied. "But what is wrong with that wench by your side?"

Ma Joong pulled the girl's skirt loose.

"Nothing," he replied, "and anyway I am not particular!"

"It would just be like you haughty Chinese to despise an Uigur girl!" the other said nastily.

Ma Joong thought it better not to make a quarrel. So he said: "Not me! I like your girls the way they are!" And as the girl made no attempt to cover herself up again, he added: "They are not prudish either!"

"Yes," The Hunter said, "we are a fine race. Much more virile than you Chinese. Some day we shall swoop down on you from north and west and conquer your entire country!"

"Not in my life time!" Ma Joong said cheerfully.

The Hunter gave Ma Joong another sharp look. Then he started on a long story to the other Uigur. The latter first shook his head emphatically. Then he seemed to agree.

The Hunter rose and came over to Ma Joong. He pushed the girl away unceremoniously and sat down by Ma Joong's side.

"Listen, brother," he said confidentially. "We might let you in on a nice job! Are you familiar with the weapons used in your regular army?"

Ma Joong thought that this was a curious question. He replied eagerly: "I was a soldier for a couple of years, my friend! I know all about it!"

The Hunter nodded.

"There is a bit of fighting coming on," he said, "and there is a lot in it for a good man!"

Ma Joong held out his open hand.

"No," The Hunter said, "not in cash. But when we start in a couple of days, as much in loot as you can grab!"

"I am ready!" Ma Joong exclaimed enthusiastically. "Where shall I join you?"

The Hunter again talked rapidly to the other man. Then he rose and said: "Come along, brother, I shall take you to our headman!"

Ma Joong jumped up and drew his robe over his shoulders. He gave the girl a friendly pat and said: "I'll be back, Tulbee!"

They left the house, The Hunter walking in front.

He led Ma Joong through two dark alleys, then entered what seemed to be a ruined compound. They halted in front of a small hovel.

He knocked on the door. There was no answer.

The Hunter shrugged his shoulders and pushed the door open, beckoning Ma Joong to follow him.

They sat down on low footstools covered with sheepskin. The room was bare but for a low wooden couch.

"The boss will be back soon," The Hunter said.

Ma Joong nodded and prepared himself for a long wait.

Suddenly the door burst open and a broad-shouldered man came running in. He shouted excitedly at The Hunter.

"What is he jabbering about?" asked Ma Joong.

The Hunter looked frightened.

"He says that the constables have just raided the east quarter!"

Ma Joong jumped up.

"This is the time for me to leave!" he exclaimed. "If they come here I am lost! I'll be back tomorrow. How can I find this wretched place?"

"Just ask for Orolakchee!" the other replied.

"I am off now. That wench will keep!"

And Ma Joong rushed out.

He found Judge Dee sitting alone in his private office, apparently deep in thought.

When Judge Dee saw Ma Joong he said with a frown: "Tao Gan and Headman Fang came in a few moments ago. They reported that the search had been a failure. Tao Gan went to the Southern Row, but they have bought no new girls there for the last half year. Did you find any clue to White Orchid's whereabouts in the northern licensed quarter?"

"Nothing that pointed to the kidnapped girl," Ma Joong answered, "but I heard a queer story."

Then he told the judge all about his adventure with The Hunter and Tulbee.

Judge Dee listened absent-mindedly. He said: "Those rascals probably want you to join them in a raid on another tribe. I would not venture out with them into the plain across the river if I were you!"

Ma Joong shook his head doubtfully but the judge continued: "Tomorrow morning I want you to accompany me and Sergeant Hoong on a visit to the country estate of Governor Yoo. But tomorrow night you can go out to the Northern Row again and try to learn more about the headman of those barbarian rascals."

Seventeenth Chapter

MRS. YOO PAYS A SECOND VISIT TO THE TRIBUNAL;
A QUEER DISCOVERY IS MADE IN AN OLD MANSION

Judge Dee had planned to set out for the Governor's country estate early in the morning. But just as he was finishing his morning tea, Sergeant Hoong announced that Mrs. Yoo and her son Yoo Shan had come to see the judge as requested.

Judge Dee had them brought in.

Yoo Shan was tall for his age. He had an open, intelligent face and an air of self-assurance that pleased the judge.

He made Mrs. Yoo and her son sit down in front of his desk. After the exchange of the usual courtesies the judge said: "I regret, Madam, that pressure of other business has prevented me from devoting as much time to your case as I would have liked. I have not yet succeeded in solving the riddle of the Governor's scroll picture. However, I have a feeling that if I knew more about the general situation in your household when your late husband was still alive, I would be in a better position to solve the problem. Hence I would like to ask you a few questions, for my own guidance."

Mrs. Yoo bowed.

"In the first place," Judge Dee continued, "I wondered about the old Governor's attitude to his eldest son, Yoo Kee. According to your testimony, Yoo Kee is a heartless man. Did the Governor realize that his son had a wicked character?"

"It is my duty to stress," Mrs. Yoo replied, "that until his father's death, Yoo Kee behaved most correctly. I would never have dreamed that he was capable of such cruelty as he showed later. My husband always spoke to me kindly about Yoo Kee. He used to say that Yoo Kee was a diligent man and a great help to him in the administration of the family property. And Yoo Kee struck me as an exemplary son who tried to anticipate his father's every wish."

"Then, Madam," Judge Dee went on, "I would like you to give me a few names of the Governor's friends here in Lan-fang."

Mrs. Yoo hesitated. Then she answered: "The Governor did not like company, Your Honour. He used to spend every morning out in the fields. In the afternoon he would enter the maze alone and stay there for an hour or so."

"Did you ever go inside?" the judge interrupted.

Mrs. Yoo shook her head.

"No," she said, "the Governor always said that it was too damp there. Afterwards he used to drink tea in the garden pavilion behind the mansion. He either read a book or worked on his paintings. I knew a Mrs. Lee, who was quite a gifted amateur painter. The Governor would often invite Mrs. Lee and myself to join him in the pavilion and discuss his pictures."

"Is Mrs. Lee still alive?" inquired the judge.

"Yes, I think so. Formerly she lived not far from our town mansion. She would often come to see me. She is a very kind lady who had the misfortune to lose her husband shortly after their marriage. I once met her when she was walking through the rice fields near our farm and she seemed to take a liking to me. After the Governor married me, she kept up our friendship, and my husband encouraged it.

"He was so considerate, Your Honour! He understood that I, as the mistress of such a large mansion full of people I had not known before, would sometimes feel lonely. I know that it was for this reason that he encouraged Mrs. Lee to come often, although as a rule he did not like visitors."

"Did Mrs. Lee break off the relationship when the Governor died?" Judge Dee asked.

Mrs. Yoo blushed.

"No," she said, "it is entirely my fault that I did not see her again. After Yoo Kee had expelled me from the mansion I felt so humiliated and ashamed that I just went back to my father's farm. I have never been to see Mrs. Lee."

The judge saw that she was deeply moved. He asked hastily: "Thus, the Governor had no friends at all here in Lan-fang?"

Mrs. Yoo mastered herself. She nodded and said: "My husband preferred to be alone. Once, however, he told me that somewhere in the mountains near this town there lived a very old and intimate friend of his."

Judge Dee leaned forward eagerly.

"Who was that, Madam?"

"The Governor never mentioned his name, but I received the impression that he had the greatest regard and affection for him."

Judge Dee's face fell.

"This is very important, Madam. Try to think back whether you cannot remember something more about that friend!"

Mrs. Yoo slowly drank her tea. Then she said: "I remember now that he must have visited the Governor once, because that was rather a peculiar occurrence. My husband used to receive his tenant farmers once every

month; everyone who had a complaint or who wanted advice could come
to see him that day.

"Once there was an old peasant waiting in the courtyard. As soon as the
Governor had seen him he rushed to him and bowed deeply. He took the
peasant straight to his library and remained closeted with him for several
hours. I thought that he might have been the Governor's friend, probably a
recluse. But I never asked."

Judge Dee stroked his beard.

"I suppose," he said after a pause, "that you kept some scrolls written
by your husband?"

Mrs. Yoo shook her head.

"When the Governor married me," she said simply, "I could neither
read nor write. He himself taught me a little, but of course I never made
such progress as to enable me to appreciate calligraphy. There must be
some specimens of the Governor's calligraphy in Yoo Kee's mansion. Your
Honour might refer to him."

Judge Dee rose.

"I appreciate that you took all the trouble to come, Madam. Rest
assured that I shall do my utmost to discover the hidden message of the
Governor's picture. Let me congratulate you on your son. He seems a most
intelligent youngster!"

Mrs. Yoo and Yoo Shan rose and bowed deeply. Then Sergeant Hoong
saw them out.

As he came back he said: "Nothing, Your Honour, seems more difficult
than to obtain a specimen of the Governor's handwriting! Perhaps we
could apply to the capital for one. The Grand Secretary must have many
original memoranda to the Throne drawn up by the Governor."

"That would take several weeks," the judge replied. "Perhaps Mrs. Lee
has a picture inscribed by the Governor. Try to find out whether she is still
alive, and where she lives, Sergeant. The information about that hermit
who was a friend of Governor Yoo is so vague that I have little hope of
locating him. Probably he is dead."

"Does Your Honour intend to hear the case of Candidate Ding this
afternoon?" the sergeant inquired.

The night before, Judge Dee had vouchsafed no further explanation of
the discovery he had made in Candidate Ding's poem, and the sergeant was
curious to know.

Judge Dee did not answer for a while. Then he rose and said: "To tell
you the truth, Sergeant, I have not yet made up my mind. Let us see when
we have come back from our expedition to the country house. Please go
out and see whether my palanquin is ready, and have Ma Joong called!"

Sergeant Hoong knew that it was no use insisting. He went out and had

Judge Dee's private palanquin made ready, with six bearers.

The judge ascended his palanquin. Ma Joong and Sergeant Hoong mounted their horses.

They left the city by the east gate and moved along the narrow road through the rice fields.

When they were approaching elevated terrain, Ma Joong asked a peasant about the way. It appeared that they should take the first road to the right.

This side road proved to be very neglected. It was so overgrown with wild weeds and shrubs that only a footpath in the middle remained.

The bearers put the palanquin down. Judge Dee descended.

"We had better proceed on foot, Your Honour!" Ma Joong observed. "The palanquin cannot pass through here."

So speaking, he fastened the reins of his horse to a tree. Sergeant Hoong followed his example.

They went on in single file, the judge in front.

After many turns they came unexpectedly upon a large gate house. The double doors had once been covered with gold and red lacquer but now there was nothing left but the cracked boards. One panel hung loose.

"Anyone can walk in here!" said the judge in amazement.

"Yet there is no safer place in Lan-fang!" Sergeant Hoong remarked. "Even the most audacious robber would not dare to cross this threshold. This is haunted ground!"

The judge pushed the creaking door open and entered what had once been a beautiful park.

Now it was a wilderness. The roots of towering cedar trees had broken through the flagstones and thick undergrowth obstructed the way. Deep silence reigned. Even the birds did not sing.

The path seemed to disappear into a cluster of shrubs. Ma Joong parted the thick foliage to let the judge pass through. They saw a dilapidated mansion surrounded by a broad elevated terrace.

It was a one-storied, quite extensive building that must once have been an impressive sight. Now the roof had caved in at several places, and wind and rain had played havoc with the carved woodwork of doors and pillars.

Ma Joong went up the crumbling steps of the terrace and looked around. There was no one about.

"Visitors have arrived!" he shouted in a stentorian voice.

The echo was the only answer.

They entered the main hall.

Here the plaster hung down in strips from the walls. A few pieces of broken, bare furniture stood in a corner.

Ma Joong shouted again. But there was still no answer. Judge Dee lowered himself carefully into an old chair. He said: "You two had better have a look round. You will probably find the old couple working in the garden behind the house."

Judge Dee folded his arms. Again he marvelled at the uncanny stillness that hung over the place.

Suddenly he heard the sound of running feet.

Ma Joong and Sergeant Hoong came rushing into the hall.

"Your Honour!" Ma Joong panted, "we have found the dead bodies of the old couple!"

"Well," Judge Dee said testily, "dead people can do no harm. Let us go and have a look!"

They led the judge through a dim corridor. It gave on to a fairly large garden surrounded by old pine trees. In the middle stood an octagonal pavilion.

Ma Joong pointed silently to a flowering magnolia tree in a corner.

Judge Dee went down the stairs of the terrace and walked through the tall grass. On a bamboo couch, right under the magnolia tree he saw the remains of two people.

The bodies must have been lying there for several months. The bones were sticking up through the ragged, decaying robes. Strands of grey hair were attached to the bare skulls. They lay side by side, their arms crossed on their breasts.

Judge Dee bent over and scrutinized the bodies intently.

"It seems to me," he said, "that the two old people died natural deaths. I think that when one of them had succumbed to weakness and old age, the other just lay down there too and died.

"I shall have the constables carry these bodies to the tribunal for an autopsy. But I don't expect any exciting discoveries."

Ma Joong shook his head disconsolately.

"If there is any information to be obtained here," he remarked, "we must get it all by ourselves!"

Judge Dee walked over to the pavilion.

The intricate lattice work of the window openings proved that formerly it had been a very elegant place. Now there was nothing left but the bare walls, and one large table.

"Here," Judge Dee said, "the old Governor used to paint and read his books. I wonder where that gate in the back fence leads to."

They left the pavilion and strolled over to the wooden gate. Ma Joong pushed it open. They found themselves in a paved yard.

In front, a large stone gate loomed against the green foliage. The curved roof was decked with blue-glazed tiles. On left and right there rose walls of thick shrubbery and closely planted trees. Judge Dee looked up at the inscribed stone slab inserted in the plaster over the gate.

He turned around and said to his companions: "This is apparently the entrance to the Governor's famous maze. Look at that stanza written there:

> A winding path goes round and round
> For over a hundred miles;
> Yet the road to one's heart
> Is shorter than one-thousandth of an inch.

The sergeant and Ma Joong looked up intently. The inscription was written in very cursive style.

"I can't identify a single character!" Sergeant Hoong exclaimed.

Judge Dee did not seem to have heard him. He stood there gazing enraptured at the inscription.

"That is the most magnificent calligraphy I have ever seen!" he sighed. "Unfortunately the signature is so covered with moss that I can hardly read it. Yes, that is it. 'The Hermit Clad in Crane Feathers.' What a curious name!"

The judge thought for a moment. Then he continued: "I cannot remember ever having heard of a person of that name. But whoever he is, that man is a superb calligrapher! Seeing such writing, my friends, one understands why the ancients praised great calligraphy by comparing it to 'the tension of a crouching panther, and the wild force of dragons sporting among rain and thunder.' "

Judge Dee passed through the archway, still shaking his head in admiration.

"Give me handwriting that a man can read!" Ma Joong whispered to the sergeant.

In front rose a row of age-old cedar trees. The space between their heavy trunks was filled with large boulders and thorny shrubs. The tree tops met on high, screening out the sunlight.

The air was foul with the smell of decaying leaves.

On the right, two gnarled pine trees on either side of the path formed a natural gateway. At the foot of one stood a stone tablet with the inscription "Entrance." Beyond it a dim, damp tunnel went on straight for a while, then disappeared in a curve.

As he was looking into this green tunnel, Judge Dee suddenly felt an uncanny fear.

Slowly he turned. On the left he saw the opening of another tunnel. A number of large boulders were piled up among the cedar trees. One stone was marked "Exit."

Ma Joong and Sergeant Hoong stood behind the judge. They did not say a word. They, too, felt the weird, threatening atmosphere of this place.

Judge Dee again looked into the entrance. The tunnel seemed to exhale a cold current of air. The judge felt chilled to his very bones. Yet the air was completely still. Not a leaf moved.

Judge Dee wanted to avert his gaze, but the dim tunnel held him hypnotized. He felt a compelling desire to enter. He thought that he could see the tall figure of the old Governor standing in the green dimness beyond the curve, beckoning him.

With a great effort the judge mastered himself. In order to free himself from this evil atmosphere he forced his gaze to the ground, covered with a thick layer of decaying leaves.

Suddenly his heart stood still. In the middle of a muddy stretch, right in front of his feet, he saw the imprint of a small foot, pointing towards the tunnel. This eerie signpost seemed to order him to enter.

Judge Dee heaved a deep sigh, then turned round abruptly. He said casually: "Well, we had better not venture into this maze without adequate preparations!"

So speaking he passed under the archway, crossed the paved yard and walked back into the garden. Never had the warm sunlight been so welcome to him.

Judge Dee looked up at a huge cedar tree that rose high over the pines. He said to Ma Joong: "I would like to have at least a general idea of the size and shape of this maze. We need not go inside for that. If you climb this tree, you should be able to obtain a view of the entire area."

"That is easily done!" Ma Joong exclaimed.

He loosened his girdle and took off his outer robe. Then he jumped and caught the lowest branch. He pulled himself up. Soon he had disappeared among the thick foliage.

Judge Dee and Sergeant Hoong sat down on a fallen tree. Neither of them spoke.

They heard a crashing sound above them. Ma Joong jumped down. He looked ruefully at a tear in his under garment.

"I climbed up right to the top, Your Honour," he said. "From there I could overlook the maze. It is circular in form and extends over several acres, right up to where the mountain slope begins. But I could discover nothing of its design. The tree tops meet nearly everywhere, I could see only short stretches of the path. Here and there a light haze hangs over it. I would not wonder if there was a number of stagnant pools inside it."

"Did you see anything like the roof of a pavilion or a small house?" inquired Judge Dee.

"No," Ma Joong replied, "I saw only a sea of green tree tops!"

"That is curious," Judge Dee mused. "Since the Governor spent so much of his time in that maze, one would expect him to have had some small library or studio inside."

The judge rose and straightened his robes.

"Let us now have a closer look at the mansion itself," he said.

They passed once more the garden pavilion and the two still figures under the magnolia tree. Then they ascended the terrace.

They inspected a number of larger and smaller empty rooms. Most of the woodwork had rotted away; the bricks showed through the plaster.

As the judge was entering a dim corridor, Ma Joong who had been walking ahead of him called out: "Here is a closed door, Your Honour!"

Judge Dee and Sergeant Hoong walked up to him. Ma Joong pointed to a large wooden door that was in an excellent state of repair.

"This is the first door we find in this place that closes properly!" the sergeant observed.

Ma Joong put his shoulder against it and nearly fell inside. The door swung open smoothly on well-oiled hinges.

Judge Dee stepped inside.

The room had only one window, barred with a solid iron grating. It was empty but for a rustic bamboo couch in a corner. The floor was swept clean.

Sergeant Hoong entered the room too and walked over to the grated window.

Ma Joong hurriedly stepped out.

"Since our adventure under the bronze bell*," he called to Judge Dee from outside, "I have become very chary of closed spaces! While Your Honour and the sergeant are inside, I shall stand guard here in the corridor and see that no well-wisher slams that door shut on you!"

Judge Dee smiled bleakly.

With a glance at the barred window and the high ceiling he remarked: "You are quite right, Ma Joong! Once that door is locked we would not easily escape from this room!"

Feeling the smooth bamboo of the couch that did not show one speck of dust, he added: "Someone has been living here until quite recently!"

"Not a bad hiding place," the sergeant commented. "This may have served as the lair of a criminal!"

"A criminal or a prisoner," Judge Dee said pensively.

He then ordered Sergeant Hoong to seal the door.

They inspected the other rooms but did not discover anything. As noon was approaching, Judge Dee decided to go back to the tribunal.

---

* See *The Chinese Bell Murders*.

Eighteenth Chapter

JUDGE DEE DECIDES TO CONSULT AN OLD HERMIT;
MA JOONG CATCHES HIS MAN IN THE DRUM TOWER

Once they were back in the tribunal Judge Dee immediately had Headman Fang called in. He ordered him to proceed with ten constables and two stretchers to the country mansion to fetch the remains of the old gate-keeper and his wife.

Then the judge had his luncheon served in his private office.

While he was eating, he called for the Chief Archivist. This was a man over sixty who had been recommended to the judge by the master of the Guild of Silk Merchants. He was a retired silk dealer who had lived all his life in Lan-fang.

As Judge Dee was emptying his bowl of soup, he asked: "Have you ever heard of an old scholar in this district who uses the pen name of 'Hermit Clad in Crane-feathers?' "

The archivist asked: "I suppose that Your Honour means Master Crane Robe?"

"That might well be the same man," Judge Dee said. "He must live somewhere outside the city."

"Yes," the other replied, "that is Master Crane Robe, as he is generally called. He is a hermit who has been living in the mountains outside the south gate as long as I can remember. No one knows how old he is."

"I would like to meet him," the judge said.

The old archivist looked doubtful.

"That is a difficult proposition, Your Honour!" he remarked. "The old master never leaves his mountain valley and he refuses to see visitors. I would not know that he is still alive were it not that last week I heard that two fuel gatherers had happened to see him working in his garden. He is a very wise and learned man, Your Honour. Some even say that he has discovered the Elixir of Life, and soon will leave this world as an Immortal."

Judge Dee slowly smoothed his long beard.

"I have heard many a story," he said, "about such recluses. Usually they turn out to be nothing but extremely lazy and ignorant men. However, I have seen a specimen of this man's calligraphy, which is absolutely superior. He may be an exception. How is the road out there?"

"Your Honour will have to walk the greater part of the way," the archivist replied. "The mountain path is so steep and narrow that even a small sedan chair cannot pass."

As the judge thanked the archivist, Chiao Tai came in. He looked worried.

"I trust that there is nothing wrong in the Chien mansion, Chiao Tai?" asked the judge anxiously.

Chiao Tai sat down and started twirling his short moustache. Then he said: "It is very hard, Your Honour, to explain how one notices a change in the attitude of a body of soldiers. I suppose that it is mainly intuition. For the last two days I have felt there was something wrong with the men.

"I checked with Corporal Ling and found that he too has been worrying. He tells me that some soldiers seem to spend more money than they should be able to account for."

Judge Dee had been listening intently.

"This sounds serious, Chiao Tai!" he said slowly. "Listen to the queer story that Ma Joong has to tell."

Ma Joong again told what he had heard in the Northern Row.

Chiao Tai shook his head.

"I fear that this means trouble, Your Honour! Our ruse of creating an imaginary regiment inspecting the border has worked two ways. On the one hand it enabled us to oust Chien Mow and subdue his men. On the other it may have convinced barbarian tribes planning to raid the city that they have to act now or never, before a garrison arrives."

Judge Dee tugged at his whiskers.

"A barbarian attack on this town would be the last straw!" he exclaimed angrily. "As if we didn't have enough difficulties on our hands already! I suspect that the mysterious trouble-maker who directed Chien Mow is at the back of this! How many men do you think we can trust?"

Chiao Tai looked thoughtful. After a while he said: "I would not count on more than fifty in all, Your Honour!"

All were silent.

Suddenly Judge Dee crashed his fist on the desk.

"It may not be too late yet," he exclaimed. "That remark of yours about a ruse working two ways, Chiao Tai, has given me an idea.

"Ma Joong, we must immediately apprehend that Uigur ruffian you were to meet last night. Can you arrest him without attracting the attention of the people out there?"

Ma Joong looked pleased. He put his large hands on his knees and said with a smile: "Broad daylight is not the most suitable time for such an undertaking, Your Honour, but of course it can be done!"

"Go there immediately with Chiao Tai!" the judge ordered. "But remember that this is to be a secret arrest. If you find that you cannot apprehend him without someone knowing it, you must leave him alone and come back here!"

Ma Joong nodded. He rose and beckoned Chiao Tai to follow him.

They went to the quarters of the guards and sat down in a corner. There they held a whispered consultation. Then Ma Joong left the tribunal alone.

He walked round the tribunal compound and sauntered along the main street leading to the north city gate. He stood about for a moment in front of a small eating house. Then he entered.

Ma Joong had been there once before. The manager greeted him by his name.

"I want my luncheon in a small room upstairs!" Ma Joong announced and climbed the stairs.

On the second floor he found an empty corner room. When he had ordered his luncheon, the door opened and Chiao Tai came in. He had entered the restaurant by the backdoor.

Ma Joong hurriedly took off his upper gown and his cap. While Chiao Tai wrapped these up in a bundle, Ma Joong ruffled his hair and bound a dirty rag round his head. He tucked the slips of his undergarments in his girdle and rolled up his sleeves. With a hasty farewell he left the room.

Tiptoeing down the stairs he went into the kitchen.

"Haven't you a spare oil cake lying about, you fat bastard?" he barked at the cook who was sweating over the kitchen fire.

The cook looked up. When he saw the uncouth ruffian, he hastily gave him a flour cake that had stuck to the pan.

Ma Joong muttered something, grabbed the cake and left the kitchen by the backdoor.

Upstairs Chiao Tai had started on his luncheon. Seeing the familiar brown robe and the pointed black cap of the tribunal, the waiter who served him did not realize that this was not the same man who had entered the restaurant.

Chiao Tai planned to leave while the manager was busy.

In the meantime Ma Joong had strolled to the market near the Drum Tower.

He loitered for a while among the stalls of the street venders, then walked over to the tower.

The dark area under the stone arches that formed the base of the Drum Tower was deserted. On rainy days itinerant merchants often used the sheltered space under the arches for displaying their wares but now they preferred the bright sunlight outside.

Ma Joong looked over his shoulder. When he saw that no one was paying any attention to him he quickly stepped inside. He climbed the narrow stairway that led to the second floor.

This was a kind of loft with large windows on all four sides. In hot weather people sometimes came up to catch the breeze but now there was no one about. The steep ladder to the third floor was barred by a wooden gate. There was no lock on it. It was closed by an iron bolt with a strip bearing the large red seal of the tribunal pasted over it.

Ma Joong calmly broke the seal and wrenched the gate open. Then he climbed up to the third floor.

The huge round drum stood on a platform in the middle of the wooden floor. It was covered with a thick layer of dust that had blown in through the open arches. The drum was sounded only in times of emergency to warn the populace. Evidently it had not been used for many years.

Ma Joong nodded. He quickly went down again. He looked around the corner of one of the arches. When he saw that no one observed him, he slipped out and made for the Northern Row.

In broad daylight the quarter looked even more miserable than at night. There was no one about. Apparently the inmates were sleeping off the night before.

Ma Joong wandered about for a while, but he failed to locate the house he had visited.

He pushed open a door at random. A slovenly clad girl was lying on a wooden couch.

Ma Joong gave the couch a kick. The girl slowly scrambled up. She gave Ma Joong a sullen look and started to scratch her head.

Ma Joong said gruffly: "Orolakchee!"

Suddenly the girl became active. She jumped from the couch and disappeared through the screen at the back. She emerged again dragging along a small dirty boy. Pointing to Ma Joong she rapidly talked to the urchin. Then she said something to Ma Joong. He nodded eagerly although he had not understood a word.

The urchin beckoned to Ma Joong. He rushed out into the street, Ma Joong following on his heels.

The boy slipped into the narrow space between two houses. Ma Joong had difficulty squeezing his large frame through. When he passed underneath a small window-opening about two feet square he reflected that if somebody inside chose this moment to crush his skull there was very little he could do about it.

A nail ripped his robe. Ma Joong stood still and ruefully looked at the large tear. Then he shrugged his shoulders; after all this was an additional touch to his disguise.

Suddenly he heard a soft voice calling from above: "Yoong Bao, Yoong Bao!"

He looked up. The girl Tulbee was looking out of the small window just above his head.

"How are you, my wench?" Ma Joong said pleasantly.

Tulbee seemed very excited. She started to whisper some words, looking fixedly at Ma Joong with her large eyes.

Ma Joong shook his head.

"I don't know what is your trouble, my girl, but I am in a hurry just now. I'll come back later!"

As he made to go on Tulbee stuck her bare arm through the window and clutched the collar of Ma Joong's robe. She pointed in the direction the urchin had gone to, shaking her head emphatically. Then she drew her forefinger across her throat.

"Yes, that they are cutthroats I know!" Ma Joong said with a smile. "But don't you worry, I can take care of myself!"

Tulbee quickly drew him near to the window. For a moment her cheek touched his. There was a slight smell of lambsfat about her, but Ma Joong still thought it was rather pleasant.

Then he softly loosened her arm and went on. When he emerged from the passage, the urchin came to meet him. He jabbered excitedly; apparently he had feared that he had lost Ma Joong.

They scrambled over a heap of refuse, then climbed over a broken down wall.

The boy pointed to a neat plaster hut standing all by itself among tumble-down shacks. Then the urchin ran away.

Ma Joong now recognized the small house he had visited the night before with The Hunter. He knocked on the door.

"Come in!" a voice shouted from inside.

Ma Joong opened the door. He stood stock still.

A tall, spare man was standing with his back against the wall opposite. Ma Joong kept his eyes riveted on the long, evil-looking knife that rested on the palm of the man's right hand. It was poised for the throw.

After a tense moment the man said: "So it is you, Yoong Bao! Sit down!"

He put the knife back in a leather sheath and sat down on one of the low footstools. Ma Joong followed his example.

"Last night," Ma Joong began, "The Hunter directed me to come here, and . . ."

"Shut up!" the other interrupted, "if I had not known all about you, you would be dead now. I never miss when I throw my knife!"

Ma Joong thought to himself that that was probably very true. The Uigur spoke excellent Chinese. Ma Joong took him for a minor chieftain.

Ma Joong smiled ingratiatingly.

"I was told that you, Sir, could help me to a job with a little money in it!"

"You are a traitor," the other said disdainfully, "and traitors think only of money. Yet you may be useful. But before I give you my instructions, I want to make one point very clear. It will be good for your health to avoid even a semblance of double-dealing. At the slightest sign you will find a knife in your back!"

"Certainly, sir!" Ma Joong said hurriedly. "You know my situation. I . . ."

"Enough!" the other said imperiously, "Listen carefully. I never repeat my instructions.

"Three tribes are assembling in the plains across the river. Tomorrow, at midnight, they will occupy this city. We could have taken this town any time we liked, but we want to avoid excessive bloodshed. Your Chinese authorities are self-satisfied and lazy, and this is a distant outpost. If the fall of this town does not create too much interest in the capital, the authorities will not be in too much of a hurry to send an army here. Fortunately for us the route to the west no longer passes through this town. So the central authorities need not worry that we shall interfere with the tribute caravans from the western tributary kingdoms. By the time they decide to take action, we shall have established our kingdom here and be in a position to ward off any attack.

"The point is that we want to take this town by surprise. Everything has been prepared for taking over the tribunal and killing the magistrate and his men. But we need a few more Chinese to dispose of the guards on the gates."

"Ha!" Ma Joong exclaimed, "that is very fortunate! It so happens that I have a friend here who is the very man for you. He was a sergeant in our regular army who had to desert and hide because he got into trouble with the new magistrate here. That fellow Dee is a nasty man!"

"You Chinese are always afraid of your magistrates!" the Uigur said with a sneer. "I am not afraid of any of them! A couple of years ago I slit the throat of one with my own hands!"

Ma Joong gave his host an admiring look.

"Well," he said, "you had better contact my friend. He is a firstclass swordsman and knows all about the passwords and military routine."

"Where is he?" the other asked eagerly.

"Not far from here, sir!" Ma Joong replied. "We found a perfect hiding place for him. He goes out only at night; during the daytime he sleeps on the third floor of the Drum Tower."

The Uigur laughed.

"That is not a bad idea!" he said. "Nobody would look for him there! Go and bring him here!"

Ma Joong looked doubtful. He said with a frown: "As I just remarked, sir, he cannot risk going out by daylight. Could not we go there ourselves? It is quite near!"

The Uigur shot Ma Joong a suspicious look. He thought for a while. Then he rose, transferring his knife from his girdle to his sleeve.

"I hope for you, my friend," he said, "that you are not planning some trick. You walk ahead. At the first suspicious move I shall throw my knife in your back and nobody will even guess where it came from!"

Ma Joong shrugged his shoulders.

"There is no need for all these warnings," he remarked. "Don't you know that we are entirely in your hands? One word to the tribunal and my friend and I are lost!"

"So long as you don't forget that, my friend!" the other said.

They went out into the street, the Uigur following Ma Joong at some distance.

As Ma Joong entered the market place, he saw Chiao Tai standing with his back to a stone memorial tablet. His arms folded in his sleeves, he leisurely surveyed the crowd. His pointed cap, his brown robe with the black sash, together with his air of authority clearly marked him as an officer of the tribunal.

Ma Joong halted in his steps.

This was where Ma Joong had to take his chances. Every moment he expected to feel the knife of the Uigur landing in his back.

Yet he could not move too quickly, for he had to make sure that Chiao Tai saw him. With cold sweat on his brow Ma Joong carefully played his role.

He made as if he hesitated for a moment. When Chiao Tai lifted his hand and slowly smoothed his moustache, Ma Joong turned around and made a detour behind the stone tablet.

As soon as he was safely under the dark arch of the Drum Tower, the Uigur joined him.

"Did you see that bastard leaning against the stone tablet?" Ma Joong whispered excitedly. "That is an officer of the tribunal!"

"So I saw," the other said dryly. "Hurry up!"

Ma Joong climbed the stairway to the second floor. He waited till the Uigur had come up too. Pointing to the broken seal on the gate Ma Joong said: "Look! That is where my friend went up!"

The Uigur pulled his knife from the sheath. He ran his thumb along its razor-sharp blade.

"Climb up!" he ordered.

Ma Joong shrugged his shoulders resignedly. Slowly he ascended the narrow ladder, the Uigur following.

As soon as Ma Joong had his shoulders through the floor opening, he exclaimed: "Well, well! The lazy dog is sleeping!"

So speaking he quickly went up the last steps. Pointing at the drum he said: "Look at the fellow!"

The Uigur came up quickly.

When his head was on a level with the floor, Ma Joong suddenly gave him a kick right in the face.

With a gasp the Uigur fell down the steep ladder.

Ma Joong let himself slide down as fast as he could. At the bottom of the step ladder he just barely dodged a vicious knife thrust. The Uigur was lying on the floor leaning on his left arm. Apparently he had broken a leg, and blood gushed from a nasty gash on his shaven head. But his eyes shone with a green light and he held his knife in a firm grip.

Ma Joong decided there was no time for the finer points. He quickly stepped behind the other. Before the Uigur could scramble around, Ma Joong had placed a kick. The Uigur's head crashed against the side of the ladder. The knife clattered to the floor. He lay quite still.

Ma Joong picked the knife up and put it in his girdle. Then he bound the Uigur's hands behind his back. He felt the other's leg; it seemed broken in more than one place.

Ma Joong went down. He left the tower and strolled nonchalantly out into the market place, heading for the stone tablet.

As he was about to pass in front of the tablet Chiao Tai stepped forward.

"Halt!" he shouted and gripped Ma Joong's arm.

Ma Joong shook his arm free and gave Chiao Tai a sullen look.

"Keep your dirty hands off me, you dogshead!" he barked.

"I am an officer of the tribunal," Chiao Tai said curtly. "I am sure that His Excellency the Judge would like to ask you a few questions, my man!"

"Me?" Ma Joong exclaimed indignantly, "I am an honest citizen, Constable!"

A crowd of idlers had gathered around them, eagerly following this incident.

"Will you come along, or must I knock you down first?" Chiao Tai asked threateningly.

"Shall we let ourselves be bullied by these running-dogs of the tribunal?" Ma Joong asked the crowd.

He noticed to his secret satisfaction that no one made a move.

Ma Joong shrugged his shoulders.

"All right," he said, "the tribunal has nothing on me!"

Chiao Tai bound his hands behind his back.

Ma Joong turned around.

"Listen," he said, "I have a sick friend. Let me give the flour-cake peddler here a few coppers to take some food to him. The man cannot move!"

"Where is the fellow?", Chiao Tai asked.

Ma Joong hesitated a while. Then he said reluctantly: "Well, to tell you the truth, last night he went up the Drum Tower over there to enjoy the fresh air. He fell down the steps and broke his leg. He is now lying on the second floor."

The crowd guffawed.

"I think," Chiao Tai said, "that the tribunal would like to see that patient of yours!" Turning to the crowd he added: "Let someone run to the warden and call him here with four men, a stretcher and a few old blankets!"

Soon the warden came running along with four sturdy fellows carrying bamboo poles.

"Warden, look after this ruffian!" Chiao Tai ordered.

He beckoned two of the men and went to the Drum Tower.

Chiao Tai climbed the stairs with the blankets over his shoulder. The Uigur was still unconscious. Chiao Tai quickly pasted a piece of oil paper over his mouth. Then he rolled him in one of the blankets and wrapped the other around the Uigur's head and shoulders. He called down the stairs. The warden's men came up to carry the limp form down.

The Uigur was laid on the improvised stretcher. The procession set out for the tribunal, Chiao Tai leading the way, dragging Ma Joong along.

They entered by the side gate. As soon as they were inside Chiao Tai said to the warden: "Put the stretcher down here. You and your men can go!"

As Chiao Tai locked the gate behind them, Ma Joong slipped his hands out of the loose ropes. Together with Chiao Tai he carried the stretcher to the jail. They laid the Uigur on the couch in a small cell.

While Ma Joong bandaged the wounded man's head, Chiao Tai cut open his baggy trousers and attached a rough splint to the broken leg.

Ma Joong hurried out to report to the judge.

Chiao Tai locked the door of the cell. He then stood with his back to the door. When the warden of the jail came along, Chiao Tai told him that he had caught a violent ruffian; he would inquire his name as soon as he had calmed down.

Judge Dee's private office was empty but for Tao Gan, who sat dozing in a corner.

Ma Joong shook him awake and asked excitedly: "Where is His Excellency?"

Tao Gan looked up.

"The judge went out with Sergeant Hoong shortly after you and Chiao Tai had left," he replied testily. "What is all the excitement? Did you catch that Uigur fellow?"

"Better than that," Ma Joong said proudly, "we caught the murderer of Magistrate Pan!"

"That will cost you a round of wine tonight, brother!" Tao Gan said contentedly. "Well, His Excellency ordered me to go and invite Yoo Kee to visit the tribunal later this afternoon. I suppose that the judge wants to question him about the death of the old caretaker of the country mansion and his wife. I had better be off!"

Nineteenth Chapter

A RECLUSE DISCOURSES ON THE PURPOSE OF LIFE; JUDGE DEE LEARNS THE OLD GOVERNOR'S SECRET

After Ma Joong and Chiao Tai had left, Judge Dee took a paper from the pile on the desk. He looked at it but did not seem to absorb its contents.

Sergeant Hoong knew that the judge was worried.

Judge Dee impatiently threw down the document. He said: "I don't mind telling you, Sergeant, that if Ma Joong and Chiao Tai do not succeed in catching that man, we shall find ourselves in a most dangerous position!"

"They have done more difficult jobs than that, Your Honour!" the sergeant said reassuringly.

Judge Dee made no comment. For half an hour he concentrated on various official documents.

At last he put down his writing brush.

"It is no use sitting waiting here any longer," he said curtly. "Evidently Ma Joong and Chiao Tai have seen a chance to arrest their man without attracting attention. The weather is fine; let us go and see whether we can find Master Crane Robe!"

Sergeant Hoong knew from long experience that action always was the best sedative when the judge was harassed. He quickly went out to order two horses.

They left the tribunal by the main gate, heading south. They galloped over the marble bridge and passed through the southern city gate.

After they had ridden for some time along the main road, a peasant directed them to a narrow path that led to the mountains. It ended at the foot of a steep ridge.

Judge Dee and the sergeant jumped down from their horses. Sergeant Hoong handed a few coppers to a wood gatherer and asked him to look after the horses for an hour or so. Then they began the ascent.

A strenuous climb took them to the top of the pine-clad ridge. Judge Dee paused there a while to regain his breath. Looking down on the verdant valley that spread out at his feet, he lifted his arms and enjoyed the cool mountain breeze that blew through his wide sleeves.

When Sergeant Hoong, too, had rested himself, they slowly descended by the winding path.

As they went down into the valley, the air became curiously still. The murmur of a brook was the only sound they heard.

They crossed the river by a narrow stone bridge. A side path led to a low thatched roof that was partly visible in the midst of the green foliage. The path took them through dense undergrowth to a crudely made bamboo gate.

Inside they found a small garden. On both sides stood flowering plants of well-nigh a man's height. The judge thought that he had never seen such a profusion of magnificent flowers.

The plaster walls of the small house were overgrown with vines; they seemed to sag under the load of the thatched roof, green with moss. A few rickety wooden steps led up to a single door of unpainted boards. It stood ajar.

Judge Dee meant to call out that there were visitors but somehow or other he felt reluctant to break the quiet atmosphere. He pushed aside the plants that grew by the side of the house.

He saw a rustic verandah made of bamboo poles. A very old man clad in a ragged robe was watering a row of potted flowers. He had a large round straw hat on his head. The delicate fragrance of orchids hung in the air.

Judge Dee pushed the branches further apart and called out: "Is Master Crane Robe at home?"

The old man turned round. The lower half of his face was concealed by a thick moustache and a long white beard; the rest was covered by the broad rim of the hat. He did not answer, but made a vague gesture in the direction of the house.

Then he put down his watering pot and disappeared behind the house without saying a word.

Judge Dee was not very pleased with this casual reception. He curtly told Sergeant Hoong to wait outside.

As the sergeant sat down on the bench near the gate, Judge Dee ascended the steps and entered the house.

He found himself in a large, empty room. The wooden floor was bare and so were the white plaster walls. The furniture consisted of a rough wooden table and two footstools in front of the low, broad window, and a bamboo table against the back wall. It looked like the interior of a peasant's house. But everything was scrupulously clean.

There was no sign of the host. Judge Dee felt annoyed and began to regret that he had come all this way.

With a sigh he sat down on one of the footstools and looked out of the window.

He was struck by the fine view over the rows of flowering plants that stood on racks in the verandah outside. Rare orchids blossomed in porcelain and earthenware bowls; their fragrance seemed to pervade the entire room.

As he was sitting there, Judge Dee felt the immense tranquillity of his surroundings slowly soothe his harassed mind. Listening to the soft humming of an invisible bee, he thought that time seemed to be standing still.

Judge Dee's irritation evaporated. He placed his elbows on the table and leisurely looked around. He noticed that above the bamboo table a pair of paper scrolls had been stuck up on the plaster wall. They bore a couplet written in powerful calligraphy.

Judge Dee idly scanned the lines:

> There are but two roads that lead to the gate of
>   Eternal Life:
> Either one bores his head in the mud like a worm,
>   or like a dragon flies up high into the sky.

The judge reflected that these lines were rather unusual; they could be interpreted in more than one way.

The couplet was signed and sealed, but from where he sat the judge could not read the small characters.

A faded blue screen at the back was pulled aside and the old man entered.

He had changed his ragged robe for a loose gown of brown cloth and his grey head was uncovered. He carried a steaming kettle in his hand.

Judge Dee hastily rose and bowed deeply. The old man nodded casually, and leisurely sat down on the other footstool, with his back to the window. After a moment's hesitation the judge sat down too.

The old man's face was all wrinkled like the skin of a crab apple. But his lips were red like cinnabar. As his host bowed his head while pouring the boiling water in the tea pot, his long white eyebrows screened his eyes like a curtain, so that the judge could not see them.

Judge Dee waited respectfully for the old man to speak first.

When he had replaced the lid on the tea pot, his host folded his arms in his sleeves and looked straight at the judge. Under his bushy brows his piercing eyes were keen, like those of a hawk.

He spoke in a deep, sonorous voice: "Excuse this old man's remissness. I rarely entertain visitors!"

As he spoke the judge noticed that his teeth were even and of a pearly white.

Judge Dee answered: "I beg your forgiveness for this sudden visit. You . . ."

"Ha, Yoo!" the old man interrupted him. "So you are a member of the famous Yoo family!"

"No," the judge corrected him hastily; "my family name is Dee. I . . ."

"Yes, yes," his host mused, "it is a long time since I saw my old friend Yoo. Let me see now, it must be eight years since he died. Or was it nine?"

Judge Dee reflected that the old man was apparently in his dotage. But since his host's mistake seemed to lead him straight to the object of his visit, he did not again try to correct it.

The old man poured the tea.

"Yes," he continued pensively; "a man of great purpose, the old Governor Yoo. Why, it must be seventy years ago now that we studied together in the capital. Yes, he was a man of great purpose who laid his plans far in the future. He was going to eradicate all evil, he was going to reform the Empire . . ."

The old man's voice trailed off. He nodded a few times and sipped his tea.

Judge Dee said diffidently: "I am greatly interested in Governor Yoo's life here in Lan-fang."

His host did not seem to have heard him. He slowly went on sipping his tea.

The judge also brought the cup to his lips. After the first sip he knew that this was the most delicious tea he had ever tasted. Its mellow aroma seemed to pervade his entire body.

His host said suddenly: "The water was taken from where the brook springs from the rocks. Last night I placed the tea leaves in the bud of a chrysanthemum. I took them out this morning when the flower opened in the sun. These leaves are saturated with the essence of the morning dew."

Then, without any transition, he continued: "Yoo set out on his official career and I went away to roam over the Empire. He became a prefect, then a governor. His name rang through the marble halls of the Imperial palace. He persecuted the wicked, protected and encouraged the good, and went a long, long way towards reforming the Empire. Then, one day, when he had nearly realized all his ambitions, he found that he had failed to reform his own son.

"He resigned from all his high offices and came here to live a life of retirement, tending his fields and his garden. So we met again, after more

MASTER CRANE ROBE AND JUDGE DEE

than fifty years. We had reached the same goal by different roads."

The old man suddenly chuckled softly like a child as he added: "The only difference was that one way was long and tortuous, the other short and straight!"

Here his host paused. Judge Dee debated with himself whether he should ask for some explanation of that last remark. But before he could speak, his host went on: "Shortly before he passed away, he and I were discussing this very point. Then he wrote down that couplet on the wall there. Go and admire his calligraphy!"

Judge Dee obediently rose and went to look at the paper scroll on the wall. Now he could read the signature: "Penned by Yoo Shou-chien of the 'Abode of Tranquillity.'" The judge knew now for certain that the testament they had found in Mrs. Yoo's scroll picture was a forgery. The signature resembled the one added to the alleged last will, but it was definitely not the same hand. Judge Dee slowly stroked his beard. Many things had become clear to him.

As he sat down again, the judge said: "If I may respectfully say so, Governor Yoo's calligraphy is excellent, but yours, Sir, is in the inspired class. Your inscription on the gate to the Governor's maze struck me as . . ."

The old man seemed not to have listened. He interrupted the judge saying: "The Governor was so full of purpose that a life time was not enough for exhausting his energy. Even when he had settled down here, he could not stop. Some of his plans for righting old wrongs were not even meant to bear fruit until years later, when he himself would be dead! Wanting to be alone, he built that astonishing maze. As if he could ever be alone, with all his schemes and plans buzzing around him like angry wasps!"

The old man shook his head. He poured another cup of tea.

Judge Dee asked: "Did the old Governor have many friends here?"

His host slowly tugged one of his long eyebrows. Then he chuckled and said: "After all those years, and after all he had seen and heard, Yoo still studied the Confucianist Classics. He sent me a cartload of books out here. I found them most useful. They made excellent kindling for my kitchen stove!"

Judge Dee was going to offer some respectful objections to this derogatory remark about the Classics, but his host ignored him. He continued: "Confucius! Now that was a purposeful man for you! He buzzed about like a gadfly! He never paused long enough to realize that the more he did, the less he achieved, and the more he acquired, the less he possessed. Yes, Confucius was a man full of purpose. So was Governor Yoo . . ."

The old man paused. Then he added peevishly: "And so are you, young man!"

Judge Dee was quite startled by this sudden personal remark. He rose in confusion. With a deep bow he said humbly: "Could this person venture to ask a question . . ."

His host had risen also.

"One question," he gruffly replied, "only leads to another one. You are like a fisherman who turns his back on his river and his nets and climbs a tree in the forest to catch fish! Or like a man who builds a boat of iron, makes a large hole in the bottom and then expects to cross the river! Approach your problems from the right end and begin with the answers. Then, one day, perhaps, you will find the final answer. Good-bye!"

Judge Dee was going to bow his farewell, but his host had already turned his back on him and was shuffling back to the screen at the end of the room.

The judge waited till the blue screen had dropped behind his host's back. Then he went out.

Outside he found Sergeant Hoong sleeping with his back against the garden gate.

The judge woke him up.

The sergeant passed his hand over his eyes. He said with a happy smile: "It seems to me that I have never slept so peacefully! I dreamt of my childhood when I was still four or five years old, things that I had completely forgotten!"

"Yes," Judge Dee said pensively, "this is a very strange abode . . ."

They climbed the mountain ridge in silence.

When they were standing once more under the pinetrees on the top, the sergeant asked: "Did the hermit give Your Honour much information?"

Judge Dee nodded absent-mindedly.

"Yes," he replied after a while, "I learned many things. I know now for certain that the testament we found concealed in the Governor's picture is a forgery. I also learned what was the reason that the old Governor suddenly resigned all his offices. And I know now the other half of General Ding's murder."

The sergeant was going to ask for some further explanation. But noticing the expression on Judge Dee's face he remained silent.

After a brief rest they descended the slope. They mounted their horses and rode back to the city.

Ma Joong was waiting in Judge Dee's private office.

As he started on his report of how he and Chiao Tai had caught the Uigur, the judge shook off his pensive mood and listened eagerly.

Ma Joong assured the judge that no one knew about the arrest. He related in great detail his conversation with the Uigur chieftain, omitting only his unexpected meeting with the girl Tulbee and her warning; he assumed, quite correctly, that Judge Dee would not be interested in that romantic interlude.

"That is excellent work!" Judge Dee exclaimed when Ma Joong had finished. "Now we have the trump card in our hands!"

Ma Joong added: "Tao Gan is now entertaining Yoo Kee in the reception hall. They are drinking tea together. When I looked in there a few moments ago, Tao Gan was fretting because Yoo Kee is talking so fast that he can't get in a word!"

The judge looked pleased. He said to Sergeant Hoong: "Sergeant, go to the reception hall and tell Yoo Kee that to my great regret I am unavoidably detained by urgent business. Offer him my apologies and inform him that I shall see him as soon as I am free!"

When the sergeant started to go the judge asked: "Did you, by the way, succeed in finding out the whereabouts of Mrs. Lee, that friend of the Governor's widow?"

"I ordered Headman Fang to see to that, Your Honour," replied the sergeant. "I thought that since he is a local man he might obtain quicker results than I."

The judge nodded. Then he asked Ma Joong: "What are the results of the autopsy on the old couple we found in the garden of the Governor's mansion?"

"The coroner confirmed that they died a natural death, Your Honour," Ma Joong replied.

Judge Dee nodded. He rose and started changing into his official robes. While he was placing the winged judge's cap on his head, he suddenly said: "If I am not mistaken, Ma Joong, you reached the ninth and highest grade in boxing about ten years ago, did you not?"

The tall fellow squared his shoulders. He replied proudly: "Yes indeed, Your Honour!"

"Now think back," Judge Dee ordered, "and tell me how you felt towards your master when you were still a beginner, say of the second or third grade!"

Ma Joong was not accustomed to analyse his feelings. He knitted his brows and thought furiously. After a while he answered slowly: "Well, Your Honour, I was deeply devoted to my master. He certainly was one of the finest boxers of our time and I admired him greatly. But when I boxed with him and he eluded my cleverest blows without the slightest effort, playfully hitting me anywhere he liked despite my frantic defence, I still admired him, but at the same time I hated him because of his infinite superiority!"

Judge Dee smiled wanly.

"Thank you, my friend!" he said. "This afternoon I went to the mountains south of this city and there met a person who greatly disturbed me. Now you have put into words exactly what I did not dare to formulate so clearly for myself!"

Ma Joong had no idea what the judge was talking about, but he felt flattered by the praise. With a broad smile he pulled aside the screen leading to the court hall. The judge passed through and ascended the dais.

Twentieth Chapter

A REBEL CHIEFTAIN CONFESSES UNDER TORTURE; A MYSTERIOUS STRANGER IS AT LAST IDENTIFIED

Three beats on the gong announced the opening of the afternoon session of the tribunal.

No one knew that anything but routine matters would be dealt with, so only a few dozen spectators had drifted into the court hall.

As soon as Judge Dee had seated himself behind the bench and opened the session, he gave a sign to Headman Fang. Four constables went to the entrance of the court hall and remained standing there on guard.

"Because of important reasons of state," Judge Dee announced, "no one shall leave this court before the session is closed!"

A murmur of astonishment rose from the audience.

Judge Dee took up his vermilion brush and filled out a slip for the warden of the jail.

Two constables brought in the Uigur. He walked with difficulty, they had to support him by his arms.

In front of the dais he let himself down on one knee; the splinted leg he stretched out in front with a groan of pain.

"State your name and profession!" Judge Dee ordered.

The man lifted his head. Deep hatred shone from his burning eyes.

"I am Prince Ooljin, of the Blue Tribe of the Uigurs!" he snapped.

"Among you barbarians," the judge said coldly, "a man calls himself a prince as soon as he has twenty horses! But that is neither here nor there.

"The Imperial Government in its infinite grace has deigned to accept the Khan of the Uigurs as a vassal, and he has duly sworn allegiance to His Majesty, taking a solemn oath with Heaven and Earth as witness.

"You, Ooljin, have been scheming to attack this town. You have betrayed your own Khan and you are guilty of rebellion against the Imperial Government.

"Rebellion is a most serious crime, it is punished with the extreme penalty in a severe form. Your only hope for having this punishment somewhat mitigated lies in telling the complete truth; this means that you must also reveal who are the Chinese traitors who promised to collaborate with you in the execution of your nefarious scheme."

"You call such a Chinese a traitor," the Uigur shouted, "I call him a just man! Some Chinese recognize that what they have taken from us must be given back. Did not you Chinese encroach on our pastures, your peasants ploughing our good grasslands and transforming them into rice fields? Have we not been driven away farther and farther into the desert where our horses and cattle die on our hands?

"I shall not reveal the names of those Chinese who realized the awful wrong that your people have done to us, the Uigur tribes!"

The headman was going to hit him, but the judge raised his hand.

Leaning forward in his chair he said quietly: "It so happens that I have no time for preliminaries. Your right leg is already broken, you cannot walk anyway. So it won't inconvenience you much if your other leg should be broken too."

Judge Dee gave a sign to the headman.

Two constables threw the Uigur on his back on the floor and stood with their feet on his hands. Another brought a wooden trestle of about two feet high.

The headman lifted Ooljin's left leg and bound the foot to the trestle. He looked up at the judge.

As Judge Dee nodded, a sturdy constable struck the knee with a heavy rounded stick.

The Uigur let out a hoarse scream.

"Take your time," the judge ordered the constable, "don't hit too fast!"

The constable struck a blow on the shin, then two on the thigh.

Ooljin screamed and cursed in his own language. When his shin was struck again he yelled: "One day our hordes shall invade your accursed country; we shall raze your walls and burn your cities; we shall kill your men and make your women and children our slaves . . ."

His voice became a wild scream as the constable hit him another vicious blow. As he raised the stick again for the final blow that would break the leg, Judge Dee held up his hand.

"You will realize, Ooljin," he said casually, "that this interrogation is mere routine. I just want you to confirm what your Chinese confederate told me when he reported on you and your tribesmen and gave away the entire plot!"

With a superhuman effort the Uigur tore away one of his hands from under the feet of the constable. Raising himself on his elbow he shouted: "Don't try to catch me with brazen lies, you dog official!"

"Well," Judge Dee observed coldly, "of course a Chinese is much too clever for you stupid barbarians. He made it appear as if he was on your side. And when the time came, he reported everything to the authorities. Soon the government shall appoint him to a lucrative post as a reward for his valuable information. Don't you see how you and your ignorant Khan were made fools of?"

When he began to speak the judge had given a sign to Ma Joong, and now Yoo Kee was led before the dais.

When he saw the Uigur lying on the floor, Yoo Kee's face turned ashen. He wanted to run away, but Ma Joong grabbed his arm in a vice-like grip.

As soon as the Uigur saw Yoo Kee, he spat out a string of curses.

"You son of a dog!" he yelled. "You vile traitor! Cursed be the day on which an honest Uigur resolved to work for a double-dealing Chinese cur like you!"

"Your Honour, this man is crazy!" Yoo Kee shouted.

Judge Dee ignored him. He calmly addressed the Uigur: "Who are your accomplices in this man's mansion?"

Ooljin gave the names of the two Uigur warriors hired by Yoo Kee ostensibly as fencing masters. Then he shouted: "And let me tell you that there are also Chinese traitors! That dogshead Yoo may have fooled me, but I assure you that those other Chinese bastards were prepared to do everything just for the money!"

He then enumerated the names of three Chinese shopkeepers and four soldiers.

Tao Gan carefully noted down their names.

Judge Dee beckoned Chiao Tai to his side. He said in a whisper: "Go immediately to your quarters in Chien's mansion and place those four soldiers under arrest. Then go with Corporal Ling and twenty men to Yoo Kee's mansion and arrest the two Uigurs there. You will then apprehend the three Chinese shopkeepers. Finally you will arrest The Hunter and his confederates in the Northern Row!"

As Chiao Tai hurried away, Judge Dee said to Ooljin: "I am not an unjust man, Ooljin. I won't stand for a Chinese receiving a reward because he betrayed you after he had instigated and abetted your crime. If you want to prevent this man Yoo Kee from getting away with his treacherous deeds, you had better tell how Magistrate Pan was murdered!"

The Uigur's eyes blazed with unholy glee.

"Here is my revenge!" he shouted. "Listen, you official! Four years ago that man Yoo Kee gave me ten silver pieces. He told me to go to the tribunal and tell the new magistrate that that very night he could catch Yoo Kee in a secret conference with an emissary of the Uigur Khan, near the ford. Magistrate Pan came along with one assistant. The latter I knocked down as soon as we were outside the city gate. I myself cut the magistrate's throat and dragged his body to the river bank."

Ooljin spat in the direction of Yoo Kee.

"Now what about your reward, you dog?" he yelled.

Judge Dee nodded to the senior scribe. He read aloud his notes of what the Uigur had said. Ooljin agreed that it was a true account of his confession. The document was handed to the Uigur and he impressed his thumbmark on it.

Then Judge Dee spoke: "You, Ooljin, are an Uigur prince from over the border and your crime of sedition concerns the external relations of our Empire. I am in no position to find out if and how deeply your Khan and the chieftains of the other tribes are implicated in this scheme of rebellion. It is not within my competence to pass judgment on you. You shall be conveyed immediately to the capital. There your crime shall be dealt with by the Board for Barbarian Affairs."

He gave a sign to the headman. Prince Ooljin was laid on a stretcher and carried back to the jail.

"Bring the criminal Yoo Kee before me!" Judge Dee ordered.

As Yoo Kee was pressed to his knees in front of the dais, Judge Dee said sternly: "Yoo Kee, you are guilty of high treason. This is a crime against the state for which the law prescribes a terrible punishment. Yet perhaps the great name of your late father and a recommendation from me might bring the authorities to mitigate somewhat the fearful fate that awaits you. Therefore I advise you to confess now and give a full account of your crime!"

Yoo Kee did not reply. His head hung low and he breathed heavily. Judge Dee gave a sign to the headman to leave him alone.

At last Yoo Kee looked up. He said in a toneless voice, quite different from his accustomed animated way of talking: "Beyond the two Uigurs, I have no accomplices in my mansion. I would have told my servants at the very last moment that we were going to take over the town. The four soldiers received a gift in money. Tomorrow, at the hour of midnight, they were to light a signal fire on the highest watchtower in the Chien mansion. They were told that this would be the sign for a band of ruffians to create a disturbance and that that was the cover under which the two large goldsmiths' shops of this city would be looted. In fact, however, the fire was to be the sign for the Uigur tribes across the river to attack. Ooljin and his Chinese helpers would then have opened the Watergate, and . . ."

"Enough!" Judge Dee interrupted him. "Tomorrow you shall have full opportunity for telling the entire story.

"Now I only want you to answer one question. What did you do with the testament you found concealed in your late father's scroll picture?"

A look of surprise flashed over Yoo Kee's haggard face. He replied: "Since the original testament stated that the property was to be divided equally between me and my half brother Yoo Shan, I destroyed it. Instead I inserted into the lining of the scroll a paper that I had written myself and that would establish beyond all doubt that I was the only rightful heir."

"You see," the judge said disdainfully, "that every one of your black deeds is known to me! Lead the criminal back to jail!"

Not long after the judge had closed the session, Chiao Tai came to his private office and reported that all the criminals had been duly placed under arrest. In the Northern Row there had been some trouble; The Hunter had resisted arrest, but had been knocked down by Corporal Ling.

Judge Dee leaned back in his chair. Sipping a cup of hot tea he said: "Ooljin and the six Uigurs must be conveyed to the capital. Let Corporal Ling select ten soldiers, and set out on horseback tomorrow morning. If they change horses at the nearest military post, they should be in the capital within a week. The three shopkeepers and the soldiers who accepted the bribe, I shall judge here."

Looking at his four lieutenants sitting in a half circle in front of his desk, Judge Dee continued with a smile: "I think that with the arrest of the leaders we have nipped this plot in the bud!"

Chiao Tai nodded eagerly.

"The Uigur tribesmen," he said, "are not to be despised as warriors in a pitched battle in the open field. They are fine horsemen and their archers shoot with deadly accuracy. But they have neither the experience nor the equipment necessary for laying siege to a walled city. When tomorrow night they don't see the signal fire on the watch tower, they will not dare to attack!"

Judge Dee nodded.

"I leave it to you, Chiao Tai," he said, "to make the necessary preparations to meet any eventuality."

With a bleak smile the judge added: "You cannot complain that you are not kept busy here, my friends!"

"The other day when we were approaching Lan-fang," Sergeant Hoong said with a smile, "Your Honour observed that our task here would be interesting because we would meet here unusual problems! That surmise has indeed come true!"

Judge Dee wearily passed his hand over his eyes.

"I find it difficult to believe," he said, "that it is only one week since we arrived here in Lan-fang!"

Putting his hands into his wide sleeves he continued: "Looking back upon the last few days I think that Chien Mow's mysterious visitor worried me more than anything else. It was evident that he was the brain behind the tyrant's activities. I knew that as long as he was free anything might happen!"

"How did Your Honour discover that it was Yoo Kee?" Tao Gan asked. "As far as I can see there was no clue at all to the stranger's identity!"

Judge Dee nodded.

"It is true," he replied, "we did not know much. Yet there were two indirect clues. First, we knew that he must be a man conversant with the internal and external affairs of the Empire. Second, that he probably lived in the vicinity of Chien Mow's mansion.

"I must confess that at first I strongly suspected Woo Feng of being our man. Woo is exactly the kind of reckless fellow who would venture on such a wild scheme. And his family background would have given him sufficient knowledge of affairs of state to guide Chien Mow's actions."

"Moreover," Sergeant Hoong interrupted, "there is Woo's queer predilection for barbarian art!"

"Exactly!" said Judge Dee. "However, Woo lived far from Chien Mow's mansion and it seemed unlikely to me that he would be able to leave his quarters regularly in an elaborate disguise without the garrulous host of the Eternal Spring Wineshop coming to know of it. Lastly, Ma Joong's talk with The Hunter proved that the plans of the conspirators were not affected by Woo's arrest."

Judge Dee pulled his hands from his sleeves and leaned with his elbows on the table. Looking at Chiao Tai he continued: "You, Chiao Tai, suggested the solution to me!"

Chiao Tai looked his astonishment at this unexpected statement.

"Yes," the judge went on, "it was you who, in connection with our imaginary army, pointed out to me that a ruse could work two ways! It suddenly dawned on me that Yoo Kee's elaborate preparations for defending himself against a barbarian attack could as well be explained as preparations for taking part in such a raid!

"Once my suspicions had been aroused I found that Yoo Kee fitted the part of Chien Mow's secret adviser very well. First, Yoo Kee is, of course, thoroughly conversant with political affairs; he grew up in the house of one of the greatest statesmen of our time. Second, his house is within walking distance of Chien Mow's mansion, he would soon see the black flag that Chien used to hoist on his gate when he wanted Yoo Kee to visit him that day.

"Then I started to ask myself a few questions. Why should a man who is afraid of a barbarian raid purchase a mansion in the most dangerous spot, in the southwest corner of the city near the Watergate? And that while he already possessed a mansion near the East Gate, a safe location where he can flee to the mountains at the first sign of danger? And why did Chien Mow take no measures against Yoo Kee when the latter took Chien's best fencing master away?

"There could be only one answer: Yoo Kee was Chien's adviser; it was he who organized the plan for establishing an independent kingdom here on the border.

"Lastly, Chien Mow told me so himself!"

"When was that, Your Honour?" Sergeant Hoong and Ma Joong exclaimed at the same time. Tao Gan and Chiao Tai stared at the judge in utter amazement.

Judge Dee looked at his lieutenants with a quizzical smile.

"When Chien Mow was dying," he replied, "we all thought that he tried to start a sentence with 'You . . . .' I should have known better! A dying man who can hardly speak does not try to formulate a complicated sentence. He only wanted to pronounce one name, the name of the murderer of Magistrate Pan. And that name was Yoo Kee!"

Tao Gan crashed his fist on the desk. He gave the others a meaningful look.

"I must add," Judge Dee continued, "that it was old Master Crane Robe who suggested this to me. At the very beginning of our conversation he misheard 'Yoo' for 'You.' At least I thought that he had misheard . . . Looking back on that strange conversation I suspect that every word of the old master was said with a purpose and had a very special meaning . . ."

Judge Dee's voice trailed off. He fell silent and for a few moments pensively stroked his beard. Then he looked at his lieutenants and continued in a brisk voice: "Tomorrow I shall close the case against Yoo Kee. The charge of high treason is the most serious one that can be made. It disposes of his murdering Magistrate Pan.

"In the same session, I shall close the murder of General Ding!"

The last announcement gave Judge Dee's lieutenants their second shock that evening. They all spoke together.

Judge Dee raised his hand.

"Yes," he said, "I have finally found the solution of that queer and complicated case. The man who actually killed the General signed his name to the deed!"

"So it was, after all, that impudent rascal Woo!" Sergeant Hoong said excitedly.

"Tomorrow," Judge Dee said calmly, "you will know how General Ding met his death."

He sipped his tea. Then he went on: "Today we have made much progress. Yet there still remain two vexing problems. The first is a practical and urgent one, namely the disappearance of White Orchid. The second is a less urgent one, but all the same it needs our full attention. I mean the riddle of Governor Yoo's picture.

"Unless we can establish that Mrs. Yoo and her son Yoo Shan are the rightful owners of half of the Governor's property, they will forever be as destitute as they are now. For since Yoo Kee will be indicted on the charge of high treason, the government will confiscate all his possessions.

"Unfortunately, Yoo Kee destroyed the testament he found in the Governor's scroll picture. So that proof is gone. Yoo Kee's confession does not alter the fact that the old Governor on his deathbed bequeathed the picture to Mrs. Yoo and her son, and 'all the rest' to Yoo Kee. The higher authorities, and especially the Board of Finance will base themselves on that oral will, and confiscate all Yoo Kee's property. Thus unless I solve the riddle of that picture, Mrs. Yoo and Yoo Shan will receive nothing!"

Tao Gan nodded. He slowly played with the three long hairs that sprouted from his left cheek. Then he asked: "At the beginning we did not know that Yoo Kee was concerned with this plan for taking the city. We only knew that he was the defendant in an inheritance suit. Why did Your Honour right from the beginning take such a great interest in the case of Yoo versus Yoo?"

Judge Dee answered with a smile: "Since I am explaining, I may as well tell you the background of my special interest in that case.

"I must state that I have always been deeply interested in the personality of Governor Yoo Shou-chien. Many years ago when I was preparing myself for my second examination, I copied out all the records I could lay hands on of the criminal cases solved by Governor Yoo when he was still a district magistrate. Poring over those I made it my ambition to learn his brilliant deductive methods. Later I carefully studied his inspired memorials to the Throne and tried to absorb his burning passion for justice and his deep devotion to the state and the people. He was for me the shining example, the ideal of the perfect servant of the state.

"How I longed to meet him in person! But that was of course quite impossible since he was a Governor and I but a struggling young candidate.

"Then Governor Yoo suddenly resigned. This inexplicable action of my hero perturbed me greatly. I have been wondering about it ever since.

"When I found in the archives here in Lan-fang the file Yoo versus Yoo, it seemed to me as if at last I would have an opportunity of coming nearer to the idol of my youth, that I would meet him, as it were, in the spirit.

The riddle of his testament seemed to me a challenge from beyond the grave . . ."

Judge Dee paused and looked intently at the scroll picture hanging on the wall opposite.

As he pointed at it he continued: "I am firmly resolved to find the secret of that scroll! Since Yoo Kee's confession, the old Governor's message has become more than a challenge. I feel it is my solemn duty to the Governor's memory to see to it that the widow and the son of the man I worshipped obtain what is rightfully theirs. All the more so since I sent his eldest son to the execution ground."

The judge rose and stood in front of the picture. His lieutenants left their seats and also gazed once more at the mysterious landscape.

Folding his hands in his sleeves Judge Dee said slowly: " 'Bowers of Empty Illusion'! How deeply it must have shocked the old Governor when he found that his eldest son had inherited his father's brilliant mind, but nothing of his noble character!

"I know every brush stroke of this picture by heart. I had hoped that the old country mansion would have given me some clue, yet I cannot . . ."

Suddenly the judge stopped. Bending forward he looked over the entire picture from top to bottom. As he straightened himself he slowly tugged at his whiskers. Then he turned around. His eyes were shining.

"I have found it, my friends!" he exclaimed. "Tomorrow, this riddle also will be solved!"

Twenty-first Chapter

JUDGE DEE CLOSES THE CASE OF THE MURDERED GENERAL;
CHIAO TAI RELATES THE STORY OF A MILITARY DISASTER

The next day, when Judge Dee opened the morning session of the tribunal hundreds of people crowded into the courtroom. The news of Yoo Kee's arrest had spread all over the town and the wildest rumours were circulating with regard to the arrest of the Uigur chieftain.

Judge Dee slowly surveyed the crowd, and pondered for a while as to how he should start the questioning. He reflected that Yoo Kee excelled in dissimulation and secret planning; he was wont to direct affairs from behind a carefully constructed screen. Often such persons break down completely once they have been forced to come out into the open.

The judge wrote Yoo Kee's name on a slip and handed it to Headman Fang.

As Yoo Kee was brought in Judge Dee saw that his surmise had been correct. Yoo Kee had changed overnight into a different person. The cloak of easy joviality that he had so carefully worn had fallen off. There was left nothing but a listless, broken man.

Judge Dee said quietly: "At yesterday's session we went through the formalities. You can now begin immediately with your confession!"

"Your Honour," Yoo Kee spoke in a toneless voice, "when a man has been left no hope either in this world or the next there is no reason why he should not tell the whole truth."

Yoo Kee paused for a moment. Then he suddenly said bitterly: "I know that my father hated me. Well, I hated him, too, although I admit that I feared him! While he was still alive, I had already made the firm resolution that I would become a greater man than he. He had been a governor; I was to be a sovereign ruler!

"For years I made a careful study of the border situation. I realized that if the barbarian tribes could be united and given some guidance, they could easily overrun the entire border region. With Lan-fang as capital I could found a kingdom astride the border. While keeping off the Chinese authorities by promises of submission and lengthy negotiations about vassalage, I would steadily enlarge the kingdom to the west by attracting more and more barbarian chieftains; thus while my power would be growing in the west, my attitude to the Chinese authorities in the east would gradually stiffen until I would be so strong that no one would dare to attack me."

Yoo Kee heaved a sigh, then went on: "I was confident that I had sufficient diplomatic skill and knowledge of Chinese internal politics to execute this scheme. But I lacked military experience. In Chien Mow I found a useful tool. He was a determined and ruthless man, but he knew he was not qualified to act as a political leader. I encouraged him to establish himself as the local ruler here and showed him how he could consolidate his position against the central authorities. He acknowledged my leadership. After our plans had materialized, I would have appointed Chien Mow as my Generalissimo. At the same time I used Chien's activities to test the reaction of the central authorities. Everything succeeded; the central government seemed to acquiesce in the irregular situation here. So I resolved to take the next step and establish contact with the Uigur tribes.

"Then that interfering fool, Magistrate Pan arrived. Through an unfortunate accident a letter I had written to an Uigur chieftain fell into his hands. I had to act quickly. I ordered Orolakchee, a cousin of the Khan and my confidential agent, to lure Pan to the river and kill him. Chien Mow was angry; he feared that the government would retaliate. But I instructed him as to how he could cover up this crime, and nothing untoward happened."

Judge Dee was going to interrupt Yoo Kee but on second thought he decided that it was better to let him tell his story in his own way. Yoo Kee went on in the same toneless voice: "I would have come out into the open then, were it not that the Khan received information of big Chinese victories over the barbarians in the north. He started to waver and finally withdrew his support. Then I engaged in complicated negotiations with minor chieftains, and finally succeeded in uniting three powerful tribes. They would attack the city if I guaranteed that the Watergate would be open and that the main points inside the town would be occupied by my men.

"When the date had been fixed, Your Honour arrived with a regiment of the regular army for inspecting the border; Chien Mow was arrested and his men dispersed. I feared that my plans had leaked out and that in the near future a strong garrison would be sent to Lan-fang. I decided to take immediate action.

"Tonight three Uigur tribes will gather in the plain. When at midnight they see the signal fire on the watchtower, they will ford the river and enter the city by the Watergate.

"That is all!"

The crowd started to talk excitedly. They realized that they had narrowly escaped being overrun by cruel barbarian horsemen.

"Silence!" shouted Judge Dee.

Then he ordered Yoo Kee: "State how many men these three tribes can put under arms!"

Yoo Kee thought for a while, then he replied: "About two thousand trained mounted archers, and a few hundred footmen."

"What part were the three Chinese shopkeepers to play in this scheme?" asked the judge.

"I never met them," Yoo Kee answered. "It was my fixed policy to remain in the background as much as possible. I ordered Orolakchee to enlist the help of about one dozen Chinese to guide the Uigur warriors to the tribunal and the gates. He located those men and guaranteed their support."

Judge Dee gave a sign to the senior scribe. He read out his record of Yoo Kee's statement, and Yoo Kee affixed his thumbmark to it.

Then the judge spoke in a solemn voice: "Yoo Kee, I pronounce you guilty of the crime of high treason. It is possible that the higher authorities will mitigate to some degree the severity of the extreme penalty in deference to the meritorious services of your late father, and because you confessed without pressure. But it is my duty to warn you that for high treason the Code prescribes execution by the process called 'lingering death,' that is, being cut to pieces alive.

"Lead the criminal away!"

Then Judge Dee addressed the court: "I have arrested all the leaders of this nefarious scheme. The barbarians will not dare to attack tonight when they do not see the signal fire. I have issued orders, however, to make the necessary preparations for any eventuality. In the course of the day you will receive instructions from your wardens what to do. The barbarians have never been able to take a walled city, so there is nothing to fear!"

The spectators broke into cheers.

Judge Dee hit his gavel on the bench. Then he announced: "I shall now hear the case Ding versus Woo."

He filled out a slip with his vermilion brush. Soon Woo Feng was led before the dais by two constables.

As soon as Woo was kneeling, the judge took from his sleeve a cardboard box and pushed it over the edge of the bench. It fell down with a thud in front of Woo.

He looked at it curiously. It was the box discovered in the sleeve of the murdered General. The corner the mouse had gnawed off had been neatly repaired.

The judge asked: "Are you familiar with that box?"

Woo looked up.

"This," he replied, "is the kind of box they sell sweet plums in. I have seen hundreds of them on sale on the market near the Drum Tower. Occasionally I have bought one myself. Thus, although I am indeed familiar with such boxes in general, I have never seen this particular one. The congratulatory inscription on top evidently means that it was offered to someone as a present."

"You are quite right," Judge Dee said, "it is an anniversary present. Do you mind tasting the plums inside?"

Woo gave the judge a bewildered look. Then he shrugged his shoulders and replied:

"Not in the least, Your Honour!"

He opened the box. Nine plums were neatly arranged on a layer of white tissue paper. Woo poked them with his forefinger. When he had found a soft one he put it in his mouth. He ate it and spat the stone on the floor.

"Does Your Honour wish me to eat more?" Woo asked politely.

"That is quite sufficient!" Judge Dee said coldly. "You may stand back!"

Woo rose and looked around at the constables. They made no move to grab him and lead him back to the jail. So he retreated a few paces and remained standing there. He looked curiously at the judge.

"Let Candidate Ding come forward!" Judge Dee ordered

As Ding knelt in front of the bench, Judge Dee spoke: "Candidate Ding, I have now discovered who killed your father. This case proved to be a singularly complicated one. I don't pretend to have disentangled all its ramifications. Your father's life was threatened from more than one side, and more than one attempt was made to kill him. This court, however, is concerned only with the one attempt that succeeded. The accused Woo had nothing to do with that. Hence the case against Woo Feng is herewith dismissed!"

A murmur of astonishment rose from the crowd. Candidate Ding remained silent. He did not repeat his accusation against Woo.

Woo cried out: "Your Honour, has White Orchid been found?"

When the judge shook his head, Woo turned round without another word and unceremoniously elbowed his way through the spectators to the door of the court hall.

Judge Dee took a red-lacquered writing brush from the bench.

"Rise, Candidate Ding," he ordered, "and tell me what you know about this brush!"

As he spoke the judge held out the writing brush to Ding, the open end of the shaft pointing straight at the young man's face.

Candidate Ding looked dumbfounded. He took the brush from Judge Dee's hands and turned it around in his fingers. When he had read the engraved inscription he nodded his head.

"Now that I see the inscription I remember, Your Honour! Some years ago when my father was showing me some rare old jade pieces, he also took out this writing brush. He told me that it was an advance gift for his sixtieth birthday from a very exalted personage. My father did not reveal his name, but he said that that person had told him that since he feared his end was near he wished to present the brush in advance; my father was not to use it until he had actually celebrated his sixtieth birthday.

"My father valued this writing brush highly. After he had shown it to me, he put it back into the locked box where he kept his jade collection."

"That writing brush," Judge Dee said gravely, "is the instrument that killed your father!"

Candidate Ding looked in bewilderment at the brush in his hands. He scrutinized it carefully and peered inside the hollow shaft. Then he shook his head doubtfully.

Judge Dee had followed intently his every move. Then he said curtly: "Give that brush back to me. I shall demonstrate how the deed was done!"

When Candidate Ding had handed back the brush, Judge Dee kept it in his left hand. With his right he took a small wooden cylinder from his sleeve and held it up so that every one could see it.

"This," he said, "is an exact replica in wood of the hilt of the small knife that was found in General Ding's throat; it is just as long as the entire dagger including the blade. I shall now insert it into the hollow shaft of this brush."

The stick fitted exactly into the shaft. But when it had gone in for half an inch, it stuck.

Judge Dee handed the brush to Ma Joong.

"Press this stick further down!" he ordered.

Ma Joong placed his large thumb over the protruding end of the stick. With evident difficulty he pressed it down till it had disappeared into the shaft.

He looked expectantly at the judge.

"Stretch out your arm and release your thumb as quickly as you can!" ordered the judge.

The wooden stick shot up in the air for about five feet, then clattered down on the stoneflags.

Judge Dee leaned back in his chair. Stroking his beard he said slowly: "This writing brush is an ingenious instrument of death. Its hollow shaft contains a number of thin coils of what I presume to be southern rattan. After he had inserted these coils the person who made this instrument pressed them down as far as they would go with a hollow tube. He poured melted resin of the lacquer tree down that tube and held the coils down till the resin had completely dried. Then he removed the tube and replaced it with this."

Judge Dee opened a small box and with great care took from it the knife that had been found in the dead General's throat.

"You will see," he continued, "that its tubular hilt fits exactly into the shaft of this brush, while its hollow blade fits its curved inside. Even if one peered into the shaft, the knife would be invisible.

"Some years ago a certain person presented this writing brush to the General and therewith pronounced his death sentence. He knew that when the General used this brush, he would sooner or later burn its tip in a candle to discard the superfluous hairs, as we all do when we start writing with a new brush. The heat of the flame would soften the resin, the coils would be released and the poisoned knife would shoot out of the shaft. It was a ten to one chance that it would hit the victim in the face or throat. Afterwards the coils would be invisible because they would have stretched out along the inside of the hollow shaft."

While Judge Dee was speaking, Candidate Ding had first shown an expression of utter bewilderment. Slowly this expression had changed to one of incredulous horror. Now he cried out: "Who, Your Honour, contrived this diabolical device?"

"He signed his name to the deed," Judge Dee said quietly. "But for that fact I would never have solved this riddle. Let me read out to you the inscription: 'With respectful congratulations on the completion of six cycles. "The Abode of Tranquillity." ' "

"Who is that? I have never heard that studio name!" Candidate Ding cried out.

Judge Dee nodded.

"It was known only to a few intimate friends," he replied. "Yesterday I found out that it is the pen name of the late Governor Yoo Shou-chien!"

Loud exclamations rose from the audience.

When the excitement had subsided Judge Dee spoke: "It so happens that on the same day both the father and the son appear in this tribunal, the son alive and the father in spirit.

"You, Candidate Ding, will probably know better than I, what deed of your father motivated old Governor Yoo to condemn him to death and to execute the sentence himself in this singular way. However this may be, I cannot proceed against the dead. I, the magistrate, herewith declare the case closed!"

Judge Dee let his gavel descend on the bench. He rose and disappeared through the screen behind the dais.

As the spectators filed out of the court hall, they talked excitedly about the unexpected solution of the General's murder. They were full of praise for Judge Dee for having found out the ingenious device. A few elderly men with experience in court matters, however, were doubtful. They could not understand the significance of the incident of the box with plums and remarked to each other that evidently there was more to this case than met the eye.

When Headman Fang entered the quarters of the guards he found Woo waiting for him.

Woo bowed deeply for the headman and said hastily: "Please allow me to take part in the search for your daughter!"

Headman Fang looked at him thoughtfully. Then he answered: "Since you, Mr. Woo, were prepared to suffer severe torture for my daughter's sake, I shall welcome your assistance. I have an order to carry out just now. Wait here for a few moments. When I am back, I shall tell you everything about our first unsuccessful search."

Cutting short Woo's protests, the headman walked to the gate and surveyed the crowd that was streaming out. He saw Candidate Ding who was just stepping out into the street. Headman Fang overtook him and said: "Mr. Ding, His Excellency would like to see you for a moment in his private office."

Judge Dee was sitting behind his desk with his four lieutenants gathered round him. The judge had ordered Tao Gan to saw the shaft of the writing brush in two. They had seen the clot of resin at the bottom of the shaft, and the thin rattan strips stretched out along its inside.

When Headman Fang had shown Candidate Ding in, Judge Dee turned to his lieutenants and said: "Your presence is no longer required!"

They rose and left for the corridor. Chiao Tai, however, remained standing in front of Judge Dee's desk.

"Your Honour," he said stiffly, "I beg to be allowed to stay!"

Judge Dee raised his eyebrows and shot a curious look at Chiao Tai's impassive face. Then he nodded and motioned to a footstool by the side of his desk.

Chiao Tai sat down and Candidate Ding made a move to follow his example. But as the judge did not ask him to be seated, after some hesitation the young man remained standing where he was. Then Judge Dee spoke: "Candidate Ding, I refrained from denouncing your late father in public. Were it not for a special reason which I shall specify presently, I would not denounce him before you who are his only son.

"I know exactly why your father was compelled to resign. The confidential documents relating to that case happened to pass through the Office of Records and Compilation in the capital when I was working there. There were no details, for not a single eye-witness to your father's black deed survived the disaster. Commander Woo, however, collected sufficient secondary evidence to show beyond doubt that your father was responsible for the massacre of one entire regiment of our Imperial army.

"When political considerations prevented the authorities from indicting your father, Governor Yoo decided that he himself would execute him as he deserved. The old Governor was a fearless man. He would have killed your father openly were it not that that would have involved the Governor's own family. Therefore he decided that the deed would be done after he had placed himself beyond the pale of human justice.

"I would not make bold to pass judgment on the Governor's actions. A man of his sort can never be measured by ordinary standards. I only wish to make it perfectly clear to you that I know all the facts."

Candidate Ding did not answer. It was evident that he knew of his father's crime. He had bent his head and stood there looking silently at the floor.

Chiao Tai was sitting quite still. He looked straight in front of him with unseeing eyes.

Judge Dee silently stroked his long beard for a few moments. Then he said: "Having thus disposed of your father's case, Candidate Ding, I now come to you yourself!"

Chiao Tai rose.

"I beg to be excused, Your Honour!"

Judge Dee nodded. Chiao Tai left the room.

The judge did not speak for a while.

At last Candidate Ding looked up fearfully. He shrank back as he saw the burning eyes of the judge bore into his.

Gripping the arms of his chair the judge leaned forward and said contemptuously: "Look at your magistrate, you miserable wretch!"

The young man looked at him with deadly fear in his eyes.

"You despicable fool!" Judge Dee spat in a voice trembling with wrath, "you thought you could deceive me, your magistrate, with your foul plot!"

With an effort the judge mastered himself. When he spoke again his voice was steady. But it had a merciless metal ring that made Candidate Ding cringe with fear.

"It was not Woo Feng who planned to kill your father with poison. It was you, his only son!

"Woo's arrival in Lan-fang supplied you with the idea for covering the crime you were contemplating. You started rumours about Woo, you spied on him. It was you who, sneaking into Woo's studio when he was out or in the midst of one of his drinking bouts, abstracted a piece of paper bearing an impression of his seal!"

Candidate Ding opened his mouth.

Judge Dee crashed his fist on the desk.

"Be silent and listen!" he barked.

"On the night of your father's anniversary you had the box with poisoned plums ready in your sleeve. When your father left the hall you, his dutiful son, escorted him to his library. The steward walked behind you.

"Your father unlocked the door. You knelt down and wished him good night. The steward stepped inside and lighted the two candles on the desk. Then you took the box from your sleeve and silently presented it to your father. Probably you bowed. The inscription on top of the box made any explanation superfluous. Your father thanked you and put the box in his left sleeve.

"At that very moment the steward stepped out again. He thought he saw your father put the key back into his sleeve, and he thought that the words of thanks he heard your father say referred to your wishing him good night. But there is an unexplained interval of two minutes or so, the

JUDGE DEE CONFRONTS A CRIMINAL WITH THE
EVIDENCE

time during which the steward lighted the two candles. Why should your father have been standing there with the key in his hand? Of course he had put it back in his sleeve as soon as he had unlocked the door. It was the box with the poisoned plums that the steward saw him putting in his sleeve. The instrument with which a depraved son planned to kill his own father!"

Judge Dee's eyes bored like daggers into Ding's. The young man had started to tremble all over, but he could not avert his eyes from Judge Dee's compelling gaze.

"You did not murder your father," the judge continued in a low voice. "Before he had even opened the box, the hand of the dead Governor struck."

Candidate Ding swallowed several times. Then he cried out in an unnatural voice: "Why, why should I want to kill my own father?"

The judge rose. He took up the roll with his notes on the Ding case. Standing in front of Candidate Ding he said in a terrible voice: "You utter fool! You dare to ask this question? You dare to ask why, while in your sordid scribblings you not only clearly mentioned the depraved woman who was the cause of your hatred for your father, but also betrayed your sinful relations?"

Throwing the roll into Ding's face the judge continued: "Re-read what you wrote in your miserable poem about 'breasts white as snow,' and 'the moon that is not marred by its spots.' It so happened that a maid servant reported to me that the fourth wife of your father has an unsightly mole on her left breast. You are guilty of the despicable crime of adultery with one of your father's wives!"

A deep silence reigned in the room.

When the judge spoke again, his voice was tired.

"I could accuse you and your paramour in the tribunal of this shameful adultery. But the main purpose of the law is to restore the damage caused by a criminal act. In this case there is nothing to restore. What we can and shall do, however, is to prevent the rot from spreading further.

"You know what gardeners do when a branch of a tree is rotten to the core. They cut that branch off so that the tree itself may live. Your father is dead, you are his only son, and you have no children yourself. You will realize that this line of the Ding clan must be cut off. That is all, Candidate Ding!"

Candidate Ding turned round. He left the office walking like a man in a dream.

A knock sounded on the door.

Judge Dee's face lit up as he saw Chiao Tai come in.

"Sit down, Chiao Tai!" he said with a tired smile.

Chiao Tai seated himself on a footstool, his face pale and drawn. He began without any preliminary, speaking in a toneless voice, as if reading aloud an official report.

"Ten years ago, in the autumn, General Ding Hoo-gwo with seven thousand men met with a slightly superior force of barbarians across the northern border. If he had offered battle, he would have had an even chance to win.

"But he did not want to risk his life. He opened secret negotiations and bribed the barbarian general to withdraw. Then the barbarian insisted that his warriors could not return to their tents without several hundred enemy heads to show their prowess in battle.

"General Ding ordered the Sixth Battalion of the Left Wing to detach themselves from the main army and take up an advanced position in a valley. It numbered eight hundred men led by Commander Liang, one of the most gallant officers of the Imperial army, and eight captains.

"As soon as the battalion had entered the valley, two thousand barbarians swooped down on them from the mountains. Our men fought bravely, but their valour was of no avail against such superior numbers. The entire battalion was massacred. The barbarians cut off as many heads as they could, stuck them on their spears and rode away.

"Seven captains had been hacked to pieces. The eighth had been stunned by a spear blow on his helmet and left for dead under his horse. He came to when the barbarians had left, and found himself the only survivor."

Chiao Tai's voice had become strained. Perspiration streamed down his haggard face. He continued: "That captain found his way back to the capital and there accused General Ding before the Board of Military Affairs. He was told that the affair was closed and that he should forget all about it.

"Then that captain threw away his army uniform. He swore that he would not rest till he had found General Ding and cut off his head. He changed his name, joined a band of chivalrous highwaymen, and for some years roamed all over the Empire searching for General Ding. Then, one day, he met a magistrate travelling to his post. That man taught him the meaning of justice, and . . ."

Chiao Tai's voice faltered. A strangled sob rose from his throat.

Judge Dee looked at him affectionately. He said gravely: "Fate decided, Chiao Tai, that your good sword should not be soiled by a traitor's blood. Another man decided that General Ding should die and executed his sentence.

"What you have just told me shall remain strictly between ourselves. But I shall not keep you here against your will. I have known all along that your heart is in the army. How would it be if under some pretext or other I sent you to the capital? I can give you a confidential letter of recommendation to the head of the Board of Military Affairs. You would certainly be appointed a commander over a thousand!"

A bleak smile crossed Chiao Tai's face.

"I much prefer," he said quietly, "to wait until in due time Your Honour has been appointed to high office in the capital. I beg to be allowed to continue serving Your Honour until my services are no longer required."

"So be it!" the judge said with a happy smile. "I am grateful to you for your decision, Chiao Tai. I would have missed you greatly!"

Twenty-second Chapter

JUDGE DEE EXPLAINS THE MURDER OF GENERAL DING; HE REVEALS THE SECRET OF THE SCROLL PICTURE

In the meantime Headman Fang had had a long talk with Woo.

Evidently Woo was interested in nothing but White Orchid's disappearance. He had completely forgotten his days in jail and the whipping he had received in the tribunal. For a few moments he listened absent-mindedly to the headman's explanation of how General Ding had met his end. Then he interrupted peevishly: "I have not the slightest interest in that accursed Ding clique. What I want to know is how we shall go about locating your eldest daughter! You realize, by the way, that I intend to approach a middle-man about our marriage as soon as she is found!"

The headman bowed in silence. Secretly he was very proud that such a distinguished young man wanted to marry his daughter. But he was shocked by his casual reference to these matrimonial plans. Like most middle-class householders, Fang was a stickler for formality, and it is a fundamental rule of propriety that the prospective groom shall not touch upon this subject directly with the father of the bride until a middle-man has approached him.

It was the headman's strict sense of propriety that had made him tell his daughter Dark Orchid to gather information about Mrs. Lee, as Sergeant Hoong had ordered. Fang did not like to execute that order himself for he reasoned that it might reflect on Mrs. Lee's good name if a man made inquiries about her.

Headman Fang hastily changed the subject, saying: "I expect that His Excellency tomorrow will evolve a new plan for the search. In the meantime you, Mr. Woo, could perhaps paint four or five real portraits of my missing daughter, to be circulated among the wardens of the other quarters of this town."

"That is an excellent idea!" Woo exclaimed enthusiastically, "I shall go back home and set to work immediately!"

He jumped up, but the headman laid a restraining hand on his arm. He said diffidently: "Would it not be better, Mr. Woo, if before leaving the tribunal you requested to see His Excellency? You have not yet taken leave of him properly, and perhaps you might thank him for clearing you of suspicion."

"Later, later!" Woo said airily and rushed away.

Judge Dee had partaken of a frugal luncheon in his private office with Sergeant Hoong waiting upon him.

The sergeant saw that the judge looked tired. He ate in silence.

When the meal was over, Judge Dee lingered over his tea. At last he said: "Sergeant, call my other lieutenants. I want to tell all of you the full story of the General's murder."

When his four lieutenants were gathered in front of him, Judge Dee settled back in his armchair and told them the substance of his private conversation with Candidate Ding.

Tao Gan shook his head in perplexity. Heaving a deep sigh he said: "Your Honour, it seems to me that never before have we been confronted with such a mass of complicated problems!"

"Superficially it looks that way," the judge replied. "In fact it was only the local background that complicated everything. Now the confused threads are gradually becoming untangled and a clear pattern emerges.

"We have but three real cases. First, General Ding's murder. Second, the case of Yoo versus Yoo. Third, the disappearance of Fang's daughter.

"Our measures against Chien Mow, our discovery of Yoo Kee's scheme, and the solution of Magistrate Pan's murder, must be viewed as local background. They are separate issues and have nothing to do with the substance of our three cases."

Sergeant Hoong nooded. After a while he remarked: "I have been wondering all along why Your Honour did not proceed immediately against Woo. At first all evidence pointed strongly to his guilt."

"At our very first meeting," the judge answered, "Candidate Ding behaved in a suspicious way. When I and Ma Joong met him in the street, he could not conceal his consternation when I disclosed my identity. Since I have the undeserved reputation of a detector of crimes, Ding evidently thought for a moment of abandoning his plan of poisoning his father and throwing the blame on Woo. Then he decided that his scheme was flawless and that after all he could take his chances. He invited us to a tea house and dished out his story of Woo's designs on General Ding's life."

"That bastard Ding fooled even me!" Ma Joong exclaimed angrily.

Judge Dee smiled and went on: "Then the General was killed. Young Ding had not the slightest idea of what could have happened. I checked that again this morning. You saw that I suddenly produced the fatal writing brush, pointing the open end of the shaft right at Ding's face. If it had been Ding who had tampered with that brush after the Governor had presented it to the General, Ding would certainly have betrayed himself.

"As it was, Candidate Ding must have been as puzzled by this mysterious murder as we were. He must have had an anxious half hour, trying to find out what had happened. Had his paramour had a hand in the killing? Was it someone who had found out about his murder plot and who would in due course ask for a substantial reward for having executed his scheme for him? Then Ding decided that his original plan of making Woo the culprit must be carried out anyway. With Woo's guilt established, Ding need not be afraid of the real murderer intimidating or blackmailing him. Thus he came rushing in here and accused Woo. Ding, however, did not realize that the false trail he had so carefully constructed was extremely poor."

"That is beyond me, Your Honour!" Tao Gan interrupted. "That box of poisoned plums pointed straight to Woo!"

"Too much so," the judge replied. "It was badly overdone and moreover based on a wholly mistaken evaluation of Woo's character. Woo is an over-clever and excitable young man of a type that, I must confess, is not very sympathetic to me. But he undoubtedly is a great artist. Such persons are usually rather vague and casual about the routine of daily life, but they show a tremendous capacity for concentration as soon as it concerns things they are really interested in. If Woo chose to poison some one, he would certainly never use gamboge, and never overlook such a blatant clue as his seal on the paper inside the box."

Tao Gan nodded.

"The final proof of Woo's innocence," he said, "was his willingness to eat the new plums I had put inside that box."

"Exactly!" Judge Dee said. "However, let us keep to the chronological order of developments. When Ding had reported the murder, I immediately went to see Woo. I wanted to compare the personalities of accuser and defendant. I forthwith decided that Woo was hardly the type to commit a premeditated murder, let alone because of such a far-fetched motive as suggested by Ding.

"I assumed that the actual killing had been done by a third person. I could well imagine that a man who had committed such a black crime as General Ding would have many enemies, and I took it that Ding utilized this fact for discrediting Woo. As to Ding's reason for persecuting Woo I assumed that they were rivals in love. The recurring portrait of a girl in Woo's paintings and Ding's love letters convinced me that both young men were in love with the same girl.

"Our discovery of the box with poisoned plums strengthened me in my conviction that Ding was scheming against Woo. I assumed as a matter of course that Ding had taken due precautions that the poison would be discovered before his father ate the plums. I reasoned that a man would never risk his father's life in order to get rid of a rival in love."

"Yes," Sergeant Hoong interrupted. "I now understand why Your Honour ruled out Woo as the culprit."

"Indeed," Judge Dee replied, "I considered Ding as a treacherous and mean character. This prepared me for the next development, namely when I discovered that Woo and Ding were *not* in love with the same girl. This fact reduced the connection between Woo and Ding to the latter's false accusation. But why then had Ding accused Woo at all? The only possible answer was that Ding himself had killed his father and planned to use Woo as a scapegoat.

"Then I formed the theory that Ding had prepared two murder weapons. One had been actually used, but I had yet to discover it. The other was the box of poisoned plums, a second weapon that Ding held in reserve in case the first would fail to work. This being so, it was of the utmost importance to find Ding's motive for his hideous parricide. Could it have something to do with the girl Ding was so passionately in love with? I sent Dark Orchid back to the Ding mansion to collect more data."

Here Judge Dee paused and slowly drank a cup of tea. Deep silence reigned in the room. Then the judge continued: "At the same time, however, I was worried about a curious inconsistency. Since Ding had made such elaborate preparations to ensure that his second weapon, the box of plums, would be traced to Woo, it was evident that he would have taken good care that also his first weapon pointed straight at Woo. I cudgeled my brain but failed to find in the actual murder the slightest clue pointing to Woo.

"Therefore I decided to return to my first theory, namely that the real killing had been done by an unknown third person, whose deed happened to coincide with Ding's despicable poison plot. As a rule I do not like coincidences, but I had to admit that this case pointed forcibly to the fact that a coincidence had occurred."

"It was a coincidence," Chiao Tai remarked, "brought about by the fact which Your Honour mentioned a few moments ago, namely that General Ding had many enemies. And after all it was indeed because of the General's betrayal of his own men that the old Governor killed him!"

Judge Dee nodded and went on: "This conclusion did not bring me any nearer to the solution of the actual murder, but it helped me in so far that I could now rule out both Ding and Woo as suspects. When I had discovered Ding's motive for wishing to kill his father, that part of the case was solved."

Sergeant Hoong interrupted: "So that was what Your Honour meant by referring to half of the murder being clear! Your Honour had connected Dark Orchid's report about the General's fourth wife having an unsightly mole on her breast with the reference in Ding's poem!"

"Exactly," Judge Dee said. "As to the other half of this case, the real killing of the General, I confess that I would probably never have solved that riddle if the old Governor had not signed his name to his deed.

"The only conclusion I had arrived at was that the General must have been killed by some mechanical device, for it was absolutely impossible for the killer to have entered or left that sealed room. But I would never have discovered the secret of the writing brush. I am no match for the old Governor's brilliant mind! You will have noticed that after the knife had left the shaft, the coils straightened out along the inside; I would not have seen them even if I had peered inside the shaft.

"When during my visit to old Master Crane Robe I learned that 'The Abode of Tranquillity' was the pen name of the old Governor, I remembered having seen that name engraved on the shaft of the brush General Ding had been writing with when he was killed. I thought of Tao Gan's suggestion about the blow-pipe and realized that the hollow shaft of a writing brush could serve the same purpose. The displaced candle taught me that there was some mechanical device inside the brush that was released as soon as the brush was heated. The rest was easy."

"What shall we do if Candidate Ding does not kill himself?" asked Chiao Tai.

"I shall accuse him and his paramour in this tribunal of adultery and torture them until they confess!" Judge Dee answered calmly.

Slowly smoothing his long beard the judge looked at his lieutenants. When no one asked more questions he continued: "Now I come to our second case, the old Governor's testament."

His lieutenants turned around and looked at the picture on the wall.

"The written testament concealed in the lining," the judge said, "was a false clue deliberately planted there by the old Governor to delude Yoo Kee. The Governor's scheme was successful, for when Yoo Kee had found the document, he did not destroy the scroll, but handed it back to Mrs.

Yoo. The landscape picture itself contains the real clue, which is much more subtle!"

Judge Dee rose and walked over to the picture. His lieutenants hastily left their seats and stood by his side.

"I vaguely suspected," the judge began, "that there was some connection between this landscape and the Governor's country estate. That was the main reason why I went out there myself."

"Why should there be any connection?" Tao Gan asked eagerly.

"For the simple reason," Judge Dee replied, "that those were the only two things which the old Governor wished to be preserved at all costs. He took clever precautions to ensure that this scroll picture should not be destroyed after his death, and he gave strict instructions to Yoo Kee that nothing was to be changed on his country estate.

"At first I thought that this landscape picture was a disguised map of the country house, indicating the location of a secret wall safe where we would find the Governor's real testament. But during my visit out there I failed to discover the slightest resemblance. Only last night I found the connecting link!"

Judge Dee looked with a smile at his lieutenants. They hung on his words.

"If you study this landscape carefully," he said, "you will notice some queer points in its composition. There is a number of houses, scattered among the cliffs. Every one of them can be reached by the mountain path, except the largest and most elaborate building here on top right! It lies on the river, but there is no road at all! I concluded that that building must have a special significance.

"Now look at the trees! Is there nothing about them that strikes you as peculiar?"

Tao Gan and Sergeant Hoong scrutinized the picture closely. Ma Joong and Chiao Tai had given up. They looked at the judge with fond admiration.

When the sergeant and Tao Gan shook their heads, the judge continued: "All the houses are surrounded by clusters of trees, painted rather carelessly. Only the pine trees are drawn in detail; each trunk stands out clearly against the background. Now you will notice that there is a numerical sequence in those pine trees. Two at the top of the mountain where the path begins, three further down, four where the path crosses the river, and five near the large house on top right. I concluded that these pine trees are landmarks that indicate a route to be followed. The two pine trees on top are the link that connects this picture with the country estate: they represent the pair of pine trees that we saw at the entrance of the maze!"

"Thus this landscape is a guide map to the maze, showing how one reaches a small house or pavilion that the Governor had built inside!" Tao Gan exclaimed.

Judge Dee shook his head.

"No," he said, "not exactly. I agree that it indicates a route to a pavilion inside the maze. Since the Governor went there nearly every day, it is evident that somewhere inside there must be a pavilion where he could read and write. I also agree that this elaborate building represents that pavilion. But I don't agree that it can be reached by following the path of the maze.

"The old Governor planned his abode inside the maze as a real secret. He would never leave important documents there if anyone who had sufficient courage and patience to search the maze and follow its regular path could find it.

"Why did the Governor make such a sharp distinction between the first and second half of the route. Why indicate the second half by a mountain river?"

"To make it more difficult!" Tao Gan replied promptly.

"No," Judge Dee said, "the Governor took special pains to indicate that the place marked by the four pines is an important point. Instead of the regular mountain path, from there on one's course is indicated by the river. The bridge is a further indication that here there occurs an important change.

"I am convinced that at this point one leaves the regular path of the maze, and enters a secret short cut that leads to the hidden pavilion, located not on the real path, but somewhere in between its curves."

Tao Gan nodded his agreement.

"What a perfect hiding place!" he exclaimed. "It is safer than any stronghold! If one did not know the key to the secret short cut, one could explore the maze for weeks on end and never find the pavilion. But the Governor and anyone else who knew the secret could probably reach it in a few minutes!"

"Yes," Judge Dee said, "your last point is very important. The Governor would not like to walk for half an hour or so along the winding path of the maze every time he went inside. This consideration suggested to me the existence of a secret short cut.

"Let us now follow the route indicated on this picture!"

The judge pointed with his forefinger to the small house on top of the mountain, with one pine tree on either side.

"Here," he said, "is the entrance of the maze. We descend those steps hacked out in the rock, and follow the path downward. The first fork has no meaning; it does not matter whether one turns right or left. Coming to the second fork, three pine trees along the side of the path indicate that we must keep to the left.

"Then we arrive at the river. This is the point where we leave the regular path of the maze. The entrance to the secret short cut is marked by four pine trees; I presume that in the maze we shall find the entrance between the second and third tree, right in the middle, just like the river in this picture.

"Somewhere along this secret path we shall find five pine trees in two groups of two and three. The Governor's hidden pavilion must be located there!"

As he spoke the judge placed his forefinger on the large house on top right of the picture. He went back to his desk and sat down.

"If I am not greatly mistaken," Judge Dee concluded, "we shall find in that pavilion a safe or an iron chest with the Governor's confidential papers, including his testament!"

"Well," Ma Joong said, "it is all a little beyond me, but I am all for a try! However, there still is our third case, the disappearance of White Orchid!"

Judge Dee's face clouded. As he sipped his tea, he said slowly: "That is a most distressing case! We have not come one step nearer to finding that girl. I regret this all the more because I have taken a liking to our headman. He is an honest, decent tradesman, a class our country is justly proud of . . ."

The judge wearily passed his hand over his forehead. Then he continued: "After dinner tonight we shall consult here together about ways and means for locating the girl. With our other cases disposed of we shall be able to concentrate on this last riddle.

"Let us now go out to the country house and verify whether my theory about the secret short cut through the maze is correct. If we find the Governor's will, I can forward it to the higher authorities appended to my official report on Yoo Kee's treason. The Board of Finance will then have to except Yoo Shan's part when they declare the Yoo property confiscated.

"Chiao Tai, you will need all the afternoon for organizing the defence of the town, in case the barbarians attack tonight. But you, Sergeant, shall accompany me with Ma Joong and Tao Gan!"

Twenty-third Chapter

THE JUDGE LEADS HIS MEN TO THE HEART OF THE MAZE;
A GRUESOME DISCOVERY IS MADE IN A SECRET PAVILION

An hour later the country estate of the old Governor presented a scene of great activity.

Constables of the tribunal were everywhere. Some were clearing the garden path; others were making an inventory of the old furniture inside the mansion; others again were exploring the back garden.

Judge Dee was standing in the paved courtyard in front of the stone gate giving access to the maze. He was issuing his final instructions to Sergeant Hoong, Ma Joong and Tao Gan. Twenty constables were gathered around them.

"I don't know," Judge Dee said, "how long the road will prove to be. I assume that it will be relatively short, but we cannot be sure. As we walk along, one constable will detach himself from our group every twenty feet or so. He will remain standing there so that he can shout to the man in front and behind. I would not like to get lost in this maze!"

Turning to Ma Joong the judge added: "You will walk ahead with your spear. I don't believe all those stories about mantraps in this maze, but the place has been growing wild for years, and dangerous animals may have made their lairs here. Let everybody be careful!"

Then they passed underneath the stone archway and entered the maze.

In the dim tunnel they were met by the dank smell of rotting leaves. The path was narrow, but two men could easily walk abreast. On both sides closely planted trees and overgrown boulders formed an impenetrable wall. The trees were of all kinds, but not one single pine tree was in sight. The branches met overhead, linked together by thick clusters of vine that often hung so low that Judge Dee and Ma Joong had to stoop in order to pass underneath. The tree trunks were covered with extraordinarily large fungi. Ma Joong hit one with his spear. An evil-smelling cloud of white dust burst from it.

"Be careful, Ma Joong!" the judge warned him. "Those things may be poisonous!"

At the first left turn the judge halted. He pointed with a contented smile at three gnarled pine trees standing close together right in the curve.

"That is our first landmark!" he observed.

"Look out, Your Honour!" Ma Joong shouted.

Judge Dee quickly jumped aside.

A spider as large as a man's hand dropped to the ground with a dull thud. Its hairy body was spotted yellow; its eyes shone with an evil green light.

Ma Joong crushed it with the butt of his spear.

Judge Dee drew his neckcloth tight.

"I would not like to have one of those fall on my neck!" he observed dryly. Then he walked on.

The path seemed to double back. After twenty feet or so it made a sharp right turn.

"Halt!" Judge Dee called out to Ma Joong. "There is our next landmark!"

Alongside the path, four pine trees stood in a row.

"Here," Judge Dee said, "we must leave the regular path and enter the secret short cut. Explore the space between the second and third pine tree!"

Ma Joong poked with his spear among the thick undergrowth. Suddenly he jumped, pushing the judge unceremoniously back.

A red adder about two feet long crept over the rotting leaves and disappeared with amazing quickness in a hole under the tree.

"A hospitable place!" Ma Joong growled. "That reptile was not included in the landscape picture!"

"That is why I told you to put on your thick hunting leggings!" Judge Dee remarked: "Have a good look!"

Ma Joong squatted and peered under the branches. As he straightened himself he said: "Yes, there is a path here. But it is so narrow that a man can hardly pass. I shall go first and push the overhanging branches apart!"

He disappeared among the dense foliage. Judge Dee drew his robes tight about him and followed with Sergeant Hoong and Tao Gan walking behind him. The constables looked doubtfully at Headman Fang. Drawing his short sword he called out to his men: "Don't hesitate! If there are any wild animals we shall take care of them!"

The passage proved only a few fathoms long. After a brief struggle with the thorny branches they came out on the main path again.

On left and right there was a sharp curve. Judge Dee first turned left. He saw a long, straight stretch ahead.

He shook his head.

"It must be the opposite direction," he said. "I don't think that a short cut would include such a long straight section of the path."

He turned back to the spot where they had come out on the path. When they had rounded the corner, they found themselves in a short passage.

"Here we are!" Judge Dee exclaimed excitedly. He pointed to left and right. Three pine trees stood on one side of the path, two on the other.

"According to the Governor's picture," Judge Dee said to his companions, "the hidden pavilion must be very near. I assume that there is a path between that pair of pine trees. The three opposite would seem to be there only to make a total of five!"

Ma Joong eagerly plunged into the shrubs that filled the space between the two trees. They heard him curse fiercely.

He emerged again, his leggings soaked in mud.

"There is nothing there but a stagnant pool!" he said disgustedly.

Judge Dee frowned.

"There must be some path around that pool," he said impatiently. "Up till now everything has checked!"

Headman Fang gave a sign to the constables. They drew their swords and started hacking the undergrowth away. The edge of a black pool appeared. Bubbles were still rising on the spot where Ma Joong had plunged in. A foul smell polluted the air.

Judge Dee stooped and peered under the overhanging branches. Suddenly he shrank back.

A queerly shaped head rose slowly from the water. Its yellow eyes looked at them with a fixed stare.

Ma Joong gasped and raised his spear. But the judge laid a restraining hand on his arm.

Slowly a huge salamander crawled out of the pool. Its slimy body was more than five feet long. Once on the bank it slithered away quickly among the waterplants.

All had received a bad fright.

"I prefer six Uigurs to that animal!" Ma Joong said feelingly.

But the judge seemed very pleased. He said with evident satisfaction: "I have often read in our old books about those large salamanders. This is the first time I have actually seen one!"

Then he scrutinized what was visible of the bank of the pool. It did not look very promising; there was nothing but a mass of mud-covered waterplants. The judge then surveyed the black water again.

"Do you see that stone there?" he suddenly said to Ma Joong. "Evidently that is the first of a row of stepping stones leading across. Let us go ahead!"

Ma Joong tucked the slips of his robe in his girdle. The others followed his example.

He stepped on the flat stone and explored the surrounding area with his spear.

"Here is the next stone!" he called out, "directly in front left!"

He pushed the low branches apart and made a step forward. Then he suddenly halted. Judge Dee, who was following close behind, collided with him. The judge would have fallen into the water if Ma Joong had not steadied him.

Ma Joong silently pointed at a broken branch. He whispered in Judge Dee's ear: "That branch was broken by a human hand, and not so long ago either. Look, the leaves have not yet dried. Someone passed along here yesterday, Your Honour! He slipped on this stone and when trying to steady himself grabbed this branch!"

Judge Dee looked at the branch and nodded.

"He may be quite near; we had better be prepared for an attack!" he replied in a low voice. Then the judge passed the word to Sergeant Hoong who was standing on the stone close by, and he in his turn informed Tao Gan and Headman Fang.

"I prefer any human being to that slimy beast!" Ma Joong muttered. Testing the balance of his spear he went ahead.

The pool proved not very large, but they lost much time because they had to locate the stepping stones one by one; some of them were just under the surface of the water. A person who knew the pattern, however, could cross the pool in a few minutes.

When they were on solid ground again, Ma Joong and Judge Dee crouched. The judge parted the branches a little.

There was a fairly large clearing, hemmed in by trees and huge boulders. In the middle stood a round pavilion built of stone, under a high cedar tree. The windows were shuttered but the door stood ajar.

Judge Dee waited till all the constables had crossed the pool. Then he shouted: "Surround the pavilion!"

As he spoke he sprang forward, ran to the pavilion and kicked the door open. Two large bats flew out with flapping wings.

The judge turned round. The constables had fanned out and were searching the bushes. Judge Dee shook his head.

"There is no one here," he said. "Let the headman and the constables make a thorough search of this clearing."

Then he went inside again, Ma Joong and his two other lieutenants following him. Ma Joong pushed the shutters open.

In the dim, greenish light Judge Dee saw that the pavilion was bare but for a stone table in the centre and a marble bench against the back wall. Everything was covered by a thick layer of dirt and mould.

On the table stood a box about one foot square. Judge Dee bent over it. He brushed the dirt off with one tip of his sleeve. The box was made of green jadeite, beautifully carved with dragons and clouds.

The judge carefully lifted the cover. He took out a small roll wrapped up in a piece of faded brocade.

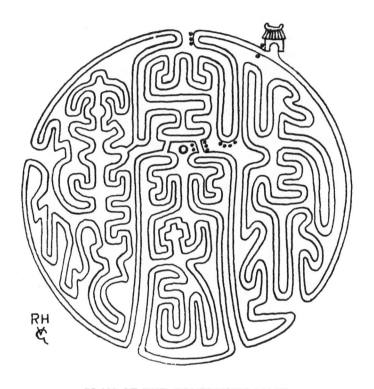

PLAN OF THE GOVERNOR'S MAZE

As he held it up for his companions to see he said in a solemn voice:
"This is the Governor's testament!"

Slowly Judge Dee unwrapped it. He unrolled the scroll and read aloud:

This is the last will and testament of Yoo Shou-chien, Member of the
Imperial Academy, ex-Governor of the Three Eastern Provinces, etc.

Revered Sir and Colleague, to you who have solved the riddle of my
picture and who have penetrated to the heart of my maze, I herewith
make my bow!

One sows in spring and reaps in autumn. When twilight is setting
over one's declining years, it behooves a man to look back and weigh his
deeds as they shall be weighed in the Hereafter.

I thought that I had attained success. I suddenly found nothing but
miserable failure. I strove hard to reform the Empire and I failed to
reform my son Yoo Kee, my own flesh and blood.

Yoo Kee is a man of wicked nature and inordinate desires. Since I
foresaw that after my death he would sooner or later bring about his
own downfall, I married again in order to fulfil my duty to my Ancestors and to ensure that our house would not perish should Yoo Kee die
in prison or on the execution ground.

Heaven blessed this marriage with my second son Yoo Shan, of
whom I have great expectations. It is my duty to see that Yoo Shan
shall continue to prosper after my death.

If I were to divide my property equally between my sons Yoo Kee
and Yoo Shan, I would endanger the latter's life. Hence on my deathbed I shall make it appear as if I leave everything to Yoo Kee. But here
I write down my real intention over my seal and signature and state
that it is my will that if Yoo Kee reforms, he and Yoo Shan shall each
receive half; should Yoo Kee be guilty of some crime, everything shall
go to Yoo Shan.

I shall hide in the picture scroll a written testament to that effect for
Yoo Kee to discover. If he faithfully executes this last will, all will be
well and Heaven will have had mercy on my house. Should Yoo Kee in
his wickedness destroy that testament, he will deem that my picture
had yielded up its secret and leave it in the hands of my faithful young
wife, till you, my wise colleague, read its hidden meaning and find the
present document.

I beseech August Heaven to grant that when you read this document
the hands of Yoo Kee shall not be stained with blood. Should he,
however, have committed a dark crime I hold you responsible for for-
warding the enclosed plea to the competent authorities.

May Heaven bless you, my wise colleague, and have pity on my
house!

Signed and sealed: Yoo Shou-chien.

"This confirms what we found in every detail!" Sergeant Hoong exclaimed.

Judge Dee nodded absent-mindedly. He was engrossed in the enclosure, a loose sheet of thick ornamental paper that had been rolled up together with the scroll.

Then he read its content aloud:

Yoo Shou-chien, who never once pleaded the cause of himself or his own, now after his death humbly pleads for such mercy as can be extended within the limits of the law for his eldest son Yoo Kee, who became a criminal through the incompetent guidance of his old father who always loved him despite his faults.

Silence reigned in the dimly lit pavilion. The only sounds heard were the shouts of the constables outside.

The judge slowly rolled up the scroll. Deep emotion thickened his voice as he said slowly: "His Excellency Yoo truly was a noble man!"

Tao Gan was scratching the table with his fingernail.

"There is an engraved design here!" he remarked.

He pulled out his knife and started scraping off the dirt. Sergeant Hoong and Ma Joong set to work also. Gradually a circular design became visible.

Judge Dee leaned forward.

"This," he said, "is a map of the maze. Look, the course of the winding path forms four stylized characters in archaic script: 'Bowers of Empty Illusion.' That is the same motto as we found inscribed on the landscape picture! This was the keynote of the old Governor's thoughts after he had resigned from official life. Empty illusion!"

"The short cut is also indicated here!" Tao Gan said eagerly. "The location of the pine trees is shown by dots!"

Judge Dee again peered at the map. He traced the design with his forefinger.

"What an ingenious maze this is!" he exclaimed. "Look, if one enters by the regular entrance and always turns right at every fork, one will arrive at the exit after having gone through the entire maze. And if, conversely, one enters by the exit, the same will happen if one always takes the left turn. But unless one knows the secret short cut, one will never discover this hidden pavilion!"

"We must obtain permission from Mrs. Yoo to have this maze cleaned, Your Honour," the sergeant remarked. "Then it will become one of the famous sights of this district, just like the pagoda in the lotus lake!"

At that moment Headman Fang came in.

"Whoever was here left before we came, Your Honour!" he reported. "We searched all through the undergrowth, but found nothing."

"Let your men also examine the trunks of the trees and look among the branches," Judge Dee ordered. "Our unknown sightseer may have hidden himself up there!"

As the headman went out again, Judge Dee looked curiously at Tao Gan. Tao Gan had squatted on the broad bench and was peering intently at the layer of dirt covering it.

Shaking his head he said: "If I did not know better, Your Honour, I would say that this dark spot here looks uncommonly like blood!"

Judge Dee felt a cold fear grip his heart.

He quickly stepped forward and rubbed his fingers over the spot Tao Gan indicated. He went to the window and looked at his hand. He saw dark red smears.

Turning round to Ma Joong the judge ordered curtly:

"Look under that marble bench!"

Ma Joong poked his spear in the dark cavity underneath. A large toad came hopping out.

He went down on his knees and peered under the bench. "There is nothing but cobwebs and dirt!" he reported.

In the meantime Tao Gan had looked in the empty space behind. He turned round with a pale face.

"There is a body lying behind the bench!" he said in a trembling voice.

Ma Joong jumped on the bench. Together they pulled up the mutilated body of a girl. She was completely naked and covered with dried blood and mud. Where the head had been, there was only the ragged stump of the neck.

They laid their gruesome find on the bench. Ma Joong loosened his neckcloth and covered up the loins. Then he stood back, his eyes wide with horror.

Judge Dee bent over the remains of what once must have been a shapely young girl. He noticed the ugly knife wound under the left breast and some badly healed scars on the arms. Slowly he turned the body over. The shoulders and hips were marked by thin welts.

As he straightened himself his eyes blazed with anger. He said in a tense voice: "This girl was killed here only yesterday. The body is quite stiff, but no decay has set in."

"How did she come here?" Ma Joong asked aghast. "She must have been already naked when she crossed the maze! Look, the thorns scratched her thighs and her legs are covered with mud from the pool. It is she who slipped on one of the stepping stones and when trying to steady herself broke that branch!"

"The main problem is who brought her here!" said the judge curtly. "Call Headman Fang!"

As the headman entered the judge ordered: "Roll this body in your gown, Headman. Order the constables to cut a few tall branches to make a stretcher!"

The headman took off his upper gown and bent over the bench.

Suddenly he uttered a hoarse cry. He was staring with bulging eyes at the mutilated body.

"This is White Orchid!" he said in a strangled voice.

Everyone exclaimed at once.

Judge Dee raised his hand.

"Are you quite certain, Headman?" he asked quietly.

"Once when she was only seven years old," the headman sobbed, "she fell over a kettle of boiling water and scalded her left arm. Do you imagine I am not familiar with that scar?"

He pointed to a white scar that marred the beauty of the shapely arm. Then he threw himself over the body, sobbing as if his heart would break.

Judge Dee folded his arms in his wide sleeves. Knitting his thick eyebrows he remained for a while in deep thought.

Suddenly the judge asked Sergeant Hoong: "Sergeant, did you find out where Mrs. Lee lives?"

The sergeant silently pointed to the prone figure of Headman Fang.

Judge Dee laid his hand on the headman's shoulder.

"Where is the house of Mrs. Lee?" he asked tensely.

Without looking up the headman answered: "This morning I told Dark Orchid to go and find out."

Judge Dee turned around as quick as lightning. He pulled Ma Joong close to him by his sleeve and whispered something in his ear.

Ma Joong rushed out of the pavilion without another word.

Twenty-fourth Chapter

A YOUNG GIRL GOES TO VIST A FAMOUS ARTIST;
A CRIMINAL IS CAUGHT IN AN UNEXPECTED PLACE

That morning Dark Orchid left the tribunal to go and find out Mrs. Lee's address as her father had ordered her.

She walked at a brisk pace along the main street leading to the eastern city gate. She had been worrying for days about her elder sister. She hoped that the walk would help clear her thoughts.

She loitered for half an hour or so among the stalls of the street venders on the crossing; then she went on to the shopping centre near the East Gate. Her father had told her that Mrs. Lee was an artist, so Dark Orchid entered the first paper and brush shop she saw.

The owner knew Mrs. Lee. He said that for many years she had been a regular customer. She was still alive. He put her age at about fifty. He added that Dark Orchid could save herself the trouble of going to Mrs. Lee's house, because for the last month or so she had not taken on any new girl students.

Dark Orchid replied that she only wished to see Mrs. Lee about a distant relative. The owner of the shop explained to her how she could find the house. It was only a few streets away.

Dark Orchid reflected that she could now return to the tribunal and report to her father. But the sun was shining and she felt loath to go back so soon. She decided to walk to the address indicated and have a look at Mrs. Lee's house.

It was located in a quiet, middle-class neighbourhood. As she looked at the well-kept houses with neat black-lacquered frontdoors, Dark Orchid thought that this probably was a quarter favoured by well-to-do retired shopkeepers.

About halfway down the street she found the name "Lee" on the gate of a fair sized house.

Standing in front of the door studded with copper nails, Dark Orchid could not resist the temptation to knock.

There was no answer. This excited the girl's curiosity and made her all the more determined to have a peep inside. She knocked again as loudly as she could. Then she put her ear against the door.

She heard the faint sounds of shuffling footsteps.

As she knocked once more the gate opened. A quietly-dressed middle-aged woman stood in the gateway, supporting herself on a silvertopped cane. She looked Dark Orchid up and down and asked coldly: "Why do you knock on my door, young woman?"

Dark Orchid knew from the lady's dress and manner that she must be Mrs. Lee herself. She bowed deeply and said respectfully: "My name is Dark Orchid, I am the daughter of Blacksmith Fang. I am trying to find a teacher who will deign to give guidance to my poor efforts at painting, and a paper shop directed me here. I made bold to come and pay my respects to you, Madam, although the shopkeeper informed me that you do not accept students any longer."

The elder woman gave Dark Orchid a thoughtful look. Suddenly she smiled and said: "It is quite true that I do not accept students any more. But since you went to all the trouble to call on me, please come in and have a cup of tea!"

Dark Orchid bowed once more. She followed Mrs. Lee as she limped across a small but well-kept garden to what evidently was the main room of the house.

While Mrs. Lee went away to fetch boiling water, Dark Orchid looked around, admiring the elegant surroundings.

The room was not large, but scrupulously clean and furnished in excellent taste. The bench on which she was sitting was of rosewood, covered with pillows of embroidered silk. The carved chairs and dainty small tea-tables were also of rosewood. On a high table against the back wall a thin cloud of incense curled up from an antique bronze burner. Over it hung a long, narrow scroll picture portraying birds and flowers. The lattice window was pasted over with spotless white paper.

Mrs. Lee came back with a copper kettle.

She poured the boiling water into a tea pot of exquisite painted porcelain, and then she sat down on the other corner of the bench.

Over a cup of fragrant tea they exchanged the usual polite enquiries.

Dark Orchid thought that despite her slight limp Mrs. Lee must have been a handsome woman when she was young. Her face was regular although her features were somewhat heavy and her eyebrows thicker than is thought beautiful for a woman. She evidently enjoyed talking with the girl. Dark Orchid felt quite flattered.

It struck the girl as curious that there seemed to be no servants in the house. When she asked about this, Mrs. Lee replied quickly: "My house is rather small. I keep only one old woman who does the rough work for me. I am a bit peculiar in this respect; I hate to have a crowd of servants around me all the time. A few days ago she became ill. I sent her home to her husband. He is an old street vender who lives round the corner. In his spare time he looks after my garden."

Dark Orchid hastily apologized once more for her intrusion which must be all the more vexing since Mrs. Lee's maid was away. She rose to take her leave.

Mrs. Lee immediately protested. She said that she enjoyed a little company and quickly poured another cup of tea.

Presently she took Dark Orchid to an outhouse. Nearly all the floor space was taken up by a huge, red-lacquered table. On shelves against the wall there stood half a dozen brush holders with brushes of all kinds and sizes, and small jars containing various pigments. Rolls of paper and silk were stacked in an open porcelain jar on the floor. The window opened on a miniature garden thick with flowering plants.

Mrs. Lee made Dark Orchid sit down on a tabouret by the side of the table and started to show her her paintings. As Mrs. Lee unrolled scroll after scroll, even Dark Orchid, who did not know much about painting, could see that her hostess was an accomplished artist. She did nothing but flowers, fruit and birds, but everything was drawn with astonishing accuracy and delicately coloured.

Dark Orchid felt greatly embarrassed by Mrs. Lee's kindness. She wondered whether she should not tell her that she had come only because the tribunal had ordered her to do so. Then she reflected that she did not know whether the judge wished this to be kept secret or not. Thus she thought she had better continue playing her role and take her leave as soon as a suitable opportunity arose.

When Mrs. Lee was rolling her pictures up again, Dark Orchid rose and looked out of the window. She remarked casually on a few plants that were trampled down.

"That happened the other day when those yokels from the tribunal came to search this neighbourhood!" Mrs. Lee answered venomously. There was so much hatred in her voice that Dark Orchid turned around and gave her an astonished look. But Mrs. Lee's face was as placid as ever.

Dark Orchid bowed and started on the polite phrases of thanks.

Mrs. Lee leaned out of the window and looked at the sun. "Well, well!" she exclaimed, "who would have thought that it is past noon already! And now I must prepare my meal. How I hate that work! Here, you look a very capable young girl. I suppose it would be impertinent to ask you to lend me a hand?"

This was a request that Dark Orchid could not refuse without being intolerably rude. At the same time she thought that she could at least redeem her imposture a little by preparing a good meal for her kind hostess. She replied quickly: "This person is extremely awkward in all things, but allow me at least to kindle the kitchen fire for you!"

Mrs. Lee looked pleased. She took Dark Orchid across the rear courtyard to the kitchen.

The girl took off her upper gown and bound up her sleeves. Then she rekindled the fire from the glowing embers. Mrs. Lee sat down on the low kitchen bench and started a long story about her husband, who had died suddenly shortly after their wedding.

Dark Orchid found a bamboo box with noodles. She chopped a few onions and garlic, and took a dozen dried mushrooms from a string hanging outside the window.

While Mrs. Lee talked on, Dark Orchid put fat in the frying pan and added the chopped vegetables and soy, stirring with the long iron spoon. At the right moment she put the noodles in the pan. Soon an appetizing smell filled the small kitchen.

Mrs. Lee fetched bowls, chopsticks and a platter with pickled vegetables. They sat down on the kitchen bench to eat.

Dark Orchid had a healthy appetite but Mrs. Lee ate very little. She put her bowl down when it was still half full. She laid her hand on the girl's knee and complimented her on her cooking. As Dark Orchid looked up from her bowl, she surprised a look in Mrs. Lee's eyes that made her curiously uncomfortable. She reasoned with herself that it was ridiculous to be shy before another woman. But somehow or other she felt ill at ease. Imperceptibly she edged away a little.

Mrs. Lee rose. She came back with a pewter jug and two small cups.

"Let us have one cup to aid the digestion!" she said with a smile.

Dark Orchid forgot her embarrassment. She had never yet tasted wine. This seemed a very lady-like and exciting thing to do.

She sipped from her cup. It was the delicious scented liquor that is called Rose Dew; it is served cold and much stronger than the ordinary yellow wine which is always taken warm.

After Mrs. Lee had filled the girl's cup a few times, Dark Orchid felt very happy. Mrs. Lee helped her to put on her upper gown and took the girl back to the reception room. She made Dark Orchid sit down next to her on the couch and continued her story about her unlucky marriage.

Mrs. Lee put her arm around Dark Orchid's waist. She intimated that married life has many disadvantages for a woman. Men were rough and had no understanding; one could never talk really intimately with them as one could with a person of one's own sex. The girl thought that there was much in what Mrs. Lee said. She felt very proud that the elder lady talked so confidentially with her.

After a while Mrs. Lee rose.

"How rude of me!" she exclaimed. "I made you work in the kitchen without thinking about your comfort! You must be very tired. Why don't you rest a little in my bedroom, while I do some work on my painting?"

Dark Orchid reflected that she ought to go home. But she did indeed feel tired and somewhat dizzy and she thought it would be interesting to see the dressing table of such an elegant lady.

As she was making some half-hearted protests, Mrs. Lee led her to a room at the back of the house.

The bedroom surpassed Dark Orchid's expectations. A delicate perfume emanated from a ball-shaped cloisonné censer that hung from the ceiling. The ebony dressing table bore a round silver mirror on a carved sandalwood stand. In front she saw over a dozen elegant small boxes of porcelain and red lacquer. The broad couch was of ebony, intricately carved and inlaid with mother of pearl. The bed curtains were of fine white gauze with designs woven in gold thread.

Mrs. Lee casually pulled aside a screen. Two marble steps led down to a small bathroom. Turning round she said: "Make yourself comfortable, my dear! As soon as you have rested, we shall have a cup of tea in my studio!"

Mrs. Lee left, closing the door behind her.

Dark Orchid took off her upper gown and sat down on the tabouret in front of the dressing table. She eagerly inspected the contents of the toilet boxes, sniffing the powders and salves. When she had satisfied her curiosity she turned to four red leather boxes that stood in a pile by the side of the couch. The boxes were marked in gold lacquer with the characters of the four seasons. They contained Mrs. Lee's robes, Dark Orchid did not dare peep inside.

She pulled aside the screen and stepped down into the bathroom. Next to the low wooden tub there stood a small bucket, and in a corner she saw the large wooden containers for cold and warm water. The lattice window had been pasted over with opaque oilpaper. The sunlight threw on it the shadows of the bamboo in the garden outside, so that the window looked like a delicate ink-painting of waving bamboo leaves.

Dark Orchid lifted the cover of the warm water container. The water was quite hot. Fragrant herbs floated on the surface.

She quickly slipped out of her robes, and poured a few buckets of hot water into the tub. When she was adding cold water, she suddenly heard a sound behind her. The girl turned around quickly.

Mrs. Lee was standing in the doorway leaning on her cane. She said with a smile. "Don't be afraid, young girl; it is only I! I thought after all I would take a nap too. It is very sensible of you to take a bath first. It will make you sleep better!"

As she spoke, Mrs. Lee looked at the girl with a queer fixed stare.

All of a sudden Dark Orchid felt very much afraid. She hastily stooped to pick up her clothes.

Mrs. Lee stepped forward and jerked the under garment from Dark Orchid's hands.

"Were you not going to take a bath?" she asked in a strained voice.

Dark Orchid started to apologize in confusion. Suddenly Mrs. Lee drew the girl close to her. She said softly: "You need not be prudish, my dear! You are very beautiful!"

A feeling of revulsion surged up in the girl's breast. She pushed the woman away with all her force. Mrs. Lee stumbled back. When she had steadied herself, her eyes were blazing in her contorted face.

As Dark Orchid stood there trembling, not knowing what to do, Mrs. Lee's cane suddenly lashed out and struck the girl a sharp blow on her bare thigh.

The pain made Dark Orchid forget her fear. She quickly stooped to pick up the small bucket with the intention of throwing it at Mrs. Lee's

DARK ORCHID SURPRISED WHILE TAKING A BATH

head. But she had not reckoned with Mrs. Lee's expert handling of her cane.

Before Dark Orchid's fingers touched the bucket, Mrs. Lee hit her a vicious blow across her hips that made the girl jump aside screaming with pain.

Mrs. Lee laughed contemptuously.

"Don't try any tricks, my dear!" she said softly. "Remember that with this cane I can stab as well as strike! You are more difficult than your sister White Orchid, but you'll soon learn to behave!"

The unexpected reference to her sister made Dark Orchid forget her pain.

"Where is my sister!" she cried out.

"Do you want to see her?" Mrs. Lee asked with an evil leer. She did not wait for an answer but quickly went inside the bedroom.

Dark Orchid stood there paralysed with fear and anxiety. She heard Mrs. Lee chuckle behind the screen.

Then Mrs. Lee pulled the screen aside with her left hand. In her right she held a long, sharp knife.

"Look!" she said triumphantly and pointed to the dressing table.

Dark Orchid uttered a piercing scream of stark terror.

In front of the mirror stood the severed head of her elder sister.

Mrs. Lee quickly stepped down in the bathroom, testing the edge of the knife on her thumb.

"You don't like me, foolish girl!" she hissed. "Therefore I shall kill you just as I killed your sister!"

Dark Orchid turned around, screaming for help at the top of her voice. She had a vague idea of smashing the lattice window and escaping to the garden.

She shrank back as she saw a huge shadow darken the window.

The window was jerked from its frame and a colossal man jumped inside.

He gave the two women a quick look, then sprang over to where Mrs. Lee was standing. He dodged the knife thrust, caught her wrist and twisted it round. The knife clattered to the floor.

In the twinkling of an eye he had bound Mrs. Lee's hands behind her back with her own sash.

"Ma Joong!" cried Dark Orchid, "she killed my sister!"

"Cover yourself up, impudent girl!" he said gruffly. "I already knew that this woman killed your sister!"

Dark Orchid felt a glowing blush rise to her face. While Ma Joong dragged Mrs. Lee to the bedroom, Dark Orchid hurriedly put on her clothes.

When she entered the bedroom, Ma Joong had laid Mrs. Lee on the couch, securely bound hand and foot. As he replaced White Orchid's severed head in the basket, he said:

"Run and open the gate! The constables will be here soon. I came ahead on horseback."

"I don't take orders from you, you bully!" Dark Orchid snapped.

Ma Joong laughed loudly. She hurriedly left the room.

When dusk had fallen, Judge Dee and his lieutenants gathered in his private office.

Woo came in and greeted the judge.

"The body of White Orchid has been deposited in the quarters of the guards," he said hoarsely. "Her head has been added to it. I have already ordered a coffin of solid wood."

"How is the headman?" the judge inquired.

"Now that he knows what happened to White Orchid," Woo replied, "he has calmed down, Your Honour. Dark Orchid is with him."

Woo bowed and went out again.

"That young man has sobered up considerably!" Judge Dee remarked.

"I can't understand what the fellow is hanging around here for!" Ma Joong said peevishly.

"I understand that he feels in some way responsible for White Orchid's tragic fate," Judge Dee observed. "That poor girl must have lived through hell while she was in Mrs. Lee's clutches. You saw the marks on her body."

"I still cannot understand," Sergeang Hoong said, "how Your Honour discovered out there in the maze that there was a connection between White Orchid and Mrs. Lee."

Judge Dee leaned back in his armchair. Slowly stroking his beard he said: "The choice was not very great. The old Governor kept the secret of the short cut strictly to himself. Even his son Yoo Kee and his young wife had never been inside. Only a person with exceptional opportunities could have discovered it.

"We knew that Mrs. Lee often drank tea in the garden pavilion with the Governor and Mrs. Yoo, discussing his paintings. I take it that Mrs. Lee once surprised the Governor when he was working on his landscape. Mrs. Lee has the trained eye of a painter; it would not be difficult for her to recognize that this was no ordinary landscape. Since she was familiar also with the situation at the entrance of the maze, she must have guessed its meaning without the Governor being aware of it."

"Probably she saw the picture at an early stage," Tao Gan observed, "when only the pine trees had been marked in. The Governor would have painted in the rest later."

Judge Dee nodded.

"Since Mrs. Lee has this abnormal interest in young girls," he continued, "she kept this knowledge to herself. She thought that it might come in useful in a time of crisis!

"Somehow or other she lured White Orchid to her house. Fang's eldest daughter was a girl of soft, pliable character, Mrs. Lee must have found it easy to subdue her. She kept her captive in her house for a few weeks. The girl's visit to the deserted temple must have made Mrs. Lee uneasy. She must have taken White Orchid to the country mansion and locked her up in that room with the grated window. Thus when the constables searched the eastern quarter and inspected Mrs. Lee's house they did not find her. That visit, however, must have frightened Mrs. Lee. She decided to kill her captive. The hidden pavilion of the old Governor was the safest place for that cruel murder."

"If we had left the tribunal an hour or so earlier that morning when we went to visit the country estate for the first time," Tao Gan exclaimed, "we could have prevented this crime! Mrs. Lee must have left there shortly before our arrival!"

"Fate decided that just that morning Mrs. Yoo would come to see me," Judge Dee said gravely. "Later, when we inspected the entrance to the maze, I saw the footprint of Mrs. Lee or White Orchid. I did not speak about it at the time, for when I stood there looking into the maze an inexplicable terror took hold of me. The soul of that poor girl who had been brutally murdered there only half an hour or so before must have been hovering over me. I also thought I saw the ghost of the old Governor beckon me from the shadows . . ."

Judge Dee's voice trailed off. He shivered as he recalled those moments of stark terror.

For a while all were silent.

Then the judge took a hold on himself and said in a brisk voice: "Well, fortunately Ma Joong was in time to prevent a second cruel murder.

"Let us now have our evening meal. Thereafter all of you had better rest a few hours. For all we know there may be a very exciting night ahead of us. It is difficult to predict what those barbarians will do!"

That afternoon Chiao Tai had with quiet efficiency organized the defence of the town. He had posted the best soldiers near the Watergate, and divided the rest over the walls of the city. On his orders the wardens had warned the population that the barbarians might attack the town that night. All able men had been busy assembling large stones and faggots of dry wood on the city wall, and making bamboo spears and iron tipped arrows. Three hours before midnight they would man the walls, every fifty men directed by one professional soldier.

JUDGE DEE ON THE RAMPARTS OF LAN-FANG

Two soldiers had been posted on the Drum Tower. As soon as the Uigurs approached the river the soldiers were to beat the huge drum with their thick wooden clubs. The dull roll of the drum would be the signal for lighting the torches on the walls. If the barbarians tried to scale them, they would meet a barrage of heavy stones and flaming faggots.

Judge Dee ate his evening meal in his own quarters. Then he slept for a few hours on the couch in his library.

One hour before midnight Ma Joong, clad in full armour, came to fetch him. Judge Dee put on a thin coat of mail under his robe and took down his grandfather's long sword that hung on the wall next to his bookshelves. Having placed his official magistrate's cap on his head, he followed Ma Joong.

They rode on horseback to the Watergate.

Chiao Tai was waiting for them. He reported that Sergeant Hoong, Tao Gan and four soldiers were posted on the watchtower of the Chien mansion. They would see to it that not a spark of fire was visible there.

Judge Dee nodded and climbed the steep stone steps to the top of the Watergate. On the battlement a burly soldier, nearly as tall as Ma Joong, stood stiffly at attention. He was carrying a long pole with the Imperial standard on top.

The judge stationed himself on the battlement. On his right he had the soldier carrying the Imperial standard, on his left, Ma Joong holding high the staff with the commander's insignia of Judge Dee.

The judge reflected that this was the first time that he had been in charge of defending the Empire's boundary against a foreign attack. Looking up at the Imperial standard fluttering in the evening breeze he felt a deep pride glow in his breast. He folded his sword in his arms and looked out over the dark plain.

When the hour of midnight approached, Judge Dee pointed to the distant horizon. Far away they saw flashes of light. The Uigurs were preparing to advance.

The lights gradually came nearer, then remained stationary. The barbarian horsemen had halted, waiting for the signal fire on the watchtower.

The three men stood there silently for over an hour.

Then suddenly lights flared up over the river. They became smaller and smaller, then disappeared altogether in the darkness.

Having waited in vain for the signal fire, the Uigurs had ridden back to their encampments.

Twenty-fifth Chapter

TWO DEPRAVED CRIMINALS SUFFER THE EXTREME PENALTY;
JUDGE DEE LEARNS THE SECRET OF AN ABSTRUSE COUPLET

The next day Judge Dee heard Mrs. Lee during the morning session of the tribunal.

She readily confessed her crimes.

Once, shortly before the Governor's death, Mrs. Lee had been drinking tea with Mrs. Yoo in the garden pavilion, waiting for the governor. Mrs. Lee had been looking over some of his pictures and found a preliminary sketch of the landscape painting. She had seen from a few notes that the Governor had written in that this picture was a guide map to a short cut through the maze.

Mrs. Lee had felt greatly attracted to Mrs. Yoo, but as long as the Governor was alive she had not dared to reveal her feelings to her. After the Governor's burial Mrs. Lee had visited the country mansion but found only the old couple there; they did not know where Mrs. Yoo had gone after Yoo Kee had expelled her. Mrs. Lee made inquiries in the countryside, but Mrs. Yoo had instructed the peasants to tell no one on what farm she was hiding with her son.

Then, some weeks before, Mrs. Lee had revisited the old country mansion when she happened to be in that neighborhood. When she had found the dead bodies of the old couple, she explored the first two stages of the short cut. She found that the clues in the landscape picture of which she had kept careful notes were correct.

Mrs. Lee had met White Orchid in the market and persuaded the girl to accompany her to her house. Once there, she soon completely cowed the shy girl and kept her captive as a victim of her whims. She made White Orchid do all the housework, beating her with her cane at the slightest provocation.

When Mrs. Lee discovered that White Orchid had slipped out to the deserted temple and there met a strange man, she had been furious. She had dragged the frightened girl to an empty storeroom where the thick walls deafened all sound. Mrs. Lee had made the girl strip and lashed her arms to a pillar.

Then Mrs. Lee had started to interrogate her, repeating again and again the same question: had White Orchid betrayed her whereabouts to the stranger? Everytime the girl denied this, Mrs. Lee had cruelly beaten her with a thin rattan stick, hissing horrible threats at her all the time. Writhing under the vicious lashes, White Orchid had frantically cried for mercy. This further enraged Mrs. Lee. She let the rattan descend with all her force on the bare hips of the screaming girl until her arm grew tired. By then White Orchid was nearly distracted with pain and fear, but she still persisted that she was innocent.

But Mrs. Lee feared that her secret had leaked out. The next morning she disguised White Orchid as a nun and took her to the Governor's country estate. There she locked the girl up in the room the old couple had been living in, taking away all her clothes to obviate every attempt at escape. Mrs. Lee visited her every other day, bringing her a jug of water and a basket of dried beans and oil cakes. She had planned to bring the girl back from there as soon as White Orchid's escapade at the temple had proved harmless.

Then, however, the constables came to search for the girl in the eastern quarter. Mrs. Lee became alarmed. Very early the next morning she hastened to the country mansion. She found her way to the hidden pavilion by means of the pine trees, compelling White Orchid to lead the way, mercilessly driving the girl on with her cane. In the pavilion she made the girl lie down on the marble bench and then thrust her knife in her breast. A perverse instinct moved her to cut off the head; the body she pushed over the edge of the bench. Mrs. Lee took the severed head back with her in a basket. In her hurry Mrs. Lee paid no attention to the box on the table.

Mrs. Lee related all this without any pressure. Judge Dee noticed that she took pleasure in telling everything and that she gloated over her cruel deeds. She also volunteered the information that thirty years ago she had murdered her husband by mixing poison in his wine.

Judge Dee felt a deep revulsion for this depraved woman. He was relieved when Mrs. Lee affixed her thumbmark to her confession and could be led back to the jail.

At that same session Judge Dee heard the three Chinese shopkeepers who had been the Uigur's accomplices. They proved to have no clear idea about the real portent of the plot. They had thought it was a plan to create a brawl and loot a few shops under cover of the confusion.

The judge had them given fifty blows with the bamboo and sentenced them to wear the heavy wooden cangue for one month.

That afternoon the steward of the Ding mansion came rushing to the tribunal. He reported that Candidate Ding had hanged himself and that the fourth wife of the late General had swallowed poison. Neither had left an explanatory note. The general opinion was that they had become despondent over the General's tragic death. The woman's suicide was favourably commented upon by some old-fashioned people who thought it a proof of supreme devotion if a wife followed her deceased husband into the grave. They opened a subscription for the erection of a commemorative stone tablet.

Over the following ten days Judge Dee devoted all his time to the liquidation of the affairs of Chien Mow and Yoo Kee. Some minor punishments were meted out to the two counsellors of Chien Mow, and those of his henchmen who had practised extortion. Mrs. Yoo had been informed of the contents of the Governor's last will. She was to be summoned to the tribunal as soon as the final verdict of the central authorities came in from the capital.

Sergeant Hoong had hoped that the judge would relax somewhat now that he had solved all three criminal cases and broken up the plot against the town. But to his disappointment he found that Judge Dee was still greatly worried about something. The judge was often in a bad temper, and occasionally revised a previous decision, which was a most uncommon thing for him to do. The sergeant could not imagine what was the cause of the judge's worries, and Judge Dee vouchsafed no explanation.

One morning the clatter of hooves and loud gongs resounded through the main street. Two hundred soldiers of the regular army entered Lan-fang with waving banners. This was the garrison force sent in response to Judge Dee's request.

Their commander was an officer who had seen active service against the barbarians of the north, an intelligent young man who impressed the judge very favourably. He presented an official letter from the Board of Military Affairs which also gave Judge Dee full authority over all military affairs of the district.

The garrison was quartered in the Chien mansion and Chiao Tai returned to the tribunal.

The arrival of the garrison somewhat heartened the judge. Soon, however, he relapsed into his morose mood. He buried himself in the routine affairs of the district and went out very little. The only time he left the tribunal was when he attended the burial rites for White Orchid.

Woo had arranged a magnificent funeral. He had insisted on defraying all the expenses himself. The painter had become a changed man. He had foresworn drinking, a decision which involved him in a bitter quarrel with his landlord, the owner of the "Eternal Spring" wineshop. The latter took this decision as a reflection on the quality of his stock. All winebibbers of the quarter sadly called this breach the end of a beautiful friendship.

Woo sold all his paintings and rented a small room in the compound of the Temple of Confucius. He spent most of his time studying the Classics, going out only to visit Headman Fang in the nearby tribunal. They seemed to have become staunch friends. Woo would talk with him for hours in the guards' quarters.

One afternoon when Judge Dee was sitting in his private office listlessly scanning some routine documents, Sergeant Hoong came in and handed him a large sealed envelope.

"This letter, Your Honour," he said, "was brought just now by a courier from the capital!"

Judge Dee's face lit up. He broke the seals and eagerly glanced through the papers inside.

As he folded the documents up again, he nodded contentedly. Tapping the papers with his forefinger he said to the sergeant: "This is the official verdict on Yoo Kee's treason, the killing of General Ding, and Mrs. Lee's murder. It will interest you that the conspiracy of the Uigur tribes has been settled on high government level, in negotiations between our Board for Barbarian Affairs and the Khan of the Uigurs; Lan-fang is safe from further attacks! Tomorrow I shall close these cases. After that I shall be a free man!"

Sergeant Hoong did not quite understand Judge Dee's last remark. But the judge gave him no time for asking questions. He immediately started to issue orders for the morning session of the tribunal.

The next morning the personnel of the tribunal started preparations two hours before daybreak. Torches were lighted in front of the main gate, where a group of constables was making ready the cart for conveying the condemned to the execution ground outside the southern city gate.

Despite the early hour, a large number of citizens were assembled there. They looked with morbid fascination at these preparations. Then mounted lance knights came from the garrison headquarters and formed a cordon round the cart.

One hour before dawn a sturdy constable hit the large bronze gong at the gate three formidable blows. The guards opened the double doors, and the crowd filed into the courtroom which was lighted by large candles.

The crowd looked on in respectful silence as Judge Dee appeared on the dais and slowly seated himself behind the bench. He was clad in full ceremonial dress of shimmering green brocade. A scarlet pelerine hung over his shoulders. This was the sign that he would pronounce capital punishment.

First Yoo Kee was led before the dais.

As he knelt on the flagstones in front of the bench, the senior scribe placed a document in front of the judge. Judge Dee drew the candle nearer and read slowly in a solemn voice: "The criminal Yoo Kee is guilty of high treason. He should properly be submitted to the lingering death, being cut to pieces alive. In view of the fact that the criminal's father, His

Excellency Yoo Shou-chien, has merited greatly from the State and the people, and in view of the fact that he has entered a posthumous plea for mercy for his son, this sentence is mitigated in so far that the said criminal shall first be killed and thereafter dismembered. In deference again to the memory of the late Governor Yoo, the criminal's head shall not be exposed on the city gate and his property shall not be confiscated."

Judge Dee paused and handed a paper to the headman.

"The criminal is allowed to read his late father's plea," he announced.

Headman Fang gave the paper to Yoo Kee, who had been listening with an impassive face. When he had read this pathetic document, however, Yoo Kee burst out into heartbreaking sobs.

Two constables bound Yoo Kee's hands behind his back. Headman Fang took a long white board that had been prepared in advance and stuck it between the ropes on Yoo Kee's back. There his personal name Kee, his crime and his punishment were written out in large characters. The family name Yoo was omitted, in deference to the old Governor.

When Yoo Kee had been led away, Judge Dee spoke: "The Imperial Government announce that the Khan of the Uigurs has sent to the capital a special delegation headed by his eldest son, to offer apologies for the outrageous scheme evolved by Prince Ooljin, begging to be allowed to renew his pledge of allegiance to the Throne. The Imperial Government have graciously accepted the apologies, and have handed over the said Ooljin and his four accomplices to the delegation, leaving it to the Khan to take appropriate action."

Ma Joong whispered to Chiao Tai: "Translated into ordinary language 'appropriate action' means that the Khan will flay Ooljin alive, boil him in oil and cut what is left into small pieces! The Khan does not take kindly to people who bungle his schemes!"

"The Khan's son," the judge continued, "has been invited to prolong his stay in the capital as an honoured guest of the Imperial Government."

The spectators started cheering. They knew that with his eldest son kept as hostage in the capital, the Khan would abide by his promises.

"Silence!" shouted the judge.

He made a sign to the headman. Mrs. Yoo and her son Yoo Shan were led before the dais.

"Madam," Judge Dee said kindly, "you have taken cognizance already of the late Governor's original testament that was discovered in his hidden studio in the heart of the maze. You shall now take full possession of all the property, also in the name of your son Yoo Shan. I am certain that under your guidance he shall grow up in the image of his illustrious father, a man worthy of the great name of Yoo!"

Mrs. Yoo and her son knocked their heads on the floor several times in succession to express their gratitude.

When they had stepped back, the senior scribe placed another document before the judge.

"I shall now read," Judge Dee spoke, "the official verdict on the case of General Ding!"

Caressing his whiskers he read out slowly: "The Metropolitan Court has taken due notice of the facts pertaining to the death of General Ding Hoo-gwo. In the Court's opinion the fact that a certain name was found engraved on the writing brush which concealed the deadly weapon does not in itself provide conclusive proof that it was that same person who transformed the said writing brush into an instrument of death, nor that as such it was necessarily destined to kill the General. Accordingly the Court rules that General Ding's demise shall be entered in the records as death by accident."

"That is a neat example of jurisprudence!" Sergeant Hoong whispered into Judge Dee's ear as he rolled up the document.

The judge nodded imperceptibly and replied in a low voice: "They evidently wanted to keep the Governor's name out of this!"

Then he took up his vermilion brush and filled out a slip for the warden of the jail.

Mrs. Lee was brought in by two constables.

During the period of waiting in jail, the horror of impending death had slowly taken possession of her. She had completely lost the attitude of self-glorification which she had displayed when confessing her hideous crimes. Her face was haggard, she looked with wide eyes at the scarlet pelerine on Judge Dee's shoulders and at the huge man who stood by the dais with impassive face. He carried a naked sword over his shoulders; his two assistants stood behind him with knives, saws and coils of rope. As Mrs. Lee realized that these were the executioner and his helpers, she tottered on her feet. Two constables had to assist her to kneel down in front of the dais.

Judge Dee read: "The criminal Lee *née* Hwang is guilty of kidnapping girls for immoral purposes and premeditated murder. She shall be scourged and then executed by decapitation. The state renounces its claim on the said criminal's property, which shall be conferred on the victim's family in lieu of blood money. The criminal's head shall be exposed on the city gate for three days, as a warning example."

Mrs. Lee started to scream. A constable gagged her with a strip of oilpaper while two others bound her hands behind her back. Finally they stuck the placard stating her name, her crime, and her punishment among the ropes.

When Mrs. Lee had been led away, the crowd of spectators prepared to leave the courtroom. Judge Dee struck his gavel on the bench and shouted for order.

"I shall now read," he announced, "the names of the temporary personnel of this tribunal."

He read out the names of Headman Fang and of the former outlaws whom he had engaged as constables and guards on the second day after his arrival in Lan-fang. They stood at attention facing the judge.

Judge Dee leaned back in his chair. Stroking his beard he thoughtfully surveyed the men who had faithfully served him during the critical days that lay behind. Then he spoke: "Headman, you and the men under you were engaged under an emergency, but you have loyally served the tribunal. Since conditions have now returned to normal, I release you of your duties, with the understanding that those among you who wish to enter permanent service shall be welcome to do so."

"All of us," Headman Fang replied respectfully, "owe a debt of gratitude to Your Honour, and I myself more than anyone else. I would beg Your Honour to continue to employ me in my present position, were it not that I owe it to my daughter to leave a city where she is constantly reminded of the tragedy that struck our family.

"Candidate Woo Feng has offered me the position of chief steward in the mansion of one of his father's friends in the capital. I feel all the more inclined to accept that generous offer since I have learned through an intermediary that Candidate Woo intends to marry my second daughter Dark Orchid as soon as he has passed his second literary examination."

"The black ingratitude of the girl!" Ma Joong muttered indignantly to Chiao Tai. "I saved her life! And what is more, I saw her as only her husband ought to see her!"

"Shut up!" Chiao Tai whispered. "You had a nice view of the wench; that is sufficient reward!"

"I beg to be allowed," the headman continued, "to leave my only son here in Lan-fang. For nowhere in the Empire could he find such a master to serve as Your Honour. I beg Your Honour to accept him, despite his slender capacities, in the permanent service of the tribunal."

Judge Dee had been listening gravely. Now he spoke: "Headman, your son shall continue to serve here as a constable.

"I rejoice that August Heaven in its infinite mercy has so willed it that a dark crime will in due course result in the happiness of two families. When the red candles are burning on your daughter's wedding, the auspicious atmosphere of a bright new future will put a healing salve on the old wounds in her father's heart.

"I regretfully accept your resignation as from tomorrow!"

Headman Fang and his son knelt and knocked their heads on the floor several times in succession.

Three constables reported that they wished to return to their original trades. All the others requested to be engaged on a permanent basis.

When these formalities had been completed, Judge Dee closed the session.

Outside the tribunal a dense crowd was waiting. Yoo Kee and Mrs. Lee had been placed in the open cart of the condemned. The placards with their names and crimes were there for all to see.

Then the gates opened and Judge Dee's palanquin was carried out into the street. Ten constables marched in front and ten behind. Ma Joong and Sergeant Hoong rode on the left, Chiao Tai and Tao Gan on the right. Four runners carrying placards marked "The Magistrate of Lan-fang" took up their position at the head. The guards sounded their copper hand gongs and the cortège moved along heading south.

The cart of the condemned, surrounded by the military escort, brought up at the rear. The crowd followed behind.

As the cortège crossed the marble bridge, the red glow of dawn shone on the pagoda in the lotus pond.

The execution ground was situated just outside the southern city gate. Judge Dee's palanquin was carried through the gate in the palisade. As he descended, the garrison commander came to meet him.

The commander led the judge to a temporary bench that had been put up there during the night. The soldiers formed a square in front.

The executioner stuck his sword in the ground and took off his jacket. The heavy muscles rolled on his naked torso. His two helpers climbed on the cart and led the two criminals to the centre of the execution ground.

They loosened Yoo Kee's ropes and dragged him to a pole with two cross bars that had been stuck in the ground. One bound his neck to the pole; the other fastened his arms and legs to the bars.

When they were ready, the executioner selected a long, thin knife and stood in front of Yoo Kee. He looked up at the judge.

Judge Dee gave the sign.

The executioner plunged his knife straight into Yoo Kee's heart. He died without uttering a sound.

Then Yoo Kee's body was sliced to pieces. Mrs. Lee swooned when she saw them start on this horrible process, and several spectators hid their faces in their sleeves.

Finally the executioner held the severed head up to the judge, who marked the forehead with his vermilion brush. It was thrown into a basket together with the remains of his body.

Mrs. Lee had been revived by burning strong incense under her nose.

The two assistants dragged her in front of the dais and threw her on her knees.

A DEPRAVED CRIMINAL ON THE EXECUTION GROUND

As she saw the executioner approach with the scourge, Mrs. Lee burst out in frantic screams. In abject fright she begged him to spare her.

The executioner and his men were accustomed to such scenes. They paid not the slightest attention to her entreaties. One of the assistants loosened her hair. He took the long tresses in his hand and pulled her head forward. The other ripped off her upper garment and bound her hands behind her back.

The executioner tested the balance of the scourge. This fearful instrument has thongs bristling with iron hooks. It is seen only on the execution ground, for no one ever survives its blows.

When Judge Dee had given the signal, the executioner raised the scourge. It fell down on Mrs. Lee's bare back with a sickening thud, lacerating the flesh from neck to waist. Mrs. Lee would have fallen on her face with the weight of the blow if the assistant had not taken a firm hold on her hair.

When Mrs. Lee regained her breath, she started screaming at the top of her voice. But the executioner struck again and again. The sixth blow laid the bones bare; blood oozed from the torn flesh. Mrs. Lee lost consciousness.

Judge Dee raised his hand.

It took some time before she was revived.

Then the executioner raised his sword while his helpers pulled Mrs. Lee up on her knees.

As the judge gave the signal, the sword swung down and severed the head from the body in one fearful blow.

Judge Dee marked the head with his vermilion brush. Then the executioner threw it into a basket. Later it would be exposed, nailed by the hair to the city gate, and remain hanging there for three days.

Judge Dee left the dais and ascended his palanquin. As the bearers hoisted the shafts on their shoulders, the first rays of the sun shone on the helmets of the soldiers.

Judge Dee's palanquin was first carried to the Temple of the City God, the military commander following behind in his open sedan chair.

There the judge reported to the tutelary deity the crimes that had been committed in his city and the capital punishments meted out to the evil-doers. Then the judge and the military commander burned incense and prayed.

They took leave of each other in the temple yard.

On returning to the tribunal Judge Dee went straight to his private office. After he had drunk a cup of strong tea, the judge told Sergeant Hoong that he could go and have his breakfast. Later in the day they would draft the report on the execution for the higher authorities.

Sergeant Hoong found Ma Joong, Chiao Tai and Tao Gan standing talking together in a corner of the main courtyard. As the sergeant joined them, he found that Ma Joong was still grumbling about what he insisted on calling Dark Orchid's infidelity.

"I had taken it for granted all along that it was I who should marry that wench!" he said sourly. "She nearly knifed me during that attack on our party in the mountains. I really liked her!"

"Consider yourself lucky, brother!" Chiao Tai said consolingly. "That girl Dark Orchid has a mighty sharp tongue. She would have led you a terrible life!"

Ma Joong clasped his hand to his forehead.

"That reminds me!" he exclaimed, "I'll tell you what I'll do! I shall buy myself the girl Tulbee. She's a fine sturdy young woman, and she can't speak a word of Chinese! Won't that be nice and quiet in the house?"

Tao Gan shook his head. His long face was even more sad than usual when he said darkly: "Don't give yourself illusions, my friend! I assure you that in a week or two that woman will be talking your head off, and in fluent Chinese too!"

But Ma Joong was not to be discouraged.

"I'll go there tonight," he said, "and anyone who wants to go with me is welcome. You'll find fine girls there, and they don't conceal their charms either!"

Chiao Tai tightened his belt. He shouted impatiently: "Can't you fellows talk about something more important than mere women? Come along, let us be off and have a real good breakfast! There is nothing better for an empty stomach than a few cups of warm wine!"

All agreed that those were wise words. They walked together to the main gate.

In the meantime Judge Dee had changed into his hunting dress. He ordered a clerk to have his favourite horse brought from the stables.

The judge swung himself on its back. He pulled his neck cloth up over his mouth and nose. Then he rode out into the street.

The streets were full of people standing about in groups. They were discussing the execution of the two criminals and paid no attention to the solitary horseman.

After the judge had ridden through the southern gate, he spurred on his horse. On the execution ground the constables were still busy clearing away the temporary bench. They had raked clean sand over the blood stains.

Once he was in the fields Judge Dee slowed down. He inhaled the fresh morning air and looked at the peaceful scene. But even in these pleasant surroundings he found no rest for his troubled thoughts.

The scene on the execution ground had as always deeply depressed the judge. He was relentless as long as he was working on a case; but as soon as the criminal had been found and had confessed, Judge Dee always longed to dismiss the case from his thoughts. He hated his duty of supervising the execution with all its horrible, bloody detail.

The plan to resign from official life that had been at the back of the judge's mind ever since his conversation with Master Crane Robe had now developed into a compelling desire. The judge reflected that he was just past forty; it was not too late to begin a new life on the small farm that he possessed in his native province.

What was better than a quiet life in peaceful retirement, devoting himself to reading and writing and giving full attention to the education of his children? What was the use of spending his every waking hour on all the wickedness and the sordid schemes of criminal minds, while life had so many good and beautiful things to offer?

There were countless capable officials to fill his place. And could he not serve the state as well by composing, as he had often planned to do, treatises setting forth in easy language the lofty doctrines of the Classics so that everyone could understand them?

Yet Judge Dee felt doubtful. What would happen to the Empire if all officials took this same aloof attitude? Was it not his duty to give his sons a chance later to enter upon an official career? Could the sheltered life on a small farm prepare those youngsters sufficiently for their future?

As he spurred on his horse, Judge Dee shook his head. The answer to his problem lay in that difficult couplet he had seen on the wall of Master Crane Robe's abode:

> There are but two roads that lead to the gate of
> Eternal Life:
> Either one bores his head in the mud like a worm,
> or like a dragon flies up high into the sky.

Ever since that strange visit these lines had been buzzing in his thoughts. Judge Dee sighed. He would leave it to the old master to decide for him. He should explain which of the two roads the judge should take.

When he had come to the foot of the mountain ridge, Judge Dee jumped from his horse. He called a peasant who was working in his field nearby and asked him to look after the animal.

As the judge turned to begin the ascent, two wood gatherers came down the mountain path. They were an old couple, their faces were wrinkled and their hands as gnarled as the dry wood they were carrying on their backs.

The man halted in his steps. He put his load of faggots down. Wiping the perspiration from his forehead, he looked up at the judge and asked politely: "Where might the gentleman be bound for?"

"I am on my way to visit Master Crane Robe," the judge answered curtly.

The old man slowly shook his head.

"You will not find him, my lord," he said. "Four days ago we found his house empty. The door was slamming in the wind, and the rain had spilt all his flowers. Now I and my old woman here use that house for storing our wood."

A feeling of utter loneliness assailed the judge.

"You can save yourself the trouble of going up there, my lord!" said the peasant and handed the reins back to Judge Dee.

As the judge took them absent-mindedly, he asked the wood gatherer: "What happened to the old master? Did you find his dead body?"

A sly smile rippled over the wrinkled face as the old man slowly shook his head.

"Men such as him," he replied, "don't die like you or me, my lord! They never really belonged to this world to begin with. In the end they fly up into the azure vault of heaven like a winged dragon. They leave nothing but emptiness behind!"

The old man shouldered his burden and went his way.

Suddenly understanding flashed through Judge Dee's mind. This then was the answer!

He said with a smile to the peasant: "Well, I belong very much to this world of ours! I shall continue boring my head into the mud!"

He swung himself into the saddle and rode back to the city.

THE END

POSTSCRIPT

A feature all old Chinese detective stories have in common is that the role of detective is always played by the magistrate of the district where the crime occurred.

This official is in charge of the entire administration of the district under his jurisdiction, usually comprising one walled city and the countryside around it for fifty miles or so. The magistrate's duties are manifold. He is fully responsible for the collection of taxes, the registration of births, deaths and marriages, keeping up to date the land registration, the maintenance of the peace, etc., while as presiding judge of the local tribunal he is charged with the apprehension and punishing of criminals and the hearing of all civil and criminal cases. Since the magistrate thus supervises practically every phase of the daily life of the people, he is commonly referred to in Chinese as the "Father-and-Mother Official."

The magistrate is a permanently overworked official. He lives with his family in separate quarters inside the compound of the tribunal, and often spends his every waking hour upon his official duties.

The district magistrate is at the bottom of the colossal pyramidal structure of ancient Chinese government organization. He must report to the prefect, who supervises ten or more districts. The prefect reports to the provincial governor, who is responsible for several prefectures. The governor in his turn reports to the central authorities in the capital, with the Emperor at the top.

Every citizen in the Empire, whether rich or poor, without regard for social background, could enter official life and become a district magistrate by passing the literary examinations instituted by the Government. In this respect the Chinese system was already a rather democratic one at a time when Europe was still under strict feudal rule.

A magistrate's term of office was usually three years. Thereafter he was transferred to another district, to be in due time promoted to prefect. Promotion was selective, being based solely on actual performance.

The magistrate was assisted by the permanent personnel of the tribunal, such as the scribes, the warden of the jail, the coroner, the constables, the guards and the runners. These, however, only perform their routine duties. They are not concerned with the detection of crimes.

This task is performed by the magistrate himself, with the assistance of three or four trusted lieutenants. These he selects at the beginning of his career and they accompany him to whatever post he goes. The lieutenants are placed over the other personnel of the tribunal. Unlike the latter they have no local connections and are, therefore, less liable to let themselves be influenced by private considerations in the execution of their official duties. For the same reason it is an old-established rule that no official shall ever be appointed magistrate in his own native district.

The present novel gives a general idea of ancient Chinese court procedure. When the court is in session, the judge sits behind the bench, with his lieutenants and the scribes standing by his side. The bench is a high table covered with a piece of red cloth that hangs down in front from the top of the table to the floor of the raised dais.

On this bench one always sees the same implements: an inkstone for rubbing black and red ink, two writing brushes, and a number of thin bamboo sticks in a tubular holder. These sticks are used to mark the number of blows that a criminal should receive. If the constables are to give ten blows, the judge will take the corresponding number of markers and throw them on the floor in front of the dais. The headman of the constables will put apart one marker for every blow or blows given.

Next to these implements one will often see on top of the bench the large square seal of the tribunal, and the gavel. The latter is not shaped like a hammer as in the West. It is an oblong, square piece of hardwood of about one foot long. In Chinese it is significantly called *ching-t'ang-mu,** "wood that frightens the hall."

The constables stand in front of the dais, facing each other in two rows on left and right. Both plaintiff and accused must kneel on the bare flagstones between these two menacing rows, and remain so during the entire session. They have no lawyers to assist them; they may call no witnesses, so their position is generally not an enviable one. The entire court procedure was in fact intended to act as a deterrent, impressing on the people the awful consequences of getting involved with the law.

The magistrate's private office was usually located at the back of the court room, separated from the dais by a screen.

It is a fundamental principle of ancient Chinese law that no criminal can be pronounced guilty unless he has confessed to his crime. To prevent hardened criminals from escaping punishment by refusing to confess even

* In the novel itself all Chinese names are transcribed in such a way, that they can be easily pronounced. In this Postscript, however, I use the regular system of transcription used in most English sinological publications.

when confronted with irrefutable evidence, the law allows the application of legal severities, such as beating with whip and bamboo, and placing hands and ankles in screws. In addition to these authorized means of torture, magistrates often apply more severe kinds. If, however, the accused should receive permanent bodily harm or die under excessive torture, the magistrate and the entire personnel of his tribunal are punished, often with the extreme penalty. Most judges therefore, depend more upon their shrewd psychological insight and their knowledge of their fellow men than on the application of torture.

All in all the old Chinese system worked reasonably well. Sharp control by the high authorities prevented excesses, and public opinion acted as another curb on wicked or irresponsible magistrates. Capital sentences had to be ratified by the Throne and every condemned criminal could appeal to the higher judicial authorities, going up as high as the Emperor himself. Moreover, the magistrate was not allowed to interrogate any accused or witness in private; all his hearings of a case including the preliminary examination had to be conducted in the public sessions of the tribunal. A careful record was kept of all proceedings and these reports had to be forwarded to the higher authorities for their inspection.

Readers of *Dee Goong An* have inquired how it was possible that the scribes accurately noted down the court proceedings without the use of shorthand. The answer is that the Chinese literary language in itself is a kind of shorthand. It is possible, for instance, to reduce to four written ideographs a sentence that would come to, say, twenty or more words in the colloquial. Moreover there exist several systems of running handwriting, where characters consisting of ten or more brush strokes can be reduced to one scrawl. While serving in China I myself often had Chinese clerks make notes of complicated negotiations conducted in Chinese and found their record to be of astonishing accuracy.

In most Chinese detective novels the magistrate is engaged in solving three or more totally different cases at the same time. This interesting feature I have retained in the present novel. In my opinion Chinese crime stories in this respect are more realistic than ours. A district had quite a large population. It is therefore only logical that often several criminal cases had to be dealt with at the same time.

In this novel I have followed the Chinese time-honoured tradition of adding at the end of the story a detailed description of the execution of the criminals. Chinese sense of justice demands that the punishment meted out to the criminal should be set forth in full detail. I also adopted the custom of Chinese writers of the Ming Dynasty of describing in their novels men and life as they were in their own time, although the scene of their plots is often laid in former centuries. The same applies to the illustrations of this novel, which reproduce customs and costumes of the Ming period (A.D. 1368-1644) rather than those of the T'ang Dynasty.

I may add that "Judge Dee" is one of the great ancient Chinese detectives. He was a historical person, one of the well known statesmen of the T'ang dynasty. His full name was Ti Jen-chieh and he lived from 630 till 700 A.D. Later he became a Minister of the Imperial Court and through his wise counsels exercised a beneficial influence on affairs of state. It is chiefly because of his reputation as a detector of crimes, however, that later Chinese fiction has made him the hero of a number of crime stories which have only very slight foundation in historical fact.

Chinese Sources

I borrowed three plots from three different 16th-century Chinese collections of crime and mystery stories. In the original none of these three plots bears any relation to Judge Dee or *Dee Goong An*. Since, however, through my translation of *Dee Goong An*, the reader has become familiar with Judge Dee and his four assistants, those three plots have now been re-written as one continuous story centering around that famous ancient Chinese master-detective. Judge Dee could be introduced into this story without much difficulty, for the magistrate-detective figures in all old Chinese crime novels. The type is more important than the name; in fact it makes little differences whether a crime is solved by "Judge Pad," "Judge Peng," "Judge Shih" or "Judge Dee."

The "Case of the Murder in the Sealed Room" was suggested by an anecdote concerning Yen Shih-fan, a notoriously wicked statesman of the Ming period who died in 1565 A.D. It is said that he invented a special writing brush capable of ejecting a deadly missile when heated near a candle (cf. A. Waley's introduction to the English translation of *Chin-p'ing Mei*, page viii). The original story states that Yen Shih-fan used this "loaded writing brush" as a defensive weapon, to be used should one of his many enemies surprise him writing in his library and if no other weapon was at hand. I described such a "loaded brush" as a weapon of attack and wrote a new story around it dealing with delayed vengeance, a motif not uncommon in Chinese novels. It should be added that when a new writing brush is to be used, the writer must first burn off the superfluous hairs around the point. To do this he holds it to a flame keeping the shaft horizontal to his eye. There is thus a good chance that a missile projected from the end of the brush will hit his face. Even if the wax holding the coiled spring inside the shaft should not melt during the actual trimming process, the writer will still have little chance of survival once he begins to use his brush, since his head would usually be bent over the paper and therefore be in the direct line of fire. This is indeed what happened to General Ding in the present novel.

Quite another motif is worked out in the "Case of the Hidden Testament." This case is based on a well-known ancient Chinese plot. A brief version occurs in the *T'ang-yin-pi-shih*, a collection of ruling cases compiled in 1211 A.D.; cf. my translation entitled "*T'ang-yin-pi-shih*, Parallel Cases from under the Peartree, a 13th-century manual of Jurisprudence and Detection" (*Sinica Leidensia*, Vol. X, Leiden 1956), page 177, Case 66-B. Another brief version is found in *Lung-t'u-kung-an*, the famous 16th-century collection of crime stories that describe the exploits of the master-detective Pao-kung, who lived during the Sung Dynasty. There the story bears the title of *Ch'e-hua-chou*, "The Taking apart of the Scroll Picture." A more elaborate version is given in the popular 17th-century collection of Chinese stories *Chin-ku-ch'i-kuan*; it is inserted there as the third tale, entitled *T'eng-ta-yin-kuei-tuan-chia-szu*, "Magistrate T'eng's marvellous solution of the Inheritance Suit." In the original story the real testament is found hidden in the scroll's mounting; the clues contained in the picture itself are an embellishment I have added. I also added the new plot of the maze mystery which—as far as I know—does not occur in ancient Chinese detective stories although mazes are occasionally mentioned in the description of Chinese palaces. The design of the maze reproduced in the present story is in reality that of the cover of a Chinese incense burner. It is an old Chinese custom to place a thin plate of copper with a cut-out continuous design, on top of a vessel filled to the brim with incense powder. When the powder is lighted at one end of the design, it slowly burns on like a fuse following the design. During past centuries, there were published in China a number of books reproducing various designs of this kind, usually representing some auspicious phrase, and often of great ingenuity. The design utilized in the present story was borrowed from the *Hsiang-yin-t'u-k'ao*, a book on this subject published in 1878.

The plot of the girl with the severed head is a quite common one in old Chinese crime stories; cf., for instance, my translation of the *T'ang-yin-pi-shih*, Case 64-A. I worked it into a story centering round sapphism, an aberration described in a number of Chinese novels and plays. The best-known example is the love story of the girl Ts'ao Yü-hua and Mrs. Fan Yün-chien, in the 17th-century play *Lien-hsiang-pan* by the famous artist and playwright Li Yü. Cruelty of women towards women servants, etc., is amply illustrated in Chinese *romans de moeurs*; I mention as an example Chapter VIII of the well-known novel *Chin-p'ing-mei*. The frequent occurrence of sapphism, and occasional cases of sadism among women in ancient China, must doubtless be ascribed to the polygamic family system, where a number of women were obligated to live in constant and close proximity. Students of sociology will find this problem discussed at some length in my book *Erotic Colour Prints of the Ming Period* (Tokyo, 1951, Vol. I, p. 146-148). I selected this motif for inclusion in the present novel partly because it enabled me to create unexpected developments and partly in order to show how surprisingly "modern" old Chinese plots can be.

The exposure of the three monks who falsely reported the theft of a golden statue, in Chapter VII of the present novel, is based on a story in the *T'ang-yin-pi-shih*, the collection of criminal cases mentioned above. This particular case will be found on page 159 of my translation, Case 57-B.

The "framework" of the present novel, *viz.* a tale of a distant town where a local bully has usurped power, also is a common situation in Chinese novels. Sometimes a clever magistrate outwits and deposes the usurper; sometimes it is the usurper who is the hero of the story. He takes over from a corrupt magistrate, and subsequently is officially confirmed in his position by a grateful government.

Finally, the role played by Master Crane Robe in this novel (see Chapter XIX) is a much-chastened version of the *deus ex machina* found in many old Chinese detective novels; they introduce a supernatural being (sometimes the King of the Nether World himself come down to earth in human shape) who helps the magistrate to solve a baffling crime by means of occult powers. This element is, of course, unacceptable to the modern reader. In the present novel, therefore, I represent Master Crane Robe as a high-minded Taoist recluse, leaving it open as to whether the clues Judge Dee discovered during their conversation were the result of a lucky accident, or of the master's inside knowledge of Governor Yoo's affairs, or, again, of the master's unusual mental powers. I chose as background of their conversation the contrast between Confucianism and Taoism. As is well known, Confucianism and Taoism are the two basic ways of thought that have dominated Chinese philosophy and religion ever since approximately the 4th century B.C. Confucianism is realistic and very much of this world, Taoism is romantic and wholly unworldly.

Judge Dee, as an orthodox Confucianist scholar-official, venerates the

Confucianist Classics, which attach supreme importance to such accepted moral values as justice, righteousness, benevolence, duty, etc. Master Crane Robe, on the other hand, advocates the Taoist principle of the relativity of all accepted values, and a life of non-action *jenseits vom Guten und Bösen*, in complete harmony with the primordial forces of nature. These two conflicting views are epitomized in the couplet of Governor Yoo about the worm and the dragon. This couplet I quoted from a Buddhist work on Ch'an (Japanese: Zen) philosophy. The Ch'an sect of Buddhism often comes very close to Taoism.

R. H. Van Gulik

A CATALOG OF SELECTED
DOVER BOOKS
IN ALL FIELDS OF INTEREST

DRAWINGS OF REMBRANDT, edited by Seymour Slive. Updated Lippmann, Hofstede de Groot edition, with definitive scholarly apparatus. All portraits, biblical sketches, landscapes, nudes. Oriental figures, classical studies, together with selection of work by followers. 550 illustrations. Total of 630pp. 9⅛ × 12¼.
21485-0, 21486-9 Pa., Two-vol. set $29.90

GHOST AND HORROR STORIES OF AMBROSE BIERCE, Ambrose Bierce. 24 tales vividly imagined, strangely prophetic, and decades ahead of their time in technical skill: "The Damned Thing," "An Inhabitant of Carcosa," "The Eyes of the Panther," "Moxon's Master," and 20 more. 199pp. 5⅜ × 8½. 20767-6 Pa. $4.95

ETHICAL WRITINGS OF MAIMONIDES, Maimonides. Most significant ethical works of great medieval sage, newly translated for utmost precision, readability. Laws Concerning Character Traits, Eight Chapters, more. 192pp. 5⅜ × 8½.
24522-5 Pa. $5.95

THE EXPLORATION OF THE COLORADO RIVER AND ITS CANYONS, J. W. Powell. Full text of Powell's 1,000-mile expedition down the fabled Colorado in 1869. Superb account of terrain, geology, vegetation, Indians, famine, mutiny, treacherous rapids, mighty canyons, during exploration of last unknown part of continental U.S. 400pp. 5⅜ × 8½. 20094-9 Pa. $8.95

HISTORY OF PHILOSOPHY, Julián Marías. Clearest one-volume history on the market. Every major philosopher and dozens of others, to Existentialism and later. 505pp. 5⅜ × 8½. 21739-6 Pa. $9.95

ALL ABOUT LIGHTNING, Martin A. Uman. Highly readable nontechnical survey of nature and causes of lightning, thunderstorms, ball lightning, St. Elmo's Fire, much more. Illustrated. 192pp. 5⅜ × 8½. 25237-X Pa. $5.95

SAILING ALONE AROUND THE WORLD, Captain Joshua Slocum. First man to sail around the world, alone, in small boat. One of great feats of seamanship told in delightful manner. 67 illustrations. 294pp. 5⅜ × 8½. 20326-3 Pa. $4.95

LETTERS AND NOTES ON THE MANNERS, CUSTOMS AND CONDITIONS OF THE NORTH AMERICAN INDIANS, George Catlin. Classic account of life among Plains Indians: ceremonies, hunt, warfare, etc. 312 plates. 572pp. of text. 6⅛ × 9¼. 22118-0, 22119-9, Pa., Two-vol. set $17.90

THE SECRET LIFE OF SALVADOR DALÍ, Salvador Dalí. Outrageous but fascinating autobiography through Dalí's thirties with scores of drawings and sketches and 80 photographs. A must for lovers of 20th-century art. 432pp. 6½ × 9¼. (Available in U.S. only) 27454-3 Pa. $9.95

THE BOOK OF BEASTS: Being a Translation from a Latin Bestiary of the Twelfth Century, T. H. White. Wonderful catalog of real and fanciful beasts: manticore, griffin, phoenix, amphivius, jaculus, many more. White's witty erudite commentary on scientific, historical aspects enhances fascinating glimpse of medieval mind. Illustrated. 296pp. 5⅜ × 8¼. (Available in U.S. only) 24609-4 Pa. $7.95

FRANK LLOYD WRIGHT: Architecture and Nature with 160 Illustrations, Donald Hoffmann. Profusely illustrated study of influence of nature—especially prairie—on Wright's designs for Fallingwater, Robie House, Guggenheim Museum, other masterpieces. 96pp. 9¼ × 10¾. 25098-9 Pa. $8.95

LIMBERT ARTS AND CRAFTS FURNITURE: The Complete 1903 Catalog, Charles P. Limbert and Company. Rare catalog depicting 188 pieces of Mission-style furniture: fold-down tables and desks, bookcases, library and octagonal tables, chairs, more. Descriptive captions. 80pp. 9⅜ × 12¼. 27120-X Pa. $6.95

YEARS WITH FRANK LLOYD WRIGHT: Apprentice to Genius, Edgar Tafel. Insightful memoir by a former apprentice presents a revealing portrait of Wright the man, the inspired teacher, the greatest American architect. 372 black-and-white illustrations. Preface. Index. vi + 228pp. 8¼ × 11. 24801-1 Pa. $10.95

THE STORY OF KING ARTHUR AND HIS KNIGHTS, Howard Pyle. Enchanting version of King Arthur fable has delighted generations with imaginative narratives of exciting adventures and unforgettable illustrations by the author. 41 illustrations. xviii + 313pp. 6⅛ × 9¼. 21445-1 Pa. $6.95

THE GODS OF THE EGYPTIANS, E. A. Wallis Budge. Thorough coverage of numerous gods of ancient Egypt by foremost Egyptologist. Information on evolution of cults, rites and gods; the cult of Osiris; the Book of the Dead and its rites; the sacred animals and birds; Heaven and Hell; and more. 956pp. 6⅛ × 9¼. 22055-9, 22056-7 Pa., Two-vol. set $22.90

A THEOLOGICO-POLITICAL TREATISE, Benedict Spinoza. Also contains unfinished *Political Treatise*. Great classic on religious liberty, theory of government on common consent. R. Elwes translation. Total of 421pp. 5⅜ × 8½. 20249-6 Pa. $7.95

INCIDENTS OF TRAVEL IN CENTRAL AMERICA, CHIAPAS, AND YUCATAN, John L. Stephens. Almost single-handed discovery of Maya culture; exploration of ruined cities, monuments, temples; customs of Indians. 115 drawings. 892pp. 5⅜ × 8½. 22404-X, 22405-8 Pa., Two-vol. set $17.90

LOS CAPRICHOS, Francisco Goya. 80 plates of wild, grotesque monsters and caricatures. Prado manuscript included. 183pp. 6⅜ × 9⅜. 22384-1 Pa. $6.95

AUTOBIOGRAPHY: The Story of My Experiments with Truth, Mohandas K. Gandhi. Not hagiography, but Gandhi in his own words. Boyhood, legal studies, purification, the growth of the Satyagraha (nonviolent protest) movement. Critical, inspiring work of the man who freed India. 480pp. 5⅜ × 8½. (Available in U.S. only) 24593-4 Pa. $6.95

ILLUSTRATED DICTIONARY OF HISTORIC ARCHITECTURE, edited by Cyril M. Harris. Extraordinary compendium of clear, concise definitions for over 5,000 important architectural terms complemented by over 2,000 line drawings. Covers full spectrum of architecture from ancient ruins to 20th-century Modernism. Preface. 592pp. 7½ × 9⅜. 24444-X Pa. $15.95

THE NIGHT BEFORE CHRISTMAS, Clement C. Moore. Full text, and woodcuts from original 1848 book. Also critical, historical material. 19 illustrations. 40pp. 4⅝ × 6. 22797-9 Pa. $2.50

THE LESSON OF JAPANESE ARCHITECTURE: 165 Photographs, Jiro Harada. Memorable gallery of 165 photographs taken in the 1930s of exquisite Japanese homes of the well-to-do and historic buildings. 13 line diagrams. 192pp. 8⅜ × 11¼. 24778-3 Pa. $10.95

THE AUTOBIOGRAPHY OF CHARLES DARWIN AND SELECTED LETTERS, edited by Francis Darwin. The fascinating life of eccentric genius composed of an intimate memoir by Darwin (intended for his children); commentary by his son, Francis; hundreds of fragments from notebooks, journals, papers; and letters to and from Lyell, Hooker, Huxley, Wallace and Henslow. xi + 365pp. 5⅜ × 8. 20479-0 Pa. $6.95

WONDERS OF THE SKY: Observing Rainbows, Comets, Eclipses, the Stars and Other Phenomena, Fred Schaaf. Charming, easy-to-read poetic guide to all manner of celestial events visible to the naked eye. Mock suns, glories, Belt of Venus, more. Illustrated. 299pp. 5¼ × 8¼. 24402-4 Pa. $8.95

BURNHAM'S CELESTIAL HANDBOOK, Robert Burnham, Jr. Thorough guide to the stars beyond our solar system. Exhaustive treatment. Alphabetical by constellation: Andromeda to Cetus in Vol. 1; Chamaeleon to Orion in Vol. 2; and Pavo to Vulpecula in Vol. 3. Hundreds of illustrations. Index in Vol. 3. 2,000pp. 6⅛ × 9¼. 23567-X, 23568-8, 23673-0 Pa., Three-vol. set $41.85

STAR NAMES: Their Lore and Meaning, Richard Hinckley Allen. Fascinating history of names various cultures have given to constellations and literary and folkloristic uses that have been made of stars. Indexes to subjects. Arabic and Greek names. Biblical references. Bibliography. 563pp. 5⅜ × 8½. 21079-0 Pa. $9.95

THIRTY YEARS THAT SHOOK PHYSICS: The Story of Quantum Theory, George Gamow. Lucid, accessible introduction to influential theory of energy and matter. Careful explanations of Dirac's anti-particles, Bohr's model of the atom, much more. 12 plates. Numerous drawings. 240pp. 5⅜ × 8½. 24895-X Pa. $6.95

CHINESE DOMESTIC FURNITURE IN PHOTOGRAPHS AND MEASURED DRAWINGS, Gustav Ecke. A rare volume, now affordably priced for antique collectors, furniture buffs and art historians. Detailed review of styles ranging from early Shang to late Ming. Unabridged republication. 161 black-and-white drawings, photos. Total of 224pp. 8⅜ × 11¼. (Available in U.S. only) 25171-3 Pa. $14.95

VINCENT VAN GOGH: A Biography, Julius Meier-Graefe. Dynamic, penetrating study of artist's life, relationship with brother, Theo, painting techniques, travels, more. Readable, engrossing. 160pp. 5⅜ × 8½. (Available in U.S. only) 25253-1 Pa. $4.95

ILLUSTRATED GUIDE TO SHAKER FURNITURE, Robert Meader. All furniture and appurtenances, with much on unknown local styles. 235 photos. 146pp. 9 × 12. 22819-3 Pa. $9.95

WHALE SHIPS AND WHALING: A Pictorial Survey, George Francis Dow. Over 200 vintage engravings, drawings, photographs of barks, brigs, cutters, other vessels. Also harpoons, lances, whaling guns, many other artifacts. Comprehensive text by foremost authority. 207 black-and-white illustrations. 288pp. 6 × 9. 24808-9 Pa. $9.95

THE BERTRAMS, Anthony Trollope. Powerful portrayal of blind self-will and thwarted ambition includes one of Trollope's most heartrending love stories. 497pp. 5⅜ × 8½. 25119-5 Pa. $9.95

ADVENTURES WITH A HAND LENS, Richard Headstrom. Clearly written guide to observing and studying flowers and grasses, fish scales, moth and insect wings, egg cases, buds, feathers, seeds, leaf scars, moss, molds, ferns, common crystals, etc.—all with an ordinary, inexpensive magnifying glass. 209 exact line drawings aid in your discoveries. 220pp. 5⅜ × 8½. 23330-8 Pa. $5.95

RODIN ON ART AND ARTISTS, Auguste Rodin. Great sculptor's candid, wide-ranging comments on meaning of art; great artists; relation of sculpture to poetry, painting, music; philosophy of life, more. 76 superb black-and-white illustrations of Rodin's sculpture, drawings and prints. 119pp. 8⅜ × 11¼. 24487-3 Pa. $7.95

FIFTY CLASSIC FRENCH FILMS, 1912–1982: A Pictorial Record, Anthony Slide. Memorable stills from Grand Illusion, Beauty and the Beast, Hiroshima, Mon Amour, many more. Credits, plot synopses, reviews, etc. 160pp. 8¼ × 11. 25256-6 Pa. $11.95

THE PRINCIPLES OF PSYCHOLOGY, William James. Famous long course complete, unabridged. Stream of thought, time perception, memory, experimental methods; great work decades ahead of its time. 94 figures. 1,391pp. 5⅜ × 8½. 20381-6, 20382-4 Pa., Two-vol. set $25.90

BODIES IN A BOOKSHOP, R. T. Campbell. Challenging mystery of blackmail and murder with ingenious plot and superbly drawn characters. In the best tradition of British suspense fiction. 192pp. 5⅜ × 8½. 24720-1 Pa. $5.95

CALLAS: Portrait of a Prima Donna, George Jellinek. Renowned commentator on the musical scene chronicles incredible career and life of the most controversial, fascinating, influential operatic personality of our time. 64 black-and-white photographs. 416pp. 5⅜ × 8¼. 25047-4 Pa. $8.95

GEOMETRY, RELATIVITY AND THE FOURTH DIMENSION, Rudolph Rucker. Exposition of fourth dimension, concepts of relativity as Flatland characters continue adventures. Popular, easily followed yet accurate, profound. 141 illustrations. 133pp. 5⅜ × 8½. 23400-2 Pa. $4.95

HOUSEHOLD STORIES BY THE BROTHERS GRIMM, with pictures by Walter Crane. 53 classic stories—Rumpelstiltskin, Rapunzel, Hansel and Gretel, the Fisherman and his Wife, Snow White, Tom Thumb, Sleeping Beauty, Cinderella, and so much more—lavishly illustrated with original 19th-century drawings. 114 illustrations. x + 269pp. 5⅜ × 8½. 21080-4 Pa. $4.95

SUNDIALS, Albert Waugh. Far and away the best, most thorough coverage of ideas, mathematics concerned, types, construction, adjusting anywhere. Over 100 illustrations. 230pp. 5⅜ × 8½. 22947-5 Pa. $5.95

PICTURE HISTORY OF THE NORMANDIE: With 190 Illustrations, Frank O. Braynard. Full story of legendary French ocean liner: Art Deco interiors, design innovations, furnishings, celebrities, maiden voyage, tragic fire, much more. Extensive text. 144pp. 8⅞ × 11¾. 25257-4 Pa. $11.95

THE FIRST AMERICAN COOKBOOK: A Facsimile of "American Cookery," 1796, Amelia Simmons. Facsimile of the first American-written cookbook published in the United States contains authentic recipes for colonial favorites—pumpkin pudding, winter squash pudding, spruce beer, Indian slapjacks, and more. Introductory Essay and Glossary of colonial cooking terms. 80pp. 5⅜ × 8½. 24710-4 Pa. $3.50

101 PUZZLES IN THOUGHT AND LOGIC, C. R. Wylie, Jr. Solve murders and robberies, find out which fishermen are liars, how a blind man could possibly identify a color—purely by your own reasoning! 107pp. 5⅜ × 8½. 20367-0 Pa. $2.95

ANCIENT EGYPTIAN MYTHS AND LEGENDS, Lewis Spence. Examines animism, totemism, fetishism, creation myths, deities, alchemy, art and magic, other topics. Over 50 illustrations. 432pp. 5⅜ × 8½. 26525-0 Pa. $8.95

ANTHROPOLOGY AND MODERN LIFE, Franz Boas. Great anthropologist's classic treatise on race and culture. Introduction by Ruth Bunzel. Only inexpensive paperback edition. 255pp. 5⅜ × 8½. 25245-0 Pa. $7.95

THE TALE OF PETER RABBIT, Beatrix Potter. The inimitable Peter's terrifying adventure in Mr. McGregor's garden, with all 27 wonderful, full-color Potter illustrations. 55pp. 4¼ × 5½. 22827-4 Pa. $1.75

THREE PROPHETIC SCIENCE FICTION NOVELS, H. G. Wells. *When the Sleeper Wakes, A Story of the Days to Come* and *The Time Machine* (full version). 335pp. 5⅜ × 8½. (Available in U.S. only) 20605-X Pa. $8.95

APICIUS COOKERY AND DINING IN IMPERIAL ROME, edited and translated by Joseph Dommers Vehling. Oldest known cookbook in existence offers readers a clear picture of what foods Romans ate, how they prepared them, etc. 49 illustrations. 301pp. 6⅛ × 9¼. 23563-7 Pa. $8.95

SHAKESPEARE LEXICON AND QUOTATION DICTIONARY, Alexander Schmidt. Full definitions, locations, shades of meaning of every word in plays and poems. More than 50,000 exact quotations. 1,485pp. 6½ × 9¼. 22726-X, 22727-8 Pa., Two-vol. set $31.90

THE WORLD'S GREAT SPEECHES, edited by Lewis Copeland and Lawrence W. Lamm. Vast collection of 278 speeches from Greeks to 1970. Powerful and effective models; unique look at history. 842pp. 5⅜ × 8½. 20468-5 Pa. $12.95

THE BLUE FAIRY BOOK, Andrew Lang. The first, most famous collection, with many familiar tales: Little Red Riding Hood, Aladdin and the Wonderful Lamp, Puss in Boots, Sleeping Beauty, Hansel and Gretel, Rumpelstiltskin; 37 in all. 138 illustrations. 390pp. 5⅜ × 8½.   21437-0 Pa. $6.95

THE STORY OF THE CHAMPIONS OF THE ROUND TABLE, Howard Pyle. Sir Launcelot, Sir Tristram and Sir Percival in spirited adventures of love and triumph retold in Pyle's inimitable style. 50 drawings, 31 full-page. xviii + 329pp. 6½ × 9¼.   21883-X Pa. $7.95

THE MYTHS OF THE NORTH AMERICAN INDIANS, Lewis Spence. Myths and legends of the Algonquins, Iroquois, Pawnees and Sioux with comprehensive historical and ethnological commentary. 36 illustrations. 5⅜ × 8½.
                                                                    25967-6 Pa. $8.95

GREAT DINOSAUR HUNTERS AND THEIR DISCOVERIES, Edwin H. Colbert. Fascinating, lavishly illustrated chronicle of dinosaur research, 1820s to 1960. Achievements of Cope, Marsh, Brown, Buckland, Mantell, Huxley, many others. 384pp. 5¼ × 8¼.   24701-5 Pa. $8.95

THE TASTEMAKERS, Russell Lynes. Informal, illustrated social history of American taste 1850s–1950s. First popularized categories Highbrow, Lowbrow, Middlebrow. 129 illustrations. New (1979) afterword. 384pp. 6 × 9.
                                                                    23993-4 Pa. $8.95

NORTH AMERICAN INDIAN LIFE: Customs and Traditions of 23 Tribes, Elsie Clews Parsons (ed.). 27 fictionalized essays by noted anthropologists examine religion, customs, government, additional facets of life among the Winnebago, Crow, Zuni, Eskimo, other tribes. 480pp. 6⅛ × 9¼.   27377-6 Pa. $10.95

AUTHENTIC VICTORIAN DECORATION AND ORNAMENTATION IN FULL COLOR: 46 Plates from "Studies in Design," Christopher Dresser. Superb full-color lithographs reproduced from rare original portfolio of a major Victorian designer. 48pp. 9¼ × 12¼.   25083-0 Pa. $7.95

PRIMITIVE ART, Franz Boas. Remains the best text ever prepared on subject, thoroughly discussing Indian, African, Asian, Australian, and, especially, Northern American primitive art. Over 950 illustrations show ceramics, masks, totem poles, weapons, textiles, paintings, much more. 376pp. 5⅜ × 8. 20025-6 Pa. $8.95

SIDELIGHTS ON RELATIVITY, Albert Einstein. Unabridged republication of two lectures delivered by the great physicist in 1920–21. *Ether and Relativity* and *Geometry and Experience*. Elegant ideas in nonmathematical form, accessible to intelligent layman. vi + 56pp. 5⅜ × 8½.   24511-X Pa. $3.95

THE WIT AND HUMOR OF OSCAR WILDE, edited by Alvin Redman. More than 1,000 ripostes, paradoxes, wisecracks: Work is the curse of the drinking classes, I can resist everything except temptation, etc. 258pp. 5⅜ × 8½.   20602-5 Pa. $4.95

ADVENTURES WITH A MICROSCOPE, Richard Headstrom. 59 adventures with clothing fibers, protozoa, ferns and lichens, roots and leaves, much more. 142 illustrations. 232pp. 5⅜ × 8½.   23471-1 Pa. $4.95

PLANTS OF THE BIBLE, Harold N. Moldenke and Alma L. Moldenke. Standard reference to all 230 plants mentioned in Scriptures. Latin name, biblical reference, uses, modern identity, much more. Unsurpassed encyclopedic resource for scholars, botanists, nature lovers, students of Bible. Bibliography. Indexes. 123 black-and-white illustrations. 384pp. 6 × 9. 25069-5 Pa. $9.95

FAMOUS AMERICAN WOMEN: A Biographical Dictionary from Colonial Times to the Present, Robert McHenry, ed. From Pocahontas to Rosa Parks, 1,035 distinguished American women documented in separate biographical entries. Accurate, up-to-date data, numerous categories, spans 400 years. Indices. 493pp. 6½ × 9¼. 24523-3 Pa. $11.95

THE FABULOUS INTERIORS OF THE GREAT OCEAN LINERS IN HIS-TORIC PHOTOGRAPHS, William H. Miller, Jr. Some 200 superb photographs capture exquisite interiors of world's great "floating palaces"—1890s to 1980s: *Titanic, Ile de France, Queen Elizabeth, United States, Europa,* more. Approx. 200 black-and-white photographs. Captions. Text. Introduction. 160pp. 8⅜ × 11¾. 24756-2 Pa. $10.95

THE GREAT LUXURY LINERS, 1927–1954: A Photographic Record, William H. Miller, Jr. Nostalgic tribute to heyday of ocean liners. 186 photos of *Ile de France, Normandie, Leviathan, Queen Elizabeth, United States,* many others. Interior and exterior views. Introduction. Captions. 160pp. 9 × 12. 24056-8 Pa. $12.95

A NATURAL HISTORY OF THE DUCKS, John Charles Phillips. Great landmark of ornithology offers complete detailed coverage of nearly 200 species and subspecies of ducks: gadwall, sheldrake, merganser, pintail, many more. 74 full-color plates, 102 black-and-white. Bibliography. Total of 1,920pp. 8⅜ × 11¼. 25141-1, 25142-X Cloth., Two-vol. set $100.00

THE COMPLETE "MASTERS OF THE POSTER": All 256 Color Plates from "Les Maîtres de l'Affiche", Stanley Appelbaum (ed.). The most famous compilation ever made of the art of the great age of the poster, featuring works by Chéret, Steinlen, Toulouse-Lautrec, nearly 100 other artists. One poster per page. 272pp. 9¼ × 12¼. 26309-6 Pa. $29.95

THE TEN BOOKS OF ARCHITECTURE: The 1755 Leoni Edition, Leon Battista Alberti. Rare classic helped introduce the glories of ancient architecture to the Renaissance. 68 black-and-white plates. 336pp. 8⅜ × 11¼. 25239-6 Pa. $14.95

MISS MACKENZIE, Anthony Trollope. Minor masterpieces by Victorian master unmasks many truths about life in 19th-century England. First inexpensive edition in years. 392pp. 5⅜ × 8½. 25201-9 Pa. $8.95

THE RIME OF THE ANCIENT MARINER, Gustave Doré, Samuel Taylor Coleridge. Dramatic engravings considered by many to be his greatest work. The terrifying space of the open sea, the storms and whirlpools of an unknown ocean, the ice of Antarctica, more—all rendered in a powerful, chilling manner. Full text. 38 plates. 77pp. 9¼ × 12. 22305-1 Pa. $4.95

THE EXPEDITIONS OF ZEBULON MONTGOMERY PIKE, Zebulon Montgomery Pike. Fascinating firsthand accounts (1805–6) of exploration of Mississippi River, Indian wars, capture by Spanish dragoons, much more. 1,088pp. 5⅜ × 8½. 25254-X, 25255-8 Pa., Two-vol. set $25.90

DEGAS: An Intimate Portrait, Ambroise Vollard. Charming, anecdotal memoir by famous art dealer of one of the greatest 19th-century French painters. 14 black-and-white illustrations. Introduction by Harold L. Van Doren. 96pp. 5⅜ × 8½.
25131-4 Pa. $4.95

PERSONAL NARRATIVE OF A PILGRIMAGE TO AL-MADINAH AND MECCAH, Richard F. Burton. Great travel classic by remarkably colorful personality. Burton, disguised as a Moroccan, visited sacred shrines of Islam, narrowly escaping death. 47 illustrations. 959pp. 5⅜ × 8½.
21217-3, 21218-1 Pa., Two-vol. set $19.90

PHRASE AND WORD ORIGINS, A. H. Holt. Entertaining, reliable, modern study of more than 1,200 colorful words, phrases, origins and histories. Much unexpected information. 254pp. 5⅜ × 8½.
20758-7 Pa. $5.95

THE RED THUMB MARK, R. Austin Freeman. In this first Dr. Thorndyke case, the great scientific detective draws fascinating conclusions from the nature of a single fingerprint. Exciting story, authentic science. 320pp. 5⅜ × 8½. (Available in U.S. only)
25210-8 Pa. $6.95

AN EGYPTIAN HIEROGLYPHIC DICTIONARY, E. A. Wallis Budge. Monumental work containing about 25,000 words or terms that occur in texts ranging from 3000 B.C. to 600 A.D. Each entry consists of a transliteration of the word, the word in hieroglyphs, and the meaning in English. 1,314pp. 6⅜ × 10.
23615-3, 23616-1 Pa., Two-vol. set $35.90

THE COMPLEAT STRATEGYST: Being a Primer on the Theory of Games of Strategy, J. D. Williams. Highly entertaining classic describes, with many illustrated examples, how to select best strategies in conflict situations. Prefaces. Appendices. xvi + 268pp. 5⅜ × 8½.
25101-2 Pa. $7.95

THE ROAD TO OZ, L. Frank Baum. Dorothy meets the Shaggy Man, little Button-Bright and the Rainbow's beautiful daughter in this delightful trip to the magical Land of Oz. 272pp. 5⅜ × 8.
25208-6 Pa. $5.95

POINT AND LINE TO PLANE, Wassily Kandinsky. Seminal exposition of role of point, line, other elements in nonobjective painting. Essential to understanding 20th-century art. 127 illustrations. 192pp. 6½ × 9¼.
23808-3 Pa. $5.95

LADY ANNA, Anthony Trollope. Moving chronicle of Countess Lovel's bitter struggle to win for herself and daughter Anna their rightful rank and fortune—perhaps at cost of sanity itself. 384pp. 5⅜ × 8½.
24669-8 Pa. $8.95

EGYPTIAN MAGIC, E. A. Wallis Budge. Sums up all that is known about magic in Ancient Egypt: the role of magic in controlling the gods, powerful amulets that warded off evil spirits, scarabs of immortality, use of wax images, formulas and spells, the secret name, much more. 253pp. 5⅜ × 8½.
22681-6 Pa. $4.95

THE DANCE OF SIVA, Ananda Coomaraswamy. Preeminent authority unfolds the vast metaphysic of India: the revelation of her art, conception of the universe, social organization, etc. 27 reproductions of art masterpieces. 192pp. 5⅜ × 8½.
24817-8 Pa. $6.95

CHRISTMAS CUSTOMS AND TRADITIONS, Clement A. Miles. Origin, evolution, significance of religious, secular practices. Caroling, gifts, yule logs, much more. Full, scholarly yet fascinating; non-sectarian. 400pp. 5⅜ × 8½.
23354-5 Pa. $7.95

THE HUMAN FIGURE IN MOTION, Eadweard Muybridge. More than 4,500 stopped-action photos, in action series, showing undraped men, women, children jumping, lying down, throwing, sitting, wrestling, carrying, etc. 390pp. 7⅞ × 10⅝.
20204-6 Cloth. $24.95

THE MAN WHO WAS THURSDAY, Gilbert Keith Chesterton. Witty, fast-paced novel about a club of anarchists in turn-of-the-century London. Brilliant social, religious, philosophical speculations. 128pp. 5⅜ × 8½.
25121-7 Pa. $3.95

A CÉZANNE SKETCHBOOK: Figures, Portraits, Landscapes and Still Lifes, Paul Cézanne. Great artist experiments with tonal effects, light, mass, other qualities in over 100 drawings. A revealing view of developing master painter, precursor of Cubism. 102 black-and-white illustrations. 144pp. 8¾ × 6⅜.
24790-2 Pa. $6.95

AN ENCYCLOPEDIA OF BATTLES: Accounts of Over 1,560 Battles from 1479 B.C. to the Present, David Eggenberger. Presents essential details of every major battle in recorded history, from the first battle of Megiddo in 1479 B.C. to Grenada in 1984. List of Battle Maps. New Appendix covering the years 1967–1984. Index. 99 illustrations. 544pp. 6½ × 9¼.
24913-1 Pa. $14.95

AN ETYMOLOGICAL DICTIONARY OF MODERN ENGLISH, Ernest Weekley. Richest, fullest work, by foremost British lexicographer. Detailed word histories. Inexhaustible. Total of 856pp. 6½ × 9¼.
21873-2, 21874-0 Pa., Two-vol. set $19.90

WEBSTER'S AMERICAN MILITARY BIOGRAPHIES, edited by Robert McHenry. Over 1,000 figures who shaped 3 centuries of American military history. Detailed biographies of Nathan Hale, Douglas MacArthur, Mary Hallaren, others. Chronologies of engagements, more. Introduction. Addenda. 1,033 entries in alphabetical order. xi + 548pp. 6½ × 9¼. (Available in U.S. only)
24758-9 Pa. $13.95

LIFE IN ANCIENT EGYPT, Adolf Erman. Detailed older account, with much not in more recent books: domestic life, religion, magic, medicine, commerce, and whatever else needed for complete picture. Many illustrations. 597pp. 5⅜ × 8½.
22632-8 Pa. $9.95

HISTORIC COSTUME IN PICTURES, Braun & Schneider. Over 1,450 costumed figures shown, covering a wide variety of peoples: kings, emperors, nobles, priests, servants, soldiers, scholars, townsfolk, peasants, merchants, courtiers, cavaliers, and more. 256pp. 8⅜ × 11¼.
23150-X Pa. $9.95

THE NOTEBOOKS OF LEONARDO DA VINCI, edited by J. P. Richter. Extracts from manuscripts reveal great genius; on painting, sculpture, anatomy, sciences, geography, etc. Both Italian and English. 186 ms. pages reproduced, plus 500 additional drawings, including studies for *Last Supper, Sforza* monument, etc. 860pp. 7⅞ × 10¾.
22572-0, 22573-9 Pa., Two-vol. set $35.90

HOW TO WRITE, Gertrude Stein. Gertrude Stein claimed anyone could understand her unconventional writing—here are clues to help. Fascinating improvisations, language experiments, explanations illuminate Stein's craft and the art of writing. Total of 414pp. 4⅝ × 6⅜. 23144-5 Pa. $6.95

ADVENTURES AT SEA IN THE GREAT AGE OF SAIL: Five Firsthand Narratives, edited by Elliot Snow. Rare true accounts of exploration, whaling, shipwreck, fierce natives, trade, shipboard life, more. 33 illustrations. Introduction. 353pp. 5⅜ × 8½. 25177-2 Pa. $9.95

THE HERBAL OR GENERAL HISTORY OF PLANTS, John Gerard. Classic descriptions of about 2,850 plants—with over 2,700 illustrations—includes Latin and English names, physical descriptions, varieties, time and place of growth, more. 2,706 illustrations. xlv + 1,678pp. 8½ × 12¼. 23147-X Cloth. $89.95

DOROTHY AND THE WIZARD IN OZ, L. Frank Baum. Dorothy and the Wizard visit the center of the Earth, where people are vegetables, glass houses grow and Oz characters reappear. Classic sequel to *Wizard of Oz*. 256pp. 5⅜ × 8. 24714-7 Pa. $5.95

SONGS OF EXPERIENCE: Facsimile Reproduction with 26 Plates in Full Color, William Blake. This facsimile of Blake's original "Illuminated Book" reproduces 26 full-color plates from a rare 1826 edition. Includes "The Tyger," "London," "Holy Thursday," and other immortal poems. 26 color plates. Printed text of poems. 48pp. 5¼ × 7. 24636-1 Pa. $3.95

SONGS OF INNOCENCE, William Blake. The first and most popular of Blake's famous "Illuminated Books," in a facsimile edition reproducing all 31 brightly colored plates. Additional printed text of each poem. 64pp. 5¼ × 7. 22764-2 Pa. $3.95

PRECIOUS STONES, Max Bauer. Classic, thorough study of diamonds, rubies, emeralds, garnets, etc.: physical character, occurrence, properties, use, similar topics. 20 plates, 8 in color. 94 figures. 659pp. 6⅛ × 9¼. 21910-0, 21911-9 Pa., Two-vol. set $21.90

ENCYCLOPEDIA OF VICTORIAN NEEDLEWORK, S. F. A. Caulfeild and Blanche Saward. Full, precise descriptions of stitches, techniques for dozens of needlecrafts—most exhaustive reference of its kind. Over 800 figures. Total of 679pp. 8⅜ × 11. 22800-2, 22801-0 Pa., Two-vol. set $26.90

THE MARVELOUS LAND OF OZ, L. Frank Baum. Second Oz book, the Scarecrow and Tin Woodman are back with hero named Tip, Oz magic. 136 illustrations. 287pp. 5⅜ × 8½. 20692-0 Pa. $5.95

WILD FOWL DECOYS, Joel Barber. Basic book on the subject, by foremost authority and collector. Reveals history of decoy making and rigging, place in American culture, different kinds of decoys, how to make them, and how to use them. 140 plates. 156pp. 7⅞ × 10¾. 20011-6 Pa. $14.95

HISTORY OF LACE, Mrs. Bury Palliser. Definitive, profusely illustrated chronicle of lace from earliest times to late 19th century. Laces of Italy, Greece, England, France, Belgium, etc. Landmark of needlework scholarship. 266 illustrations. 672pp. 6⅛ × 9¼. 24742-2 Pa. $16.95

A CONCISE HISTORY OF PHOTOGRAPHY: Third Revised Edition, Helmut Gernsheim. Best one-volume history—camera obscura, photochemistry, daguerreotypes, evolution of cameras, film, more. Also artistic aspects—landscape, portraits, fine art, etc. 281 black-and-white photographs. 26 in color. 176pp. 8⅜×11¼.
25128-4 Pa. $14.95

THE DORÉ BIBLE ILLUSTRATIONS, Gustave Doré. 241 detailed plates from the Bible: the Creation scenes, Adam and Eve, Flood, Babylon, battle sequences, life of Jesus, etc. Each plate is accompanied by the verses from the King James version of the Bible. 241pp. 9 × 12.
23004-X Pa. $9.95

WANDERINGS IN WEST AFRICA, Richard F. Burton. Great Victorian scholar/ adventurer's invaluable descriptions of African tribal rituals, fetishism, culture, art, much more. Fascinating 19th-century account. 624pp. 5⅜ × 8½. 26890-X Pa. $12.95

HISTORIC HOMES OF THE AMERICAN PRESIDENTS, Second Revised Edition, Irvin Haas. Guide to homes occupied by every president from Washington to Bush. Visiting hours, travel routes, more. 175 photos. 160pp. 8¼ × 11.
26751-2 Pa. $9.95

THE HISTORY OF THE LEWIS AND CLARK EXPEDITION, Meriwether Lewis and William Clark, edited by Elliott Coues. Classic edition of Lewis and Clark's day-by-day journals that later became the basis for U.S. claims to Oregon and the West. Accurate and invaluable geographical, botanical, biological, meteorological and anthropological material. Total of 1,508pp. 5⅜ × 8½.
21268-8, 21269-6, 21270-X Pa., Three-vol. set $29.85

LANGUAGE, TRUTH AND LOGIC, Alfred J. Ayer. Famous, clear introduction to Vienna, Cambridge schools of Logical Positivism. Role of philosophy, elimination of metaphysics, nature of analysis, etc. 160pp. 5⅜ × 8½. (Available in U.S. and Canada only)
20010-8 Pa. $3.95

MATHEMATICS FOR THE NONMATHEMATICIAN, Morris Kline. Detailed, college-level treatment of mathematics in cultural and historical context, with numerous exercises. For liberal arts students. Preface. Recommended Reading Lists. Tables. Index. Numerous black-and-white figures. xvi + 641pp. 5⅜ × 8½.
24823-2 Pa. $11.95

HANDBOOK OF PICTORIAL SYMBOLS, Rudolph Modley. 3,250 signs and symbols, many systems in full; official or heavy commercial use. Arranged by subject. Most in Pictorial Archive series. 143pp. 8⅜ × 11. 23357-X Pa. $8.95

INCIDENTS OF TRAVEL IN YUCATAN, John L. Stephens. Classic (1843) exploration of jungles of Yucatan, looking for evidences of Maya civilization. Travel adventures, Mexican and Indian culture, etc. Total of 669pp. 5⅜ × 8½.
20926-1, 20927-X Pa., Two-vol. set $13.90

AMERICAN CLIPPER SHIPS: 1833–1858, Octavius T. Howe & Frederick C. Matthews. Fully-illustrated, encyclopedic review of 352 clipper ships from the period of America's greatest maritime supremacy. Introduction. 109 halftones. 5 black-and-white line illustrations. Index. Total of 928pp. 5⅜ × 8½.
25115-2, 25116-0 Pa., Two-vol. set $21.90

TOWARDS A NEW ARCHITECTURE, Le Corbusier. Pioneering manifesto by great architect, near legendary founder of "International School." Technical and aesthetic theories, views on industry, economics, relation of form to function, "mass-production spirit," much more. Profusely illustrated. Unabridged translation of 13th French edition. Introduction by Frederick Etchells. 320pp. 6⅛ × 9¼. (Available in U.S. only)
25023-7 Pa. $8.95

THE BOOK OF KELLS, edited by Blanche Cirker. Inexpensive collection of 32 full-color, full-page plates from the greatest illuminated manuscript of the Middle Ages, painstakingly reproduced from rare facsimile edition. Publisher's Note. Captions. 32pp. 9⅜ × 12¼. (Available in U.S. only)
24345-1 Pa. $5.95

BEST SCIENCE FICTION STORIES OF H. G. WELLS, H. G. Wells. Full novel *The Invisible Man*, plus 17 short stories: "The Crystal Egg," "Aepyornis Island," "The Strange Orchid," etc. 303pp. 5⅜ × 8½. (Available in U.S. only)
21531-8 Pa. $6.95

AMERICAN SAILING SHIPS: Their Plans and History, Charles G. Davis. Photos, construction details of schooners, frigates, clippers, other sailcraft of 18th to early 20th centuries—plus entertaining discourse on design, rigging, nautical lore, much more. 137 black-and-white illustrations. 240pp. 6⅛ × 9¼.
24658-2 Pa. $6.95

ENTERTAINING MATHEMATICAL PUZZLES, Martin Gardner. Selection of author's favorite conundrums involving arithmetic, money, speed, etc., with lively commentary. Complete solutions. 112pp. 5⅜ × 8½.
25211-6 Pa. $3.95

THE WILL TO BELIEVE, HUMAN IMMORTALITY, William James. Two books bound together. Effect of irrational on logical, and arguments for human immortality. 402pp. 5⅜ × 8½.
20291-7 Pa. $8.95

THE HAUNTED MONASTERY and THE CHINESE MAZE MURDERS, Robert Van Gulik. 2 full novels by Van Gulik continue adventures of Judge Dee and his companions. An evil Taoist monastery, seemingly supernatural events; overgrown topiary maze that hides strange crimes. Set in 7th-century China. 27 illustrations. 328pp. 5⅜ × 8½.
23502-5 Pa. $6.95

CELEBRATED CASES OF JUDGE DEE (DEE GOONG AN), translated by Robert Van Gulik. Authentic 18th-century Chinese detective novel; Dee and associates solve three interlocked cases. Led to Van Gulik's own stories with same characters. Extensive introduction. 9 illustrations. 237pp. 5⅜ × 8½.
23337-5 Pa. $5.95

Prices subject to change without notice.

Available at your book dealer or write for free catalog to Dept. GI, Dover Publications, Inc., 31 East 2nd St., Mineola, N.Y. 11501. Dover publishes more than 400 books each year on science, elementary and advanced mathematics, biology, music, art, literary history, social sciences and other areas.